Unborn

Heavenly Emissary Interventions

Lona Schäfer

Before I formed you
in the womb
I knew you
(Jeremiah 1:5).

RIVER BIRCH PRESS

Daphne, Alabama

ISBN 978-1-956365-00-9 print
       978-1-956365-01-6 e-book

For Worldwide Distribution
Printed in the U.S.A.

River Birch Press
P.O. Box 868, Daphne, AL 36526

CONTENTS

INTRODUCTION

Although *Unborn* is a work of fiction, it was developed with every effort to maintain medical and biblical accuracy throughout. My use of fiction is intended to communicate truth. Yet, applied in this way, fiction has its risks because it blurs the distinction between literary license and false teaching; I never want to stand on that ground.

It's only natural that *Unborn* began as a fetus. A young hospital pathologist friend unknowingly gave birth to this book when she described a human fetus—about the size of a golf ball—brought to her for dissection. With deep reverence, she spoke of details visible at its tender age of six weeks: a forest of neat, orderly hair, tiny fingers and toes.

Her description stirred a mix waiting in abeyance, becoming the pathway to this story. *Unborn* offers a unique perspective to the sanctity of life.

PROLOGUE

NOVA'S LAMENT

I didn't want you to die, Eve. I really didn't. I'm immune to the sadness of it, as people pass from one realm to another. Well, I was, anyway. Somehow, you were different. Thinking back on that day, I now see that your death set in motion a stream of changes in me, igniting a sensitivity I'd never known.

The "incompletes" hadn't bothered me before. That is, those human lives within the womb who'd lost their chance to breathe, to smile, or feel the warmth of a mother's love, to contribute. As a heavenly overwatcher with an assignment, life for me was once so efficient, filled with purpose and accomplishment. Before you came along, Eve, I merely observed them as lives lost in clinics and back alley dens joined with those lost to cancer, anger, accident, or natural cause. Once long ago, it seems I could casually process and package those expired lives, sending them on their way.

What amazes me most is the ordinariness of your intended life, Eve. You were to be attractive, but not striking, with unremarkable hair, height, and eyes. Also, a wing-shaped birthmark on your left leg and a slight lisp, a speech impediment that was to win your lover's heart. Your role was to caress the lives of others so meaningfully, leaving a trail of joy wherever you went. When you spoke, even while sleeping, you smiled. You would've drawn others to yourself simply through your quiet presence. Pure goodness and serenity were to follow you all the days of your life.

But, no. You were aborted like so many millions each year.

I suppose it's my ability to see both sides of the coin, as they say, that bothered me. I saw your path weave in and out of so many lives, leaving flower petals and butterfly sweetness everywhere—but of course, those petals and the winged nectar never happened. Now, there are only tears where you were meant to be.

That became a revelation for me, a defining moment. The instant I stopped to examine you, Eve, that's where my travails began. Your floating, blissful existence, like so many others jarringly wrenched away, ended with a bolt of pain that thrust you into my awareness. I know this, though—your young mother, Kristin, now deeply regrets the choice she made. You know, the one that abruptly ended the gentle sway and warmth that you once knew within her womb, the muffled music heard occasionally, and the sweet amniotic sustenance.

Why were you different, Eve?

Before, I could wrap and process 50 million lost lives each year. But somehow I got stuck on you. Maybe it was God's way of telling me that I'd earned my wings, just like ol' Clarence in that Jimmy Stewart movie. Not that I was happy about it, though; the change was terribly unsettling.

Before, I slept peacefully and didn't tire, but that changed too. Just paging through your intended life exhausted me. One thing led to another before I realized what was happening. I began to see a cascade of lives, rushing into the unknown. You were in that tortured mass with arms outstretched, eyes pleading. That was the moment I shed my first tear for you, seeing you there, calling me helplessly.

No one had ever seen me before, there on the sidelines. But you did. Your cry set everything in motion.

– *Nova*

1

MIDNIGHT VISAGE, SHARED

HANNAH WAS EXHAUSTED. As she went to bed that evening, she had a foreboding sense of darkness that was like staring, cold and naked, into a gaping abyss. A restless sleep brought no comfort.

The new day began horribly, two hours too soon when she woke from the nightmare, still smelling the fetus. It was that intense, and its recollection persisted through vigorous toothbrushing. She was up instantly and out of bed.

Why two nights in a row? She was pushed into consciousness the night before from a bad dream, brief and with fewer details—though at the time she hadn't known, couldn't have known, it would be the precursor to last night's vivid nightmare. The most recent one was similar at the beginning but quickly surpassed the other in its intensity, including an olfactory signature, pungent and raw. It hung with her, still clinging to her senses.

Now awake but sluggish, Hannah forced herself toward optimism, considering the day before her. She could at least appreciate that today's class, a requirement to maintain her pathology assistant certification, took place at the teaching hospital where she worked. Travel was required for most of the others. Her laboratory/office was just a few floors from the classroom, so there was at least that satisfaction.

A breakfast bar and instant coffee would suffice today; she was in no mood to belabor the day's edgy beginning. Fortunately, her husband could prepare the kids for their day. A sticky note attached to the back of a chair (Up early. Gotta go. Remember their lunches) was enough to release her from routine duty. Her irritability was energizing; better to channel it and better to go.

A 90-minute jump on the commute's usual departure time was a small reprieve. The typical 20-minute commute took less than 15 today. Attempting to clarify the dream, she decided against the radio's distraction. As she turned into a parking space, she plucked the last tendrils of recollection from the vivid images that jumpstarted her day.

Hannah was soon sliding the key into her office door. Inside her lab, she could see a shoebox-sized FedEx package on her desk. The box sparked no curiosity; she frequently received new lab tools or documents. She nudged it aside to make room for her handbag, a pebbled leather beauty she bought for herself in Santa Fe a year ago during a symposium for the American Association of Pathology Assistants.

Her attention was drawn to the coffee maker just beyond it. At least, now there was something that felt like her comfortable ritual.

She used a small beaker to measure just the right amount of fragrant beans, dumped them into the grinder, and from there into the coffee machine. She placed her mug in its slot to receive the quiet trickle of coffee. *Ahh, fuel.*

Hannah's lab was six floors below the fourth-floor classroom—her destination, soon enough. It amused her to think about how pathology and anatomy labs, her turf, were typically at a medical facility's lowest level.

"God forbid we have dead bodies or fresh-off-the-surgical-floor specimens hovering over working professionals or patients in clinical suites,'" Hannah once told a co-worker. "Something hellish about that. I'll never have a corner office with a window. I'm tethered to dungeoned corpses."

Her sister laughed at that one. While both of them chose pre-med, Hannah veered off into pathology after completing her MS in anatomy and pathology. Kristin continued on with her studies to achieve her M.D., with degrees in surgery and obstetrics. She completed her education in California where she also acquired what their father once characterized as an "altered state of morality." There, Kristin was inspired by the women's movement and decided upon "a responsibility to help women." She rose quickly to become the lead physician at a birth control enterprise based in San Francisco.

On the last day of Kristin's most recent visit with her parents, fraught with tension, she spoke little to them, instead, spending much of her time absorbed with work-related email and phone calls.

As Kristin waited for a taxi to ferry her to the airport (unwilling to accept a ride with either—or worse—both parents), she told them that, "Unless women can freely decide whether or not to continue a pregnancy, it's impossible for us to control our lives, to enjoy our sexuality, and to participate fully in society." Her mother cried. Her father, fuming, opened the door.

Hannah loved her sister. As kids, they were close. Life, learning, and amusement were all about science. One year they hosted a "medical care" tent for neighborhood pets that attracted the involvement of a veterinarian who lived two streets over. Hannah and Kristin grew to be more like their parents each year—inquisitive, engaging, confident, and mostly untroubled.

The girls gradually became aware that their parents—Jack and Miriam Soelberg—were mostly regarded as old school for their conservative beliefs and lifestyle. They attended church as a family; well, until Kristin entered what Jack described as her years of "Sybil unrest" for the 70s portrayal of a patient with multiple personality disorder. It was at the same church where Hannah Soelberg later met and married Chet Methaney, her husband of five years and the father of their two children, Matthew and Sarah.

In her junior year of high school, Kristin's life had spiraled in and out of many unhappy relationships. And now: no kids, no strings attached.

THE COFFEE was perfect and, with the PC activated, the cascade of emails that awaited Hannah's attention was no surprise. An hour slipped by unremarkably with only occasional sounds from the hallway as others began their day. Hannah took a final glance at her watch and switched off the reading lamp.

She entered the stairway and climbed up rapidly. Arriving at Room 410, she was one of the last to enter the classroom. Hannah scanned faces, looking for anyone familiar among the 30-some pathology assistants, anatomists, and a handful of young physician interns.

She spotted Samantha and an empty seat beside her. Hannah waved and aimed for the chair, taking another swig of coffee. The ceramic mug, lack of a jacket or coat, and of course the university lab smock with her name embroidered below it quickly told the others she was at work, on home turf.

Samantha saw Hannah coming her way. "I haven't seen you for months. What a nice surprise!"

"Yes, I know," said Hannah, taking the seat next to Samantha. "I thought the same thing exactly. Been too long." The two knew each other through postgraduate classes and occasional social mixers. For a few years, they'd been close to BFF status, but their paths had diverged.

"Long distance commute for you today! What, 20 seconds in the elevator?" teased Sam as she pulled a notebook a bit closer, making more room for Hannah. She knew that Hannah had accepted a position at the university shortly before completing grad school.

Samantha worked twenty-some miles away at a community hospital. Hannah noticed that Sam looked like she needed another cup of coffee too.

Hannah hadn't noticed the course title projected onto the big screen until she was seated: Pathology Law 301 and Other Oddities. It was one of many Harley-isms. Professor Evan Harley's eccentric humor was on display, and he was sure to flaunt it throughout the day. Hannah knew Dr. Harley better than most, as his office was just two doors from hers, and, after all, he was her supervisor. She happily excused his peculiarities, and he laughed at hers, such as her preference to call him Harley.

"It's just such a cool name," she told him. "Dad once had a Road King. I loved that bike. And now, here you are—Doctor Cool." She'd had plenty of time to assess the man carefully, determining quickly that he was a genuinely fine guy, a brilliant anatomist, and a B+ instructor. And, not a shred of vanity, a rarity in any med center setting. As far as Hannah could tell, Harley had four or five sets of clothing. They just aged. She figured he must comb his hair for church because on Mondays, it was neatest. Each week, for the three and a half years of her observation, the mass of mostly grey hair led a mutiny that looked truly Einsteinish by Friday.

"My thoroughly lifeless patients don't care about my appearance," he once said to a gaggle of bioscience visitors. He expected laughter. "Oh, just a dad joke," he added after a few moments of silence. "My kids didn't like my, um, deadpan humor, either. But you do get it, right?"

As a tenured department chair, Harley couldn't be unseated. The way he looked at it, his appearance meant nothing. He cared only about his family, staff, work, faith, and maintaining a steady income of NIH funding for the department. Few anatomy departments nationwide enjoyed the income of Harley's department due entirely to his ability to write compelling proposals for National Institutes of Health research grants. His applications were brilliant and meticulous.

And now, Harley was just getting started. After a brief introduction and a few notes about the facility (where to find bathrooms, cafeteria), he slipped into gear. *He wasn't the most inspiring instructor,* thought Hannah, *but he got the job done.* She was among the few who appreciated his comedic personality.

Department rumor had it that if a staff candidate didn't laugh at least once during an interview, they were off the list, regardless of their credentials. The way Harley saw it, humor was a necessity. And, by God, if he didn't detect in a candidate some sense of humor—whether lively (a good start) or even self-deprecating (better yet)—then they had no place in his department.

All facets of death were a constant companion among those who worked in the field of anatomy, and humor was its ideal counterbalance. Before her first week was over, he told Hannah, "Don't take life too seriously. It ain't nohow permanent." He added that the quote was attributed to Pogo, a cartoon character, but Hannah never paid any attention to comics.

Hannah told her husband, Chet, about it that evening—including some of Harley's hiring eccentricities—and he laughed wildly.

Soon, Harley droned steadily, predictably into the world of new governmental regulations applicable to the practice of anatomy, pathology, and—for the interns—medicine. The best part of his morning lecture had to do with a video that was shot covertly in a restaurant by a journalist acting as a buyer of fetal tissue while speaking with the director of an abortion clinic. They discussed the cost of fetal tissue, parts, and pieces for sale. Harley pulled it up on his laptop, then hit a button that transported the scene onto a large screen. Most had seen or heard about the video through social media.

"After its release, third-party verification proved that the video was indeed genuine," commented Harley, doing his best to feign neutrality.

In the video a rather gaunt, hollow-eyed clinician, who identified herself as the director of a family planning clinic in one of America's largest metro areas, made little attempt to hide the fact that she was selling—well, accepting compensation for—human flesh, bodies whole and in part. The greatest profitability came from the sale of fetal specimens for highly specialized purposes; just a vial of cells could sell for thousands. It was all illegal, but the woman believed at the time that she was merely making another secure, secret sale.

As the video ended, one student raised a hand. "There's no denying it's a growing field," he said. "But to get the best parts, preferably from near-full-term babies—well, fetuses—I found it interesting to learn that popular, time-saving techniques are mostly ruled out. That means no to abortions via saline injection or mechanical vacuum. Surgical abortion's a must, that is, for many pharmaceutical or bioprocurement buyers."

"That's right," acknowledged another student. "The bigger, more complete the parts, the better, and with greater payoff at the end. I saw that, after the video posted and was verified as real, special congressional hearings were held."

"Yes, that's true. They confirmed that some clinics purposefully delay abortions so that they can sell entire fetuses, or more developed tissue for greater reward," said Harley. "I heard from a pretty good source recently that baby parts at 40 weeks are four times more valuable than those harvested at 20 weeks. I also learned about a researcher who paid a procurement firm about $3,500 for a late fetal brain with spinal column intact. No doubt, abortionists and the organizations that support them make it very difficult to verify that. Of course, where there are laws and regulations and governmental oversight, black markets thrive. That means not only the market for fetal tissue and organs but also secret abortion parlors and a thriving supply from developing countries. And, China."

One facet of the purposeful delaying of abortions was

what interested Hannah the most. She'd learned a year earlier in a candid conversation with Kristin that she and her colleagues could profile patients—those who'd go to near-full-term, then abort, with remarkable accuracy. This meant a higher-cost abortion and a much higher return for fetal tissue. "Of course, you never heard it from me," Kristin added.

As Kristin explained it, the youngest women were less likely to discern the intent of a clinic's delay tactics. They were more likely to carry a child to near full-term with little protest. Some lacked the intellect or financial means to file a complaint or hire an attorney should the tactic be discovered. Also, those in sound physical condition with a reduced risk of complications leading up to or during the abortion procedure were deliberately steered toward late-term abortions.

The duplicitous "need" or "best timing" for their abortion was then revealed to patients somewhere during the third trimester, with results that guaranteed higher profitability to the clinic and to the abortionist. "The clinic makes money selling abortions, not the pill," added Kristin. "Annual bonuses are tied to our ability to increase abortions; later-term all the better. Where else would I get a salary to support the good life here in California?"

Leaning over to speak close to Sam's ear, Hannah whispered, "And yet, as relevant as that video and this conversation is today, you can bet that few others taking courses like this would catch a glimpse of that video in class. Harley's the real deal."

Sam acknowledged the comment with a nod to Hannah as Harley shifted his conversation toward another topic: neonatal abstinence syndrome (NAS)—a term for a group of problems a baby experiences when withdrawing from narcotics. "We won't spend a lot of time on this one; after all, as pathologists, we're not concerned—professionally, that is—with living babies," said Harley.

HALF AN HOUR LATER, Harley glanced at the clock. "Aha. I see we're already at the half-way point. So, students, tadpoles, and scholars, let's break for lunch. See you back here in 45 minutes."

Leaving the class, Hannah and Samantha walked toward the elevator past clusters of young, preoccupied interns on rounds, focusing their attention on questions posed by attending physicians. Nurses and administrators all moved with harried expressions.

On the ground floor, they approached an Amish family making their way through the antiseptic confines of the hallway. They shuffled as a group, almost matching steps.

It wasn't uncommon to see Amish families here; north central Ohio has one of the nation's largest concentrations of Amish. When Amish arrive at the facility, occasionally by horse-drawn buggy but more frequently by paid drivers, they often enter with looks of wonderment. Hannah noticed this wasn't the case today.

A young, bearded father, accompanied by four girls and three boys, walked solemnly toward an accounts payable window. They were morose, tearful. The girls held hands as they wiped their eyes. Their father gripped a small, badly scuffed briefcase wrapped with several strands of bailing twine knotted at the top. This was an apparent settling of accounts, the Amish way, with a briefcase passed between church families with just one grim purpose.

Most of those in the hallway knew from stories of giant sums paid in cash by members of the Amish faith. The man's wife and the mother of seven, all born at home, had entered the oncology wing a week earlier. Refusing morphine, she'd see her children once more, briefly, and would leave in a body bag before nightfall.

At the hospital's center, Hannah and Sam could smell the kitchen long before they could see it. They passed the cashier on their way in, aiming toward an uncrowded corner of the cafeteria. As they took seats, Hannah complained of a headache.

"Tough night, huh?" asked Sam as she unpacked her lunch bag. "Kids weren't sleeping?"

"Not that," said Hannah. "Just a bad night; didn't sleep well. All things considered, it's nothing compared to what we just saw. Who knows what awful thing just happened to that Amish family."

Sam acknowledged the comment with a nod. "For sure. Those poor kids, looking so miserable."

Hannah was momentarily quiet, then bowed her head. It was an "Oh, yeah" moment for Sam, who simply looked down at her hands. Soon the two spoke as they ate, catching up. Family goings-on, their careers, and Sam's just-purchased, first-ever new car. Sam's husband, Rob, had recently left a law practice to begin his own.

There was a short lull; Hannah pulled a grape from a plastic bag. "I had a freaky dream two nights ago," she said, interrupting the easy stream of conversation. "And that was just the introduction to last night's doozie." Sam looked at her with curiosity.

"I got outta bed for a drink of water, maybe around four-thirty or so, trying to shake it off but couldn't go back to sleep," Hannah added. "The darndest thing is that, in the dream I had two nights ago, I received a tray from the OR with a note telling me to do a typical necropsy. In the tray was a nonviable stillborn [one with no chance of survival].[1] Strange, too—at just 12 or 14 weeks of age, it had a name on the tag—'Eve.'"

Hannah glanced at Sam momentarily. Sam, suddenly with a worried expression, averted her eyes to stir bread crumbs with a finger.

"So, in the first dream," continued Hannah, "I held it in the palm of my hand, noticing every detail. The smell—well, you know it—seemed stronger than usual. I can still feel its weight. It was one of those moments when you can't help but admire such a perfectly formed fetus. I began to examine the finest hairs on its shoulder and head under the magnifier... then I woke up."

Hannah paused when she noticed that Sam's finger, still plowing through crumbs, began to quiver.

"Then, last night, the dream started the same way, but moved beyond where the first one ended," added Hannah. She put her head in her hands, plastic fork extended between two fingers of her right hand, and emitted a sigh. She paused a few moments, expecting to look up into Sam's eyes. But when she lifted her head, Sam was gone. Huh?

Samantha had left silently, retreating to a restroom down the hall. She hurried into a stall and slammed the door. A few minutes later, knowing that Hannah would be alarmed at the abruptness of her departure, she went to a sink, splashed water into her face, and dabbed at her eyes with a paper towel. Did it show?

"I'm so sorry, Hannah," she said as she returned, visibly shaken. "I had to go. Didn't mean to leave so quickly."

"Oh…it's fine." Hannah was puzzled but had no intention of returning to the story. That was sort of rude, but hey, she was talking shop during lunch, after all.

They ate in silence for a few minutes, Sam looking oddly flustered. Her hands were still shaking, but Hannah was too tired to ask about it.

Then Sam spoke, startling Hannah with a question: "So, this baby—well, the fetus—was a second trimester and intact?"

Sam's return to the topic was mildly surprising. Hannah registered it as something of an apology for her abrupt departure. Maybe professional curiosity.

"Yes. Well—the crazy thing was that in last night's dream, the baby twitched, then moved its arms and gasped. . . and then its hands, both of them, reached toward me," continued Hannah. "If that wasn't bad enough, both eyes opened at that moment, looking right through me. Then it began to scream. That's when I woke up."

Hannah glanced up at Sam, alarmed to see her so shaken.

"My God, Hannah. Don't say another word," said Sam. "I had exactly the same dream last night—and the one before. The first one, brief, the next—awful. Just as you described it. The baby's eyes were filled with tears and had a look of alarm and incredible sadness. The outstretched fingers and the scream. That's why I had to leave so quickly. It was such a shock. I didn't know what to say."

"What? You're freaking me out now," said Hannah. She stared at Sam, each of them completely dismayed.

They saw that others from the class were preparing to

leave the cafeteria. Reluctantly, they gathered their things. "I think we'll have to talk about this again," said Hannah.

"Yeah, I suppose so," Sam replied.

2

MALBAS' TREASURE

BACK IN THE CLASSROOM, Hannah sat as in a fog. The remainder of their class moved sluggishly. At 4:30, they were dismissed. Hannah and Sam agreed to call each other soon.

As she unlocked her office, Hannah looked inside and immediately saw that things weren't as she expected them to be. The forgotten FedEx box was centered on her desk, and the cantilevered reading light was on, illuminating the top of it.

Startled by its appearance there, she recalled vaguely that she had seen it in the morning and pushed it aside with her purse. She looked quickly to see if anything else had been disturbed.

She threw her class notes into a chair, set the coffee mug aside, then grabbed her handbag to check its contents. The inner purse, cards, and cash were all there. She knew she hadn't left the light on.

The box.

She brought it closer. The label was addressed to Hannah Methaney. It must've arrived early that morning, probably placed in her office by mail delivery. The facility's post office personnel, and Harley, were among the few with keys for her lab.

The sender's information was torn in transit. Hannah split the side and center seams carefully, then lifted out another box within it, taped shut. She pulled the tape to see a flash of gold or brass, maybe a tool, cradled in shredded paper.

Hannah removed and opened a card resting on top. It read:

> Hannah, dear, you've come to mean so much to me, though we've not yet met in person. I'm so glad you chose a path unlike your sister's.
>
> I believe that zero is but a fiction. That nothing is always still something. That while there may be eyes that yet cannot see, there is no cosmic stillness; ears that cannot yet hear, but not cosmic silence; bodies that yet cannot feel, but not cosmic cold. I believe that even as we know alienation, pain, evil, and death, there is real hope of healing, wholeness, repair, harmony, and truth. Even at the heart of darkness, there is light.
>
> Because you are accepted and loved, you can help me affect the metamorphosis to good. You alone are (or will soon be) in a position to help. Just remember: we are all loved immeasurably.
>
> The only possibility of human life lies in mutuality, participation, acceptance of the gift, the giver, joyous acknowledgment of them, and becoming. Not death—no, that is not the issue—but lifelessness in all its forms is the enemy.
>
> Sorry about the nightmares. Guard the cross; it will be reclaimed. —*Nova*

Hannah felt weak. She'd been standing to read the card, but reached back frantically for the desk chair, pulled it toward her, and dropped onto the seat.

She was losing all sense of color, and darkness narrowed her vision. She was shaking, with a rapid, shallow heartbeat. Reflexively, Hannah dropped her head between her legs, barely maintaining consciousness.

Gradually, Hannah brought herself out of the near-faint spell. She raised her head slowly. Her water bottle was within reach. Moving sparingly, she unscrewed the cap and took a drink. Stability returned.

Hannah fumbled for the box, bringing it toward her. She moved the shredded paper aside to see an elegantly inlaid bone or ivory handle to an unfamiliar tool. Eighteen to twenty inches long and gracefully curved near the end, the golden metal culminated in a small cup at the end. Could it be a vintage church candle snuffer? She grasped it gently, removing it by the handle.

She tipped the tool toward her to look inside the small cup, expecting to see some sign of carbon or wax. But there inside the clean, reflective curve of the cup, perfectly centered, was a small drill bit (corkscrew?) crafted of the same metal. Sensing a connection between the screw device and the handle, she brought both parts of the handle together like a piston to see that it was a two-handed tool. Two hands were required to operate the instrument that slowly rotated the corkscrew inside the cup.

Could it be a surgical instrument? Well, not with the polished bone or ivory handle; impossible to sterilize. Well, at least to modern standards.

Hannah tapped her cellphone's screen to check the time.

She was alarmed to see that 30 minutes had passed since she left the classroom. She called Chet and, as he picked up, she heard the decelerating whine of a table saw.

"Hey—you can't still be at work, right?"

"No, no. I'm in the garage. Matt needs a piece of half-inch plywood for—"

"Okay, okay, you had me worried there. I'm still here in my office, leaving in a minute. Just wanted to let you know. Did you make dinner by any chance? I could eat some plywood if that's all you've got."

"Yup. All taken care of," he assured her.

"Okay. Great. I'm texting you a photo. See you as soon as I can get there."

She took a photo of the object, texting it to Chet with a note: "Any clue what this might be? See U soon." She placed the tool back in the box. Initially, she planned to leave it on her desk but decided to take it with her.

Hannah turned off the desk lamp, grabbed her purse and the box, and fished for keys. As she opened the door, she glanced back. She scanned the room, making sure nothing was out of place, then flipped off the light switch, closed the door, and locked it.

It was the beginning of a beautiful fall evening, ideal for her to open the windows. As she drove, her mind wandered through the day. She recalled the conversation with Sam, Harley's class, then the message within the card and the tool.

A mile or so from home, she approached a red light at an intersection she knew well. That's when Hannah had an unusual sensation—the neck-hair-bristling awareness of being watched. The only other car at the intersection beside her to the left was a dark sedan, also with open windows. The music that came from the car was odd primitive drumming.

The man at the wheel wasn't looking at her, but as her gaze lingered momentarily on him, she noticed peculiar things. Darkly clad and with dark, tightly cropped hair—40 or 45? He had long sideburns and a trimmed goatee. And though it was twilight, he was still wearing sunglasses. Some sort of hot-shot, jazz wannabe. She realized she'd taken her eyes off the light for too long and glanced up quickly, expecting to see green. It was still red.

Hannah ventured another glance to her left, but this time the man was looking directly at her. Slowly, he lifted the glasses up with one hand and stared at her with acute, penetrating eyes. In that second, it seemed that every hair on her body stood erect. His gaze was explicit, direct, absorbing her. Immediately, she knew he was the source of her discomfort moments ago.

In just the second or two that they looked at each other, she noticed in him a complete lack of emotion. Yet, his eyes were drilling into hers. And something about them, even at that distance and in the day's waning light, was disturbing; his pupils were irregular, horrifying. Then, still looking directly at her, he said "Hannah" just loud enough to be heard above the drumbeat.

She felt a sudden weakness as a deep wash began to envelop her eyes, starting with the collapse of her peripheral vision, then moving inward. Hannah's head dipped weakly just as a horn sounded from behind. She snapped her head upward to see the light turn green. The dark sedan was gone. *What's…happening…to me?* She began to accelerate robotically, forcing herself to concentrate with her eyes, hands, and feet. *Move, move.* Hannah confirmed that no sedan was ahead of her in the forward lanes, right or left. Not in the rear or side mirrors. Nowhere in sight.

In a stupor she forced herself on. Just one more turn and then to Hampton Avenue, halfway down to their driveway on the left. She tabbed the visor button for the garage door. Open. Ignition off. Then, while her head hung weakly, she stabbed blindly at the visor's garage door tab. Close. Close!

EARLIER THAT MORNING, the gravel parking lot at Tuck's Garage and Autobody on Market Street in Akron was jammed with troubled cars. The lot provided plenty of blind spots to the few video cameras mounted on telephone poles. From the building's open bay door, Ben Tuckweiler's awareness of anything outside the shop was limited, especially since his only part-time helper was already 15 minutes late. At the moment, Tuck was engrossed and frustrated with an ornery Dodge Charger cowl panel and A-pillar replacement.

He certainly wouldn't have noticed what appeared to be a common black crow under the best of circumstances. The large black bird sat atop a telephone pole outside Tuck's lot, peering in the direction of Bruchtel Avenue. Other birds veered in a wide swath around it in an undulating formation. When the crow spotted a young man walking in its direction, it spread his wings, dropping quickly into Tuck's lot for the transformation.

Though Tuck's 28-year-old understudy would have arrived on time—his mother woke him, fed him scrambled eggs and marbled rye, then prodded him out the door for work—he'd chosen precisely the wrong shortcut. The young man's leisurely walk of two blocks ended when he decided to slip between two cars in the far corner of Tuck's lot. The last thing he recalled before his spirit was released was the painful constriction of his neck. He reached up to untie the pressure, but the hands from behind were too tightly entwined.

A man in dark clothes with stylish Oakley sunglasses, kneeling behind one of the cars, gradually released the hapless lad. When the body's convulsions stopped, the man adjusted his sunglasses, dusted his knees, and pushed the corpse under an old Volvo coupe. The killer then opened the driver's door of a black '09 Toyota Camry, towed to Tuck's three weeks earlier for a new transmission system. After throwing his derby hat into the front passenger seat, Malbas (the dark angel's given name) sat behind the wheel.

Adjusting the rearview mirror to see himself, Malbas was satisfied that there was no dirt on his impeccably clean black shirt. His tightly trimmed scalp and facial hair were spotless too. He smoothed the dark goatee and admired the stylish shades. "Baaaaad," he mumbled. He was pleased with his appearance; after all, an apex predator should look intimidating. He examined the side mirrors for view, then turned his attention to the strange nylon strap hanging to his left side, unsure of its purpose.

Malbas had never driven an automobile before, but his actions were precise. Ignoring the peculiar metal key hanging from a string on the rearview mirror, he placed a hand on the dashboard and closed his eyes. Wires below the dash sizzled, and the engine ignited. Foot on the brake, he moved the car into drive and slowly accelerated, turning the wheel with fluid ease to navigate through the parking lot and out onto Market Street. Tuck was busy hammering away at the A-pillar while contemplating the possibility of having to fire another tardy employee.

When police reviewed the video recordings after the body was found, the only thing truly puzzling was the car's departure from a section of Tuck's lot where inoperable vehicles were parked. "I coulda sworn that Camry's tranny was shot," stammered Tuck. But of course, by that time, Tuck had bigger fish to fry. A pack of feral dogs had gathered noisily around the old Volvo two hours earlier. A police investigator told Tuck the dogs had molested only the young man's tongue and the bagged lunch his mother had prepared.

The man in the black Camry, driving east, found himself in Medina. There, on Reagan Parkway, Malbas pitched the Camry's license plate into a storm drain and quickly removed the one from a late model VW bug parked nearby. He fastened the bug's plate to the back of the Camry.

Jumping back into the sedan, Malbas quietly seethed. What an outrage that Nova had outmaneuvered him with the tool's delivery to Hannah!

Hannah hadn't been on his radar, but she certainly was now. He knew he needed some time to think through his next move and to contemplate several more steps beyond it.

Malbas wanted an indulgence, an earthly delight; what better way to celebrate a fresh kill? Recalling the smell of food that he alerted to near the town square, Malbas drove back a few blocks to a spot across the street from a pizza parlor. He remembered what a colleague had told him about "one of earth's greatest pleasures—pizza with anchovies, smothered in cayenne pepper flakes."

While placing the order for a large pizza, Malbas told the man behind the counter to triple the anchovies. The man nodded, making note that it was an order he'd never before prepared. As for the man's request for "lots of red pepper flakes," he told the customer he'd have to add the peppers himself.

"Drink, sir?"

"No thanks, never took to it," was the customer's reply as he paid with cash.

As he was the only customer in the pizzeria at the time, the three men behind the counter watched in disbelief as the man with sunglasses and odd derby hat took his pizza over to the counter that held the utensils, bottled parmesan cheese, and cayenne pepper dispensers. He sniffed the top of a barrel-shaped red pepper shaker, unscrewed the cap, and dumped its contents onto one side of the pizza. He then reached for its twin, unscrewed the shaker top, and emptied its flakes onto the pizza's other side.

Using a knife, Malbas smoothed out a pencil-thick layer of flakes and seated himself at a table. The cooks were astounded to see that he smiled while tilting his head back, savoring the taste of each mouthful. They were momentarily distracted with calls. When the cooks looked up again, their customer was gone. All that remained of the pizza was a sparse sprinkling of cayenne pepper flakes.

By late afternoon, the driver of the black Camry closely tracked Hannah's car, heading homeward. Malbas knew only that this was the appointed day for the beginning of revelations. His task: to assure an outcome that wouldn't interrupt the steady outpouring of human souls. His performance was being monitored.

He considered his task an unpleasant one, yet he was one of the more qualified for such an important mission. Not that direct interactions here on earth are disagreeable—quite the contrary. His work was the very essence of devotion, similar to what Americans refer to as patriotic duty. All to the betterment of darkness.

Malbas knew that several players were involved. Those poised against him included the churched humans. And, of course, Nova and Gabriel, both despised adversaries. But he'd prepared well and had long ago dealt with Nova, a real lightweight during her formative years.

For the meantime he'd stay close to Hannah, now the possessor of his beloved surgical tool.

As THE GARAGE DOOR DESCENDED, Hannah sat with her mind in a fog. What just happened? A moment later, smells from the house began to penetrate the car. Gradually, she unstrapped and opened the door. The smell, something delicious, was just enough to force her into a sense of recovery, security, and comfort—so richly unexpected. Was someone baking?

When Hannah entered the house, wanting simply to collapse, she found all three members of her family standing at parade rest before the dining room table, looking directly at her. Their left arms were tucked behind their backs, the opposite arms with a dish towel draped neatly across the forearm, extending tight to bellies and feet spread below each shoulder. Waiters, waiting. Smiles one, two, and three.

Still not a word. The table was set with extra chairs in place. Candles, too! At nine years of age, Sarah's smirk and barely-constrained giggle belied the…"Surprise!" In unison, they timed the greeting with additional voices that could only belong to her parents.

An instant later, her father and mother appeared from concealment behind a kitchen wall. "My darling girl," said her mother.

Hannah had forgotten her own birthday.

"Mom, Dad . . ." as her eyes met theirs. "Sarah, Matt, Chet!" They all came for her at once with hugs and kisses. "Oh, Mom, Dad—you made such a long trip, just for this?"

"Just for this," said her father. "After all, you turn 34 only once in your life!"

Their eyes conveyed radiant joy—a love for her that had always been there. It was one of few constants in her life, cherished and deeply embedded. Well, of course, her own family as well. She'd done everything within her ability to replicate the warmth of her family experience for her own children. And for Chet, whose love was a perfect match for hers, having grown as one of five siblings, the youngest of the bunch. His parents knew no greater responsibility than to raise their kids right: home-schooled, with mom at home, and within the conventional structure and accountability of an extended church family.

It had been eighteen months since she'd seen her parents. The distance between north central Ohio and Indianapolis was five or six hours, without stops.

Her parents, Jack and Miriam, lived about as close to Fort Benjamin Harrison's old campus as her father could manage among a friendly cluster of his military companions. Their wives were some of her mother's best friends.

"We're not in just any ol' suburbs. We're in the 'burbs of Uncle Ben's Rest Home," Jack had said to Matthew a few years earlier, referring to a term of endearment given to the post by those fortunate enough to get an assignment there before its closing in '91. As he'd often do, he then smiled and gave a quick wink to Matthew—a mannerism that trans-ferred to Hannah genetically.

Jack had attended advanced military training at Fort Benjamin Harrison twice in the 70s and 80s. He completed his 31 years of Army service at Fort Meade, MD, reluctantly retiring as a full bird colonel. They settled near Indianapolis because he and Miriam came to enjoy the town (refusing to call it a city), their proximity to the grand old re-greened park that had now replaced Fort Ben, and the familiarity of their home church.

Tonight, her parents looked dog-tired but otherwise wonderful. It was so good to see them. The day's stress and the effect of bizarre occurrences began to slide off in heavy release. It was great to be home. And this....

Chet asked: "Surprised?"

Before Hannah could reply, she glanced at her son Matt. She could discern the slightest agitation in her 12-year-old son's expression. Something's off, awry. Aha, for sure: he had a secret.

"Yes. What a surprise! But, Matthew, my loving son, you're...not...telling me something." Hannah dropped her bag and crouched down, moving toward him steadily in a tackler's position, eyes locked on his. He tried to stand his ground but laughed uncontrollably as soon as her hands met his, grappling as wrestlers might before they tumbled to the floor.

"Okay, okay!" he screeched. "They're staying! Grammaw 'n' Gramps are here to stay! They bought the Miller's home!"

Hannah wriggled free, turning to look at her parents. Her gaze expressed disbelief, then joy and wonderment. "Oh Mom, Dad—what? Really? Dad—all your buddies, left behind? You really did this? And just a few houses away?"

Her eyes danced to her mother, Miriam. Nodding, she

happily confirmed it. Her father's smile and wink locked it in.

"We wondered who'd bought it when the Sold sign went up!" stammered Hannah, looking at her parents.

"Well, you wondered. We knew," offered Chet. More hugs, with her father adding, "As for those ol' buds of mine, they can visit anytime."

Hannah spun toward Miriam. "Mom, the Miller property has such beautiful trees and flower gardens, just what you've always wanted!"

"We left before sunup to meet the realtor for a house tour, then settlement, all arranged by your incredibly organized husband," said Jack.

"We now have a set of keys," added Miriam. "The home and property are immaculate. Your husband sure picked a winner. Sight unseen for us until a few hours ago. Three bedrooms too—so an office for Jack in addition to the guest room. We're so blessed. Of course, we saw all the photos online, and Chet made sure of everything else—checking out the foundation, roof, plumbing, electrical, and HVAC."

Hannah looked at Chet. "All this time, a secret! And to find out today. All I wanted was something to eat and crawl into bed."

"Aw, honey—a bad day?" asked her mother. "No, Mom. Well, not anymore."

"They get to stay in Tommy's room," said Sarah excitedly. And then, immediately recognizing her mistake, in a sad whisper, she added, "I mean the guest room." She sighed and her eyes swelled. Hannah moved toward her as Sarah bunched her shoulders and hung her head. Hannah was quickly at Sarah's side, hands on her daughter's shoulders. Barely audibly, Sarah muttered, "Sorry, Mom."

"Oh, sweety, it's okay," said Hannah, holding her warmly. "Grampa and Gram remember it as his room, just as you do, and we'll all pray for Thomas tonight."

The solemn moment gathered them all around Sarah, whose lower lip shook, eyes still tearing. Hannah and Chet's third child, at just 14 months, died of SIDS a year-and-a-half ago—the cheerless occasion for her parent's last visit. The family had just begun to rise from the awful depression of Thomas' sudden departure.

A few minutes later, Matt attempted to break the spell with a recollection from their tour of the Miller home that morning. "Mom, you'll love the house. Gramps told me I can explore heaven any time I want!"

His innocent double-entendre blurted out hit the adults quickly. Hannah's expression darkened, searching for an explanation. She could only utter, "What?"

Hannah's eyes went to Chet's, then to her parents. Miriam explained with a forced smile. "In the Miller's— our—home, there's a storage area in one of the hallways. You need a ladder to get into it, or to be hoisted there on shoulders. Either way, Matt and Sarah immediately gave it the name. So 'heaven' it is!"

Hannah glanced from face to face. Unexpectedly, tears began to pulse from her eyes. She was weak again. Sobbing, she held out an arm, taken immediately by Chet.

Chet comforted Matt, who'd just begun to interpret his own mistake—the wrong words.

"Mom, Mom," yelped Sarah, with tears of her own. "You're happy, right?"

Chet lowered Hannah to a sitting position on the floor. Looks of concern spread among them all. "Yes, sweety," she said between sobs. "I'm just—a bit unsteady right now."

Miriam went to the kitchen for a box of tissues and pressed a few into Hannah's hands. "Oh, dear, just the wrong words. Everything's happening so fast. It's a bit over-whelming for all of us."

"Yes it is, Mom," Hannah sniffed. Blowing her nose, she looked up from face to face. "This is incredible. It's the best birthday, ever."

Her father put a hand on her shoulder. "It's a heck of a way to show happiness," he said.

"Well, almost the best birthday," added her mother. "You know, the best one of all happened 34 years ago in Austin."

"I was the happiest soldier in the Southern states," continued her father, still trying to break the spell.

"And me, a southern belle with two beautiful daughters," added Miriam, quick to move with it.

Hannah blew her nose. "That's it. No more tears." With a quick, upward look and a nod to Chet, she added, "Help me up, hon. I'm ready for a birthday party with whatever it is that smells so good."

As Chet helped Hannah back to her feet, she glanced at her parents, asking, "Has anyone shared the news of your move with Kristin?"

"We did," said her mother. "We told her, but she said that work just wouldn't let her come at the time. She promised to return east this winter or spring at the latest."

Hannah and her sister had grown apart not long after high school—and it was her sister's choice to keep the distance between herself and her only sibling, knowing that Hannah had developed, well, traditionally and with care to nurture her relationship with Jack and Miriam.

3

MALAISE

HANNAH NOTICED THE CHANGE in her sister when Kristin was in 11th grade, a transformation she attributed to Kristin's acquaintance with a new student, a senior from out of state. Whitney was the daughter of college profs; somehow, she and Kristin connected. Almost immediately, Jack and Miriam had to deal with a new, troublesome reality. Kristin was enamored with Whitney's freedom and intellect, her politics, and especially her instant popularity with the boys. And she had her own car. Rather than studying at home alone, her previous modus operandi for years, Kristin was often out late with Whitney. They were inseparable.

"She doesn't appear to be drinking or on drugs, but her attraction to guys has certainly taken an upturn," Miriam said to Jack late one night as they waited for her to return home. "That could be good, but it all depends on who she's interested in. I sure wish she'd spend more time with us at church. There are plenty of young fellas there who've shown interest in her."

"I don't like the sudden infatuation with Whitney," replied Jack. "But if I make any attempt to have adult conversation with our almost-grown daughter, she makes it clear that my opinion isn't wanted. Maybe it's just another phase.

Maybe you need to push a bit harder for some honest conversation with her, hon."

A few months later, just before Whitney's graduation—which Kristin exclaimed would leave her "behind to an untenable, final year in this stinking pit of a school"—Whitney and Kristin disappeared for three days. When Kristin didn't return home from school Friday afternoon and wasn't answering her phone, Miriam called Whitney's parents, having to leave a message. They didn't know Whitney's phone number.

Jack and Miriam asked Hannah to call her friends and friends of friends who knew Kristin or Whitney. Information began to trickle in that the two girls had isolated themselves among their peers. There were rumors they'd taken an interest in some young men at the community college. Recently, they were seen together leaving the men's dorm. Both girls were tugging at their clothes with their hair in disarray.

There was more. Turns out that Kristin was seen one Saturday morning, four or five weeks earlier by a girl named Audrey and her father who'd joined a prayer vigil at a family planning clinic, a facility where abortions were performed. Apparently, Kristin was driven to a parking space just inside the clinic's gate, maybe assuming that the clinic's location a few miles from home would assure her anonymity. The guy at the wheel appeared to be a few years older than Kristin.

Just before Kristin entered the clinic alone, she glanced at the gate and the 10 or 12 people gathered there for prayer. Momentarily, Kristin locked eyes with Audrey. Audrey seemed vaguely familiar, but Kristin couldn't place the face. She then dashed inside.

A few minutes later, the guy who'd driven her got out of the car to light a cigarette. He made a call. "Hey, Carol! How ya doin' . . ." was all they heard as he shut the door, then drove away. He returned a few hours later. Kristin emerged, drooped and withdrawn. She stood, looking for the car, then ventured another pathetic, peripheral glance at the gate. Ride-guy merely flashed his lights. Kristin, sore as she was, shuffled to the car and let herself in.

As they left, they noticed the number of people at the fence had doubled. Many flashed signs: "We're praying for you." "God loves you and your baby." "God knew you before you were born." "Your baby is God's gift."

Hannah had no choice but to share the convincing evidence of the abortion with her parents. However, at the time, she omitted references to Kristin's choice of friends or her fascination with the occult. But it was bad enough. Her parents were devastated.

By 10 that evening, with all of them deeply concerned, there was little choice but to call the police. They weren't too alarmed, saying that it was likely she'd be coming in the door before too long. Miriam and Jack sent Hannah to bed by 11 that night, assuring her that it would be okay, yet their quarrel woke her shortly after one am. She'd never heard her father so upset. Miriam was attempting to console him, though with little success. When there was quiet, she could tell her mother was crying, occasionally with guttural spasms and moaning.

"It's all connected, somehow," she heard her father say. "I know there's more to this than we can see."

THE NEXT DAY, with new calls to the police and then a visit

by two officers who came to get Kristin's description and a photo, they settled in for an uneasy lunch when Miriam's phone rang. In her clamor to get the call, she dropped the phone, disconnecting the line.

Hannah had never seen her mother so distraught. Crying pitifully over her clumsiness, Miriam reconnected with the recent caller. Fumbling with the phone's buttons, she activated the speaker. They learned immediately that it was Whitney's mother, Amanda, who sounded completely at ease. "Oh, the girls went to our new summer home near Brown County State Park. They decided to take the day off from school to make it a long weekend."

"You're freaking kidding me!" howled Jack as he grabbed the phone from Miriam. "And you're just letting us know now! We called you last night! Why didn't we learn from them what's going on? She just disappeared," he added angrily.

There was a long silence at the other end of the call, then a muffled conversation they couldn't make out.

Whitney's father came on the line. "Mister, um…I'm sorry, I forget Kristin's last name."

"Soelberg," replied Jack.

"Okay, Mr. Soelberg. This is Ian Paulson. Let's please cool down. You're shaking Amanda up unnecessarily. Look— Whitney told us she wanted to take Kristin to the lake house, and we assumed that Kristin okayed it with you."

"You assumed!" Jack bellowed. "You and Amanda, who's now unnecessarily shaken because I'm upset; yeah, that's accurate. Our daughter disappeared more than 24 hours ago, apparently with your daughter, and for all I know they're sleeping with guys out there! Even the police—"

The line went dead. Adrenals churning, Jack poked at the phone to reconnect to no avail. Apparently, Whitney's parents then called their daughter. Ten minutes later, Kristin called her mother. In a groggy and irritable voice, Kristin told them, "I had to get away and I knew you and Dad wouldn't let me go."

Miriam and Jack turned to Hannah, asking her to give them some privacy. Reluctantly, Hannah headed for her room, but when she turned the corner, she hid within range to hear both the phone's speaker and her parents. It was clear that Kristin, defiant, had no interest in staying on the line. "I have a life too. I'm responsible and have good grades. You really freaked out Whitney's parents! They also said something about the police!"

Jack was fuming. He attempted to take the phone from his wife, but she held him at bay with an icy stare, an unambiguous butt out.

Miriam attempted to have a quiet, restrained conversation with her daughter. "So you're telling me guys aren't spending the night, and there's no drinking or other stuff involved?" Kristin was silent, prompting Miriam to say, "I'm still here. Just talk with me."

Five minutes after the call began, it ended with Kristin's promise to return on Sunday. Jack called the police a few minutes later, informing the duty officer that Kristin was located. At church the next morning, Jack agonized quietly. Miriam spoke discreetly with close friends about her struggle, asking for prayers.

A few hours after dinner, Kristin entered the front door, looking tired and disheveled. She gave her parents a quick look, saying only that "Whitney's the best friend I've ever had." She ran quickly up the stairs, slamming her bedroom door.

THAT SUMMER, Kristin applied for and was accepted to cyber-school for her senior year, saying she couldn't take "all the petty drama" at school. Hannah learned in her junior year at high school that Kristin had created her own role as an outsider. The hardest part of it was to learn that, in no uncertain terms, her sister fell ponytail-over-sneakers for some guy at the community college, a guy who Whitney introduced her to. Shortly after taking her to the clinic, he was accepted at the state university and wasn't seen again.

Hannah was firm in her own confidence and convictions, so the taunting looks she received from some students in the hallway and occasional mocking remarks, she mostly sloughed off. But impressions were made, and she'd formed a deep sense of sadness for her sister. Not so much for the choices she was making—it was her life—but for the social derision and contempt that trailed behind her, at least on home turf.

One thing really bothered Hannah, and she knew that it must have been central to her parents' concern—the baby. Kristin had made some awful decisions and had gotten herself into a lifestyle her parents were deeply troubled with.

As a result, a baby was sacrificed. Who was there to stand up in the baby's defense? Hannah heard her mother punctuate fitful, late-night conversations with, "Our grandchild," as Jack listened quietly.

Kristin's torment and contempt for life deepened after the abortion, which also coincided with Whitney's departure after graduation from high school. It was a crucible moment for Kristin. She entered a dark period of her own design that included mostly black apparel, far fewer social outings, and refusal to attend church with her parents. It was a malaise so profound that she also began to read about the occult and demonology. She advanced from casual reading and dove into it with vigor—with laptop time that eclipsed any previous phase of interest or fascination.

One day while Kristin was out, Jack confiscated her laptop, iPad, and phone. He soon learned that Kristin had protected the devices with layers of security to block access. Kristin discovered his treachery (her word for it) within a few hours, decrying the theft of her belongings with a fuming tirade.

Jack had prepared Miriam in advance, saying only that his suspicion was aroused when intel from their firewall, which he could check easily, confirmed attempts to breach the barrier, both on her part and from the outside. Jack wasn't adept at computer work, but he did discover that many of the sites Kristin had tried to enter, and some that she had successfully navigated access to, had addresses and URLs that indicated occult content. And some among those he could open had an evil that, for as long as he could tolerate the content, gave him heart palpitations and twitching fingers.

The following day, Jack gave the devices to Manny, a Department of Defense IT friend who, like Jack, led an adult class at church. Manny agreed to do some forensic work to diagnose what sort of online activity Kristin had been involved with.

A few days later, Jack's fears were confirmed when he received a call from Manny, saying, "It's not good. In fact, it looks awful. Pure rot and filth. Kristin's late-night interests took her deeply into social media groups well within Satan's reach," continued Manny. "It's hard to believe she could do schoolwork on so little sleep; some of her online forays lasted well into the night. Phone calls, too—long calls to a few numbers on the west coast. One of the numbers matches the 'blog father' of a really wretched site. Overall, the content is scary as hell.

"As you and I agreed, Jack, I swept the devices. They're clean," he added. "I also increased your firewall settings to high security. I saved some of the information on a thumb drive to review when there's time—though I've got to warn you, there's some stuff here you may not want Miriam to see. Up to you as her parents, Jack, but I believe Kristin needs to spend some quality time with a pastor or Christian counselor. And maybe a good psychiatrist."

The next day, Jack and Miriam met with Manny. Gone were Kristin's secret passageways to groups, the address book, and her entire phone directory. Jack and Miriam swapped out the phone for one with a new number. They returned to Manny's for one more touch, the coup de grâce to any effort by Kristin to find the trails that he and Manny had pillaged and burned. When Jack returned the devices, he told Kristin that an online monitoring bug was installed in all of them, impossible to remove. As long as he was paying for the devices and her service, those were his conditions. He also planted a note in both the iPad and laptop:

Kristin, your mother and I and Hannah love you to the depth of our souls and forever will. You're in the midst of a torturous time, and we want to help in whatever way we can. Please don't turn from us or away from God, who loves you more than you can even imagine. Let's set aside the anger, please, long enough to talk.

Your mother and I don't know what to say to convince you that we are here to support and love you. We know you want your independence, and you'll soon have it as a beautiful young woman. Just tell us: what can we do to help? As your parents, we're also your stewards, a role that's both a privilege and a promise to God. We are so in love with you.—*Dad*

He concluded the note with:

Be alert and of sober mind. Your enemy the devil prowls around like a roaring lion looking for someone to devour. Resist him, standing firm in the faith, because you know that the family of believers throughout the world is undergoing the same kind of suffering (1 Peter 5:8-9).

That evening, as Jack and Miriam prepared for rest, they knelt at the bed. "Oh, Lord God, Heavenly Father, please be with us tonight, and through this troubled time in our lives," prayed Jack. "Please, Lord, be with both of our children, but especially with Kristin as she is so troubled. Please touch her with your love so that she knows the warmth of your presence."

"Thank you, Father, for hearing us," added Miriam. "Kristin's anguish is so foreign to us. We've lived for so many years with happiness, thanks to you. As Hannah flourishes and has embraced your love, Kristin seems to have abandoned it, though we know your Holy Spirit is suffering with her, wanting nothing more than to bring her closer to your loving Son. Please hear our prayers."

Restless, Jack went downstairs to wrap up some work. Thirty minutes later, Jack quietly climbed the stairs but noticed that Kristin's light was still on, visible below her door. He knocked lightly and was surprised that it swung open.

"Hey."

Kristin was propped up in her bed with a book.

"Whatcha reading, hon?" he asked.

"Hobbit," she replied but still hadn't taken her eyes from the book.

"I read it when I was about your age," he said quietly. "And that took me quickly into the trilogy. Tolkien's amazing, isn't he?"

Kristin's eyes crept from the page and met his gaze. "I like it."

"Babe, your Mom and I, well—like the note said—we love you so much. There's nothing we won't do for you."

Kristin's arms came up over her knees as she drew them tight. She hung her head, then emitted a whimper. "I know." Jack felt an urge to move and, as he cautiously made his way toward her, he prayed silently, *Lord, please guide me now when I need it most.*

Jack sat lightly on the edge of Kristin's bed and slowly moved a hand to her shoulder. At the mere touch of his hand, her shoulders heaved. Soon they were both awash in tears, and not a word went between them for a while. Jack wrapped her with both arms.

"Sweety, you know this feeling, right now, isn't just a stray emotion. It's from the heart—both of ours, and it was planted there a long time ago, even before you were born," Jack said. "You know, after all, God knew you before you were born. He called you to this life, and he gave you to us to protect and to nurture. You'll soon be on your own, and though we love you dearly, we need to fulfill our role to guide you while you're still here with us and then release you—hopefully a stronger woman with God's support.

"That stuff you'd been so interested in, honey—it was pure filth, the devil's playground, and an awful deception. You blundered in, innocent and unprotected," added Jack. "Your mother and I couldn't have it. We want you to love life and explore and to learn, but not in that awful place. It's a dangerous black hole of the worst kind. We know you knew it wasn't the place to be. God's arms are open wide to you, and His love is limitless."

Kristin looked into her father's eyes. His had begun to clear, but hers burned with distress.

"Let me ask just one thing, honey," continued Jack, still with one hand on her shoulder. "Someday, in a situation when you feel even worse than this—and that day will come because life's sure to throw unpleasant, uncomfortable surprises at you—remember this moment, then raise your eyes and heart to God and simply say, 'Please be with me, Lord. Show me what to do.'"

He waited a moment as new tears throbbed outward and fell from his daughter's eyes. But she held his gaze.

"Promise me, honey. Promise me that you will."

"I promise, Dad."

Jack held her again with both arms and then placed a kiss on her forehead. As he turned to leave, with a silent prayer sent aloft, Kristin's bedside light went out.

For a short while, things improved at home. Kristin spoke briefly with their pastor, though he was mostly dismayed. "I doubt there's much I can help with unless she wants to open up."

Kristin's attitude and a rededication to schoolwork improved. Her parents began to wonder if they'd dodged a bullet.

4

SUBTERFUGE

SADLY, THE BULLETS CONTINUED to come. Jack and Miriam learned that each day required a sense of alertness. Fatigue rode with it. Kristin's final months of cyber school were fraught with challenges.

With sad regularity, Kristin brought disunity and division into the family. It was the continuation of a bleak and desolate time for Jack and Miriam. Hannah was bewildered. Miriam wore the stress most noticeably. She threw herself into Bible study and joined a group of women whose children (or others) were involved with drinking or drugs—the closest she could come to a support group for the situation they'd found themselves in. Jack dove into his work.

Effortlessly, Kristin graduated from cyber school with honors. She was accepted at CSU, Sacramento, pre-med. Her lifestyle changed even more dramatically when she was in her 20s during graduate studies and then med school at UC Irvine. In those rare instances when Jack and Miriam learned of Kristin's experiences, they were torn to see that the substantial investment they'd made in their daughter's education placed her in a cauldron of vehemently anti-Christian, pro-socialist/communist, pro-choice stew. Jack's contempt for the country's system of higher education festered.

Kristin's visits home became less comfortable for herself and others. She spoke vaguely of people that she connected with socially and intellectually. There were occasional references to students, profs, and eventually, colleagues who she "fit in with ideologically and politically."

She once told Hannah that she'd been "transformed by a new society" of people who flaunted their disdain for America—its values, ethics, patriotism, liberty, and religion. "In the USA, freedoms and material wealth are overrated and in the hands of the wrong people," she said.

"It's a Trojan horse subterfuge," Jack complained to Miriam one evening. "It's so infuriating that we've opened the gates for these monsters, disguised as educators, who prey on and indoctrinate our children. They're given grand salaries to corrupt kids with trash like—get this [he read from a course syllabus on his iPad]—'Phallic studies' where they learn about the 'significance of the phallus, the relation of the phallus to masculinity, femininity, genital organs, and the fetish, the whiteness of the phallus, and the lesbian phallus.' And this wee teaser: 'Orgasmic enlightenment!'"

Jack was sweating, pacing. "Hon, you'll blow a gasket if you keep this up," said Miriam.

Knowing she was right, Jack took a few deep breaths and sat down. He went on to say that he received Kristin's list of UC Irvine courses. "She emailed 'em to me by mistake, then attempted to recall the message. Last semester, she took a three-credit course, simply titled 'Queer,' offered by the Department of Gender and Sexual Studies. Who allows this garbage?" He challenged Miriam with wide eyes. "We do! Because we pay for it! Lots and lots of money for that filth. And yet, she's jaded and privileged—and we're the enablers.

"Kristin's steeped in ingratitude, and she's intolerant—exactly what she believes we are! Talk about entitlement and lack of objectivity! Those smug, self-righteous, elitist, bullying profs have indoctrinated and brainwashed our daughter and countless other impressionable kids," he added. "It makes me sick to my stomach, hon. No wonder we're the laughing-stock of other nations."

When well-meaning people asked about Kristin at church, Miriam's remarks were clipped, circumspect. Hannah and Kristin spoke by phone on rare occasion; Kristin preferred the impersonal convenience of texting.

After Hannah gave birth to Matthew, she simply quit trying so hard to connect with her sister. Occasionally, when she thought about Kristin, usually at night before dozing off, it was too late to call. Though Kristin's clock was three hours earlier, Hannah didn't want to risk a long call, even though it wasn't likely. Sleep was a precious commodity, so she protected it.

Occasionally the sisters spoke by phone on a Saturday or Sunday, but Hannah became exasperated with that, sensing that Kristin would rather be elsewhere, anywhere, but on the phone with her own sister. Before she knew it, another six months had gone by, then a year. Hannah sent cards for Kristin's birthday, always personalized with updates and best wishes, usually with a photo or two. Kristin rarely reciprocated.

Then Sarah was born, strengthening Hannah's desire to keep a fairly tight regimen with nap and bedtimes, a schedule she was careful to maintain as the kids grew. Before she knew it, another Christmas season had come and gone with no real word, nothing substantive, loving, or insightful from Kristin.

So when Kristin called one Sunday evening, at an oddly

ideal time with both kids having just gone to bed for the night, Hannah was happy to speak with her.

Hannah gave Chet a quick signal and took her phone outside. She sat on the front porch as Kristin talked about her most recent promotion and a new leather sofa she found recently. Oh, and a guy she'd grown quite close to, and who'd proposed to her—Dr. Gilgamesh Arzhang, a pulmonary surgeon. Hannah learned that he was older by a dozen years, a divorcee with no kids, six feet tall, and a distance runner with a collection of paintings and prints. He had an affection for Dada, abstract, and surrealism; he owned several signed Dali prints, an original Miro oil, and a huge Calder tapestry.

Gili also had a very entertaining three-year-old Hill Myna bird. The bird's name, inexplicably, was Festus O. Yossarian. "The bird, and its name, are a bit eccentric—like he is," laughed Kristin, referring to her fiancé. Apparently, the Asian bird was riotously engaging, the life of the party with a broad range of screeches and whistles, and a vocabulary that grew by three to five words a week.

"Sounds like my son Matthew," was Hannah's reply, trying to show interest in Kristin's fascination with the bird.

"He calls him Fester."

"Huh?" said Hannah, not sure what her sister had said.

"Fester. Short for his full name," Kristin explained, chuckling. "Gili only reveals his full name—Festus O. Yossarian—when he wants to impress someone. The name has something to do with a character in the book, *Catch 22*."

Kristin excused herself, saying that she was needed and would be right back. A few minutes later, the phone was dropped loudly, then picked up. "I had to help Gili with something."

That's when Hannah heard the first slurring of Kristin's

words, taking her back several years to an evening when Kristin had successfully snuck back into the house, smelling of alcohol and sweet smoke, a pungent odor she later identified as marijuana. Recollection of that night swirled amidst the words that Kristin spoke now, with Hannah considering another dimension to her sister's jovial conversation: It's 5:45 there on Sunday evening, and Kristin's already buzzed.

"Those photos you sent a few munts ago, Hannah— they're so cute, and, and with you 'n' Chet smilin' so proud, it's such a picture of idyllic happiness," said Kristin. "Oh, I'm just going on, Hannah…."

"Hey, that's okay, girl. I hope things are well. So tell me more about this fabulous guy," asked Hannah, hoping to learn more about the mysterious man who could become a relative. As Kristin spoke, Hannah wondered how he might treat her sister. It certainly didn't sound like he had an aversion to drinking, which would've done Kristin some good. Hannah hoped he'd be a good influence on her sis, although if the last couple of minutes were any indication, it didn't sound promising.

There were other odd interruptions during the hour-long call, including one that sounded like an amorous scuffle. And more drinking; Kristin made no attempt to disguise that. Her sister's speech continued to deteriorate, but she was able to communicate sufficiently, despite the effects of alcohol and whatever else was involved. Hannah knew not to ask about it; her sister would surely end the call. At least they were talking, and Hannah was gaining some insight into Kristin's life.

Toward the end of their conversation, Kristin feigned fatigue, saying that it had been a long weekend of "social gatherings" and would she please tell Jack and Miriam about her engagement. Kristin rarely referred to her parents as Mom and Dad, preferring instead to use their first names.

"Sure I will, sis. I'll be glad to." The line went dead.

5

GABRIEL, REVELATIONS

TONIGHT WAS HANNAH'S 34TH BIRTHDAY. At dinner, especially now with her parents here at home, there was so much to be thankful for.

Sarah spoke about neighborhood goings-on and her guinea pigs—a boar and a sow—that recently had pups.

"Boar and a sow, huh?" asked Jack with a wink at his granddaughter. "Yup, I googled it," she replied.

Matt told his grandparents excitedly about school, some new friends, and about the church school's new teacher for middle school students, Miss Jinny.

"Um, that's Miss Rothermel to you, sir," corrected Chet.

"Dad—she told me to call her Miss Jinny, or just Jinny. She said I was very mature for my age and liked my choice of cowboy boots," replied Matt without missing a beat.

"She's too old for you," inserted Sarah with a smile that bounced around the table a few times as Matt fidgeted with his napkin.

"Well, I'll admit she's a fine addition to the teaching staff, and she really has a way with kids," Hannah explained to her parents. "Hey, Mom, Dad—would you like to join us this Sunday for the service and maybe for church school too?"

"Miriam and Jack glanced at each other and without hesitation said they'd like to do that. "You've spoken so much about Grace Church over the years," said Miriam. "We'd love to."

After dinner, everyone helped Jack and Miriam get settled in. The kids were cheerful and effervescent.

Then, as Matthew and Sarah were getting ready for bed upstairs, Jack asked Chet if they wanted to talk before turning in. "Sure. I think Hannah would like that a lot," he replied. "She seemed really troubled by something earlier. I haven't had the time to ask her about it." Jack nodded appreciatively.

A short while later in his room, Matt told his grandfather, "It's just so hard to believe that you and Grams are here to stay."

"We're so happy too, Matthew—to be here with you all." Jack gave Matt a big hug, saying, "Goodnight, champ. I love you."

Miriam entered and sat on his bed, stroking his hair. "I love you, wonderful young man." They left, turning out the lights and leaving the door ajar.

They both visited Sarah's room, telling her what a delight it was to tuck her in. Sarah introduced them to her favorite stuffed critters, Bob the Owl, Bun-Buns, and Mr. MonkeyMan. "They'll keep you company all night long, won't they?" asked Jack.

"Oh, unless they decide to go an adventure tonight," she replied, smiling.

Miriam chuckled, saying that they've all had enough adventure for the day. "I think they'll stay put because, after all, we get to have breakfast together. They wouldn't want to miss that, would they?"

Sarah thought about that for a second and said, "I think you're right, Grams. I love you so much."

"Goodnight Scooter," said Jack, giving her a gentle squeeze. Miriam leaned in to kiss her granddaughter. "Night-night, sweety."

THE ADULTS GATHERED in the den a short while later. They spoke a bit more about the kids, the trip, and the Miller's home—now in the family, complete with the kids' favorite hideaway, dubbed Heaven.

Jack chuckled, adding, "I'd have never thought of that one. Those kids are such a blessing."

Miriam glanced at Jack and said, "Speaking of blessings, Jack and I have something we'd like to share."

Miriam initially groped for words. They were sitting side-by-side on the couch. Jack's hand went to her shoulder, and he gave her a light squeeze. "We decided it's time, right?" Miriam looked at Jack with a contemplative smile in return. They were quiet for a moment, simply looking at each other. Chet and Hanna exchanged glances.

"Mom?" said Hannah.

"Jack and I decided a while ago that, with this opportunity of being here with you—we'd share something," Miriam said. "We've talked lots about it between ourselves, knowing that we'd make the move here and be closer to you and Chet and the kids. The timing of everything worked perfectly. God gave us a home that sold quickly, and though that was bitter-sweet, we knew we wanted to make this move. We had few complications, trouble-free travel, and then this, the perfect reunion. The only disappointment is Kristin's inability to be here.

"But if she was here right now, at this moment…I think it would be harder to say what I want to speak with you about," she added. Miriam glanced again at Jack with a look that confirmed her resolve to continue.

"Just about 34 years ago, your Dad and I had a tough decision to make, Hannah. At least, let me say—others made it tough for us. I was almost full-term with you," she added with a look of love that melted Hannah's heart. "In the three or four months before you were born, we'd had several meetings with my gynecologist, then the obstetrician who brought other specialists in to speak with me. Consistently, they told me that you were a high-risk pregnancy."

Hannah's expression grew deeper. She could barely take her eyes off her mother. She glanced at her father momentarily, long enough to see that he wasn't giving her the satisfaction of a conspiratory wink (so this was for real); his expression was uncharacteristically reflective.

"Essentially—following my heart complications after Kristin was born, which both of you girls know a few scant details about—they told us that you most likely had chromosomal abnormalities, and also that having you would put my own life at risk," added Miriam. "They all but assured us I'd die giving birth to you.

"They wanted me to abort. To abort you," she added, looking at Hannah, then attempted to hide the beginnings of a tear with a smile, but her trembling lower lip gave it away; it was the same pulsating nerve that replicated itself two generations later in her granddaughter, Sarah. Jack moved a bit closer, but Hannah leaped from her chair to wedge herself between them in a three-way hug that turned into a slow-motion carousel of arms, hands, and tears.

51

Miriam continued while looking at her daughter with soft eyes. "One physician gave us hope. He was a brilliant and sympathetic doc; neither of us can recall his full name. But it was Gabriel, not Gabe—and we seem to remember everything else about meeting him at the clinic and just about everything he told me that day, maybe ten weeks before I gave birth to you.

"He began by saying, 'I see your need for concern, and it's not difficult to see how this whole situation's weighing on you.' He wanted to offer a second opinion. But first, he asked us to join him in prayer. We were astounded. He led; his prayer was simple and eloquent. Jack and I added to the prayer with petitions for you and your sister and for our family to grow in God's love. When we were finished, the physician closed the prayer and said something to us like, 'As believers, we needed to place our worries with God, to turn them over to Him.'

"He also wanted us to activate the prayer chain at church," added Miriam. "Back then, I thought: a what? I'd never before heard words like that from a physician. He seemed perfectly comfortable saying them. He also sensed that our faith journey was just beginning.

"Gabriel then used a stethoscope to listen to my heart and looked through my chart again, even though it seemed to us that he did this merely to appease our concerns. We now believe that he somehow knew I'd be fine, and that you'd be healthy too. That's when he turned to me and said that my body was strong, and that my prenatal tests weren't worrisome. His words meant so much to us, to me, and left an impression that's lasted forever. Of course, he confirmed our decision to have you," she said, stroking her daughter's hair.

Miriam added that the physician wasn't with them for more than several minutes. "We've tried so many times to recall his last name and the exact words of his prayer. But I can tell you this, honey—it was incredible and so loving. He took our worries and concerns, personalized so insightfully, straight to God's attention. After we closed the prayer, he winked at Jack as though he knew it was Jack's own signature and said he'd see us again. But in the moment before he left, he added something that Jack and I remember with clarity. He said, 'There'll be many special moments in your life, to come. So much. Twins too, eventually.'

"A second later, he left—leaving us to ponder what he meant," continued Miriam. "Within a minute the nurse returned. We should've asked her then who the doctor was. We both remember him as Gabriel—handsome and fairly tall, with piercingly blue eyes and a voice that was incredibly warm.

"At the time, your father and I both considered ourselves to be Christians, though we weren't going to church regularly," Miriam added. "So we didn't even know what a church prayer chain was. But the physician's encouragement for us to pray became the foundation of our real love for Christ. That spilled into our much deeper love for each other and for both of you girls—especially you, Hannah. Not because we loved you more, but because you brought us together in Christ.

"We prayed a lot and began to enjoy our place in a community of believers, something we didn't have previously. The very next Sunday, when we attended church, we asked about a prayer chain. They started one for us that day, and it paved the way for our many years there as members of the congregation.

"Amazingly, a week later when I called to tell the doctor—Gabriel—that we'd made our decision to go through with the pregnancy, to have you, he wasn't there," added Miriam. "In fact, we couldn't leave a message for him at all. After dozens of calls and return visits to the hospital to see other physicians and specialists, no one could give us a last name for him. No one recalled him in any way. Not even the nurse who was there the day he slipped into my exam room, asking to speak with me. Even the hospital administration; believe me, I called them all. They all thought I'd lost my mind."

Miriam seemed almost lost in the retelling of her experience from so long ago. Quietly, she continued: "Jack and I can tell you without any reservation that we're convinced that Gabriel met with us, spoke from his heart, changed our lives—and gave you yours."

A few moments later, as Chet watched all three of them close together, Miriam added, "Jack and I decided, whatever the consequence, I'd give birth to you, Hannah. Naturally, after so many tests and talks with specialists, we knew you'd be a girl. So, we named you. That strengthened my resolve. When you were Hannah, there was no turning back, no consideration for what may come; I was going to have you.

"Should the predictions and warning of the other physicians come true...I'd give you to Jack, and he'd raise you with Kristin. But somehow, deep inside, with Gabriel's assurance, whoever he was, we knew things would be okay."

At the end of her mother's astonishing revelation, Hannah's expression turned inward. Her thoughts had placed her on the edge of a powerful vortex, with an undertow only she could feel. Hannah began to sob as tears mounted a new assault, an automatic reaction over which she had no power. Quickly, Chet moved to Hannah's side. The day's experiences spun relentlessly. As her mind reviewed the tumultuous events of the day—a single day—a headache and crushing sense of anguish poured in. As she sobbed convulsively, Chet, Miriam, and Jack surrounded her.

Jack and Miriam had no way of knowing or predicting Hannah's reaction to the revelation of events before her birth. They anticipated the very opposite of it, expecting from Hannah a mostly happy response, with interest in the strangest part of it—Gabriel's role. Through the years, they'd been so fascinated by his appearance and the impact of what he had to say that both of them were sure Hannah's reaction would be joyous.

Now, seeing their 34-year old daughter coiled into a fetal ball and sobbing uncontrollably was completely unexpected. No one spoke. They held and patted Hannah, offering comfort while looking at each other for answers. Chet signaled that he had no idea, no way of knowing why Miriam's story had struck an exposed nerve. Jack and Miriam wondered separately what their appearance, and the move, might have to do with it—combined with the impact of the story of Hannah's close brush with death before her birth. And of course, there was Tommy's death, too. Was this all mixing into some awful, toxic brew?

Jack leaned closer to Chet and whispered, "Would you like us to leave the two of you alone for a while?" Before Chet could answer, Hannah spoke through her sobs: "No, Dad, please don't. I have to tell you something."

Through her tears, Hannah began with a retelling of her day, beginning with the repeated nightmare. The delivered box, unopened. Harley's class, with some context-setting details, including a reference to the video taken by a guy posing as a bioprocurement pro. Then, lunch with Samantha and her revelation that they shared the same nightmare. The numbness she felt and the disbelief, knowing that she and Sam needed to talk again soon. *How could such a thing be possible?* Then, the discovery of changes in her office, knowing that she hadn't left the light on, or the box centered under it with the shiny tool inside. The note and her drive home.

Miriam was visibly stunned. Her expression settled into a look of astonishment when Hannah spoke about the guy in the car next to hers. Miriam asked, "Are you sure he spoke your name?"

"Yes, Mom. Clear as a bell," replied Hannah as she slowly stood. "My purse and the box are in the car."

Chet gently grabbed her hand and said, "Lemme get those. Just sit, hon." Moments later, he returned with the box and her purse, placing them next to her.

Hannah opened the purse and pulled the note from it, handing it to her mother. Miriam was stunned by the note and passed it to Chet. After reading it, Jack asked Hannah, "How well do you know Doctor Harley? Is there any chance he concocted some ridiculous scheme, a joke?"

"Dad, it occurred to me for a second, but it would be so unlike him. Way off character, and not his nature. And, anyway, what about the dreams that Sam and I shared? And the guy in the car?" Hannah reached into the box and withdrew the tool. She handed it to her father; they all marveled at its beauty.

"It feels like an awful hallucination," said Hannah. "The note and the tool, and the dreams—mine and Sam's—all fit together somehow. How, and why, I haven't a clue. Just thinking of the guy in the car, he's no less real than the dream. At least I saw and heard him while I was awake. Really freaked me out too. And the note. It's so mysterious and poignant, with its reference to the good I can do and the path I've taken, unlike Kristin's."

"Well, she's not exactly mentioned by name," Chet pointed out while scanning the note.

Miriam asked, "What sort of tool is it?"

"I have no idea, Mom," said Hannah. "Surgical, I think. But old—because you couldn't properly sanitize a bone or ivory handle. It occurred to me before leaving that I should show it to Harley. But as I left, I checked. His office was locked."

"It's highly specialized," said Chet, turning the tool over in his hands. "Loads of old home construction tools existed 50 and 100 years ago that aren't in use or reproduced today. Of course, we now have modern tools that improve the function and performance of the old ones. This tool, whatever its purpose, is incredibly well made. The moving mechanism of the handle, as the drill bit turns and extends, or retracts, is no doubt intentional and works precisely. I'm impressed."

"What's Kristin got to do with any of this?" asked Jack. "Talk about intentional: her presence in the letter seems to be as much by design as the operation of that freakin' drill bit. And what's this about a cross?"

57

6

TROUBLED RECOLLECTIONS

IT WASN'T LONG after their child had died that Hannah and Chet had the room repainted. They purchased new furniture, repurposing the bedroom as a guest room. By 10:30 that evening, Jack and Miriam were finally preparing to close out a long day there in Thomas' room. As he threw his shirt onto a chair, Jack spoke to Miriam.

"Hon, there's one facet to this I didn't talk about tonight because it's so unclear to me. This business of the note that Hannah shared; I once received a note—as best as I can recall—that connects with it in some strange way." Miriam, already in bed, opened her eyes to look at Jack just before he turned off the light.

"Please tell me it's nothing that I need to lose sleep over," she replied.

"No, don't. Besides, my memory of it's already decades old. The note's in a box—one of several marked for my office," he said. "I kept it because it was such an oddity. I'll look for it as soon as we unpack. Well, goodnight hon." Miriam was already asleep.

Jack's need for coffee and early-up routine put him in the kitchen just before Hannah was leaving for work. "Mornin' Dad," she said with a hug. "I smelled the coffee. I'm pretty sure I can make a short day of it today. I look forward to helping you move in. Let's get pizza for tonight, huh? Give Mom my love." Travel cup in hand, she slipped into the garage and left for work.

The next few days passed in a cheerful blur. The now-rejoined family, minus only Kristin, joyously appreciated each other's company. Midweek, the movers arrived with their furniture and more boxes, so they threw themselves into the task of making the new house a home.

During church on Sunday morning, their pastor made a special announcement just before his opening routine. "Our family has grown. You all know the Methaneys, Chet and Hannah, Matt and Sarah. But you may not know that Hannah's parents, Jack and Miriam Soelberg, have just moved here—in fact, just a few houses from Chet 'n' Hannah's place. You'll be glad to know that Jack and Miriam asked me this morning about joining the church without even hearing what a wretched messenger I am! Will the Methaneys and Soelbergs please stand?" Moments later, a jubilant noise arose as the Soelbergs were briefly the center of attention.

As the service drew to a close, Miriam leaned toward Jack to whisper, "This sure feels like home, doesn't it?" That evening, still with no further discussion of the strange events of the previous week, Jack decided to open boxes in his new office while Miriam read the Bible.

Jack's office boxes, layer by layer, were peeled back like sedimentary strata—documents and awards, photos and articles, each adding clarity through his military years. He found the box he was looking for, containing a collection of military orders, citations, and memorabilia. In it was a file from the year Hannah was born.

Jack's military career began in '68; he was drafted after completing a BA degree. He went through basic training at Fort Dix, then infantry training. At the age of 23, he and more than a hundred other soldiers stepped off a large air transport into terrain unlike any they'd seen before. The air in Vietnam was as thick as the tangled jungles they'd soon be fighting in.

As a young infantryman—though still a few years older than many enlisted troops and some of the officers—Jack entered 'Nam at the beginning of the horrific Tet offensive. He and several other XXIV Corps cherries (new, replacement troops) were lifted by helicopter to fill spots vacated by soldiers killed in and around the U.S. Marines Corps base at Khe Sanh. They were there to reinforce Marines who'd fought fiercely against the North Vietnamese and Viet Cong.

Jack was stationed at a forward operating base as a rifleman and machine gunner. It was brutal, with hard experiences that woke him, wide-eyed and sweating, years later. One of those experiences, just weeks after his arrival was to witness, from just 40 feet away, his commanding officer (CO) being blown off the ground when a single artillery round came in near the HQ bunker.

The captain, Maximus Miracle, AKA "Captain Miracle," or "Captain Max," was only a few years older than Jack. He'd just stepped out for a chat with his troops. Seconds later, he landed with one leg attached. Medics rushed in immediately. They first performed CPR. "Breathing! Heartbeat!" yelled one medic while another shrieked for a gaggle of wide-eyed soldiers to stand back. "Disperse, will ya? Break up! Who knows if they don't have an observer nearby?"

"Freakin' cherries," commiserated the medics of the astonished newbies. "They'll get us all killed."

Though another artillery round didn't come in, they learned too quickly that the enemy did indeed have close eyes on them. When the captain's medevac helicopter lifted off, an antiaircraft gun began firing on it from the adjacent hill. Fortunately, the bird took only one hit that grazed the cabin. The troops quickly called in air support on the hill, silencing the distant gun. They learned later that their captain survived and would return home. His replacement arrived before Captain Miracle was flown from the hospital ship, the USS Repose, anchored 20 miles off the coast of Da Nang in the South China Sea.

Had it not been for air support on several occasions and a guardian angel he thanked profusely, Jack knew he'd have had no chance of returning home, at least alive.

A year later, with a shrapnel wound and Purple Heart, Jack returned to the states and entered officer candidate school. He sped from the rank of sergeant to a commissioned second lieutenant, then received further training at Fort Benning, Georgia. Jack was back to 'Nam, though to a much-altered war and with the "end game" (more accurately, a retreat) in full swing.

After 30 years in service, Jack Soelberg retired from the US Army at Fort Meade in Maryland. He and Miriam returned to their home in Indianapolis.

As JACK OPENED box after box in search of a letter he vaguely recalled, every folder and citation provided a glimpse back through his many years of military service. Occasionally, he stopped to peruse a document or article.

Before Jack could find the letter he was searching for, a very specific memory came back to him. He'd received the letter he was searching for the day of Hannah's birth.

Jack recalled that he was sitting at his desk, reading the letter over and over, when a call came through from Miriam. She called to say that it was soon time for him to pick her up. Hannah was on her way! Miriam had already seen to Kristin's care through the mother's group and needed a ride to the hospital.

"Dora from next door can take me if you can't," she'd said.

"Nonsense; I'm on my way," he replied.

They arrived at the hospital two hours before she gave birth, and miraculously, their new baby girl was healthy. Miriam, however, received a radical hysterectomy. Their second child, Hannah Christine, would be their last. Jack remained with her there through the night. Miriam and the baby wouldn't return home for four days.

As these recollections were streaming in, Jack thumbed past a few magazine articles and there—as though reaching out to him from the distant past—was the letter he sought. The edges were yellowed, and each corner a bit worn, but otherwise it was in good condition. The letter was addressed to him, dated two days before Hannah's birth.

Jack—Congratulations to you and Miriam on this very special day. Number two! What a blessing.

Life's harmony is in the balance you find between the inpouring of God's endless love and your provision of His love with others, especially family. You and Miriam are purposefully blessed with new life. Years from now you'll see—in a new light—that one of your loved ones will need both my shielding and yours because essential, intended lives will be at risk.

Surely, God's offer of eternal life matters, but so do earthly lives and their divine mission, God's holy commission, among men. Yet, too many are wrongly taken.

We are chosen to be trustees of those lives given to us and the lives of others who come within our influence. We must be vigilant, as guardians of divine provision.

Allow joy in Christ to be your river of affirmation. It's flowing bountifully to you. I was by your side in Ban Phuong in November of '68, shield in hand.

Psalm 58:3—*The wicked are estranged from the womb.* — *Nova*

Through his many decades, Jack could count very few emotional trenches as deep as this one. A cascade of anguish enveloped him at realizing how closely this message connected current events with those on the day Hannah was born. His dismay intensified as he re-read and considered the message and its poignancy to this very day, its immediacy and impact.

Jack sat down at his desk to think, head lowered into his hands. Even now, attempting to piece it together was dizzying. Who could hold or discern insights like these then—and now? How had their lives become entangled in something so mysterious? And the reference to Ban Phuong! The "shield in hand" notation took him to the worst day of the worst month of his first year in 'Nam, and certainly the most shocking in graphic clarity to the horrible impact of war.

Through sheer willpower, Jack trudged deeper into sealed archives, memories of the war that he'd deliberately buried in his mind. Ban Phuong, November of '68, was his most laboriously sealed memory. Though he could never fully forget what happened on Thursday, Nov. 28 that year, he'd done his best to pack, seal, and quarantine it for all time. Recalling the day, Jack remembered taking point on patrol for the squad. Behind him were his closest buddies—Speedy, Roscoe, Ringo, and Billy Yank; together, they were the Five Amigos.

On the morning of Thanksgiving Day, '68, coming into the last few months of his tour as a newly-minted buck sergeant, Jack remembered that it was the last time their entire platoon, all four squads, patrolled as a unit. The day before, there were airstrikes near the village of Ban Phuong in response to intel of a VC encampment. The battalion commander's instructions were to assess the bombing's effectiveness.

Jack was chosen to lead the patrol from base camp along trails toward the small village. With almost 10 months in the country, Jack was now regarded as one of the more experienced soldiers in the unit, well-suited for the point-on-patrol position.

It was no place for Jack's M60 machine gun, AKA the "Jackhammer"—a belt-fed, 24-pound weapon he could use on his own, given his six-foot frame—so he'd exchanged it for a lighter M16 and a few grenades that he hung on a canvas chest rig.

There were 32 soldiers on the move, down by a dozen from injuries and attrition. They were overdue for some new guys, but this was no time to argue about that. He recalled that the company XO was with them, predictably toward the rear, with an ARVN interpreter. With his remaining time in the country so short and with friends Speedy and Roscoe behind him, each separated by 20 feet or so, Jack's alertness choked out all other thoughts or emotion. Every movement ahead or in his peripheral vision became a potential threat. A few hours into the patrol, the stress was palpable and seemed to propel him into a nauseous hyper-drive. There was always the risk of an ambush around the next bend, tripwire, or punji pit. He'd seen the damage they could do.

Some of the soldiers behind him could sense Jack's apprehension, noting the way his head would spin toward the slightest sound. His several hand-signaled warnings (fist up at shoulder level) to stop, take a knee—all false alarms.

Every combat-experienced soldier went through some form of it. Had the law of averages, at last, weighed against him? He'd seen too many short-timers take the hit, zipped into a body bag just weeks or days before their scheduled flight home.

When they rested, Roscoe teased, "Ease up, Jacko. You won't get hit unless the bullet has your name on it."

"Yeah, but I ain't seen that one laying on the ground yet," countered Jack.

A sergeant chimed in: "It ain't the bullet that has your name on it that you've gotta worry bout, Jack. It's the ones marked, 'To whom it may concern.'"

They knew a settlement was nearby from a previous patrol months earlier. What they didn't expect was to wade into a napalm-brutalized landscape, smoldering from jellied gasoline dropped the day before. The black and leafless areas that fueled the inferno gave off an acidic pong that concentrated the stench of death. The soldiers did their best to stay on the footpath, wading through wet, ankle-deep ash and grime, hemmed in by naked tree trunks, oozing sap, some with pools that held boiled centipedes and roaches.

About 400 yards from the first hooch they came to, just beyond the napalm's reach, they discovered two hurriedly camouflaged holes. Their two best tunnel rats, Ringo and Billy Yank, quickly stripped down to pants. Both were lowered head-first into the dark spider holes 60 feet apart, having no idea what they might encounter.

The platoon posted defense while they waited, with no occurrence, only to learn from the returned soldiers that their enemy had left in a hurry. In one tunnel, a few bowls of rice were newly congealed. In the other, bedding, clothes, several rifles, and a box of grenades were hastily abandoned. Thank God, no traps.

After confiscating what they could, they blew the tunnels and radioed command. The soldiers were instructed to continue on into the village, being told they'd have air support if need be. As they got closer to the village, the signs of the previous day's bombing were unmistakable: giant, twisted craters and shredded trees, elephant grass blasted flat, the absence of forest sounds. The first hooch was obliterated.

The soldiers walked around additional craters and beyond two or three more hooches, some of them smoldering. Their platoon leader placed a different soldier on point. Jack was glad to move to the rear and to exchange the carbine for his treasured M60. The craters were plentiful and the damage more severe as they moved out, seeing that—here, where the concentration of bombs was heaviest—nothing could have survived.

Clearly the work of B52s, heavy bombs had churned up the lush jungle. Twisted and destroyed pieces of NVA military gear and equipment were mixed with body parts and appendages strewn in all directions. Tire rubber Ho Chi Minh sandal prints, pools of jellied blood, body drags, and fleshy clumps of skin radiated outward, eventually forming paths of retreat, confirming that the intel was good; this had been a large encampment. After posting security, the XO made assignments to assess the enemy's makeup and size. The remains of a command post were found with big, blasted vats of rice, shredded boxes of ammo, and blood trails that led out like spokes of a wheel. All dead and wounded were gone.

By midafternoon, while planning a return to base camp, many of the soldiers had collapsed in craters to smoke and eat. Gradually, their perimeter defenses relaxed, assuming no nearby threat, a terrible mistake given the flattened terrain. A small NVA element—knowing of the Americans' penchant to evaluate the effectiveness of a bombing mission—had crept back to a concealed position, 80 or 90 yards from the large gathering of GIs.

Without warning, two machine guns opened up on several groups of soldiers. Bullets tore through them before one squad could mount a counterattack. By the time they reached trampled grass and piles of still-hot metal casings, the enemy had vanished.

Three soldiers were dead in one crater. In another, there were two dead and one wounded. A stone's throw from one of the craters, Jack was throwing up, surrounded by fallen comrades.

Just minutes before the attack, Jack had joined several other soldiers, his closest friends, to sit against a low and oddly pristine mud wall, built as one of the NVA's defenses for the command post. Moments later, he was surrounded by dead and bleeding soldiers, with medics hurriedly at work to save lives. Large bandages were applied, tourniquets twisted tightly, and morphine injected. Jack shook regurgitated food from his lap while he checked and rechecked his limbs. It was their blood, not his, splattered across his boots and fatigues.

Jack cried for the first time in 'Nam. His best friends were gone or fighting for their lives. Ringo, dead; Billy Yank, dead; Speedy, badly wounded, face and chest. And Roscoe, whose legs and torso were a ragged mess, a femoral artery gushed uncontrollably. Jack heaved miserably, tears pouring from below his hands, clamped tightly to his face in shame. Ringo and Billy Yank had only three weeks remaining in their tour. How? Why?

Medevac choppers, the "dustoffs," touched down to collect dead and wounded. As the remaining group prepared to pull out, Jack swept tears aside to look back at the wall to see the line of stitched pockmarks left by bullets as they raked through the soldiers. How could it be that he'd been spared? There was no explanation. The outline of his own body— stenciled in place by the blood and gore was unmistakable, his torso completely hemmed in. How could it be?

"I was by your side…shield in hand."

A week before he left 'Nam, Jack learned that both Speedy and Roscoe had died. Uno Amigo; he was the last.

Shaking from his effort to recall the events of Thanksgiving '68, and with fresh tears running freely, Jack moved unsteadily from his desk and pulled the tape off of another box, filled with citations and photos from that first year in 'Nam.

Halfway into the pile of papers, including the *Stars and Stripes* story of the assault that took the lives of his friends, Jack found the other materials he was looking for: two-color 8x10s given to him by a camera-toting journalist weeks after the attack. One of the photos was taken earlier, back at base camp with the five amigos; the other of the bloodstained wall, complete with his stenciled outline. He'd kept it only because it was a reminder of how precious life is.

He then walked, trance-like, to Miriam's purse in the kitchen. She'd asked Hannah for the note that arrived in the box with the tool. Jack pulled the letter out and returned to his desk where his now-decades-old note lay open. When he placed them side by side, he was stunned to see that they appeared to be written by the same hand. Letters were formed exactly alike. He turned on his laptop, fingers vibrating with adrenalin and grief, went online, and began reading.

"How on earth could this be?" He seemed oblivious to his own outburst.

Miriam entered the office, gently placing a hand on his back. Jack looked up through bloodshot eyes to see a look of deep concern on her face. "Hon, you okay?" He didn't reply but shoved the laptop back to make room for the letters, then pushed them together at the center of his desk. She looked from him to the letters, then leaned over to scrutinize them. "Jack—who's Nova? Why am I mentioned here, and what's this about 'number two?'"

"I'm as confused as you are, hon," he replied, still trembling. "This is a baffling thing, a mystery I can't solve." Miriam swiveled his chair to see him, shocked at his appearance and agitation.

"The note that Hannah got today reminded me of something I stashed away 34 years ago. I began to mention it to you several nights ago when we were still at Hannah's place, but it was too late. You were almost asleep. So I searched for it, finding what I was looking for in one of my boxes," he explained, pointing to the old note.

"This one, here," he said, poking the old note, "arrived just an hour or two before you told me to it was time to take you to the hospital 34 years ago. I never told you about it because we had more important things on our plate and, at the time, it just seemed unbelievable—way too strange to share with you then. But I kept it and a few things related to it. Now I'm freakin' baffled that this has come back to life. Just look at the writing, Miriam. It's identical. Yet I've had the older note for decades! I'm gonna scan the notes and get them to an old friend who knows some handwriting experts."

Jack got out of his seat and ushered her into it. Miriam carefully read each note as he stood beside her.

"Jack, you never said a word about this. And, now, after all these years...."

"Hon, that's right. I thought way back then how strange it was," he replied. "A week, a month, a year later—it just moved further back, and the kids were growing, my job getting more demanding. Until today, I'd forgotten about it. My head hurts. I'm gonna' get some Tylenol. Take your time. I'm sorry. If I'd have known this would come back to us, you'd have learned of it long ago." He left her at his desk. She found him 15 minutes later sitting in the den, reclined, eyes closed.

"I'm not asleep," he said without opening his eyes.

"Jack, can you tell me about these photos?"

"I figured you'd ask," he said. "Those were supposed to dissolve in time too—buried in the box with the note and the article, stuff I thought I might never see again, yet something kept me from pitching them. Now they're important, somehow. And they may even fit into the mystery of Hannah's horrible day."

"I don't know that I've ever come across anything so confusing," said Miriam. "Hannah and Kristin know nothing of this, right?"

"Not a thing. And, as freaked out as Hannah was, there's no way I was gonna mention it," he responded. "Besides, I had to find this stuff to get reacquainted with it. Now my head's spinning, Miriam. Think of it: my first year in 'Nam is in there with the reference to how I was protected. Takes me right back to what I told you about long ago, that day when we were on patrol and then being with my best buddies when the machine guns lit into us against that wall."

"You mean…the note Hannah got today refers to something in these photos?" she asked, holding out the color photos. One was a faded picture of the five amigos, shirtless, smiling, and seemingly carefree amidst the warzone. All happy but aged beyond their years.

"You showed me this photo once before, a long time ago," Miriam said, holding up the photo of Jack with his good friends. In the image, the soldiers sat atop a ring of sandbags that wrapped around a big .50-cal at Bravo platoon's home away from home—Ringo tapping on his thigh to whatever rock was blaring from the radio at that moment, Speedy with a celebratory cigar, Billy Yank whittling on a piece of palm, and Roscoe who'd just popped the top of his jungle-temp Pabst Blue Ribbon, foaming profusely. And, Jacko with his signature smirk.

"But this one, never. You never showed me this one," she added, moving closer to him. "Jack—is this what it looks like?" No other image could so effectively convey for Jack the personalized horror of war: the blood-stenciled wall. Jack's recollection of the foot-thick barrier was etched permanently in his memory. He was certain that if a man's life flashes before his eyes in the moments before death, this horrific movie would be among them.

In the days after the attack, he tried to recall the burst of machine gun and the awful moments at the wall—but his subconscious refused to let it go. But it hit and hit hard in his dreams—a ghastly slow-motion bloodbath.

"I shouldn't have kept it, Miriam," he said of the photo. "But I had to, for them. I never wanted to see that wall again, but I kept the picture just to know it was there. The last time I pulled it out was the day we gave our lives to Christ. Good that we did because I was so angry at God for so long. I've thought and prayed about that wall and what happened there so many times. It's hard not to cry. I told you about the attack on that awful night; I couldn't stop crying. You saw the newspaper article with this photo. That's the wall where it happened."

"You mean…right there," she said, pointing at gruesome patterns on the bloodied wall, many of the outlined shapes so horribly perforated—all but one. Miriam looked closely at the one imprint not riddled through. "That's…where you were?" He could only nod through new tears. "Oh, hon," she said, wrapping him in her arms. She flipped the image over on his desk to hide it. That's when she saw that he'd written long ago on the backside: "I'll love you guys forever—*Jacko.*"

Minutes later, Jack willed himself to regain control. "Hon, there's more. But now it's hard to know where to pick up." He paused, wiping his eyes. "The note—the one from Hannah's birthday—you're mentioned in it, by name, and the kids, indirectly. Somehow, now, the reference to 'intended lives wrongly taken' in your old note from Nova appears to point to abortion. There's no other explanation. And, also in Hannah's note, there's the mention of Kristin's 'chosen path,' maybe another reference to abortion. And here we are 34 years later rejoined with this godawful thing."

Miriam went to Jack's office to retrieve the note Hannah had given to her earlier. "Right up top, it points to Hannah's choice not to go the route that Kristin did," she said. "Both notes are spiritual and from a position of the sanctity of life. There's an unusual, almost poetic, intellect to them—and the mention of Hannah's nightmares, also shared by her friend, Samantha. Finally, mention of a cross and scriptural reference: Psalm 58:3. 'Wicked are estranged from the womb.'

"Jack, this is frightening." She stood, looking at the photos for a few minutes. "Hon, could you join me in the kitchen?" She left him to gather the other note, the article, and the photos. They sat at the kitchen counter in silence, Jack holding his head, Miriam re-reading the article.

"What's that tool got to do with any of this?" she asked.

He mumbled, "I haven't the faintest idea, unless…."

"Unless what?"

"Unless that beautiful golden tool with the cute little drill bit has a ghastly purpose," he replied.

"Like what?"

"Heck, it seems pretty sinister if you think about it. In my mind, I've eliminated so many possible uses, coming up at last with surgery. Animal? Human? What if…just what if it's an abortionist's tool?" he asked. "Maybe Hannah didn't want to say so initially, whether she knew or merely guessed at it, because it'd terrify you and draw us closer to what seems to be some freakin' horrible, cosmic nightmare.

"It's happening right now, you know," continued Jack. "I

did some online research for some of this earlier today. Right here in the USA, thousands of babies died today. Tomorrow, thousands more. It's endless, and our daughters are at opposite sides of this damnable thing: Hannah's role, as a scientist, to save lives; Kristin's role as a physician quite frankly is to make the death machine more efficient, and to hell with her adherence to the Hippocratic oath."

"The what?" asked Miriam.

"It's an oath of ethics taken by physicians—one of the best-known of Greek medical texts. Physicians swear to uphold specific ethical standards, including and especially acknowledging the sanctity of life. They're sworn to save lives.

"I was reading about the oath before you came in and was stunned to see several different, original copies of it. It's incredible," he said. "A twelfth-century manuscript of the Hippocratic Corpus, the oath, is written on papyrus or something like that in the shape of a cross; the words actually form a cross on the manuscript. But the oath dates back much further to within a decade of Christ's time. The earliest version of the oath forbids abortion. A 275 AD version of it, if I recall it right, keeps the prohibition of abortion, yet other versions somehow contradict that—allowing the practice of killing babies. Yet, again, middle-aged versions of the oath explicitly prohibit abortion. And now—here's the killer—that prohibition is omitted from most of the oaths taken at US medical schools today, once again allowing abortion, or simply by omitting reference to it, new generations of docs are discreetly given consent through omission.

"You and I know abortion to be wrong, Miriam. It's one of the worst, if not *the* worst, of modern-day depravities," he added. "So, tell me, how could the menace of this horrible sin afflict us, again—you and me—here and now? This time, it's real close to home, and somehow includes Hannah and Kristin. With your near-abortion 34 years ago, well, we stood in the way of those who wanted it. And now, with all this other stuff thrown in the pot, I'm just stupefied by it. There's no easy explanation, and it seems that Hannah and Kristin, especially, are embroiled in something substantial.

Miriam and Jack did not rest well that night.

THE NEXT MORNING, Jack removed his scanner from a box and wired it to his laptop. He placed the notes atop the scanner's plate, then saved them as PDFs. His email to Harry, who'd spent a long career in Army intel, was brief:

> Greetings old friend. Blast from the past. Hey, I know this is oddballish, but I wouldn't ask if it weren't important. Could you please have these notes reviewed by a handwriting expert—the best you've got? Are these notes penned by the same person? Anything else that sticks out, please let me know. I'll gladly pay whatever the cost. And if you're ever in Ohio, lemme know. There's a spare bedroom here for you and Jan. And a microbrew nearby. All the best. —*Jack*

That afternoon, Jack's computer emitted a bugled reveille signal. Incoming email:

> Best to you, too, you ol' fart. Hope you and Miriam are well. Central Ohio, huh? Jan and I knew the lure of grandkids would be irresistible for you both. Isn't it great?
>
> Those letters sure are strange. The best handwriting expert I know agreed to take a look, so I

passed the documents along to her. She's still active duty, soon to retire. As a favor, she looked at them today and says that you've unquestionably got notes from the same letter writer. Apparently, there are also some clues as to the writer's character—very interesting stuff—but you'll have to call her after a trip overseas. She leaves tomorrow for Brussels and will be back in a few weeks. Here's her contact info: Brigadier General Kay Zavala, INSCOM, Ft. Belvoir, VA. Kay's a handwriting savant, best in her trade. She may tell you some oddballish things about those letters; don't dismiss them too easily.

Best. —*Harry*

Jack made note of the need to check with her in two weeks. He then examined her credentials on LinkedIn's military portal.

7

FETUS AND CHOCOLATE MARTINIS

KRISTIN CALLED her sister one evening several days after Hannah's birthday. "Hey, sis. Sorry I didn't send a card or call. I was traveling and just forgot," said Kristin. With her recent promotion, Kristin's responsibilities as the organization's top clinician for the western region included visits to meet with staff around the country. Kristin was talking cheerfully while sipping something with ice cubes.

"Gili's out with his buds, so the cat can play," Kristin said, expecting a reciprocal giggle. Hannah yawned; it was nine o'clock, almost her bedtime. She realized that Kristin was well into her altered state at six pm, Pacific time.

It required no prodding on Hannah's part to learn that Kristin was being groomed for the position of clinical director, then CEO. Kristin was flaunting it: "I'm not even 37, and they see me as Cynthia's, well, Cyn's replacement in just two or three years."

OBGYN physician and administrator Dr. Cynthia Moloch, the organization's CEO and executive director for the past 12 years, the architect of rapid growth, currently had supervisory responsibility for hundreds of employees and managed all operations and resources. She planned to retire soon.

In an earlier call, Kristin let it slip that Cynthia enjoyed having Kristin as a drinking buddy. And, for the past couple of years, Kristin had been by Cyn's side, learning the intricacies of managing ever-expanding staffs and responsibilities. "Every few months, she gives me a bigger role, a new title, and then we go on tour. I've had two freakin' raises in the past year, sis, and Cyn promised to double my bonus in December."

"You must be doing something right," replied Hannah, trying to sound enthusiastic.

"Money's better than I could've imagined," added Kristin. "Cyn went with me 'n' Gili to an artist's wine and cheese event in Santa Barbara last weekend. With Gili's encouragement, she bought a big, original oil for close to half a million—must be six feet high. I think she was trying to impress him. She says Gili knows art better than anyone. He later told me it was the nicest piece on display. Says she got it at a terrific price."

Hannah couldn't think of a reply for that, other than to say, "I hope she has room for it."

"Oh, she does, and it's only her first original," Kristin added, taking another icy sip. "Her place is big and modern, with loads of wall space for more art. She says it's her last ambition before retiring—to decorate the remaining walls with original works, with Gili serving as her art advisor—and then she wants to hand the reins to me."

Hannah tried to engage with her, but the growing disparity between their lives had become an irritant. She wanted to sleep, and Kristin wanted to talk, her inclination when catching a buzz.

"The only thing troubling me is that, in our meetings,

Cyn hammers the clinical managers for underperformance, insisting that they need to do more to raise revenue," said Kristin. "Even though most of the clinics are on par with profitability over the past couple of years except the four clinics in Texas where the freakin' conservatives and Bible-thumpers are really causing problems.

"Cyn's been applying pressure for the clinics to increase the number of terminations like never before," continued Kristin. "But, at the same time, she's handing out raises to headquarters staff routinely, then pressuring the base to fund HQ. She keeps saying to the clinical managers that 'we aren't a charitable organization' and 'soft services aren't profitable,' pushing the clinics to perform more abortions.

"That's where the real money is," she added. "And then, usually in closed door sessions with clinical managers, she pushes the dagger in with a twist: she wants more late-term operations, with bigger fetuses to provide a much wider range of harvesting options and higher profitability. There's gray area legally—and some of the clinics are reluctant. But Cyn insists on it, saying that she holds their careers in her hands."

"She's, um, determined, isn't she?" stammered Hannah, now attentive, thinking that Kristin's CEO must be a narcissistic monster. She was about to ask if Kristin was sure she wanted to follow in this woman's footsteps when her sister launched into a new topic.

"We've also been spending more time at lunches and dinner events with procurement agencies—the folks who buy fetal specimens," said Kristin. "You should see it: Those guys really lay it on lavishly with great food and, my oh my, have you ever had a chocolate martini, Hannah? Last night's affair was incredible. There was duck, Japanese wagyu beef filets or whatever they were, and yummy 'licious choc-tinis. I think I've gained five pounds in the past few months!

"Last night's soirée for a dozen of us from HQ was one of the best, ever. Cyn was in her prime, and toward the end of the night practically dragged me away from the bar to show me off," slurred Kristin while sipping.

Okay, thought Hannah, *this has become really annoying. Maybe I should say something to her about the alcohol....*

"...so he and Cynthia go way back."

"Um, who's he?" asked Hannah. "Sorry."

"The guy who owns the firm that hosted the party; the fetal tissue procurement agency," added Kristin. He's one of the top body-buyers in America. Well—fetal specimens. Meaning his firm, that is."

"So, Kristin, how important is the connection for you?"

"Well, Cyn wanted to see the chemistry between the two of us, most likely, and I think we got along fine—me 'n' the dude, that is. Eventually, he talked about his kids and his dog, and I talked about Gili 'n' Festus the bird." She laughed, then spouted, "Oh, dang. Bit of a spill....

"But, there's no doubt that, as Cyn pushes for higher profitability, the link between our organization and buyers of fetal tissue will become more important," she went on. "The more abortions, the better. And the more late-term abortions the better because of the secondary market for mature fetal tissue—even more lucrative than the abortions. The biggest barriers right now, according to Cyn, are the darned governmental regs and clinical managers that want to do things the old way with greater emphasis on counseling, mammograms, health checks, and contraceptives as opposed to ratcheting up the frequency of highly profitable surgical abortions. And, of course, parents."

"Parents?" interrupted Hannah.

"Yeah, Cyn always says that parents are a barrier to service," explained Kristin. "They get in the way too often; they're suspicious of their grown children or of our motives by meddling in our work and best intentions."

Hannah almost corrected her with a "Best for who? Some of those mothers are just kids," but stifled the idea. Eventually, Kristin ran out of things to say.

Hannah's exhaustion, mixed with the horror of her sister's revelations, had taken her just paces away from a sense of dread. She fought it back, refusing entry. Yet the baby writhed closer, gaining clarity.

8

MOLOCH: DEATH TO WEE INTRUDERS

As HANNAH TOSSED fitfully in bed, attempting to fend off visions of a screaming fetus, three women and two men were gathered before a Mac in a small recording studio just a few blocks from Stanford's main campus in Palo Alto, California. They made preparations to watch a 90-minute video of Dr. Cynthia Moloch, the attractive, divorced, and mid-50s CEO of one of the world's largest "family planning" organizations (and Kristin's boss).

David began his introductions. "Thanks for meeting us, ladies, and for your help over the past couple of days. Our research, training, scripting, and preparations were well rewarded. Jonathan and I reviewed the video of Cynthia briefly last night after leaving the restaurant. We came here to see it once through, real quick, just to be sure of the audio and video. There's only so much we could see on the iPad and with little indication of the sound quality, but it looks like everything went well.

"Denise—huge thanks for importing this into your system here, and for getting ready so quickly tonight. Just think, 24 hours ago Cynthia was just finishing her meal."

Of the five gathered around the Mac, Denise—who managed the studio—had been most helpful during the past several weeks in preparing David and Jonathan for their roles last night, even to include visits to the restaurant, a mock table with ideal seating arrangements in her studio, and camera and audio equipment selections. Walking away with good video and audio feed from a busy restaurant, while the subject was unaware of the recording and with only hidden electronics, was a challenge Denise was well prepared to help them with.

"I took a quick spin through the video just an hour ago, and I think we've got great material to work with," said Denise. "No glitches, and most importantly, the audio is as good as we could've hoped for under the circumstances. We'll be able to clean up the main audio feed with no other edits necessary."

David had begun his preparations months ago, establishing an ersatz company with call center, website, and business cards, counterfeit LinkedIn and social media credentials, and calls to many pro-life friends in the medical and bioscience fields. Among them was a Texas-based clinician who, mid-way through her career, owned abortion clinics. For more than a decade, she plied her craft capably. Then, during a church message that spoke to her heart, she broke down as "giant plates were lifted from her eyes" to reveal the horrible sin of her chosen profession. She gave her life to Christ, begged forgiveness, and abandoned her practice. Soon after that, she opened a women's clinic to offer free, pro-life counseling and services and a women's shelter.

So by the time David was to meet with Cynthia Moloch for the first time, at length, he was ready should she have tough questions. She didn't.

David, a happily married, mid-40s trauma nurse, father of

three, and a Bible school teacher at church, had studied for his role as a "fetal tissue procurement pro" and now CEO of the fictitious firm, WindStar Biomed.

With his medical background, and through several weeks of preparation, David knew just enough about the intricacies of abortion practices and technology, and the many types of medical research that created a market for fetal tissue. He could hold his own. He had an engaging smile and genuine attentiveness. And, through three earlier meetings with the subject of last night's video, he'd won the trust of the "Queen of Abortion," a moniker Cynthia was given by the three women gathered around the Mac.

LAST NIGHT, with confidence that he'd fully won her trust, David arrived at the eatery with Jonathan, posing as the fictitious procurement firm's VP of operations. It was Jonathan who wore the camera and carefully wired audio recording gear.

During their rehearsals leading up to the dinner with Dr. Moloch, Jonathan practiced how to activate the camera and two concealed microphones, becoming a bit more familiar with the equipment each time.

"The original audio track's only of modest quality, no thanks to the unavoidable background noise of the busy restaurant. But we've got a few tricks up our sleeves to remedy that," said Denise.

The quality of the video was excellent. "So crisp! We could see Dr. Moloch's eyelashes if we had to," said Layla. She began to make notes about video sequences, carefully watching the timer. "I can't believe the quality of that button-cam picture. Nice choice, Denise."

"The sound will improve toward the end of the recording," said David. "A group near our table created some noise, but they eventually left and that made a real improvement to the audio quality.

David looked at Jennifer and nodded. She touched the keyboard, and the screen jumped to life. The video began. The group watched, transfixed, as Dr. Cynthia Moloch set her eyes upon David repeatedly and smiled.

"Why, David. You fetching schemer, you!" said Layla. The group laughed easily at Layla's comment.

Dr. Cynthia Moloch seemed to appreciate the connection she was building with David and Jonathan. Though, especially, David.

"She was enchanted. David thawed her into a puddle," confirmed Jonathan. More laughter.

The video continued to move on the big, 30-inch Apple monitor. Dr. Moloch had a confidence that came not from an acquired, hard-won experience and skill but rather a well-honed, self-possessed bluster. Clearly, she'd refined it and was comfortable with how others perceived her.

"Okay—time out—she's just about to order her second cosmo," interrupted Layla. Jennifer, who operated the FinalCut Pro video editing software, stopped the recording. Layla noted that Cynthia Moloch had her second Absolut cosmopolitan at nine minutes and 32 seconds into the recording.

In the monitor, Moloch had just spoken to the waiter: "Thank you, kind sir. Please keep an eye on my glass." Layla made more notations on her pad.

"Fortunately, with the software, we can eliminate 50 or 60 percent of the background noise with no difficulty," assured

Jennifer. "When we get to the edits, the sound will just about match the quality of the visuals. I know it's tempting to stop and go as we watch this for the first time. But I'd like to run through it once with few interruptions if that's okay."

With the video temporarily on hold, Jennifer looked around and received confirming nods from the group. "Okay with you, Casanova?" she teased, looking at David who, the night before the engagement with Dr. Moloch, was given the oh-so-suave moniker by the group as they prepped him for his role.

"Oh please. No more theatrics. And you'll notice that I wore my ring," he said, waving his left hand. "Carol's got a great sense of humor but wouldn't appreciate all the banter."

Jennifer nodded, then wagged her finger. "Noted. Now, shall we move on?"

The video began again. "So, Cynthia, Jonathan's background and mine now unite through the connections of friendship and a passion for winning investment in our enterprise," said David. "So, please feel free to dive into any level of detail about your work that you like. We'll know to back off if Jonathan turns green. I doubt it, though. The color of currency suits him well."

"You've got a great sense of humor, Dave. But please call me Cyn," said Moloch, warmly. "You're right, there are elements of my profession that can quickly overwhelm a person's sense of curiosity and well-being. Typically—except for those of us in the business—it isn't proper table talk, but if your colleague's amenable, I'll educate you." She smiled at Jonathan.

Moloch's second drink arrived. David received another as well. She was oblivious to his order for the non-alcoholic

"Distinguished Guest" that he nonchalantly pointed to on the drink menu; the waiter simply nodded his understanding. "I'll have the same as him," said Jonathan, as rehearsed, when the waiter prepared to leave.

With just a bit of prompting, Cynthia Moloch began to talk about the organization's successes, nationwide, and growing profitability.

Nineteen minutes into the video she said, "Our clinical managers are finally getting it. Kristin Soelberg and I are getting them dialed in. She's my closest associate and the one I plan to name as my successor when the time's right. We've identified the last pockets of resistance among the regional clinical staff. I've had to put two managers on notice and fired one in Chicago just last week. We're rooting out the ones who're stuck in their old tendencies to steer women toward options such as adoption. Or to offer help with unprofitable diagnostic and health services.

"Some of the old-timers also prefer to let abortions trickle in on a natural basis, rather than to push patients toward them," she added. "So, I'll train them away from old habits or show them the door. I call it 'calibrating.' I'm in the midst of it now, making a real move toward steady increases in abortions, favoring late-term terminations which, by the way, sets the stage for our relationship." She again glanced at David, smiling warmly.

"Almost a suggestion in that one," interrupted Jennifer, with shared laughter. "Sorry, couldn't resist."

The video continued as Cynthia casually sipped on her third drink while speaking about their operations and how she'd set the foundation for an increase in abortions by 25 percent within the following year and 40 percent the next.

"I plan to retire soon, leaving plenty of time to have some fun. And, by that time, I plan to double our late-term abortions. Maybe more. It's a methodical process, and I'm determined to make it happen," she said. "All the pieces are now in place, and the numbers are moving nicely. As you know, abortions are the largest unregulated business in our nation, and with improving profitability, so I'm pushing our staffs to strike while the iron's hot.

"With your interest in larger fetal specimens, we'll be able to deliver exactly what you want, when, and with improved quality," she said.

"That's great news. So, how're you doing it, Cyn? How are you pushing the numbers so successfully?" asked Jonathan.

She took a drink and smiled confidently. "I can be demanding and meticulous. By the time I leave, I could patent the process," she said, chuckling. "Among other things, I instruct my clinical managers how to bore it into their staffs, to find a girl's, well. . .fragility, and work on it. Frankly, they aren't given alternatives. Or, if so, only as a last resort. Our patients are reminded how much trouble it is to have a baby and to raise them.

"Part of the process of increasing terminations at our facilities happens through good ol' sex education. We have a goal of three to five abortions for every girl between the ages of 13 and 18. It's ambitious, I know, but most of us work on straight commissions, so the more abortions we get per customer, the better off we all are financially. For our clinics to reach financial goals, I developed a process of educating— well, convincing—young girls from the earliest age possible to view their sexuality in a new light.

"Thanks to new and permissive educational systems foisted upon oblivious children and their parents, we're allowed to start with kindergarteners. That's where our carefully groomed 'educators' who're strategically planted in many public and private schools across the country, begin the process of indoctrination. They typically put children in a circle, asking them all the same question: 'What do your parents call your private parts?'

"You and I know that every family has a different name for private parts," she continued. "So by the time we reach the third or fourth child, it's clear to those children that they simply don't know what it is they've got between their legs. Lots of confusion there, of course, and the kids' parents certainly aren't enlightening them at this age. But that weakness is where we begin. We tell them: 'Boys, this is what you have, and girls, this is what you have, and don't be ashamed of your private parts.'

"The aim of sex education at the earliest ages is to erode a child's natural modesty. Everything is calculated to separate the children from their own values and those of their parents," added Moloch. "By third grade, children were shown explicit 'how to' diagrams for sexual intercourse. By fourth grade, children are encouraged to masturbate, either alone or in groups of the same sex. It was during the fifth and sixth grades that I led our staff educators to provide the missing link between sex-ed and abortion.

"Our goal was to get them to be sexually active as early as possible and to get girls on a low-dosage birth control pill that we knew, quite frankly, they'd get pregnant on," she said with a wry smile. "You see—for low dose birth control to provide any level of protection, it has to be taken at the same time every single day. We all know there's not a teen in the world who's capable of maintaining a tight regimen like that."

Moloch explained that a girl on the pill who thought she was "safe" typically had sex more frequently than those not on the pill.

"Quite simply, that pill doesn't work, enabling us to accomplish our goal of three to five abortions, per girl, between the ages of 13 and 18. And, with our best educators who tend to be the most convincing, when the girls they've taught become pregnant, they believe they have only one real option," she said. "Those same girls will call our clinics because they believe we empathize with them, we understand them, we're familiar, and we're 'pro-choice.'

"To improve things, and to sell as many abortions as possible, we now train our call-in desk counselors to lead distraught callers toward abortion as the best, easiest solution. Our call center ladies are instructed rigorously about how to lead girls into our clinics. They have scripts designed to overcome every objection.

"I knew the sex-ed strategy was working when a young woman visited one of our clinics for her ninth abortion," she continued, smiling broadly. "The system's working. I'm rather proud of our accomplishments, and everyone that takes part in providing the service benefits financially. And, now, with fetal specimens involved—someone I know jokingly referred to them as 'aftermarket parts'—the downstream benefits are multiplied, with even greater reward."

"Cyn, I'm so curious, and you've probably encountered this, so I'll ask," said David. "Aren't parents throwing up objections?"

"Oh, sure. Some of them do, if they know about it," Cyn

replied. "It's rare for them to learn anything from the kids because, after all, none of the children want their parents at school. Even worse—a parent at school asking tough questions, making a scene. But, if they get that far, and put up a good argument, and especially if they articulate well—tipping us off to new levels of threat we may not want to deal with—we quickly and apologetically retreat, noting carefully which child is involved. Funny, though: we find that most parents, who learn anything of this, blithely ignore the specifics of what sex education entails or simply don't want to be bothered with it."

"Really?" asked Jonathan.

"Sure—they trust the system," replied Moloch. "Their lives are already too stressful in one way or another. Meanwhile, we have total access to their kids, with essentially free roam from school administrators to have our way with 'em."

9

COSMOGIRL, PURSUING TRESPASSERS

DINNER WAS EXCELLENT. David, Jonathan, and Cynthia were now picking at the remains of their salads. Jonathan tried to delay his need to visit the restroom. His departure meant that the audio and video recording would come to a stop, but he could no longer delay it. He politely excused himself. The camera moved as he turned the corner heading for the restroom, opened his blazer, and hit the power button, disabling the audio and video. The video resumed when Jonathan reactivated the camera.

Not wanting to stir curiosity, Jonathan took his time walking back to the table. As he returned, Cynthia and David were having a warm discussion. He noticed that she'd moved her chair a bit closer to David's. Jonathan had to adjust his position to accommodate the slightly new angle for video.

"Ah, looky there," said Layla as the video returned to Cynthia Moloch. "Our CosmoGirl's acquired a new drink, number four, I do believe. She's got a healthy tolerance to them."

"It appears to be her special affliction," agreed David.

On the monitor: "Jonathan, we've ventured from the school classroom back to the OR," said David, steering the conversation in a new direction. Cyn was just saying some-

92

thing that you'll want to hear. Though, this will be tougher for tender ears. Well, yours. So it's good we've eaten," he added with an assuring smile. She nodded and took a deep pull on the cosmo.

"I was telling Dave that, back at the clinic, there are other facets to our methodology," said Moloch. "For instance, we never allow a patient, or staff members for that matter, to see a baby during ultrasound procedures. As you know from Abby Johnson's story in the movie, *Unplanned*, that alone can be a turning point. It's such a shame that her book, and the film, became so popular. Agh!

"Suffice it to say that women who're having abortions should never be able to see the ultrasound video or photos," added Moloch. "It's the same for our staff. The physician may need to, though without even telling the patient we're using ultrasound. And, if absolutely necessary, the assistant. But that's it. I've even instructed my staff to turn off the volume for heartbeats whenever possible. The last thing we want to do is to humanize the little intruder."

"She stopped. Why'd she stop?" asked Layla, thinking for a moment that this might be the end of the video feed.

"She's just getting warmed up," assured David. "I'm pretty sure she'll reach for her glass."

Moloch took a slow drink, relishing the cool taste. "I think that bartender can read my desire for perfection," she said, looking at both of her hosts. Just the right amount of lime, a dash of Cointreau, a spit of orange, and oh…that Absolut."

Denise stopped the video. "Just curious. Were you guys aware of how much she was drinking? She's not gonna' do anything embarrassing before the night's over is she, David?" Denise looked teasingly at him.

"Naw, nothing like that. She's a quiet but effective killer, so nothing unbecoming the Queen of Abortion," replied David. "But you're right. She sure enjoys those cosmos."

Following a moment of silence, Denise started the video.

Finishing her fourth cosmo, Dr. Moloch glanced up for a few seconds, eventually catching the eye of the waiter, who quickly returned with a refill. "I've instructed our counselors to build supernatural empathy with their patients and to cry with the girls, well, patients, at the drop of a pin. The counselors are to learn what's driving their interest in a termination and to reinforce and amplify it."

Forty-two minutes into the video, Cynthia saw the waiter passing by and simply nodded toward her long-stemmed, triangular glass. Cosmo number six was rushed in. Both of the drinks for Jonathan and David were also replenished.

"By now, she must think you have no idea how many cosmos she'd had," said Denise, having frozen the video momentarily.

She then tapped a key, reactivating the video.

"We're not pushing, pitching, promoting, or selling soft services or counseling," Moloch said. "We sell abortions, and we get right down to business, yet in a way that still preserves the illusion of empathy and understanding. The goal of our compassion is to drive patients toward the one decision that's best for them: termination.

"Typically, patients have two key questions: 'Is it a baby?' and, 'Does it hurt?' Our answers are consistent and emphatic: simply, no. Counselors are instructed to lie as sweetly as they need to—whatever it takes to secure a patient's consent and to collect as much of the fee up front as possible," she added. "That way, they're locked in."

"We do appreciate consistency," interrupted Jonathan. "Buyers of fetal tissue now include some of the leading university med centers and private biomeds, many of which are at the cutting edge of med research, Cyn. They have private or NIH funding, and no one in the chain wants to push the question of where tissue samples are coming from. Sort of a, 'don't ask, don't tell' policy."

Cynthia welcomed Jonathan's conspiratorial comment. "We all learn to improve those deliverables," she acknowledged. "Our role, and our partnership, will be built on that commitment."

"Stop the monitor just a sec," said Layla. "Sorry, I had to say. Unquestionably, any sense of guardedness on Cyn's part was dissolved by the cosmos. But, will her spilling the beans be admissible in court if she's, well…drunk?"

"She hasn't even slurred her first word," said Jonathan. "That doesn't happen 'til near the video's end. I don't know the legal facets of this, but she's clearly in control at this point, feelin' no pain, and telling all."

The video began again at the marker for 68-minutes, 33-seconds.

The table next to theirs was just receiving a new round of drinks. The closest guy to Cynthia made a happy ruckus of it, encouraging his guests to order another refill immediately. Their laughter and merriment overwhelmed the audio feed entirely for a few minutes. The distraction wasn't ignored by Cynthia, who seemed to enjoy their good cheer.

The soundtrack picked up with Cynthia Moloch looking at David, saying, "Life's good, isn't it?"

"Yeah, for those given the chance to exit the birth canal in one piece," countered Layla.

Denise stopped the camera. She hung her head, shaking it slowly. "That'd be clever if it wasn't so horrible," she said before starting the video again.

On the monitor Cynthia Moloch resumed, looking at Jonathan. "The women, or patients, are told that we're dealing with 'products of conception' or 'globs of tissue.' As the concerns of pain, I've instructed counselors to assure patients there's only mild cramping. In reality abortions can cause a wide range of experiences, from minor pain and cramps to excruciating pain and a host of psychological issues. With that, though, I see I'm on the wrong track. Let's move back to products and deliverables.

"So, Jon, since some of this may be new for you—and just tell me if I'm going too far or offering too much detail—I'll just provide a quick explanation of what's involved beginning with first trimester terminations," she added, sweetly. "Then, second and third. It's at the later stages where we harvest the best, most valuable tissue—those of greatest value to you and Dave.

"In most cases, girls have a choice between medical or surgical abortion procedures during the first trimester. Medical abortions—non-invasive—are only available up through nine or ten weeks of gestation. For the first seven weeks, there's methotrexate and misoprostol, or MTX. This combination of meds isn't as frequently used here in the states anymore with the availability of mifepristone and misoprostol, commonly referred to as RU-486, the abortion pill. And there's mifeprex.

"There are also manual vacuum aspiration, or MVAs—a procedure used as early as three to 12 weeks from a girl's last period," she said. "It's considered one of the least invasive procedures with the need only for local anesthesia at the cervix.

"Then there are surgical procedures used to terminate pregnancy up to 16 weeks from the last period," she continued. "Suction curettage, dilation and curettage—or, a D-and-C—or vacuum aspiration.

"On those days when clinics offer terminations, we like to set it up to handle first trimester abortions efficiently," continued Moloch. "Conservatively, abortionists can do 10 to 12 an hour for four hours—meaning easily 40 or more abortions in a day. Usually, more. Sometimes, many more. An abortionist once told me that he did 27 first trimester terminations in one hour. A clinic average for second trimester terminations, more time-consuming and costlier, might be 12 to 15 in a day. Or more. Usually more.

"As for money, we all make money. An abortionist typically makes one-third of the cost of an abortion," she added. "So, take for example first trimester abortions, which might cost the patient $500 or more. Each two- to five-minute procedure nets the abortionist, say, $150 to $200 of that. That's easily $6,000 to $7,200 in a four-hour day. Just for the abortionist. The rest of it goes to the clinic. And if parts 'n' pieces factor in, especially with older babies, there's a lot more money on the table."

As she reached for her drink, Jonathan saw his opportunity for a question, one stemming from their detailed preparations over the past few weeks. He asked, "What about the possibility of prostaglandin, Cyn?"

Not missing a beat, she looked at him and explained: "Vaginal prostaglandin, or 'E2' suppositories, are effective for mid-trimester abortion or fetal demise in the third trimester.

No sooner than that, and they're safe and effective. In fact, Jon, we have a girl who's won her, well, frequent flyer miles. She's 16. We've given her E2 four times already. Each time, effective.

"And, as I'm sure you know, the D-and-E—well, dilation and extraction—is the most common type of second trimester abortion," she added. "In a D-and-E, the girl's cervix is dilated broadly because the baby's too big to remove merely with a suction machine. Once she's sufficiently dilated, termination begins by rupturing the amniotic sack.

"We can then dismember the little trespasser, pulling it out in pieces, both by suction and with forceps to tear parts outta there until it looks like the physician's extracted everything," she said.

"Occasionally, a baby's skull is too large to remove, so the abortionist crushes it with forceps. We know that the baby's skull has fully collapsed when its brains flow out of the uterus—like a light gray-white porridge. This is called the 'calvaria sign,' and it signals that the skull will then be much easier to remove."

Then, she looked at Jonathan and said, "You okay with this? Too much info, dear boy?"

Jonathan replied. "I'm okay. I assumed we'd get to this level of detail. Whew, I think I'll have another of those drinks, though." David smiled just perceptibly at Jonathan's remark, secure in their conspiratorial sobriety. Seeing his opportunity for a restroom break, David began to rise, saying, "Be sure to get a refresh on mine too."

Moloch wasn't about to pass up another round. At the time, there was a noisy interruption from the nearby table. More drinks were delivered there, and as David returned, he dodged the agile waiter, who was momentarily unaware of his presence. The waiter moved deftly while balancing a tray of empty glasses with one hand and an arrangement of newly filled glasses in another. The trays rose and fell with practiced ease as the waiter accommodated David's return to the table.

"Where were we?" asked Moloch.

"I think we were watching Jonathan turn green with your explanations of second trimester procedures, Cyn," replied David. They laughed, and she resumed.

"Let's see," said Moloch, now aglow and with a luminous smile brought on by the triggering of endorphins. It was apparent to the group gathered around the monitor that Cyn was nourishing a compulsion and that the Absolut was satisfying the need precisely.

"Stop the cam," said Layla. "She's reaching nirvana. There it is: CosmoGirl's signature—the Absolut smile. Now, let's just hope she can keep it together to give us some more useful info."

"She'll get there," assured Jonathan.

Denise hit the go key. Moloch was still stuck, trying to recall the point where the conversation ended.

"Oh, I know, Cyn. The calvaria sign," prompted David as their drinks were quietly placed on the table.

"Yes, yes." She smiled confidently. "Once everything seems to be removed in the D-and-E, we can feel around inside the uterus with forceps and a curette. Then the suction machine can be used again to vacuum up whatever debris might still be in there," she continued, now emptying her sixth cosmo.

"Cyn," said Jonathan, trying not to look at all shocked, but yet sincere, "how do you know everything's…out?"

She smiled. "It's a good question. With a D-and-E, all the removed baby parts are put on a tray where they're reassembled. This makes certain that the entire baby's accounted for, and no parts are left behind.

"One way to enhance a D-and-E is to kill the baby—um, I mean fetus—beforehand, maybe a day or so before the procedure. We call it a 'ditch.' It's accomplished by inserting a long needle through the mother's abdomen and into the heart of her baby. Then, a chemical agent, usually digoxin, is injected through the needle, causing the child's death. A key advantage is that the feticidal agent—well, the digoxin— softens the child's body, making dismemberment and removal much easier.

"Ditching has one potential downside. Because the chemical used to kill the baby is toxic, it's critical that the abortionist inserts the needle into the baby and not the mother. One way to verify if it's in the right place is for the physician to let go of the syringe before injecting the drug. If the syringe begins to jump around independent of the mom's movements, that's the baby squirming and the sign of success.

"May I confess, I find this amusing," she continued. "We have a doc that calls this part 'harpooning the whale!'" She laughed, oblivious to her solitary enjoyment of the wretched joke.

Moloch went on to explain that a variation of the operation is called an "intact D-and-E." She said that with an "intact," the baby isn't pulled out in pieces but removed in its entirety. Physicians often use a feticidal chemical to kill the baby first, or they'll position the baby so that the skull can be crushed. On rare occasions, the baby may emerge alive, in which case they're simply clipped with a scissor behind the skull to sever the spinal cord. Some abortionists prefer to drown the child, crush its tracheal tube, or snap its neck.

"One of the challenges is that, with a D-and-E, the physician is essentially blind unless we guide the effort with ultrasound."

"Blind, Cyn?" said Jonathan.

"Well, we can only sense the state of things through looking and tactile orientation—by feeling for the baby through the mother's skin," she replied. "Of course, the more advanced the baby, the more we can tell about the baby's placement or orientation inside the uterus. Imagine reaching into her nether regions with a sopher clamp—a grasping instrument with rows of sharp teeth—to latch onto anything you can get ahold of. Is it part of the mother that we've just latched onto or part of the baby? After 18 or 22 weeks of gestation, the uterus is quite thin and soft, so we've gotta be careful not to puncture the walls of the mother's uterus. Oh, it happens.

"Once the abortionist has grasped something inside, hoping it's the baby, she'll squeeze the handles of the clamp to lock the jaws, setting them, and then pulls—really hard. What happens is that you feel something release, and then out pops a fully-formed arm, maybe three or four inches long, or a leg of about the same length. Then, the procedure is repeated over 'n' over, reaching in repeatedly to latch onto whatever is in there. Eventually, the jaws grasp and bring out a spine or pieces of the intestine. Then the heart and lungs, neck and head. That's the toughest part, by the way: the head may be about the size of a golf ball, and by this time, it's just bobbing around in there freely.

"The bigger the head, the tougher the challenge with a

sopher clamp which can only open so far," she continued. "An option is a larger Bierhof forceps, which helps, though some practitioners prefer the smaller clamp. After many terminations, Jon, a skilled abortionist gets the hang of it quite naturally, so our practiced tactile skills just take over. Many of us do these operations so routinely that we could do them in our sleep. Often, I like to listen to soothing music in the operating room. Of course, the wee intruders—who'll often be able to hear too—have no idea what's about to hit them.

"Now, when the clamp crushes and we see that white goo or porridge leaching out of the cervix, that was the baby's brains. You can then extract the skull pieces. It's not uncommon to pull out the baby's little face floating in the flotsam."

Jonathan's head dropped. Moloch noticed it and said, "Aw, it's not so bad, sweety. Don't be gloomy. It's all over 'n' done with in a jiffy. And then the mommy, now a free woman, gets to go home to her lover and her job, or schooling, with no interruption. And all of us in the clinic get our piece of the pie too. And, come to think of it, you boys will share in the rewards as well."

"Please stop that freakin' thing," said Jonathan. Denise tapped a key to freeze the video.

Recalling the moment resurrected emotions from the night before. There were tears in Jonathan's eyes, and his expression was sullen. "I have a monster headache, and I can only hope that this nasty exercise was worth the effort," he said. "Do we really have to go on?"

"I know how awful this is," said David. "We didn't know exactly what we were getting into, but I can assure you—with all of this as the lead-up, when she gets to the final stages of tissue buying, you and I both know we accomplished what we set out to do."

Denise, Layla, and Jennifer quietly looked at Jonathan, who resignedly shrugged his shoulders. "You're right. Go ahead; I guess there's not much more to it, anyway," he said. Layla reached over to place an Aleve next to his glass of water.

Denise tapped the play key, and the video sprang back to life on the monitor.

"Another type of second trimester procedure is known as an instillation," continued Moloch. "With these, the physician sticks a long needle through the mother's abdomen and into the baby's amniotic fluid sac. Lots of fluid is drained from the sac and replaced with either saline or urea solutions.

"This usually kills the baby pretty effectively, but it may take hours, and many women say that they can feel their baby thrashing around—sometimes quite violently," she added. "We don't often sell—well, avail—the fetal tissue under those conditions because children killed by instillation generally show extensive chemical burns, and it affects the integrity of tissue for many research purposes."

"Chemical warfare inside the mother's womb!" shrieked Layla. Again, Denise stopped the video.

"This is ghastly," said Layla. "And she's utterly immune, this witch of a woman, to the godawful horror she brings to those babies and to their mothers. How is it the mothers aren't tormented?"

"It is awful," agreed David, looking at Layla, then the others. "And it's precisely why we're doing this. Please don't lose sight of that. God's placed on our hearts a very real sensitivity to the horrific worldwide murder of children. That's why we're here. None of us may sleep well tonight, but our purpose is to do everything we can to reveal the horror of abortion. Just think of the raw terror of what's going on behind those clinic walls with such young girls. And those helpless babies are being torn to shreds.

"Needless to say, we'll do everything we can to maximize the impact and usefulness of this video. So, when we're done tonight, go home and hug your kids, hug anyone at home, and thank God that we have this opportunity to fight the good fight. It's not a battle that many could endure, or would want to, as you can tell by these revelations. But we can do this, and we must."

David brought both hands to his forehead, massaging his temples and eyes. Then he spoke slowly, almost in a whisper, "Satan's reach has breached the holy sanctuary of the womb with a deception so convincing that mothers willingly sacrifice their own helpless babes."

It was quiet. Layla reached for the box of tissues.

In a cloud of sorrow, Denise struggled with her own tears while fumbling for the right key. She'd reached her saturation point. Jonathan noticed her trembling hand and hesitation. He placed a hand on her shoulder, another solemn moment for the group.

With sad resignation, Denise found the right key and tapped it.

On the monitor, the group watched as Moloch resumed: "Another type of second trimester procedure is called induction. With these, the mother's given a drug, usually prostaglandin or oxytocin, that causes her to go into labor. Most often, the physician will kill the baby to avoid the possibility of a live delivery. Sometimes, the labor-inducing drug given to the mother will kill her child. But if the baby emerges alive, it's usually placed in a steel tray to let it die on its own, or like I've said—for the abortionist to kill it.

"Finally, there are the good ol' standards, the hysterectomy and abdominal hysterotomy, for second trimester abortions, performed in hospitals—procedures that have been around for a long time. But today, for every million babies aborted here in the US, maybe 5,000 are eliminated in this manner these days. They're rarer because of the need for hospitalization, a higher expense and greater risk of complication, and death—to the mother, that is. So, you see, we've made things so much better!

"During a hysterectomy abortion, the mother's entire uterus, including the baby, is removed. The abdominal hysterotomy, also called a uterotomy, is similar to a C-section," she continued.

Moloch shifted in her seat. She attempted to straighten her posture, though the alcohol's gravitational effects were gradually winning.

Cynthia looked at her hosts, glad to see that they returned her smile, reading their expressions as genuine appreciation for her mastery of the subject. Perhaps, too, real respect that she cared to share further insights into her climb to surgical stardom. And now, of course, administrative prowess.

There was an awkward silence for several seconds, and perhaps a signal that the evening was drawing to a close, though Cyn's quick glance at the remainder of her drink was recognition that she could go either way with it.

She tipped her cosmo back entirely, swiped the crystal edge of the glass with her tongue, yawned, then glanced at her watch. "Oh my, it is getting late. But you've got me going on a topic I'm passionate about," she added, with a practiced though wobbly look of deep commitment.

"Let's see—where was I?"

"Third . . ."

"Yes; I could use a third and final drink," she said, smiling. "Oh, who's counting?"

David and Jonathan smiled in return.

David caught the eye of the waiter, who began walking toward him immediately, his attention now more acute with fewer patrons in the restaurant. The video's sound quality had also improved accordingly, thanks to the departure of the boisterous group at the neighboring table. When the waiter arrived, David said, "We'll have a new round, please."

"Yes sir. And will there be dessert, anyone?"

David and Jonathan looked to Moloch who blew a kiss to the waiter and said, "I thought you'd never ask, dear. I hear your Crème Brûlée is heavenly."

"Yes, ma'am, it is. The finest in the West. We have two recipes. One is a luxurious getaway for traditionalists. The other, an invention of our master chef who spent some time in Asia; there's a hint of ginger in it. Would you like to sample either of them?"

"Dear me, no, kind sir," crooned Moloch. "I'm delighted to have an order of your very finest. I've avoided dessert all week long, so I'm ready for something gingery and adventurous."

Jennifer groaned. Sensing a comment, Denise tapped a key to stop the video. "Would you smack her or shut her up?" said Jennifer. "I'm gonna puke. And what's this now—she's entered her boudoir voice phase? Suddenly, she's all sexy and funny and spicy while talking about chopping up children?"

"I know, I know. It's insane. Let's move on," said David, the voice of reason. "We've only got several more minutes to go."

David looked at Denise and nodded. She tapped a key to reactivate the video.

The group watched as the waiter nodded appreciatively. "You won't regret it, ma'am." He then looked at David and Jonathan. "Gentlemen?"

"We'll have the same, please," said David.

The waiter nodded, clicked his heels theatrically, and spun off toward the kitchen.

Cynthia's expression—eyes now at half-mast, face still turned toward the waiter—took on the look of one smitten by the man who'd soon bring not only the heavenly dessert she craved but also her next (and final) cosmo.

She turned toward Jonathan and David, smiling. "Yes, yes. We can talk about third trimester. And, please, boys, don't let me have another cosmo! I do love them, but I've got a few things to tackle tomorrow morning."

David smiled reassuringly while hoping for a content-rich conclusion to the video.

Go for it Cyn, thought Jonathan. *It's time to divulge.*

10

HELL, MALBAS, AND THE ARTS

IT WAS 7:45 PM IN CALIFORNIA; 10:45 in Ohio. Cynthia Moloch was blissfully unaware of the brewing storm that awaited her. For years, it had gathered strength on a distant horizon, invisible to those whose lives would be swept into the vortex.

Dr. Moloch was sure to get her share of the turbulent, hellish monster. Now, in the eye of her storm, the Queen of Abortion was fully unaware of the implications for herself and those closest to her—namely Kristin, heiress to her throne.

In Ohio, Hannah woke again shortly after turning in for the night, unsettled through vague recollection of a bad dream. She knew that if her evenings through the past couple of weeks were any indication of what she could expect tonight, she'd wake briefly, irritated but unable to reassemble the pieces, then gradually drift back into a fitful sleep.

For weeks, Hannah's days were fogged through incomplete rest. She drank coffee to compensate and occasionally sacrificed her lunch, favoring a nap with the door closed and phones silenced.

One evening, after speaking with Chet about her "imbalance," Hannah went to bed early, hoping to quiet the tempest or whatever it was that continued to buffet and prod her when she most needed the rest. At the time, he was sitting up in bed, surrounded by Bible study reading material.

"I wish you hadn't poked the bear with your research into that freakin' box, and the 'Nova' message. And that awful tool," said Chet. "Maybe it was all some whacked out sorta joke."

"No, Chet. What about the message and its reference to Kristin, and the guy in the car," she replied weakly, too tired for debate as she pulled up the covers, easing her head into the pillow. He then kissed her on the forehead and massaged her neck and shoulders. Then he returned to his reading and prayer.

Hannah was so proud of her good man. "I love you, Chet, but now I've gotta lay me down to rest," she said.

TWENTY-FIVE HUNDRED MILES AWAY, Hannah's sister Kristin was engrossed in a different sort of challenge.

Kristin was aware that her boss, Cynthia Moloch (Cyn), was meeting with a couple of fetal tissue procurement pros for dinner. Cyn's dinner with them coincided with the beginning of Kristin's three day, LA arts soirée with Gili.

Cyn had granted Kristin an early start to a long weekend—this weekend—that Gili had been planning for months. Kristin and Gili would soon be among a large gathering of social elite at the most popular annual art event in LA with artist receptions, exhibits, and lofty social affairs. This was Kristin's first visit with Gili to the "LA Awake" arts fair.

Weeks earlier, Kristin expressed concern: he was so connected to the arts scene in LA and had many good friends there. She was only new to the arts and awkward among people who seemed to speak a foreign language. "To them I'm some sort of freak, an extraterrestrial," she pleaded.

"Oh, please," he countered. "They'll love you because I do. And their language is no different than your clinical, reproductive mumbo-jumbo. Besides, I'm teaching you more about the arts each day."

That much was true. With Festus chatting away contentedly, Gili tutored Kristin in the arts as they happily consumed sangria one evening, martinis the next. A few nights ago, he waggled his eyebrows while holding a tightly wrapped joint. "Some fine 'sheet,'" he said, and after sharing it outside on the porch after dinner, he told her he needed 20 minutes to coach the bird. Soon, Festus regaled them with a new phrase. The bird cheerily intoned "Some fine sheet" at any provocation. Gili was delighted.

Kristin gradually acquired a taste for art. Gili appreciated her eclectic interests, from old art to contemporary. Paging through a giant, lavishly printed da Vinci volume one evening, she froze at the artists' detailed embryological drawings, focusing on "Fetus in the Womb."

"Gili, this is more than 500 years old! It's incredible," she said. As they paged through his extensive collection of art books, he noticed that she also admired the work of Rembrandt and Michelangelo, modern sculptors Henry Moore and Alexander Calder, and painter Andrew Wyeth. She especially liked Wyeth's painting, "Christina's World." Among them all, her favorite was the Dutch post-impressionist Vincent van Gogh.

On this evening, their routine was much like many before it: browsing sites online, looking through costly fine art books and catalogs, or scanning the work of lesser-known artists in Gili's well-preserved collection. His valuable originals and prints were located throughout the spacious flat's main areas. Kristin was astonished on her second trip to his home—now ostensibly hers—to follow Gili to a downstairs hidden panel. Behind it was a vault door, and beyond that, an underground room wrapped with humidity-controlled glass-and-steel drawers for artwork he'd collected for more than two decades. It was a volume of work that she believed could easily fill a museum.

"It's an investment," Gili explained to her. "I buy the work of aspiring artists, cheap. Some of them make it big. Others, maybe not. The collection was appraised last year at 20 or 30 times my investment. Some folks like stock and bond portfolios; I prefer to bank my money this way."

Gili enjoyed his status as a long-celebrated participant in the LA Awake arts fair. He'd fallen into his role as a celebrity by accident. His first wife, a woman he married a dozen years earlier, was one of the state's most promising sculptors. A decade younger, beautiful and incredibly talented, her work captured the attention of art critics and commentators worldwide. Shortly after she sold some of her work to the MOMA and Guggenheim museums, a curator from the Louvre offered her a year-long residency in Paris with a substantial salary and the planned commissioning of a large bronze.

Mary left Gili and fell in love with a Christian artist who lived in the same flat on Rue Étienne Marcel; it was there that she also committed her life to Christ. They later moved to LA, a return for her to the roots of her artwork and family, yet now as a Christian whose work celebrated her change in life. Currently, she sculpted at their canyon home, spent lots of time at a foundry, and opened a small gallery.

As for Gili, his trips to LA were invariably lavish buying events. Typically, he slept with young artists, women whose work he purchased at a pittance—some of whom were sure to see him back in LA with a new honey in tow. He was well aware of his ex-wife's gallery but never stopped in, even though it had a presence along one of the main art walk thoroughfares.

Gili's main event each year became his pilgrimage to the arts event. It drew thousands of high-heeled visitors over the weekend, streaming between downtown galleries in a contemporary artwork tour de force.

He'd done his best to prepare Kristin for her first trip with him to the flamboyant affair. Though they'd planned it for many weeks, he did manage a surprise. On the morning of their departure, he told her there were "fringe benefits" to traveling with him but wouldn't elaborate.

A few hours later, a car honked its horn from the semicircular drive. She looked out to see a limo. "A car's here, Gili." It was a chauffeured Rolls-Royce. That's when it hit her: she was helpless to resist despite concerns not only of her own awkwardness to art but also her uneasiness in such a unique social group. He thrived in it; she withered.

Soon, they mounted stairs that led into a sleek airliner's luxurious cabin. Gili explained that the chartered jet—a Gulfstream 650—would make the 350-mile trip in just 30 minutes, easily getting them to LA in time for the first dinner reception.

They sat facing each other in large leather recliners. He waggled his eyebrows, this time pantomiming erotically. "The mile-high club awaits us," he said excitedly as the pilot moved the jet through its pre-flight ritual. "This…" he added, waving his hands about the leather and mahogany-clad cabin, "is ours and ours alone as we make our way to LA, darling."

But Kristin's discomfort only took on an edge, knowing now that the arts event, with all its odd and eccentric people, would soon be upon her. And, though fascinated by the jet's compact opulence, Kristin withdrew. She wanted a martini, then another, which he mixed for her at the bar.

By the time he began to push himself toward her, the pilot started his descent. Gili was unhappy about it, making her promise that she'd consider him more favorably later that evening. "And, maybe on the way home Sunday too," he added. "C'mon, sweetness. From the moment I booked the jet, I've imagined doin' the dirty to win club membership." Kristin replied with a noncommittal nod and thin smile.

They taxied to a private hanger. The stairs opened and they were again greeted by a chauffeur. In moments, the car was making its way toward the city. Gili was elated to be back soon among friends, yet annoyed and sullen at having lost his bid for club membership. He looked out the limo's window without saying a word.

Kristin quickly spotted a bottle of Simi Valley Merlot and held it out for Gili; he reached for the limo's corkscrew and opened it for her without looking in Kristin's direction.

After 10 minutes of silence, Gili reached down into a container of iced drinks and fished out a small bottle of champagne. With a dull pop, he poured its contents into a crystal flute and drank it silently.

Weeks ago, he explained to Kristin that he was a patron member of a museum's Curator Kinship group, requiring an annual gift of $5,000. "It's the group I feel the greatest connection to. There are higher levels of financial support, but a gift of $25,000 a year automatically pushes me into a loftier group of corporate donors. I tend to like the younger set, so I've made it clear to museum managers that, though I'll donate loads more than any in my group, I want to stay where I am. I like exactly the level of adoration I receive."

As the chauffeur brought them to their first destination, Kristin's self-medication gradually led her to the realization that mixing martinis and wine had been a poor choice. "Please get me to the restroom," she said to Gili as they made their way through the lavish reception. She spent the next half hour in a bathroom stall as Gili made excuses for her—as he would through much of the weekend. Kristin was clearly out of her element, feeling like a lone mouse among hyper-energized ferrets, or foxes, maybe.

Kristin was soon immersed in a bizarre cultural stew that she disliked and was gradually unable to tolerate. Gili called it a simple rite of passage. She feigned a headache on Saturday morning after breakfast in bed, suggesting they reconnect for lunch—or later. He left promptly but called her in the midst of a restful succession of Andy Griffith reruns while still in her bathrobe. He insisted that she meet him for lunch at a downtown eatery.

What Kristin didn't know was that she'd be celebrated as among the newest inductees into "Overthrow," an artist and art philanthropy group. Gili made introductions prior to lunch, explaining to a gathering of a hundred or more that he was engaged to Dr. Soelberg, and that she was an enthusiastic patron of the arts. She was promptly mobbed by young artists, all eager to leave an impression or make a sale.

They walked between many of the galleries. By midafternoon she'd sampled three different champagnes and eaten every imaginable hors d'oeuvre, though she drew the line at living bugs and baby octopi writhing in caviar. A headache, "serious as a heart attack," she told him, was gathering in some back quadrant of her head; the front of it too busily engrossed in conversation with young artists. They sought her opinion about composition, the differences between surrealism and post-impressionism, or "art as cult divine." She couldn't maintain this charade much longer!

As Kristin made her way toward the restroom, she spotted a young woman quietly sitting in a chair near three draped easels. She made no attempt to engage Kristin. What a relief. Yet Kristin was drawn to her, curious.

"Why is your work covered?" asked Kristin.

Without lifting her eyes, she replied, "They're a triptych."

"I've heard it before," said Kristin, trying to be pleasant. "An old religious arrangement with three parts, right?"

The woman pulled her jet-black hair to one side and stood. She slowly uncovered the first easel, then the second and third. The horrific art portrayed a scene so hideous and grisly that Kristin found it difficult to view. Naked people and parts of human bodies were strewn about as though in some hellish theater. Animal demons tortured and ate people. Grotesque monsters cavorted among dismembered men and women, tangled in an unearthly orgy. Kristin was startled when the woman spoke again, though still with downcast eyes.

"About 500 years ago, Hieronymus Bosch titled these 'The Garden of Earthly Delights.' I call it psychedelic damnation. It's a live reproduction."

"Live?"

With no reply, the woman returned to her chair, still without looking at Kristin. Kristin was about to leave, recalling her need to use the restroom. That's when the first movement caught her eye.

Kristin gasped and took a step back as she watched the three parts of the triptych come alive. She hadn't noticed that each of the framed paintings was instead a flat panel, and now the horrific scenes came to life, with naked humans squirming and thrashing in horrific, silent agony. Then, sounds began to emerge from small, hidden speakers; quiet screams, groans, and cries of torment lifted from behind the triptych.

It was then that the artist turned her face toward Kristin. Immediately, Kristin saw that the pupils of her eyes weren't like anything she'd seen before—rather than spherical, they were horizontal slits. She found herself looking into the face of a human goat.

Kristin dashed for the restroom, then avoided walking by the woman again as she moved toward the exit.

Just before she made her retreat from the LSD Gallery (her best description of it), one of the featured artists blocked her path. He/she was a ghastly, horned freak of some sort. Kristin had become inured to the ubiquitous tats and piercings favored by artists and even facial implants. But this character, whose artwork was dark and self-loathing—and who Kristin carefully avoided during the gallery visit—stopped her mid-stride with a loud meow and then tucked into a crouch at her legs, rubbing against her calf.

Gili and several others thought it was hilarious. Kristin recoiled. She looked to Gili for help, but he was having too much fun at her expense. The intimidating, mostly green cat person with multi-horned crown, split tongue, filed teeth, ear stubs, and substantial breasts rose before her to a height of six-and-a-half feet. It emitted a guttural purr, then frolicked theatrically just inches from her face and smiled broadly, its teeth and wiggling tongue in full effect. Suddenly, it pulled both of Kristin's hands into its own gooey chest. "I've waited for you. Gili said that he would bring me a new pet."

Kristin darted out the door to a burst of laughter.

Outside, she attempted to blend in with others making their way between galleries. That's when she noticed a small gallery with very few people inside. An attractive woman stood in the open doorway, dressed in white. Kristin noticed the cross on a necklace. The woman smiled sweetly at her as she passed. Moments later, Kristin turned, pacing back toward the woman against the crush of oncoming walkers, all avoiding the gallery or even eye contact with the woman in white.

"Hi. My name is Mary. Welcome to LifeLine Gallery." Kristin greeted her, offering her name, and asked if she could take a look inside. "My pleasure. I hope you like our gallery. As you'll soon see, it's unlike the others."

Inside, Kristin saw the work of several artists, some of whom were speaking intently with visitors. What a contrast to most of the artists she'd met over the weekend. Wholesome and engaging, the artists here were eager to speak with visitors—vibrant with easy smiles and welcoming eyes.

Kristin stood mesmerized before a large oil titled "God's Amazing Grace." From the cross, Christ's eyes bore into the viewer's yet with love and compassion.

Mary came to stand beside her. "Its message is powerful,"

she said to Kristin. "The quality of this piece is stunning, isn't it?"

Kristin stared at it, mesmerized.

"We're featuring a sanctity-of-life exhibit this month, Kristin," Mary continued quietly. "The topic isn't accidental. This year, we wanted to counterbalance the city's main art event, one in which it seems anything goes. Are you visiting galleries as part of the big arts event?"

"Well, yes, I suppose you could say that," replied Kristin. "I'm sort of, well, swept into it."

Kristin smiled at Mary, looking into her eyes. Mary's face was a picture of purity with porcelain skin, her eyes clear and smiling.

"Some of the work in this exhibit may be a bit hard to contemplate, but certainly no more than much of the work we see here in LA routinely," added Mary. She casually touched Kristin's hand. Her fingers were warm and soft, and unlike the rude cat-person's abrupt approach just minutes earlier, Mary's touch was welcomed. Mary steered Kristin's gaze to another large oil painting titled "Adam and Eve."

"Oh my, you wouldn't believe what a relief it is to see the Garden of Eden represented this way. At the last gallery I was at, an artist displayed a triptych by Bosch, I think, titled—

"'The Garden of Earthly Delights,'" Mary supplied the title. "And you saw the paintings come alive?"

Kristin nodded.

"A bit hard to view, isn't it?" added Mary. "As are her eyes. She calls herself Hell."

"She what?"

"Her given name is Helen," continued Mary. "She

changed it to Hell. That happened around the same time she hooked up with her new boyfriend, a guy named Malbas. He wears only black clothes and usually hides his eyes behind sunglasses. But he reveals them for effect, just as Helen did for you. She told a friend of hers that his eyes are real goat eyes. Helen bought contacts to distort her eyes to 'be in solidarity' with him. Sadly, she also went from being a rather quiet, mostly likeable person to being the haunted, disturbed person she is today. Night and day difference between them: Helen and Hell. I pray for her every day."

Kristin shook her head, attempting to clear her recollection of the deeply troubled artist and her work. "Well, this," said Kristin, pointing to the multicolored oil painting, "is a much nicer garden to be in. What a pleasure to see art with such beauty and grace. This painting's so colorful and lively and has such. . ."

"Clarity of purpose?" asked Mary, completing the thought for Kristin.

"Yes! That's exactly how I feel. It's a gorgeous painting. Unfortunately, my fiancé seems to like some pretty bizarre stuff, and I doubt he'd appreciate the biblical theme. I must admit I've surprised myself a bit with this one. It's just so bright and refreshing, and yet of course the implication seems to be innocence before . . ."

"The fall," added Mary, again completing Kristin's thoughts so easily.

"Yes," replied Kristin, this time not as surprised by Mary's insight.

"That's the implication, but yet the message is delivered with candor," added Mary. "It seems like so much of today's art is an assault of some sort, painful to experience. At least this art connects us to God's love even if, thematically, it's tough love. After all, Adam and Eve were forced to leave that heavenly garden."

Kristin's eyes began to pool. She turned away, attempting to hide her emotion, but Mary was quick to catch it. She walked away, swiftly returning with a tissue.

Kristin accepted it and wiped her eyes. Mary stood quietly beside her.

Seeking a distraction and a bit of normalcy here in the quiet gallery, it occurred to Kristin that Mary might know an answer to a question she'd had since first seeing the artwork of Vincent van Gogh online. "Do you happen to know if there are galleries here in LA that have any van Gogh originals?"

"Sure. Two or three museums here have his work, and host traveling exhibits occasionally," responded Mary. "So you like his art?"

"I find his life's story fascinating, and that he was so incredibly talented, despite his troubles," said Kristin.

"If there was an artist I could spin time back to be with, to guide and comfort, he'd be at the very top of my list," said Mary, smiling warmly. "He was a man of faith, yet so tortured during his last years. Fortunately, there's a wealth of information about him, much of it through his deeply personal and revealing letters—those he wrote for about a decade, up to the death of his brother Theo."

Kristin had inadvertently moved toward another work of art which gradually sharpened as her tears cleared. She looked up to see a painting of a woman, crying, in a field of green. Kristin let out a quiet yelp as tears poured from both sides of her face. Mary guided her into a chair and held her trembling shoulders, leaving only briefly for more tissues.

"There's more going on than just…the art, isn't there, Kristin?" asked Mary, placing a hand on Kristin's shoulder. Without asking permission, Mary lifted the moment in prayer. "Oh, dear Father in heaven, please be with Kristin now. Comfort her in this time of turmoil, whatever it is."

Kristin reached up to place a hand on Mary's. Minutes later, sensing recovery, Kristin blurted out, "Who are you, Mary?"

Before Mary could answer, footsteps drew closer then stopped nearby. Dr. Gilgamesh Arzhang appeared at first concerned, then perturbed when Mary turned toward him.

"Oh, it's you. I should've figured. Your gallery. What's going on here, Mary?" he demanded.

"Hello, Gil," she replied bluntly. "No need for your concern."

Kristin looked up into Gili's eyes, then at Mary, confused. Red and swollen, her eyes showed uncertainty before she could verbalize it.

"We know each other," explained Mary. "This man has led pickets here in front of LifeLine, complaining that our art is angry, demeaning, and intolerant."

"Right. And you still call this 'art,'" snarled Gil. "Kristin, let's go." He tugged her from the chair.

This time it was Mary's turn for confusion. "My fiancé…" was all Kristin could say to Mary as Gili pulled her toward the door. Mary quickly pressed a fresh tissue and business card into Kristin's hand.

Kristin managed to get the card into her purse and glanced back to see Mary framed by the gallery door, her face etched with sadness.

Throughout the remainder of the day, Kristin was with Gili, more or less, though a distance grew between them that she hadn't felt before. Gili became gruff and impatient. After traveling by cab to one exhibit, she asked questions about an artist's work. He threw up his hands with a gesture that said, "How stupid!" He then ridiculed her before the artist. For the remainder of the day, she nursed a headache and kept a low profile.

Later that evening at a dinner event, Kristin was sure that Gili was drawn to an elegant brunette who seemed perfectly at ease among the throng of art lovers. She returned to that track repeatedly, a recording stuck in a groove: art lover. Art. Lover. Is that who this woman was? Had Gili admired her openly and spoken sweetly with her? Have they known each other? The woman laughed easily. Her body language was fluid and inviting.

Gili was brooding and reserved for the remainder of their time together as events wore on.

"Who's that?" she asked shortly before they left for the hotel.

"Who?"

"The tall woman there—the brunette with the snake tat on her shoulder surrounded by adoring men. It's quite a tattoo. Gee, I wonder if there's something Freudian in it."

"I don't know," he replied as he shook his head dismissively. A few moments later, he growled, "I'm gonna get a new drink."

The nearest route to a new drink would take him toward the woman with the elaborate snake tattoo. Kristin noted that the brunette watched Gili get up from his seat. Initially, he moved toward her, and then recalling that eyes may be tracking his movements from behind, he veered to the left. He disappeared around the corner. Moments later, Kristin looked for the brunette, but she was gone.

ON SUNDAY AFTER LUNCH, Kristin noticed that when Gili purchased a large, original oil painting, a nude by George Condo, and a signed Max Ernst litho—which she considered a gaudy, bad dream in a frame—the brunette had reappeared. This time, Kristin saw their shared glances and the woman's acknowledgment of the $126,000 purchase price for both pieces that Gili so casually wrote a check for.

When the limo picked them up an hour later, the chauffeur could barely tuck the wrapped frames into the car's spacious trunk. On their way to the airport, Gil spoke excitedly about the original Condo, one he'd wanted for a decade.

He admired it, even wrapped, as it occupied a center-of-cabin position in the luxurious jet. And he continued to admire it as he coaxed Kristin onto a leather ottoman ten minutes after liftoff.

11

MOLOCH'S METHODOLOGY

THE WAITER KNEW that the table of three—David, Jonathan, and Dr. Cynthia Moloch—would soon call it a night, so he prepared for the drinks and Crème Brûlée with a bit of ceremony. Noticing that the woman studied him, his movements were buoyant. After setting used dishes and glasses on a portable tray, he refilled their water. He produced a small silver tool that deftly lifted and removed crumbs from the table. The waiter then lifted the tray and spun on a heel to fetch the drinks and dessert.

"How cute. He must've had that little street-sweeper in an apron pocket," she said, giggling. David and Jonathan smiled.

A moment later, the waiter returned with a crowded tray. He served Cyn first, placing the drink before her. She reached for it immediately. After leaving her dessert and the small spoon, he served the gentlemen.

Moloch held her glass aloft, just a bit askew, saying, "Here's to th' third trimester." The toast wasn't reciprocated, but she was too buoyant to care. The men smiled, quietly acknowledging her with their eyes.

"'Third tri's the most exciting, fellas," she added with a smile. "We do our procedures pretty much as we would in the second tri. But because the babies are bigger and more likely to survive, we modify. Of course, there's the need for more, um, dilation. Also, the chemicals we use to soften the baby and make it easier to pull apart and remove are used in greater volume. The drugs are also given earlier so they have a longer time to soak into the baby's tissue and bone. And to increase the likelihood of killing the baby, higher volumes of herbi-, no—feticidal drugs are used."

"Okay, stop. She's confused and slurring her words now," interrupted Layla as Denise froze the video. "It's a small victory to know that, at last, this wretched woman with an insatiable thirst for cosmos has more than one flaw."

"More than one?" asked Jonathan.

"Well, guiltless killer, number one," added Layla. "Number two: sloppy speech—that is, after seven cosmos. Did I tell you how much I detest that woman?"

"We've got to take a step back," said David. "It's been on my heart that we need to pray for her. Pray that her reign as the Queen of Abortion comes to a conclusion and that God can help bring an end to the slaughter of children. Sure, she's only one player, but she's a substantial one. Remember Christ's words in the midst of unimaginable pain: 'Father forgive them, they know not what they do.' Of course, we can do our part to challenge what they're doing, and that's what this is all about. We've got to keep in mind the need for a prayerful, godly confrontation."

The group quietly nodded in agreement.

"Okay, let's hit the last leg of this video. Ol' Cynthia's just about to put her evidentiary icing on the cake," added David.

With a tap of the mouse, Denise brought the video back into play.

"So you've managed to increase the numbers of third trimester terminations at clinics in many states; is that right, Cyn?" asked David.

"Yes, many states now permit late term abortions, even as a baby's in the birth canal. So, my methodology's synchronized with this and paying off sweetly," she replied. "More, bigger babies mean more valuable aftermarket parts."

"But, Cyn," interrupted Jonathan; "is it possible to reduce or eliminate...."

She lifted a hand and said, "Ah, lemme guess, Jon. It's the presence of drugs that concerns you. Researchers place highest value on untainted, pristine fetal tissue. Yes, yes. I'll get to that momentarily."

Holding the small spoon in her right hand, she made a delicate sweep of the dish before her, then brought a first taste of the Crème Brûlée to her lips. She closed her eyes briefly, savoring the sweetness.

"Sometimes, the procedure itself is modified," she continued. "One of the commonest—is that a word? [giggling]— is an intact D-and-E, also known as D 'n' X, for dilation and extraction, or partial-birth abortion. It's also referred to as a dismemberment abortion.

"When this is done in the third trimester, the abortionist maneuvers the baby into a breech position," she added. "So, Jon, that means feet-first, to pull the baby out of the uterus up to its head—leaving the baby's head just inside, and that's not an incidental position. The viable baby is still unborn.

"An alteration to this procedure is that the baby's head is left inside to sustain blood flow to the body—all of which can be harvested," she said. "The fresher the parts, the better for you.

"For many D 'n' Xs, though, the abortionist typically shoves a scissor into the base of the baby's skull to create a hole—just prior to the baby's exit," Moloch added. She then poised her spoon above the amber, caramelized crust and pushed it in. She brought it to her lips, and her eyes fluttered as she tasted the sweetness. "They can then insert a suction tube into the hole to suck out the gelatinous brain, ensuring that the baby—I mean fetus—isn't born alive. It also helps make the head smaller, easier to remove."

Jonathan and David froze, unable to acknowledge her.

Oblivious, Cyn paused with a vacant glance upward as though contemplating something pleasant or profound. "I just know those babies, if asked, would be glad to know that they've helped to make this a better world," she said dreamily, spoon casually in hand, like a cigarette. A bit of Crème Brûlée dripped onto the linen tablecloth. David and Jonathan tried not to notice it.

"Technicians at our clinics are supposed to ask patients if they'd like to donate the fetal tissue for science. We usually do in order to keep things legal, though it's a bit of a nuisance. I've taught our staffs that it's imperative to emphasize the value of fetal tissue, never a baby's tissue, for humankind and scien-, um, scientific research," continued Moloch. "This gives the patient an opportunity to appreciate the role their baby could play in advancing the good cause, ending cancer, arthritis, or diabetes. Very often, they don't care. Many of the youngest girls are quick to dismiss it, being so far from their momentary concerns.

"Everything we're involved with here, at least from my perspective, is a bit like 'playing God,'" she added. "Sure, there's a discreet subterfuge involved, but it's all part of the plan. We get to help our patients decide on abortions, even if it takes some coaxing, and even if that means we need to begin the process of grooming them at a very early age. And, along with the decisions they make, our roles and ambitions in the healthcare business are affirmed and rewarded."

Denise smashed a finger into a key to freeze the image on the screen and scurried to the restroom. Layla's first instinct was to rush to her aid. Instead, David simply held a hand toward her and whispered, "Wait. She may need a moment alone." For a few minutes, the group simply sat in silence.

David stole a glance at the screen. Moloch's face froze as she completed the word, "denied," her eyes half closed. Her expression, caught inadvertently, was contorted in a way that he could never have imagined otherwise. He shook his head to clear the thought, though he knew it was valid. She looked truly possessed, demonic. *What have I gotten us into?* David thought to himself.

Denise returned to her seat at the computer. She'd washed her face. Her eyes were red and tired. "Sorry, I needed a minute."

"I think we all did," replied Layla quietly.

Denise looked at the screen and then did a double-take. She glanced at David who was looking directly into her eyes, apologetically.

Denise's resolve and determination had returned. "Denied. Moloch said it herself. Playing God," blurted Denise. "Meanwhile, it's unclear whether the mother, the father—if he's more than just a sperm donor—and even the potential grandparents, are aware that their now-dead loved one's bodies are being used in this way, whole or in part. Just beautiful. And what about the real God? I think I can assume his opinion here." She then held her hand out, mimicking Cynthia's hand with a spoon and boudoir voice, "It's a better world."

David glanced at the Mac and nodded to the group. "Well, what we do know is that abortion clinics are supplying fetal body parts in greater quantities, worldwide, although they're not allowed by federal law to sell the tissue here in the US. Yet, that doesn't change the fact that it's a thriving market here," said David. "Abortions continue to gain traction in urban areas, with more Black babies aborted than born. Imagine that!

"For the clinics, there are plenty of loopholes to generating funds," he continued. "There's the cost of securing the tissue with 'consent fees,' the costs to cover an abortion facility's expenses, or funds needed to assure the tissue is precisely what's needed for research. Or, preparing the tissue exactly as specified, and even transportation—sometimes with a very tight schedule so that the tissue remains fresh.

"All of it comes with high cost, easily making up for legal mandates not to 'sell' tissue," he added. "There's money to be made at every angle. I learned that if a tube of liver tissue, for example, were tailored specifically for the right medical research, it might be worth $20,000, with the likelihood of much of it paid for with public funding. That is, public funds. Your tax dollars and mine, for the good cause. Hey, at 20K for just one tube of flesh, do you think there's profitability in it for those in the abortion industry?

"According to one congressional report," continued David, "some senators involved in an investigation reported that in a year's time, one research facility paid a procurement firm almost $43,000 for fifty-some containers with fetal brains, hearts, upper and lower limbs, livers, and other organs. All documented.

"Another little research project I learned about through a real, live tissue procurement firm, involved baby scalps sold to researchers. They were scalping the babies and grafting the tissue onto immune-suppressed mice, the purpose of which was to learn about the effectiveness of certain medicines in treating male pattern baldness.

"So, our dearest Cyn, who loves her cosmos and Crème Brûlée, is just one of many players in this godawful market," added David. "I learned that her clinics are arranged in some sort of federation model so that the folks at corporate—like Cynthia and her cadre of managers—have the protection of plausible deniability. The business structure also assures that, if the crap really hits the fan, they have the ability to cut 'em loose entirely, like snipping a wart. And to move assets easily. Problem solved, saving the organization as a whole."

David noticed that Denise, Layla, and Jennifer were squirming. "I'm sorry, but the horror doesn't end there," he added. "There are new reports of living babies being used for taxpayer-funded research at a university in Pennsylvania. There are many other accounts about fetal experimentation that require fetuses delivered alive so that body parts can be harvested fresh. An army of defenders deny it. Some of the best insights come in from abortion clinic personnel and even abortionists who've defected; they offer ghastly revelations, but the pro-choicers all link arms in denial.

"Of course, we've all heard about the terrible results of David Daleiden's trial in '19, having lost the lawsuit brought against him for the secret videos he made while interviewing abortionists. His efforts—some of the most praiseworthy investigative journalism by a citizen journalist—were called by the left to be a 'manipulative, malicious campaign,' and he took quite a hit.

"Unfortunately, that's a very real concern for me and Jonathan. A lawsuit, that is. Because there was no way to quietly solicit support for this mission, we chose to move forward prayerfully. And, as you'll soon see with Moloch's final revelations, we have such damning information that there'll be no squirming away from it," David added. "Please keep us in your prayers."

"I came across something a few nights ago, online at *LifeSiteNews*, while preparing for our dinner date with Cyn," said Jonathan. "There's now convincing evidence of another awful twist. Recently, a California abortionist testified that there's 'no question' that abortionists are allowing babies to be born alive in order to harvest their organs. In fact, the abortionist claimed that David Daleiden and his collaborator Sandra Merritt presented only the 'tip of the iceberg.'

"Apparently, the abortionist—who was brought in for the defense of Daleiden and Merritt—has plenty of experience to draw on; he'd performed some 50,000 abortions. The abortionist who testified in Daleiden's defense once despised him, claiming that he'd 'like to take down that SOB.' But when he saw and verified the authenticity of the videos, he was eager to speak in Daleiden's defense."

"Unquestionably, Daleiden and Merritt are national heroes," said David. "What he did gave us the recipe for pursuing Cynthia. I've watched her closely and have been on the sidelines for months to prepare for last night's video. By the time it all came together, we knew that she was sufficiently relaxed around me—to say the least, thanks to her appetite for cosmos—and I had a pretty good notion of how to play it. What we didn't know was how nicely the pieces would fall, and thank God it's all there in the video."

For a moment, the group was quiet. The mention of David Daleiden's legal woes cast a brief shadow on the evening's conversation.

"David, what're the risks to us? After all, we're all involved in refining the video," asked Jennifer. Layla, Jonathan, and Denise turned their heads to David.

He studied their faces, looking directly into each set of eyes. "We have the full assurance from one of the most prestigious law firms in the country that we'll be under their wings if and when things get uncomfortable," David replied. "Jonathan and I will be in the hot seat, not you." David turned toward Layla, Denise, and Jennifer. "Even if we're pressed, Jonathan and I will not let you fall into the hailstorm we're sure to experience. We also know we've brought this against the pro-choice movement with God's blessing. So, as Paul said, 'If God is for us, who can be against us?'"

"We can't know exactly how this'll play out," added Jonathan. "Clearly, Moloch gave us the whole package—everything we need. She just dug herself in deeper by the minute. The truth is all there. We're confident it'll be a game-changer for the pro-life movement.

"So, soon we can go back to our normal lives," said David. "I hope we'll all recover from the stress these preparations put us through. Relax, at last. Take comfort in knowing the video went as well as it could have. Thank God for that. Soon, I'll be back in touch with some of the strategic, pro-life counselors I've had the pleasure to meet with and to get advice from. I'll share this with them and let it percolate for a while.

No copies of the video go anywhere until we're ready. But, when it does, the crap will no doubt hit the fan.

"Ultimately, I'll decide when and how to deliver the video to Cynthia's attention, to the media, and elsewhere," said David. Looking quickly at his watch, he asked the group to take a quick break. "We'll resume with the video's last few minutes right away."

The group reassembled around the MAC, as before. "We've got just a few minutes more to go with the recording, but before we do that, I'll share a few thoughts," said David. "Sadly, our culture's love affair with abortion began with our parent's generation—the Vietnam-era 'flower children.' They were the loudest voices, the zealots beating drums when our very own Supreme Court set a ruling in 1973 now referred to simply as Roe v. Wade.

"So, about half a century ago, the court opened the flood-gates to these horrors, and look at how we've 'advanced' since then," he added.

"There are also pseudo-religious leaders who preach about the blessing of abortion. They refer to abortionists as heroes and 'modern-day saints.' The horrors of abortion are softened and trivialized, and now also dressed in some sort of crazy, upside-down spirituality."

"Mother Theresa once said that a 'Nation that kills its children in the womb has lost its soul,' added Jonathan. "After last night's outing with Cynthia, I went online to look for some of Mother Theresa's thoughts on the topic of abortion.

"At one point she said, 'Please don't kill the child. I want the child. I'm willing to accept any child who would be aborted and to give that child to a married couple who will love the child and be loved by the child.' It shattered her to know that acceptance of abortion had become like a rampant cancer," continued Jonathan. "Mother Theresa also said something like 'Abortion is profoundly anti-women. Three-quarters of its victims are women; half the babies and all the mothers.' She also said 'It's a poverty to decide that a child must die so that you may live as you wish.'"

"And that sets us up nicely to watch the last couple of minutes of Cynthia Moloch, patron saint of the pro-choice movement, as she tackles her last cosmo," inserted David. "She'll then walk us through some incriminating rules of engagement. Are we ready to resume?"

"She's now on cosmo number seven," said Layla. Everyone turned to look at her. "Oh, I know. I'm a bit obsessed with counting them," she added defensively. "But if you once had a drinking problem, you'd understand."

David gave Layla a supportive smile. He then glanced at Denise and nodded. Her finger tapped a key, and the Mac came alive with the now all-too-familiar visage of Cynthia Moloch, smiling toward her hosts as she took a long sip of the cosmo, oblivious to her hosts' preference for water.

"Abortion is a quick, immediate fix, and an opportunity for girls—I mean women—to put their own needs first," said Cynthia. "If they made a mistake—maybe forgetting to take the daily pill, or their partner didn't wear a condom when he said he was—we can fix it. We're here to help.

"And, that, my dear fellas, puts us in a position to help each other," she added, glancing merrily at her hosts. "As you know, the government's stomped all over our freedoms, so we have to use some creativity in how we, um, accomplish it. For example, we've learned to exaggerate the time it takes to properly separate and categorize specimens, to classify and package them. Even to separate the all-natural, organic, gluten-free specimens from those that may have drugs in them."

"Gluten-free?" asked Jonathan. "As in…edible?"

"Oh! Sorry—it's our waggish, in-house term for untainted, pristine, drug-free specimens," she replied. "This goes to your earlier concern about specimens that have no drugs or contaminants, Jon." Leaning forward conspiratorially, she added, "We only nibble the specimens occasionally." She tossed her head back, laughing.

Moloch continued, still smiling. "You 'n' your researcher customers place a higher value on drug-free specimens, so we're careful to separate and label them that way—and, of course, placing a premium on their value."

She hunched her shoulders and leaned forward again, mustering as serious an expression as her condition would allow. "That means the fees associated with the sale, I mean the procurement of those fetal specimens, are higher. I keep forgetting, so help me when I slip: baby parts aren't for sale. We make them available to you for specific fees to cover our services. Clean, exactly to specification, and free of impurities. Also, packaging and transportation. That stuff costs us money, and you help us recover those costs, and then some. Of course, you mark up your costs and pass them along to your buyers.

"We all get what we want," added Moloch. "Our lady clientele move on, and their extra baggage is disposed of. My 401K improves, my mortgage is reduced, and you can upgrade the Ford to a Ferrari.

"Researchers get what they want too," she said. "Our assurance of a steady stream of body parts 'n' pieces is what they're looking for. Consistent availability of fetal tissue, required for a wide variety of research, becomes the foundation for their NIH grant proposals to lock in big money. Or, bids for lucrative pharmaceutical company contracts. Whether through enterprise or public funding, the contracts assure millions 'n' millions of dollars for healthcare, pharmaceutical research, and other purposes—money that builds research wings, hires more scientists, pays for mortgages, bonuses, and designer cars. It's a win-win solution for a happier world."

Cynthia reached for her purse, then fiddled with her phone, dropping it once. David swiftly retrieved it from the floor and gave it to her. "That damn thing's spring-loaded," she squawked. "What's your email address, Dave?"

He provided it and, after a few concentrated taps, she looked at him, smiling. "I just sent you a fee agreement for the 10 or 12 most frequently purchased fetal specimens," she explained. "Whole bodies, brain and spinal cord, heart, lungs, liver, kidneys, skeletal muscle, eyes, bone marrow, umbilical— whatever the need, we can meet it.

"There are two categories: one where drugs may have been used during procedures; one without, and with higher cost," she added. "With that, boys, we can get started. If you have other needs, we can easily negotiate from there. Oh, and I've gotta pee."

Jonathan and David began to rise from their chairs as Moloch placed her napkin on the table.

"Don't be silly boys. Stay, sit, be comfy," she said with a broad smile.

They watched as she walked unsteadily toward the men's room while tugging at her skirt. Just as she reached for the handle, the door opened, and a surprised waiter emerged.

"Aha! You've helped me avoid embarrassment, kind sir," she said to the bewildered waiter. He was quick to reach for her arm when she spun precariously toward the women's restroom.

"Oh, you are a sweety," she crooned. Steadied, she added, "I'm okay now. Thank you."

As Moloch pulled the door open with some difficulty, Jonathan and David looked at each other.

"I think we've got everything we need," said David.

"Whew—she's a trip," replied Jonathan. "Hey, I'll head to the restroom too. I'm going to disconnect this gear."

"Good idea," replied David.

David signaled the waiter, who handled the credit card transaction swiftly. David gave him a generous tip, and it was acknowledged.

Moloch returned to the table, looking relieved but a bit disheveled. David smiled, explaining that Jonathan took the opportunity to use the restroom as well. He rose while saying, "We've had a terrific meeting, Cynthia. Thanks so much."

A moment later, Jonathan appeared. Within minutes, they tucked Dr. Moloch into a cab and were making their way to the studio.

"Well, now we know why national statistics show that health services such as cancer screenings, breast exams, and so many other prenatal services have plummeted at family planning and reproductive services clinics," said David. "Cyn said it herself: they clearly prioritize abortions, coaxing girls and women alike toward the profitable fix, the 'solution' they most want to provide—abortions.

"Prenatal care is virtually nonexistent at those clinics," he added. "The study I read about referred to calls made to dozens of clinics to learn that many have eliminated prenatal services altogether. I recall a quote from a clinic receptionist, something like, 'I know it's a bit deceiving, but we don't have services—you know—for women who want to carry through to delivery.' Our friend Cyn has solved that mystery for us. Clearly, the all-in solution for women is the one they encourage. It's become a real moneymaker for them. Aftermarket sales only sweeten the pot."

AFTER A LONG DAY at work, Hannah arrived home exhausted. Chet and the kids knew the moment they saw her that she needed some quiet time. Chet warmed her dinner and poured a fresh glass of cold grapefruit juice, a favorite refresher.

After a brief prayer, mustering just enough energy to say, "Thank you, dear Lord, for bringing me home to my family, and for this meal," she ate slowly. As she did, Hannah glanced at her phone for the first time in several hours. She activated two voicemail messages from Kristin: "Hey sis. Gimme a call." Then, "Sis, I gotta share something with you. There's trouble."

Sighing, Hannah brought Kristin's number up and called. Kristin answered immediately. "Thanks for calling back. Tough day?" Kristin didn't wait for Hannah's reply, launching into an explanation. "We had a pretty freaky scare today, sis," said Kristin. "We may have legal woes on the horizon. Cyn, my boss, went to dinner recently with some new fetal procurement pros, or people posing as them. There'll likely be media exposure, and we may be headed to court."

"Whoa. How's that, Kristin?"

"A new bioprocurement firm's CEO and another exec

took her recently to a swanky place for dinner. Long story short, she probably had one or two too many drinks. They were prodding her for information, and she was just trying to be helpful. Toward the end of the evening, and like I say with a few too many drinks, she thought she recalled maybe divulging too much. But, in the right way, just trying to help and to educate them.

"So, this morning an envelope was given to her secretary by a courier. In the bag was a thumb drive with a video taken by a camera hidden in a jacket button or something like that. It confirmed Cyn's worst concerns. She's tense, but the lawyers say not to worry and that their retainer's got plenty of flexibility to deal with it."

"Have you seen it, sis?"

"No. Cyn's kept it from me, from everyone," said Kristin. "But the lawyers have seen it. Sounds like she's mighty embarrassed. She told me enough about it to give me a bit of shock. It's maddening that she only told the truth, even though she may have revealed some things that ride a fine line between what's legal and what's not.

"Why are our laws so restrictive, Hannah? Tell me that, sis. Well, anyway, she hopes they're just some sort of small-time, fly-by-night blackmail operation. There's some sort of slush fund that Cyn built for something like this."

Kristin began to slur her words and excused herself, admitting that she needed to refresh her drink. A few minutes went by with some background noise that sounded like baby talk to the bird, Festus. Kristin fumbled with the phone, dropped it twice, then resumed her conversation as though she'd been on the phone with no interruption.

"So, apparently our lawyers are now talking about threatening to sue them—the procurement firm, blackmailers, or whatever they are—for breaking confidentiality while recording undercover videos and whatever else," continued Kristin.

"Of course, Cyn's discussion with the two dudes was all about aborting babies, harvesting and selling body parts. In a note that came with the video, the accusers call us an organ trafficking ring. And the video's exactly the sort of thing she and the organization don't want released."

12

LIFELESSNESS IN ALL ITS FORMS

FOR A FEW WEEKS, Hannah, Chet, Jack, and Miriam agreed to (mostly) ignore the strange tool and its cryptic note. They'd hoped that the mystery of the tool might answer itself in time. Hannah stashed the box on a shelf in the garage, saying to Chet and her father, "I do not want that thing in my house, whatever it is!"

When Harley informed her one afternoon that a group of interns had to reschedule a visit set for the next morning, Hannah knew it was the opportunity she'd waited for. She stopped him in the hallway. "Doc, now that you have a hole in your schedule, could I have 20 or 30 minutes of your time tomorrow?"

"Sure. Anything I should be concerned about?" he asked.

"No, I've got something I'd like to show you. It's at home but arrived on my desk last month. I'll bring it with me in the morning."

THE NEXT DAY, seeing his office door ajar, Hannah grabbed the box, walked down the hall and into Harley's office.

Hannah closed the door behind her. She watched Harley closely when she explained that the box in her hands was delivered the night before his most recent pathology seminar.

She told him that she'd arrived early that day, and the box was on her desk.

"Doc—you didn't put it there, did you?"

"No, I didn't," he replied. "Why? What've we got here?"

She placed the package on his desk, took a seat in front of him and watched his face as he first studied the Hannah Methaney label, properly addressed to her lab, then opened the box.

Seeing the shiny metal device resting in its packing material, he set the note aside. He pulled the device from the box. "Huh. It's been quite a while since I've seen one of these and only behind glass in a museum in Budapest. No, it was in Vienna; that's right—it was a museum there, among a collection of specialized surgical tools."

"Really? What is it?" she asked.

"Well, its purpose is pretty gruesome, actually," said Harley. "It's used to drill a hole in a baby's head to collapse the skull for extraction during an abortion. I'll see if I can find it." He set the tool aside, turning his attention to the PC. With some tapping of the keyboard and movement of the mouse, Harley quickly found a very similar one, held privately, in the Grantham Collection. She got up to stand beside him, leaning down for a closer look. Sure enough, it was very close to the one on Harley's desk.

Harley continued his search. He then found the Museum of Conception and Abortion in Vienna. On their website, he searched for the tool and found it. "There it is. Why, this one's a twin. It reads: Luer Cranial Perforator, circa 1858 to 1868. Missing."

"Huh," said Hannah. "What do they mean by 'missing'? Removed? Stolen?"

"Not sure. And, Hannah, this is strange. Look at the tool you just brought in, then look at the photo here on my monitor. Check out the striation in the ivory handle. Here—I'll enlarge the image." He then picked up the tool and spun it in his hands. "If I turn the device just so…here it is." The museum's missing tool appeared to be exactly identical to the one in Dr. Harley's hands.

"So, I may have a rare, antique abortion tool that's been missing from a museum's collection in Vienna," said Hannah. "That's crazy; how could that be? Doc, how many of those tools do you think may be in existence today?"

"No telling, but I'd guess not many," he said. "The folks at the Grantham Collection, or at the museum in Vienna might know. There's also a museum in Chicago." With a few additional taps on his keyboard, Harley brought up a website for the International Museum of Surgical Science. "You could also check with them."

DR. HARLEY WAS ABOUT to return the tool to Hannah when he noticed a sliver of metallic chain, just visible at the bottom of the box. He pulled it up to reveal a simple, beaded steel necklace and a small crucifix. Hannah's mouth dropped open as she stared at it. "Wait—that was in the box? We must've missed it with all the shredded paper." Dr. Harley handed it to her. Hannah examined the small, silver pendant with a stamped, bas relief image of Christ, hung on the cross.

"Was there some sort of documentation?" asked Dr. Harley. "Mind if I take a look at this?" He pointed to the paper.

"Go ahead," replied Hannah. "It was the only thing in the box, other than the tool. And the cross—we completely missed that." Hannah pulled out all the paper strips to be sure they hadn't missed anything else.

A minute later, Dr. Harley looked up directly into Hannah's eyes. "This is deep. It appears that you have a secret overwatcher, this 'Nova.' Does that name ring a bell with you?"

"No, nothing. We're completely stumped. I've shared it with Chet and my parents."

Harley tapped keys and read from his monitor: "Nova: a star showing a sudden large increase in brightness and then slowly returning to its original state. Well, it's someone who clearly knows you and your sister. Nova, it seems, may have a real dislike for Kristin's path, or profession. And it also appears that you're in a unique position of some kind, perhaps one of real importance. The message seems to come from Christian teachings, and there's a reference here to…nightmares?"

Hannah looked at Harley, returning a weak smile. "We're perplexed. Maybe someday I'll explain that. Doc, I gotta say, initially I thought maybe you'd put the box on my desk as a joke. Well, you know—a Harleyism."

"Ha! So you know the term too?" he replied. "Woe to the intern that first bestowed that one upon me!"

Hannah smiled and shrugged her shoulders. Glancing at her watch, she added, "I've got a meeting in ten minutes. Gotta scoot. Thanks much, doc."

"Talk to me toward the end of the day, Hannah. Are you free at four o'clock?" he asked.

"Yep, I am," said Hannah. "What's up?"

"Just something that came to mind," he replied. "Let's get back together then. Same place, same channel."

Dr. Harley watched her leave. Then, joining his fingers behind his head, he leaned back in the chair and closed his eyes, thinking: Nova, cosmic stillness, heart of darkness, metamorphosis to good, immeasurable love, enemy is lifelessness in all its forms, nightmares. He checked his watch. He had 90 minutes before class began. He could easily drive home, pull the paper, and return.

Hannah moved through her day lethargically. Visions of the tool, and now the cross, and contemplations of their meaning were renewed. Cranial perforator, 1858!

She was on the phone with a lab manager from the second floor when she glanced at the clock: 4:05. Dang. She excused herself from the call, then walked to Harley's office. "Sorry I'm late, doc."

"No sweat," he countered. "Have a seat. I, um, have something I'd like to show you. "Hannah, you know I'm a Christian. And I know you are, as well. I'm very glad about that. Unfortunately, there aren't enough of us here or in academic circles worldwide."

He paused uneasily. "Well, it just so happens that it's not the first time I've seen the name 'Nova.' Not long after you received the box with the note and tool, I found a sealed envelope with my name on it—at home, so I knew you hadn't put it there. When I read this, I prayed about it, asking for understanding, meaning, or insight. I'd almost dismissed it. And then you came in today with your note, the tool—and the cross."

Hannah was startled by Harley's revelation. He reached across his desk, handing her a note. In it, she read:

Dear Evan –

Events are unfolding, and you have a role. Hang onto your faith. Embrace it with fervor.

Hannah deeply respects you. Yet she's soon to enter a cosmic storm. She and others are embroiled in events that will give her little rest, even in slumber. In time, she'll tell you about it. Please support and pray for her.

Oh, Dies Irae—day of wrath. A humbling consideration, but no longer foreboding through time. Each generation places greater trust in Satan's realm, and now they laugh at infanticide. But for many, it's grace, not wrath, that opens the path of our choosing. The fear of losing our way can be illuminated as we yearn for the day (that is not now or may ever be again here on earth) when the womb is sacred.

Even the Son of God began his incarnation as an embryo, sacred at the moment of conception. Behold, children are a gift of the Lord, his greatest endowment. The fruit of the womb is both a gift and a reward. The privilege comes with great responsibility—stewardship.

Know that we are all loved immeasurably, and even at the heart of darkness, there is light. So I'll ask that you convey the need for Hannah to give the crucifix to her sister. It has a role and will ultimately return to its rightful owner.

Lifelessness in all its forms is the enemy.

– *Nova*

Hannah dropped the note. She couldn't move. Even her

mouth was clamped shut by a force unknown to her. Tears pushed out on their own.

"Hannah. Hannah…are you alright?" Harley moved quickly to her side, kneeling beside her chair. Then she moved, slowly working her neck muscles to break up what felt like some form of paralysis. Gradually, she brought her hands to her face as tears pulsed and cascaded freely. Her shoulders shook as she whimpered quietly. Dr. Harley placed a hand on her shoulder.

"Oh dear, I'm so sorry. I should've anticipated this."

"No, no, doc," she managed to say. "I've…got…to put these…pieces together."

"When I saw the chain in the box earlier today and pulled on it to discover the crucifix, I knew unquestionably that the letter I'd received was connected," he said.

A few minutes later, with a box of Kleenex in her lap, Hannah dabbed at her swollen eyes and mopped tears from her hands and neck. "This will mean more, later, as I learn more about whatever it is I'm heading into. It's complicated; my father received a note from Nova decades ago. Whatever's happening, it appears that it's advancing at a faster pace, and I'm in it, like it or not. And Kristin is too."

"What about the nightmares, Hannah?"

"They're work-related in a way. Somehow tied to my work and Kristin's," said Hannah. "A fetus screams and the images are, well, vivid."

"I'm so sorry," he replied. "Let's hope the cross is planted purposefully, perhaps as a symbol of His presence and guardianship."

Hannah nodded. "I sure hope so. Doc, may I borrow this letter?" she asked.

"No need. I made a copy of it for you." She returned his original, now spotted with tears.

Back in her office, she quickly gathered her things and put the copy of Harley's letter in her purse. In the hallway, she closed and locked the door. Absorbed in thought about Nova's letters and her secrets, it occurred to Hannah a few miles from home that she couldn't recall leaving the parking lot or navigating the several stoplights along her trek.

As she pulled up to the last light a mile from home, Hannah suddenly felt a sense of dread. That's when she realized that it was this time of day and at this light several weeks earlier that she'd encountered the ominous stranger who knew her name. She looked to both sides and was momentarily relieved to see that no car was there. Then she glanced in the rearview mirror, and immediately her body tensed.

The driver of the dark sedan had stopped close to her rear bumper. He was again wearing sunglasses. The music was loud; she was aware of the steady pulsation of drums. Within seconds, she could hear her own heartbeat hammering furiously. Hannah realized that she couldn't move. It was happening again—a paralysis she was helpless to shake. Seconds later, she was somehow aware of the light's change from red to green. She tried desperately to roll her neck, to raise her hands. She attempted to press on the accelerator but couldn't. She wanted to lock the doors or dial 911.

Car horns began to sound, some moving slowly beyond her on both sides. She could vaguely see long-held glances in her periphery as they moved by. The sedan was still there, visible in the rearview. The music blared as Malbas opened his car door. What she could see in the mirror horrified her: she watched in slow motion as he left the vehicle and moved toward her.

At that moment, as though time were held in suspension, Hannah realized that prayer was her best defense. The man appeared frozen as she silently asked for God's interference and guardianship. And just as quickly, she was released. As the man reached for her door, he spoke. "Hannah."

She managed to hit the accelerator just as he touched the door handle. Her car jumped from the now-yellow light. Frantically, she watched the rearview mirror as she sped away. A minute later, the garage door opened and closed. Turning off the ignition, she sat in the car to gather herself, playing back the scene at the stoplight. That's when she realized there had to be a connection between the letters, the nightmares, and the man in black.

SAMANTHA'S LAST CONVERSATION with Hannah was six weeks earlier. She thought occasionally about their trip to the hospital cafeteria and the startling revelation of the shared nightmare. Soon after the seminar led by Dr. Harley, Samantha and her husband took a week-long vacation. It helped to wipe the slate clean, easing her back into work and, most importantly, nighttime rests with no interruption.

She and Hannah hadn't reconnected, even though at the time they knew they'd stumbled onto something important, awful, or both. Easier to simply let it slide.

Shortly after two am, Samantha woke with a jolt. She ran to the bathroom. Staring back at her in the mirror was a tortured image of herself—eyes puffy and red with facial skin still pulled tight. Her fingers reached up to massage her temples and that's when she noticed the tremors, a shaking she hadn't experienced before. Images of the fresh nightmare flitted in and out of her mind and—just as Hannah had begun to describe weeks ago—the fetus in a steel tray wriggled in tortured agony, tiny hand extended, then emitted a scream.

More of the dream revealed itself while she sat on the toilet. Briefly, she could wind and rewind the tape, though each rewind shed detail. The baby's world beforehand was one of pure, fluid comfort, suspended warmth with blissful sensations that included even the occasional awareness of muted music, her mother's movement, a taste of the host's spicy foods, and energized recognition of sugars consumed. Then, abruptly, Sam was aware—and feeling, as the baby did—shockwaves of agony as the baby was prodded with a suction tube and steel instruments. Each time the tools probed or attached, the baby winced in pain, helplessly moving away from alien steel, head arched back with mouth agape.

Still shaken and sleep-deprived, Samantha drove to work early. On her PC, she searched for evidence that a fetus could feel pain during abortion procedures.

She quickly found convincing information at *Live Action News* and *ProLifeAction.org*. She explored further, finding *LifeNews.com, nrlc.org, abortionNO.org, DailyWire.com,* and *PreciousLife.com.*

Sam learned that a revered OBGYN, still in practice today after decades of work, proved that preborn babies feel pain. Unquestionably, there was the potential for horrendous pain as the baby matures—a scientific certainty shared by many embryologists, pediatricians, researchers, and other medical professionals. After all, the baby has a brain and a nervous system with nerve endings.

She also found a video, *The Silent Scream*, produced by the late Dr. Bernard Nathanson. She watched in horror as the video replayed exactly the scene she'd witnessed in her nightmare hours earlier. In the ultrasound, a baby's head arched back, mouth ajar as horrific pain shot through its tiny body during an abortion procedure. Suddenly, a door opened and closed down the hall, causing her to jump. Calming herself, she plowed on. She learned that ultrasound technology played a pivotal role in converting many abortion providers to Christianity, a change that often led to abandonment of their career as abortionists.

Apparently, Nathanson had been an abortionist who presided over 60,000 abortions and was also the founder of the National Abortion Rights Action League. He fled from his vocation as a result of the invention of ultrasound, forever changing the fact that, previously, abortions were a blind procedure. With ultrasound, those conducting abortions could see in graphic detail how fetuses made futile attempts to move away from the abortion instruments, and whose heads rocked back in pain, thus the name of his film.

Through the years, shocked by what they now could view, many abortionists have forever dropped their tools in the tray, never to pick them up again. One said that he was "shaken to the very roots of my soul by what I saw."

Samantha also found references to Dr. Maureen Condic, a professor of neurobiology and anatomy at the University of Utah School of Medicine. Condic now has a successful career studying neural development and providing expert testimony for state and national legislative proceedings. The physician has publicly testified about the science of fetal pain, confirming that there's no question to it—preborn babies have a mature perception of pain at 20 weeks gestation. Condic was quoted (in *Live Action News*) as saying,

> We're all horrified by the pictures of infants that were brutally killed by convicted murderer [Philadelphia abortionist] Kermit Gosnell. And yet we tolerate the same brutality—and even worse—for humans at 20 weeks of development. Imposing pain on any pain-capable living creature is cruelty, and ignoring the pain experienced by another human for any reason is barbaric."

The neural circuitry underlying the most basic response to pain is in place by eight weeks. It is entirely uncontested in scientific and medical literature that a fetus experiences pain in some capacity from as early as eight weeks.

Samantha discovered a statement by the American College of Pediatricians: "At conception, a distinct, living, and whole human organism is formed." Tara Sander Lee, PhD, a leading molecular geneticist agreed, stating, "It's a scientific certainty the human life begins at the moment of fertilization."

She could take no more. System overload and exhaustion conspired against her. Sam rose abruptly, retreating to the restroom where she splashed cold water on her face. Just as she returned to the hallway, her boss rounded the corner. He stopped in his tracks when he saw her. Sam had no trouble explaining her need to return home. "I thought I could make it through the day, but I don't think I can."

That evening, Samantha cuddled close to her husband, Rob, insisting they watch a romantic comedy together, hoping that easy humor, popcorn, a glass of milk, and a happy ending might erase the online images, reducing the chance of another nightmare. By 9:30, Sam was asleep. At three, she awoke panting, covered in sweat.

Sam's dream had increased in horrifying clarity and depth. Shaking, she searched frantically on bookshelves for their only Bible, finally locating it on the lowest shelf in the spare bedroom. Using the "Bible helps" guide in front, she quickly found comfort in Isaiah 41:10 (fear not), Psalm 118:6-7 (the Lord is with me), and then finally, Psalm 23 (The Lord is my shepherd) which she read repeatedly.

Before the sun rose, she dialed Hannah's number at work, fully expecting to leave a brief message. The phone rang once, and Hannah answered. "Hey. What's up?"

"Sorry to call so early," said Sam. "I expected to leave a message. I woke early this morning—two in a row, actually—after some awful dreams and thought we should talk."

"Oh, girl. I've been meaning to call you too. You okay?"

"I don't have a clue what to think, Hannah. The nightmare has returned."

"Hey, Sam…could you come over to our place tonight? We were going to take the kids to the discovery museum, but Chet could take them by himself," said Hannah.

That became the plan; Hannah would make dinner. She explained to Chet that Sam's need was urgent. He already knew of the coincidence of their nightmares. Taking the kids out would be the least he could do to help.

When Sam arrived at Hannah's home, the meal was ready. The smell in the kitchen was overpowering. Ziti with Hannah's own sauce; she claimed its goodness was all about the use of fresh garlic and farmer's market sausage. Hannah served the meal.

When Hannah was seated, she quietly looked into Sam's eyes. "Would you join me for grace, Sam?" she asked. Hannah then reached over to place her hand on top of Sam's, then asked the Lord's blessing. And though Hannah was quickly aware of Sam's jittery nerves, telegraphed through her fingers, she pressed on.

Hannah's prayer concluded with, "Lord, please bless us with discernment when we discuss our shared experiences. Help us understand what's happening, and how best to deal with it according to your will. And, Lord, when it's right— please allow us to return to restful, peaceful sleep." Hannah lifted her eyes to look at Sam. She withdrew her hands while offering a smile, beckoning her to speak.

"Thank you for the prayer. I was going to mention something right away, but dinner was ready, and then I knew you'd want prayer," said Sam. "I need to ask a question."

"Sure. What is it, Sam?" replied Hannah.

"Is there some sort of creeper in the area?"

"What do you mean? Did something happen?" asked Hannah.

"Well, I don't know. I was at the last light on my way here, and some guy in a black or charcoal sedan pulled up beside me. Classy sunglasses, dark hair. He motioned for me to roll the window down. He turned the music down just enough for me to hear him say something like, 'Sam—are you out this way for a visit?' He didn't look at all familiar, and my senses were shooting bottle rockets by that time, so I left quickly, not saying a word. There's a chance he followed me here."

Hannah got out of her chair and went to the front window. The drapes were open; she stood to one side, looking into the street.

Hannah returned to the table and sat down to look intently at Sam. "Did you say, dark sedan, sunglasses, and dark hair? And he somehow knew your name?" Sam nodded her head, looking concerned. Hannah excused herself again, this time to text Chet. The message: "Nothing to worry about, but odd - when u get closer to home w/the kids, keep an eye out for someone that may be following you, or driving 2 close. I'll explain later."

"It's possible I've seen the same guy," said Hannah, rejoining Sam. "Nothing ever came of it, and I've checked the area for sex offenders, that sort of thing. No one real close that's worrisome. But I may call the police tomorrow just in case."

Chet texted back: "You + Sam OK? What's up? Need us to come home?"

Hannah replied: "No. PLEASE don't. We're fine."

Hannah made every effort to dismiss the importance of Sam's experience. Though she knew their similar encounters with the guy in the dark sedan were distressing, it was the other shared experience with the dream that they needed to get to. As Sam's host, Hannah felt a responsibility to keep that on track. As they ate, they discussed an upcoming seminar they'd both attend, family goings-on, and books they're reading.

After their meal, they moved to the den, glasses of water in hand. There, Sam knew it was time to talk about the dreams. She shared the details of both recent nightmares, the second of which seemed to be fueled by the online research she did at the lab. Then, just before she called that morning, she'd found comfort in Psalm 23. Hannah acknowledged that with a warm smile.

155

Hannah told Sam about the tool she discovered on her office desk the day they met at Harley's seminar. She described the unmarked box and the note and cross that accompanied it. She mentioned her father's revelation from long ago—the first note from someone who appeared to be the same writer. Then, Harley's comments, their research into the tool, and his note from the same Nova.

They both had mild tremors while comparing the gruesome specifics of each other's dreams. Hannah was taking notes. Both experienced a strange sense of dread when they realized the exact coincidence of the nightmare's many details, now captured in Hannah's notes. And, of course, their description of the guy in the dark sedan matched precisely.

"There's got to be a reason for this. Why you and me, Hannah?" asked Sam.

"Well, there's more to it Sam, and I can only hope that if we're talking about it, we're meant to, and perhaps that'll satisfy whatever, whoever it is that's planted this awful dream," said Hannah. "I've asked God for an understanding and discernment, but nothing yet."

"Planted the dream?" stammered Sam. A look of astonishment swept her face. "How could that be?"

"I don't really know, but I can tell you this," replied Hannah. "Our nightmares, their meaning, the tool on my desk, the notes and the cross, even the guy in the car—I'm convinced they're somehow connected. We are, after all, in the devil's world. He's alive and roaming freely, but if we stay out of his reach, he can't harm us. He can try to frighten us; fear is just one of his many weapons." Hannah folded her hands and looked at Sam quietly. She paused before speaking again.

"Sam, I believe without a doubt that God has a hand in this—so it's not something entirely evil at work here, if that's what you're afraid of," said Hannah. "I really, truly believe God's involved. It's supernatural, but in both good and bad ways. We've got to steer clear of the shipwrecks and undertow. Think of it as following God's lighthouse beam."

"I think I see what you mean, Hannah," said Sam with a sigh.

"I have the distinct feeling that there are other aspects to this, yet to be revealed. Hey, you're still shaking," noted Hannah, startled at how Samantha was rocking in place, holding her arms in a tight wrap around her chest, trembling uncomfortably. She went to Sam and held her shoulders.

"I'm afraid," muffled Sam through tears, now running freely down her cheeks.

"Hey, hey," said Hannah, pulling her close. "My father's explained a lot of this to our minister at church. He and Mom have begun a prayer circle with several people, praying hard for an explanation or settlement; something."

"Is that why you're so strong?" asked Sam through her tears, burying her head in Hannah's arms. "I can't go on like this."

Hannah's tears ran with Sam's as they held each other. "Oh, Sam, don't you know that your greatest comforter is right here, waiting for us to ask for help?"

Sam's crying stopped momentarily. With wet, red eyes she looked at Sam. "You mean…."

Hannah was nodding. "Yes. That's right. He's right here with us, right now. Let's have a prayer."

Sam could only nod unsteadily.

Hannah placed her head against Sam's, then lowered her

face and closed her eyes. They sat quietly before Hannah began her prayer.

"Dear Lord Jesus—please join us now. We need you, Lord. We're frightened by all of these events and the horrible dreams. There's something hidden and deep at work, and we need your protection. You gave your life for us and now we are here, seeking your comfort, guidance, and protection."

Hannah held onto Sam as she prayed. Then she stopped. Hannah felt what came to her as a prayerful answer, with an affirmation—It's time, and Sam's ready.

Hannah knew what to do, led by loving guidance. She'd been in this place before, experienced when comforting each of her children after little Thomas' death. Shortly after that, both Matt and Sarah committed their lives to Christ, led by Hannah and Chet in experiences not unlike this one.

Hannah gently pushed Sam back to look into her face, yet Sam's eyes were closed. "Sam, I need to ask you: If you've not yet given your life to Christ, will you? You could make your commitment to Christ, right here and now." Sam's eyes opened, and she nodded vigorously.

"Okay, but Sam, you've got to say it. I'll lead; just say as I do, okay?"

"Oh, Lord God, Heavenly Father . . ." offered Hannah.

Sam said, "Lord God, Heavenly Father . . ."

"I want to accept your loving Son, Jesus into my heart," continued Hannah.

"I want to accept your loving Son, Jesus into my heart," repeated Sam, sniffing but alert and watching Hannah's every move, new tears gently pulsing down her cheeks.

"I know that Jesus died and was raised from the dead for me, and all humanity—to save us from our sins. I commit my life to you."

"I know that Jesus died and was…raised from the dead for me. And all humanity. To save us from our sins. I commit my life to you," added Sam, whose shaking quickly dissolved.

Hannah lifted her hands to Sam's face, wiping her tears. She then rested them, wet, on Sam's hands. Looking into Hannah's eyes, Samantha began crying again but through a smile broader than Hannah had ever seen before on her friend's face.

They were both awash in tears when a door swung open as Chet and the kids burst in noisily from the garage. They took a quick look at the two women and stood still. Chet put his hands on the children's shoulders, pulling them tight to his side. "Is everything okay, Mom?" whispered Sarah.

"Yes, everything's fine," said Hannah with bright acknowledgment through her tears. "My good friend Samantha just gave her life to Christ. It doesn't get much better than that, does it honey?"

With that, Chet and the kids swept in, joining them on the couch. Hands yoked shoulders, and Chet spoke. "Lord God, we thank you so much for this moment—for Samantha's commitment to you. Please strengthen and guide her. Amen."

Matt and Sarah looked about them, knowing this was a very special moment. They both smiled at Samantha, who reached for each of them, knowing how special these children were. If only she could have some of her own.

"Hey kids," said Chet softly. "Say goodnight to Samantha. Go finish your homework and then get ready for bed. I'll be up soon, alright?" Matt and Sarah looked with delight again at Sam, patted their mother (Sarah leaning in for a kiss), then left for the stairs.

Chet excused himself, making for the kitchen. Minutes later, Hannah and Sam could hear the sounds of dishwashing.

"Sam, what you've done tonight is the most important step you've taken in your life. I can promise you that," said Hannah.

"You mean…it's that easy? But, what do I do now?" countered Sam.

"Well, Sam, yes—but there's more. Lots more. It's both a commitment and an adventure, and the reward lasts forever," answered Hannah. "There's so much more to come, and an obligation with the greatest benefit of all. It's a lifelong change that you've asked for, and Christ's arms are open wide. He's waited your entire life for this very moment." After a brief pause, Hannah said, "Lemme ask you this, Sam: how will Rob feel about it?"

"You mean, what will Rob do?" asked Sam.

Hannah nodded.

"I don't know for sure. He was raised in a church as a kid," said Sam. "We were married in a church, and we visited two churches since. I've told him everything, and he's been concerned through it and supportive. I believe that if he sees the goodness of this in me, he'll be okay with it."

"That's good, Sam. Do you think he would join you? Could he? A marriage united in faith, with a husband and wife who commit their lives to Christ together, is the best foundation for a marriage and faith to grow. Because, after all, if you move together as one in your faith walk, you'll be united in the greatest adventure of all. There's nothing else like it, Sam."

"It would be a change for Rob, but I think he'd be open to it once he's heard about my night here with you," said Sam. "Would you and Chet help us?"

"We'd like nothing more, Sam," replied Hannah. "I'd like to introduce you both to our pastor. Do you think you could join us for church on an upcoming Sunday?" Sam and Hannah went over some of the specifics, service time and the church address. Adult class afterward. Sam smiled, imagining the impact of her change and the possibility of (Hannah's words) a new "church family."

"Sam, I have something for you," said Hannah, walking to a shelf filled with books. She pulled a new Bible from the wall. Returning to the couch, she said, "You may have one at home, but this is my favorite study Bible. I always keep an extra on hand for a special occasion. I'm thrilled to give it to you.

"Oh, and when you're in the Bible, here are some important starters," she added, paging through the Bible. She went to a table for a pad of sticky notes. She wrote references to specific scriptures, then stuck them inside the book.

"Look these up as soon as you can, Sam," added Hannah. The notes referred to John 3:16, Exodus 34:6-7, Deuteronomy 6:4-5, Isaiah 53:6, John 14:6, and Matthew 28:18-20.

"Also, we'll talk about the meaning of repentance when we meet with the pastor," continued Hannah. "Acknowledging our sins is an important step, whatever those sins may be. We'll have lots of time to talk about that soon. Keep a notepad handy as you read. Got questions? Just write them down. If I can't help you, I'm sure our pastor can."

Both stood and hugged. Chet had just come in from the kitchen, joining them as they walked to Sam's car. Placing her phone on the seat next to her, Sam said before closing the door: "I'll call if anything's odd along the way."

13

THE WOMB IS SACRED

DR. EVAN HARLEY ARRIVED EARLY at work one morning in preparation for a trip. As he tied up loose ends, he reached into his briefcase and removed a folded note. He used his master key to open Hannah's office door, turned on the light, and placed the note on her desk.

SEVERAL MILES AWAY, Jack Soelberg leaned back in his chair, staring intently into his computer screen while completing his email to Brigadier General Kay Zavala at Ft. Belvoir.

> Greetings, Kay. By now, you've seen those strange letters from Nova. Our mutual friend, Harry, helped to pass them on to you. We're perplexed, especially considering current events that tie to them, including a recent note to an anatomist who my daughter Hannah works for at the med center near here (copy attached). Harry told me that, at first glance, they seem to come from the same writer—and that, as the best handwriting expert in our noble military, you're his top choice. By any chance, would you have some time to discuss this within the next week or so, Kay? I hope your trip to Brussels was rewarding. Best regards.
> —*(Ret.) Col. Jack Soelberg*

Jack then entered Kay's email address and punched send.

A few seconds later, Kay Zavala turned her attention to an incoming email, read it, and opened the PDF attachments.

"So there's more to this Nova," whispered Zavala. "So strange!" Kay scanned her calendar then emailed some dates and times to Jack.

Jack returned to his desk 30 minutes later and was surprised to find her reply. They settled on a period of up to an hour the next day. He slept better that night, knowing at least that he'd have an expert to talk to.

The next afternoon Kay called him early, eager to discuss Jack and Harry's early years, then sharing some of her own background with news of her many trips to and from Europe. "Thank God I didn't draw the straw for Afghanistan. My family wouldn't have seen much of me if that had happened. In several months, Jack, I'll hit the Army's big 30 anniversary of being here. The work's both tiring and invigorating, but now at the age of 58, I'm ready to hang it up," she said.

"One of the things I get brought into occasionally are court appearances as a forensics expert, so I've always got part-time work if I want it. The FBI's way behind schedule and the Association of Forensic Document Examiners knows my name, whereabouts, and exact date of retirement," she added, chuckling.

Switching to the main track, she then said, "Hey, Jack— those Nova letters sure are strange. The latest one to Dr. Harley again references your daughter, Hannah, and seems to take a swipe at Kristin too, right?"

"Yes, that's right, Kay. One of the earlier notes referred to her explicitly," he replied. "She's an OBGYN, now second in charge of managing a rather large family planning staff, including in-house and independent abortionists. Pretty awful stuff."

"The letters are undoubtedly written by the same hand," she said. "I'm near certain they're written by a woman, based on distinctive individual and style characteristics. Looking closely at structural consistencies, connecting strokes, slant and baseline alignment—pretty standard stuff, actually— there's consistency in all facets, even her temperament, though that's only an educated guess. She's very intelligent, sincere, and has strong moral character, likely with powerful influence from her faith. She expresses that freely. It appears that she's in position as something of a saint, or guardian angel."

"You can tell all of that just by looking at those few pages, Kay?" asked Jack. "I'm amazed, and very appreciative."

"Well, Jack, you can understand the rest of it as well as I, and yet with a great deal more insight because of your closeness to it. Let me ask you something, and sorry to get personal. Harry explained to me that the earliest note from Nova came to you a few years after your near-death experience in 'Nam, right? So, by any chance, Jack, was there a woman somehow involved in your life then—there in the field, or at home who you shared intimate details with?"

"No. Miriam and I have been married for decades, not long after my return from 'Nam as a grunt gunner. No other woman anywhere in sight, there or at home. Does that help?"

"No, I guess not, but it narrows the field. Just a question I had to ask," she replied. "Okay, some observations—maybe of little consequence, but I've come to appreciate how these things can contribute to the bigger picture. There's a very odd trait that I've not encountered before, but again, it may be nothing. Nova's writing uniformity is an anomaly, especially considering its consistency through the years. No stress is apparent, yet great emotion—say, empathy—is everywhere. I'd say she has an enormous heart, one that's found you and your family. You appear to have an over-watcher of sorts. So, whoever she is, she's either extravagant with her empathy and goodwill, or she's impossibly clever in her deception.

"If anything at all comes to mind, Jack, or if you get any new letters, please let me know," added Kay. "You've won my interest. You have my number and email."

A FEW DAYS LATER, Kristin returned from her third trip to the bathroom on Friday evening, even though she'd avoided drinking much water. She was a bit concerned at this new development, feeling bloated and uncomfortable and having to pee more frequently. Not enough exercise? The onset of a cold or flu? And if that was the case, she'd need to drink considerably more water—maybe with some immune system booster for good measure. Rough week.

Kristin made a note to get some echinacea capsules and tea the next day while running errands. Oh, it was probably just hormonal swings; she expected her period any time now. She'd missed the last one but dismissed it to the extra-heavy workload, travel, and strenuous gym workouts.

It didn't help that last night's nightmare left her with only five hours of sleep. Kristin's day began around four am. She awoke with a jolt, sweating, vaguely recalling the image of a fetus, brought out whole, like many she'd seen before. Yet, there was life and an outreached hand. Then, prodding her awake, she remembered the eyes and lurid scream.

Kristin shook as she made coffee, knowing that a return to sleep was impossible. She was first into the headquarters facility that day.

THE HOUSE WAS QUIET when Kristin entered it many hours later, though Festus sensed the need to contribute avian noise and entertainment. Remarkably, the observant bird was restless when she was. He watched her continuously, taking it all in.

Gili had business in LA again with gallery visits. He couldn't call because of a later dinner engagement with his "cigar and cognac fellas." Well, that's what he told her, anyway.

Kristin was in no mood for wine, typically a source of comfort. She looked at the tall counter display of fine, lavish reds, a rack that held 18 bottles on their side—Merlot, Cab, Shiraz, Carménère, Monastrell, and Malbec. The wines were just a small collection chosen from the hundreds of bottles in Gili's spacious tasting room below—any of which they both enjoyed. Strangely, even the thought of wine sickened her.

Kristin was certain that she'd gained weight over the past few weeks. Maybe too much fine dining. She made a note in her phone to call the gym for an extra-long appointment with her fitness trainer.

Dried mealworms were Festus' favorite snack, and she gave them to him plentifully while he whistled and jabbered in appreciation. In the den, Kristin grabbed the stack of bills to pay—a task she accepted shortly after agreeing to live with Gili at the house. Any mail they knew requiring payment, check or electronic, went there.

Papers now in place at the counter, she grabbed the

checkbook, taking it with her to the Mac. She first did the online banking. Ten minutes later, notations made, she returned to her seat at the counter and pulled the first envelope and opened it, verifying the PGE utility payment against the number noted in the computer.

Next was an envelope with art on its cover. Kristin immediately recognized it as a van Gogh. She turned it over to open it, thinking that Gili left a message, knowing the likelihood of her tackling the bills this weekend. On the card's back page was an inscription: "Pieta of Jesus and Mary by Vincent van Gogh." She found a folded note inside...

Dear Kristin,

Sorry about the circumstances of your early rise this morning. Sadly, the unpleasant dream fits into your present circumstance and an outpouring of love that's now moving in your direction.

The baby you've seen, Eve, has become a catalyst for change. I'm merely the messenger. Events are unfolding, and you have a role. Hannah's struggles are now entwined with yours, a journey that will ultimately give each of you tasks in God's now-moving plan.

I know you love Vincent's art, Kristin. Mary conveyed that in her prayers.

Today, there's a man who lives in the D.C. area. He writes and preaches with passion. In one of his books, *Soulprint*, Mark Batterson offers something I couldn't possibly have expressed better: "Every work of art originates in the imagination of the artist. And so you originated in the imagination of God....You are His masterpiece...You are His painting, His novel, His sculpture." The you he speaks of is you, Kristin.

Van Gogh once said, "Christ is more of an artist than the artists. He works in the living spirit and the living flesh; he makes men [and women] instead of statues." God is painting a picture of grace on the canvas of your life.

Batterson asks, "Have you ever felt captive?" The question applies to you, dear. Batterson adds that God wants to finish what he started with you, a mission that began long before you were brought into this world. You need to break free from the bondage of captivity and sin that have held you back and—even more dangerously, from your calling.

It's a very specific call to action. The lives of so many are at stake: loved ones, intended souls yet to be—who otherwise will be terminated.

Your guilt, shame, and anxiety have enslaved you, holding you captive. Some mistakes can and will bury you, Kristin. But, for you, God has commanded me to be sure that won't happen. What's more: He loves and forgives you, but He's pressing now for an urgent change in your life. You'll need to muster every ounce of courage and resolve to bring it about. I'll be with you each step of the way, but you've got to do your part.

Finally, I need to encourage you to be like Saul (who became Paul). Read Acts 9: 1-31; there are many similarities in your lives and a metamorphosis that's dying to find you.

The womb is sacred.

Yours, now and forever, —*Nova*

Kristin pushed her chair back forcefully and skittered quickly to the bathroom, not knowing if she'd merely sit to pee again or grab the bowl with both hands. Her bowels were churning.

Twenty minutes later, she emerged, wiping tears. The aftertaste of mouthwash, used to suppress the rotten taste of vomit, soured. Before she left, she had the urge to pee again, wondering if there was an ounce of moisture left in her body.

Back at the kitchen counter, she held the note again unsteadily. How could this be? She dialed Hannah's number, only to get her voicemail. "Hey, sis. Please give me a call." She called Gili's number. Voicemail there too, but she chose not to leave a message. He'd know that she called. She went to the bedroom to find Mary Bruneau's card, LifeLine Gallery. The number was for the gallery; she left a message: "Mary, this is Kristin Soelberg. We met several weeks ago. It was a bad day for me. I, um, have some questions for you. Here are my numbers. I'll also email you. Thanks, Mary. — Kristin."

With no Bible in the house, she opened the Mac's Safari for a search, keying in Acts 9:1-31.

In Acts, Kristin learned that Saul, a tyrant waging war against the Lord's disciples, was on his way to Damascus, seeking permission from the high priest to take early believers as prisoners to Jerusalem. A light from heaven flashed, and he fell to the ground, then a voice said to him, "Saul, Saul, why do you persecute me?"

"Who are you, Lord?" Saul asked.

"I am Jesus, whom you are persecuting," he replied. "Now get up and go into the city, and you will be told what you must do."

Saul was blinded, which led to his amazing transformation. When he reached his destination, his sight returned, and he took up his new call of evangelism in Jesus' name. He was now called Paul, a devout disciple of the risen Christ.

This was madness. Nova's note was a very bad joke or something completely beyond comprehension. Kristin returned to the bathroom, losing whatever remained in her stomach. The dry heaves left her empty, unsteady, and exhausted.

She forced herself to drink water, sitting again at the kitchen counter to the background sounds of TV news—anything to force the bewildering card further from her mind. She cursed Gili for ignoring her call. She sat, head hung low, attempting to make sense of the note.

Eventually, she moved to plug in her phone for a charge and went into the downstairs theater. Seated before the giant flat screen there, she scrolled through the new movies, found one, and spread out as comfortably as possible. Meaning to take her phone with her, Kristin soon fell asleep on the leather sectional. While she slept, the phone rang continuously. First, Hannah, then Mary. Each tried to reach her several times.

Many hours later, the nightmare of the baby came again, this time with greater clarity. She woke suddenly, panting and covered with sweat. She ran upstairs and into the bathroom while also aware that her breasts were oddly sensitive. That discomfort triggered a sudden thought. In a daze, as she scrolled through the awful dream, Kristin dug deep into a drawer of toiletries. There were the packets with the clinic's logo. Pregnancy test strips.

"This can't be," she mumbled. She knew that urine is

most concentrated in the morning, assuring greater accuracy. Urinating on the fabric strip, she saw the results minutes later. Positive. She did it again, the positive result confirmed. She fumed, *No wonder I've missed my period twice and feel so bloated.*

That's when she knew that Gili's forced sex in the jet 10 weeks earlier had been without protection. Had to be. And now she's carrying his child.

Well, that's easily remedied.

Kristin's mood swung from miserable to furious that morning. She reached for her phone on the kitchen counter and saw she had two missed calls, Hannah's and Mary's. but there was nothing from Gili. Too early to return their calls, but she dialed Gili's number anyway. One ring, and it went to directly to voicemail. She arched back to throw the phone toward the wall, stopping only at the last moment. She tabbed a quick note to Gili: "Just go ahead and disappear. Ignore my call. You 'n' your freakin' limos and plane. Some gift they turned out to be. Your bird's history." That one, sufficiently cryptic, brought a smug grin.

She put on some sweats, grabbed a key, a large bottle of water, and precautionary pepper spray, then went out for a walk. She was vaguely aware of a single crow that seemed to fly with her, always tracking her path. As she became more attuned to its movements, she noted that the bird seemed to follow her deliberately.

Oddly, no other birds were nearby, so there was little chance of confusing it as just another crow. As she neared Gili's home, she saw an opportunity when the bird settled atop a phone pole. Kristin picked up a palm-sized rock and threw it at the bird. So strange—it merely watched the rock that missed by just three or four inches. When she picked up another stone, the bird was gone.

Kristin's Fitbit logged almost five miles on her return. After a shower, she started to heat water for tea when the phone rang. Mary. "Good morning, Kristin. I tried you a few times last night. So sorry we didn't connect."

"Oh, I fell asleep, forgetting to take my phone with me," said Kristin, sounding morose.

"Hey, you don't sound so good. Bad night?"

"Well, you know Gili pretty well, I suspect. He left for parts unknown."

"Oh, I'm so sorry. Our marriage wasn't meant to be," said Mary. "I left him and changed my life forever. In Paris I fell in love, traveled Europe, found Christ and a real calling in sculpture. Still smiling! I take it you're…engaged?"

"Well yes, but I now have some real reservations, despite his charm. I suspect he's seeing other women, and I've already learned I'll never hold a candle to his art collection."

"Senseless surrealism and pagan art, most of it," replied Mary.

"Huh? What's that mean, Mary?"

"There's actually an art form by that name—pagan art—though I use it simply as a broad reference to most of the work that he's enamored with: modern stuff, lot of nonsense, most of it with no redeeming value. And little appreciation for the greatest form of art on earth, the Christian faith," replied Mary. "Gil's most interested in the sad and immoral lifestyle of many artists today, expressive of so much filth and misery, yet with no regard for the greatest artist of all."

Kristin cringed, recalling Nova's letter: somehow, she was His painting, His novel, His sculpture. And van Gogh:

"Christ is more of an artist than the artists. He works in the living spirit and the living flesh."

"Does the name 'Nova' ring a bell with you?" asked Kristin.

"No, I'm sorry. It doesn't," answered Mary. "Should it?"

The phone was quiet. Mary waited, then heard sniffling at the other end. "Oh, hey, Kristin—what's wrong?"

"I'm pregnant," Kristin whimpered. "Gili. It happened on the way back from the arts fair."

"Don't tell me he got you with that scheme about the Mile High Club or whatever he calls it. What a rat. Oh, I'm sorry. I shouldn't've said that," added Mary.

"No, it's fine. He really is a rat."

"God works in mysterious ways, Kristin. If the seed for your love of God was planted in an event like the arts fair, just think what more he can do for you when you turn to him with purpose."

"Did you just say…'seed of love?'"

"I did. Oh, but I'm not referring to Gil! Listen, you've come into my prayers lately, Kristin," Mary added. "And now, this revelation. I'm so sorry to hear of your latest news if you are, yet I know there's sure to be goodness in it. Your disappointment can turn to the greatest joy if you take it to Christ. The seed I refer to is the beginning of your love for Christ. Has anyone ever spoken to you about Christ's unconditional love for you?"

"Yes, a long time ago," said Kristin, thoughtfully. "Somehow, I think he knew a day like this would come. My father. Well, Mom too. But there are other things in play now that make this so uncomfortable."

"What're your plans?" asked Mary.

"I can't have his baby, especially now that Gili's given me so much to be concerned about—his lifestyle and fidelity."

"Adoption?" asked Mary.

"No."

"You mean…abortion?"

"You don't know, Mary, do you?" replied Kristin. "I run one of the largest family planning and abortion enterprises in the world. It's my job. Well, it'll soon be my responsibility; the CEO's planning her retirement. I've put everything into this."

"Oh, Kristin. I didn't know. That's very bad news. For you."

"What? What do you mean, Mary?"

"What you just told me is one of the saddest things I've ever heard." There was a long silence. "Has anyone spoken with you about the consequence of a sin so egregious?"

Kristin was stunned. Her mind reeled. Her initial impulse was to end the call. Though denying what she heard was easiest, she somehow knew the truth of it. Like a small fissure, expanding, the realization of Mary's indictment hit her hard and continued to flow into her heart. It was an overpowering force that tapped her strength. Unsteadily, she walked past Festus, nearly toppling the bird's freestanding perch. She collapsed into a sofa.

With the phone propped near an ear, Kristin was vaguely aware of Mary's words, attempting to penetrate her thoughts. Yet, recollection of her father's request from long ago overpowered it: "In a situation when you feel even worse than this—and that day will come, because life will throw unpleasant, uncomfortable surprises at you—remember this moment, then raise your eyes and your heart to God and simply say, 'Please be with me, Lord. Show me what to do.' Promise me, honey. Promise me that you will."

Closely tied to that was her father's reference to 1 Peter 5:8-9:

> *Be alert and of sober mind. Your enemy the devil prowls around like a roaring lion looking for someone to devour. Resist him, standing firm in the faith, because you know that the family of believers throughout the world is undergoing the same kind of sufferings.*

Mary waited quietly on the line, praying for Kristin. She heard muffled tears and, in the background, Gili's bird yammered unintelligibly.

"Kristin. Gil's home is in Palo Alto Hills, right?" asked Mary. "I'm visiting a foundry today only an hour from there. Give me your address, please. I could be there around noon." Barely audibly, Kristin gave Mary the address then pulled a pillow over her face.

Minutes later, Kristin's phone rang. Certain it was Gili, she grabbed the phone, screaming angrily. Her sister Hannah replied, "You want me to try later?"

"Oh, sis. I'm sorry."

Hannah's big news about Jack and Miriam's move brought only a slight surprise. Kristin, preoccupied, spoke, whimpered, and cried into the phone. An hour later, with tears at both ends of the line, Kristin finally got off the couch to find the note from Nova, slipped it onto the scanner's glass plate, sending it to Hannah's computer.

During the call Kristin conveyed the depth of her anxiety. A storm had swept into her life unexpectedly, shredding everything known and familiar. Kristin spoke of Mary's call, explaining who she was and how they'd met (Gili's ex-wife). Then, news of her pregnancy. The recurring nightmares. Hannah was just as shocked as Kristin was, wanting nothing more than to join her for Mary's visit. Sadly, the miles made that an impossibility.

How could this be? thought Hannah. The nightmares, identical to hers, and Sam's. And now a new message from Nova. Hannah withheld some of the details of their developing mystery, thinking it would overwhelm her sister.

Before the call ended, Hannah prayed with her sister—an impossibility, earlier. Kristin was miserable, but she was sober. Uncharacteristically, Kristin was weak, vulnerable, and attentive—exactly what Hannah had hoped for if she could prescribe a state of mind and soul, and finally a need to receive the goodness of Christ. Maybe, just maybe, Kristin's drinking was the result of career discomfort, albeit while superbly managing a high-performance death machine. Hannah was both distraught and elated with the news of Kristin's plight. This had to be God's doing.

Hannah made a copy of Nova's latest letter, then texted her father. "Dad, are you + Mom in? I'll walk over. I've got news + something to show you." Minutes later, she met with her parents in their kitchen, the copy of Kristin's letter from Nova in hand. "Mom, Dad—I just prayed with Kristin. She's pregnant."

Miriam looked at Jack; though he was expressionless, she felt perplexed and concerned, yet there was consolation in it: maybe God will use this for good.

Later, Jack sent an email to Kay, the Army's top forensic document examiner, attaching a copy of Nova's latest message—the longest of them to date and the first with artwork.

He and Miriam had agreed earlier: should one more note arise, or more news of this wretched dream shared by both women (Hannah and Sam, and now possibly Kristin, too?)— they'd seek counsel from their new pastor. It was time to ask for help and advice. Hannah and Chet supported the idea fully, knowing their pastor's gift of discernment.

14

FESTUS THE ENTERTAINER AND THE GIFT OF GOD'S WORD

YEARS EARLIER, BRIGADIER GENERAL KAY ZAVALA would've ignored the request from a friend-of-a-friend. But she'd reached her star and was now looking forward to a new phase of her life—retirement. It felt good to contribute her knowledge and skills beyond the borders of military duty. And, besides, the notes from Nova, whoever or whatever she was, were fascinating. She'd never before seen anything like Nova's odd, enigmatic handwriting style or consistency. There was strength of character and moral grounding in her words and writing style.

Kay hoped not only to help but to learn more. The notes, coming to her from retired Colonel Jack Soelberg, were more than just intriguing. They were deep and mysterious. She wanted to help solve the riddle of who Nova was. There was, however, one nagging thought—something was missing. A piece of the puzzle. She made a note to probe further with Jack.

THE TEXT CAME IN AT NOON, telling Kristin that Mary was only ten minutes out. Kristin had since eaten some cereal with fruit, gradually gaining strength. She hustled to the porch and sat in a chair overlooking the driveway. As she greeted Mary with a hug, her phone alerted her to a call. She silenced it without looking. Soon, Kristin was preparing iced teas in the kitchen. They were just getting warmed up to Kristin's crisis when the phone rang again.

Mary looked down at Kristin's phone. The screen identified the caller as Gili. They shared a glance with sour expressions.

"May I?" asked Mary.

Kristin merely nodded, amused.

"May I help you?" asked Mary.

Gili was thrown off by Mary's voice—an unwanted intrusion. He didn't reply, so Mary made sure he understood the meaning of it.

"If you're looking for Kristin, she's with me." Mary activated the speaker. Both women waited. Regaining his balance, Gili lowered his voice for effect. "What in the world are you doing with Kristin?"

"Oh, so now you've found your voice, have you?" replied Mary. "It's a nice touch, Gil. Why, it's suitably menacing."

Kristin smiled broadly for the first time in days.

"Lemme speak with Kristin," he growled. He got no reply.

In the background, both heard the presence of another person with Gil, a woman calling for his attention.

Kristin grabbed a notepad and scratched: "Tall brunette—snake tat on her shoulder?"

Mary looked at Kristin, silently expressing a question. Kristin covered the microphone. She whispered in Mary's ear and got a look of recognition.

"So, Gil, the person you're with—might it be a tall brunette with a snake tat on her shoulder?"

The line went dead.

Minutes later, while they luxuriated in their sneak attack, Kristin's phone received a text: "You wench. I'll see you in 10 minutes."

Both women laughed. They knew him too well. It was a vacant threat, a feint each had experienced previously.

Kristin left her phone on the counter as Mary's visit became more comfortable by the minute. Mary said, "I've heard about Gil's palace from some, um, artists who've been here.

Kristin asked Mary if she'd like to see the house.

They began with a trek into the living room where Mary went straight to the bird. "So this is the famous Festus O. Yossarian," she said, holding a finger out to see if he'd accept a perch, which he did. They chattered together for a while. The bird took an immediate liking to Mary. "I won't tell Gil of our relationship, I promise," she said, chuckling at his banter.

"Curiosity killed the cat! I'm too drunk to taste the chicken," replied Festus.

"One tequila, two tequila, three tequila, floor," said Mary.

Festus cocked his head, taking it in. He replied, "Here's to our wives and girlfriends, may they never meet!"

"Ask me no questions, and I'll tell you no lies," responded Mary. By now, both women were laughing heartily.

"Lead me not into temptation; I can find the way m'self," jabbered Festus.

"Well, that's prophetic," said Mary, chuckling. "Gil's bird, for sure."

"Woman's like a tea bag. Like a tea bag," he added, delighted with the attention. Mary's laughter bloomed.

"I think Gili was still teaching him that one—about the tea bag," Kristin explained, smiling.

"I think it's an Eleanor Roosevelt quote," said Mary. "A woman's like a tea bag. You can't tell how strong she is until you put her in hot water."

"That one may be prophetic, too. And, even prescriptive, come to think of it," said Kristin.

Mary smiled and placed the bird back on his perch. "Don't leave me now, just when the gettin's good," scolded Festus.

Kristin and Mary went from one room to another, Mary quietly shaking her head at the ostentatious display of art. Downstairs, they wandered about in Gili's humidity-controlled art archives, the showy wine tasting room, and the expansive theater. On their way up the back stairway, Mary stopped at a bronze sculpture—a life-sized bust of Gil's head, lips parted in a smile—clearly made in his youth. Kristin had seen it before but paid little attention to the casting.

She looked at Mary, who stood quietly staring, expressionless.

"That was a long time ago," Mary said.

Was it an observation or an explanation? Kristin studied Mary.

"Like all of my bronzes, it began as a clay bust," added Mary. "He'd just gotten out of bed. I was still rather new to sculpting, and slow, so I kept him there for quite a while, forcing him to wait for breakfast. I thought I was in love, but he corrected me a few months later."

Upstairs, the two decided on the back porch, pulling chairs close. The weather was ideal. Mary saw *The Hobbit*, by Tolkien, parked on a table. "You reading that?" she asked.

"Re-reading," replied Kristin. "It's an escape."

"I enjoyed it too," said Mary. "Did you ever read C. S.

Lewis? His work is just as imaginative; the two authors were good friends."

Kristin recalled the author's name. "Did he write the Chronicles of…."

"Narnia," added Mary. "Yes, he's the one."

"I started to read that series when I was maybe 16 or 17 and loved it," continued Kristin. "Until a friend, Whitney, told me that it was an allegory modeled to parts of the Bible, with the lion as Christ. I dropped it immediately because she dissed it. I was so vain."

"Too bad," said Mary. "The Chronicles are a Christian narrative, an allegory, with the retelling of Christ's life, crucifixion, and resurrection. I loved the books. Lewis' work led me to other good literature, and the search eventually took me to the Bible."

Mary spoke freely of her love for Christ, describing her years in Paris and falling in love with the man she married after leaving Gil. "My two men—my husband and Christ—they lit a fire that's only grown. And here I am today, witnessing to my new friend, here in Gil's home. Life'll throw some zingers, won't it?"

For hours, their conversation wandered easily into each other's lives. Kristin shared many details from her last month with painful insights into her career, even revelations from her past—pointing out how she'd developed into the family's pariah and fugitive. She spoke of her teen years, wild times with Whitney, her early abortion, flirtations with the occult, and drugs. She expressed love for her sister and her parents. She then spoke about Dr. Gilgamesh Arzhang's baby. Mary noticed that, unconsciously, Kristin's hands moved to her belly. Finally, Kristin spoke of the horrific nightmares and the letter from Nova—someone who'd also sent messages to her sister and a friend of hers. Kristin got up to fetch a box of tissues. Before too long, several were rumpled, twitching in the breeze below their chairs.

Kristin gave Mary the letter from Nova.

Mary began to read it, then stared, motionless, when she saw her own name. "My prayers," she whispered, looking up at Kristin, perplexed. "Incredible. This Nova knows me and my prayers. My private prayers.

"Kristin, I'm almost certain that intimate prayers, offered from the heart and quietly lifted to God, are private, confidential—between you and God, Christ, and the Holy Spirit," continued Mary. "I don't believe that even the devil, who has immense powers here on earth, can put an ear to our prayers, at least if they're not spoken. I've lifted you silently in prayer for weeks, since the day we met. I even confided your love of Vincent's art. That's here, in this letter too."

Tears formed in Mary's eyes. "This is bigger than we are, Kristin. I've encountered Christ in my life but maybe never before so forcefully. Nova's got to be an envoy, an angel, or something supernatural. I just don't know, but I do know you're in the midst of something significant. I'm stunned by this. Not frightened, Kristin, because this must be God's doing. But you've got to be attuned to what's being asked of you. Have you asked God for answers in prayer?"

"No. I haven't found the time. And, well...I wouldn't know how."

"We'll have to fix that," responded Mary. She pulled her chair close to Kristin's, knees touching. "You do know it's written that 'where two or three gather in my name, there am I with them'—don't you?"

"That sounds familiar, but it's been a long time," replied Kristin.

"It's in the book of Matthew, on your reading list for tonight!" smiled Mary.

Mary extended her arms, gently placing Kristin's hands in hers. She looked intently at Kristin and said that she'd merely start the prayer. Her petition was deeply personal, melodious—fragrant words spoken like a sonnet, warm and lovely in every way. Kristin found herself affirming Mary's words at key junctures, led by an emotion or a presence she hadn't felt in many years, a sweet stirring of her soul.

When Mary's voice gradually dropped off, Kristin added, "Father, thank you. Thank you for Mary and the gift of her love for you. Lead me as you will, Lord. I'm so ashamed of my distractions, and forgetting who you are and of your love for me. Help me find you again. Amen."

The exchange between their eyes, while still holding hands, was a moment each knew they'd never forget. "Thank you, Mary. You can't imagine how much that means to me."

"You're welcome," said Mary, reaching for a tissue. "There's one more in there for you," she added with a smile. Kristin emptied the box, dabbing at her eyes. Mary quietly reread the letter.

"Kristin, this letter's just amazing," said Mary. "What's written fits perfectly if you think about it. Nova's reference to the preacher and writer, Mark Batterson; I've read several of his books. He's brilliant. Do you have any of them?"

Kristin shook her head with an expression that seemed to express regret.

"Hey, you've got to start somewhere," assured Mary. "Be sure to get Batterson's 'Circle' books and Soulprint. Branch out from there. Check out John Bevere, too—especially his book titled *Driven by Eternity*. It's powerful and changed my life."

Kristin affirmed the advice with a smile.

"Sounds like you've got some other things to work through too," added Mary. "What'll you do about work? And, the baby?"

"Those are tough ones," said Kristin. "My sister may have some good advice for me. I'll reach out to her. Maybe even my parents. It's time for a change and some serious reflection."

"Prayer, too—okay? Call me anytime if you want to pray together." Mary took her phone and, tapping it for just a few seconds, said, "I just texted you my cell number and email. Tomorrow, I'll text you a list of good books to get."

Kristin made a large salad and lemonades, recognizing how nice it felt without mid-day alcohol. Mary held Kristin's hand again when she prayed before they ate. She laughed warmly when Kristin said she'd never prayed so much in a single day. "It'll grow on you," Mary replied. As they finished their meal, Festus released a series of loud catcalls, prompting Mary's return to the living room.

"One tequila, two tequila," said the bird.

"He remembered!" exclaimed Mary.

"One tequila, two tequila," repeated Festus.

"Three tequila, floor," countered Mary.

"This suspense is terrible. I hope it'll last," added the bird. The women laughed.

"He's quite the charmer, huh?" asked Mary.

"Just like Gil," replied Kristin.

After making Mary a copy of Nova's letter (Mary said she wanted to pray into it), they walked together to Mary's car.

Before getting in, Mary opened a back door, pulling out two hefty books. "I got these for you on my way here," she explained. "My only regret is that these will always be attached to the pain and discomfort of this day. But if you change the perspective of it, as I believe you will, you'll have opened the door to the greatest joy you'll ever know. Let these light your way." She gave the first one to Kristin.

Kristin scanned the book's title: Charles F. Stanley *Life Principles Daily Bible.* She looked at Mary who explained, "I've had one like it for a decade. I read it cover to cover every other year. I used to be intimidated by the Bible—especially the Old Testament. For ages, I tried to read Scripture daily, but I found it too intimidating, like trying to climb a wall. But this is a daily reader," she added, knocking on the book with a knuckle, "it provides small, daily portions of the Old Testament, New Testament, Psalms and Proverbs. It broke the barrier. There are 365 short portions—one for each day of the year. Stanley's narration and insights are invaluable. It's how Scripture came alive for me."

She hesitated, smiling at Mary with her eyes, then added, "We can't love the Lord fully, and he can't love us fully, until we immerse ourselves in his Word."

Kristin cradled the Bible. Mary held the other book toward her. Kristin opened it and read, *David Jeremiah Study Bible.* She looked at Mary.

"It's the perfect partner to Stanley's daily reader," Mary explained. "Stanley's Bible isn't in order, or assembled, as most other Bibles are. That's why you'll want one that's built traditionally—Old Testament to New. So, this one is much easier to use as you dip into studying and researching God's Word. Jeremiah's insights are invaluable."

Kristin admired the books, then gently placed them on the hood of Mary's car.

"Oh, I just remembered something," added Mary. She picked up the Charles Stanley Bible to open it. She thumbed through it, stopping at a group of pages for July 17.

"I had to search a bit for this at the bookstore earlier, but I knew I'd find it. This is from 2 Chronicles 30:9," said Mary, glancing at Kristin. "Listen to this. 'The Lord Your God is gracious and compassionate, and will not turn His face away from you if you return to Him.' I wanted this passage because of what Charles Stanley had to say about it—and especially because of your life, Kristin. Having left your faith, and then coming back to it after those years when you were, well, developing your profession."

With sad eyes, Kristin looked expectantly at Mary.

Mary continued. "Here's what Charles Stanley says about 2 Chronicles 30:9. "Some people worry that they have committed the unpardonable sin (Matthew 12:31), but God will never turn away anyone who genuinely repents of his sin and places his faith in Christ."

Kristin looked down. Mary reached toward her and gently lifted Kristin's chin. Their eyes met. "That's for you," whispered Mary.

"Thank you, Mary. These mean so much to me because they've come from you, on this amazing day," said Kristin. "I really appreciate your words, your mentoring and friendship. I can't wait to put them to use. I'll begin my daily reading today."

For a few moments, they simply stood side by side, enjoying the quiet of a lovely day.

Breaking the silence, Kristin smiled to ask, "Hey—wanna bird?"

Mary laughed. "No—I think Gil 'n' Festus are good for each other. At least he cares for that silly bird."

Kristin stood in the driveway, hugging the Bibles, until Mary's car disappeared around the bend. She returned to the house, placing the books on the kitchen counter, then glancing at her phone. No calls, no messages. For the rest of the afternoon, she gathered her things, filling three of Gili's new, rawhide suitcases with clothes (he'd thrown her worn luggage away, saying that he'd be embarrassed for anyone to see them). She added her toiletries, books, and Mac.

She noticed that the cover page for the David Jeremiah Bible was flipped open. She glanced at it to see an inscription: "To Kristin—Life's greatest joys, and adventure, start right here. Best yet, it leads to Forever. John 3:16. In Christ's love—Mary." Kristin paged to John 3:16 and read the words she hadn't seen for decades. She then closed the book and held it again to her chest, eyes closed.

Kristin glanced at the pile of her belongings assembled in the kitchen. She grabbed her purse and both Bibles, walked to the garage, and placed the armload into her car's passenger seat. After a few more trips, Kristen returned to the house to fill Festus' food and water. She lifted him on a finger, then walked slowly as they examined each other. Smiling, she deposited him in the one room of the house that Gili had posted as "off limits" to the bird—the master bedroom.

Festus looked at her curiously, as though to say, "Really? You mean it?" The bird loved hopping on couches and beds; his nature was to mess wherever he went. As he tested the bed's bounce, Festus' last glance in her direction seemed to express his gratitude. Following a few joyful leaps, he defecated on the plush comforter, then hopped onto the pillows, rolling luxuriously.

Heading for the door, smiling, Kristin yanked the engagement ring off her finger, placing it into a small pot of water she set on the stove. As she was leaving the kitchen, she spun around to pull a fat, permanent ink marker from the desk drawer. On the light granite countertop, next to the pot, she wrote, "Here's a memento from Eleanor Roosevelt (but I'll omit the heat). Any questions, ask Fester."

She pulled the car out of the garage then returned to the front door. After assuring the door was locked, she pitched the keys into a low bush then drove to a favorite eatery. She placed a call to Cynthia, getting voicemail. "Hey, I need some time. I'm looking for a new apartment. If Gili calls, you know nothing, okay? I'll talk with you soon."

While Kristin ate, she used her iPad to search online for immediately available apartments—preferring something modest and relatively close to work. She then booked herself into a hotel.

THE NEXT DAY, Jack, Miriam, Chet, and Hannah met with their pastor. Jack had hoped for a reply from Kay with some new insight, but her answer hadn't come. They took the Nova letters and a detailed timeline crafted by Miriam, referencing events that seemed to connect to the evolving mystery. Hannah took the tool and cross, still nested in its packaging.

They opened the meeting with prayer. Initially, they tried to prune the explanations, reluctant to exploit the pastor's time. But he was eager to dive in, asking more questions than Jack and Miriam had thought possible. Hannah and Chet shared knowing glances, well aware of their pastor's skills.

Their pastor read and studied the letters, made copies of them, and scrutinized the tool.

KAY ZAVALA HAD FRIENDS in high places, and she tapped some of them for any information about the mysterious Nova. She made calls and sent emails to experts within the intelligence community. There were no quick hits, but she continued to send out feelers.

Kay turned her attention to email that afternoon, delighted to see that Nova had upped her game with artwork and a longer note than any before it. She sent a simple acknowledgment, an email to Jack Soelberg:

> So now your daughter in Cali's received one! I'll be back in touch ASAP. Best—Kay.
>
> PS—I had a strange feeling not long ago that something's missing, Jack; some odd piece of this puzzle. By any chance, is there some sort of physical evidence I've not yet learned about? The letters: anything unusual about the paper they're on? Or, did one of them come with something—anything? A cross is mentioned.

Jack received the email, thanking Kay for her continued interest in their mystery. He added that they just returned from their pastor, hoping for insight there.

He went to the kitchen for a coffee, then resumed his email to Kay:

> Hannah and Chet assure us their pastor (well, ours now) is a solid guy with the gift of discernment. Hannah also has a tool and a small crucifix on a necklace. I'd forgotten to tell you about those (see attached

photos). Hannah received them months ago with her first note from Nova. She and her boss, an anatomist, researched the tool. Apparently, the very rare device, one of only three known to exist, was once in a place called the Museum of Conception and Abortion in Vienna, Austria. Some time ago, it was reported missing. No one seems to know how. And then it showed up in a box addressed to Hannah at work. It's an abortion tool, a Luer Cranial Perforator, made in the mid-1800s. Pretty ugly stuff. It's designed to drill into and collapse a baby's skull. New ones are even more ghastly and efficient. Hope this helps, Kay

—Jack

Kay replied later that day, confirming that knowledge of the tool and cross could be very helpful. Nothing yet, but that she'd explore it.

HANNAH'S LONG WEEKEND had been a good one. She knew great weather was predicted, so she and Chet made a four-day weekend of it to enjoy quality time with the kids. No emergencies, and the church service and class on Sunday—there with her mother and father—felt like blessings mounted high. When she arrived at her office Tuesday morning, she quickly spotted a folded note on her desk.

She reached for the note, dreading the worst, another note from Nova. But she immediately recognized Evan Harley's handwriting.

Hi, Hannah. I'll be out 'til Friday. You're in charge! Good news, kiddo: our latest NIH grant was approved. For you, there's a 20% bump, beginning with the next paycheck. You've earned it! And, our expanding programs and research call for a new assistant pathologist. Know of anyone? See you in a few days. All the best. —*Harley*

WITHOUT MUCH DIFFICULTY, Kristin found a furnished apartment within an easy walk of the headquarters building. The rental market was tight, but her money made easy work of it. Earlier that day, she and Cynthia spoke about work, the growing issue stemming from Cyn's taped conversation with the phony bioprocurement pros, and Gili's call to Cyn.

"Did he sound desperate?" asked Kristin, amused. "Well, yes and no," replied Cynthia. "He was upset that you allowed Festus in the bedroom; he threw away an expensive comforter and the pillow cases, had the carpet cleaned, and said something about a magic marker and having to wait two weeks to have the countertop refinished. He was unhappy about the missing luggage. As for the ring, was there symbolism in the pot of water? Maybe a reference to Eleanor Roosevelt?"

Kristin smiled. "Long story," she replied. "If he calls back, you can tell him I threw the keys into a sage plant near the front door."

"Okay. Well, thinking back to his call, if there was any sort of desperation, I'm pretty sure it was an affront to sleep alone. You rocked his boat," added Moloch. "Are you sure that you want to put him in the rear view mirror, Kristin? His beautiful home—to say nothing of his fine physique—all the art, 'Fester' the entertainer, the wine collection, and your common interests?"

"Oh, I'm done with all that," said Kristin. "It's time, I can assure you. Common interests—not so many after all."

Moloch provided greater detail into the unfolding crisis at work. "I could kick myself for liking those guys," she said. "Apparently, they plan to reveal the entirety of their videotaped interview soon, with announcements to the media and an online posting of the entire thing. Our lawyers have offered millions to shut them up, to no avail."

A FEW DAYS LATER, Kristin slipped in for a visit with Cyn and to make a quick sweep of her desk. Moloch told her to prepare for a trip to Seattle, then Indianapolis; there were issues with clinic staffs at both locations. Kristin felt that travel would do her some good. Shake out the cobwebs.

The next couple of days were almost refreshing. There were a few texts from Gili; no: Gil. She now preferred Mary's simpler moniker, less endearing.

Kristin gradually developed a new routine. But before things got too comfortable, she was packing bags for her trips north to Washington, then east to Indiana. It all felt so incongruous for Kristin—the return to work and new travel plans amidst the personal and professional crisis she found herself in the midst of. She felt she had to plod ahead while waiting for an answer, a message, anything that offered clarity. *God, please give me an answer,* she prayed.

In Seattle, pro-lifers were camped out along the main clinic's fences. They weren't noisy or combative, but their prayer vigil was in its third week, receiving some measure of media attention. The scene brought foggy recollection of her first experience, long ago, with prayerful protesters at a clinic. Each person folded in prayer—so similar to her recollection of a small army of prayer warriors at the very clinic she would visit the next day.

Inside, senior staff complained that protesters were shrinking the number of abortions and reducing their ability to hold to Moloch's rigid quotas. "We're getting tougher questions from our patients too," grumbled a clinician. "Many more are now asking for referrals to adoption agencies."

Kristin did the best she could to dispel their concerns, but staffers noted that her contributions were pale, lacking conviction. She seemed distracted, though they weren't about to say anything to Moloch about that. Everyone knew that Dr. Kristin Soelberg was favored to take the top spot soon.

The flight to Indianapolis was rough. Just one passenger, peering out a port-side window, noticed an inscrutably dark presence that easily kept pace with the aircraft—a large black crow. The bird flew casually along the jet's body and appeared to have interest with its passengers, or some of them.

Kristin's business class seat was little comfort during the turbulent flight, so rocky that the crew couldn't provide refreshments. The captain told them over the PA system that a fierce tailwind was at fault. He told them they'd move up to 34,000 feet, hoping to find better conditions. The tempest persisted.

After turning off the microphone, the captain leaned over, speaking quietly to the copilot he'd met for the first time just an hour ago. "Did you see that freakin' crow? I just saw it two feet from the glass, port side, flying like it had no concern in the world."

The copilot turned his head slowly toward the captain, hoping it might help him comprehend what he knew was an impossibility. Unless, of course, the captain was joking. Or mad, drugged, or both. He stared at the pilot, attempting to hide his apprehension. Getting no reply, the captain added, "I hope you said your prayers this morning."

Immediately, the jet lurched into a ragged dive, spilling bottles and cups. "Dang! Maybe there's someone on board who God's angry with," the copilot impulsively replied. For two years, the younger pilot had been first officer of a large Air Force fueler and had never before been tossed about so violently. After landing, the copilot attempted to disguise his shaking.

The captain was no less shaken, though what bothered him most as he prepared to leave the cockpit was his recollection of the crow at 30,000 feet. When he told his wife about it on the phone later that evening—describing the bird's every detail and movement—she wondered if the strain of commercial piloting had finally taken its toll. "Hon, are you taking your meds? How long's it been since you spoke with your counselor?"

A certain traveler in a window seat, identified in the passenger manifest as Dr. I. M. Gabriel, had joined Kristin's flight of 82 souls bound for Indianapolis. A woman in her 40s sitting next to him, traveling to her brother's funeral, noted his incredible poise through the horrifying, chaotic flight. She'd never flown before. When the flight became turbulent, Gabriel asked her to place her hand in his. They were so warm. He quoted Scripture and spoke softly to her of his commitment to the "Lord of Lords."

Before the flight ended, she gave her life to Christ. If anything, the turbulent flight went too quickly. In addition to his azure blue eyes, she noticed only three other things during the entire journey. No, four: she lost all fear while she was with him, he appeared briefly to have mild concern about a large black crow flying just a few feet outside their window, and he also seemed to pay special (protective?) attention to an attractive young woman three seats up on the opposite side of the aisle. And he wore no wedding ring.

As they were disembarking from the flight, she turned to thank him (and to slip her phone number into his hands) but he was gone. For the rest of her days—with just the slightest excuse or provocation—she'd tell the story of the mysterious, vanishing physician who'd impacted her life so substantially.

15

MALBAS MAKES HIS MOVE

WEAK AND SHAKING after the choppy flight, Kristin's earlier inclination would be to grab a drink at the bar. But, somehow, the allure of alcohol had lost its pull on her. It certainly wasn't the result of consideration for the baby—its days were numbered.

Kristin's thirst grew as she moved toward baggage claim. After gathering her luggage, she looked frantically for a drinking fountain. No water fountain in sight. Frustrated, she spun toward the shuttle point for car rentals. On the bus, she thirstily contemplated, then dismissed, a half-finished bottle of Dasani rolling around in the luggage rack.

At the rental station, the vending machine offered all variety of high-sugar sodas but no water. After getting the keys to a rental car, Kristin decided that, with three or four hours to burn before turning her attention to work, she'd visit familiar territory. She tapped their old address into her phone's CarPlay. In seconds she learned that she was just 20 minutes from the only home she really knew.

As Kristin approached the roads around what used to be Fort Benjamin Harrison, now reshaped into an expansive green space, she reminisced. It had been many years since she was last in Indianapolis, and this was an odd surprise. Less than a mile from their old home, she diverted, taking a detour to park along Shafter Road within Fort Harrison State Park. There, she took a contemplative walk, recalling euphoric days when she and Hannah would skip along this road to their father's office. They'd take him lunch. Or frolic in the office, amusing staff personnel. And, occasionally they'd beckon him outside, with Mom, to picnic nearby.

Still thirsty, she thought she'd walk to a convenience store for a bottle of water. But a movement caught her eye. Standing with his back against a tree trunk, one knee protruding, was a man in dark clothes. He had dark hair and wore shades, trying perhaps a bit too hard to look relaxed. She angled away from him, taking another route toward the store. When Malbas moved in the same general direction, Kristin spun quickly, making her way to her car. She hopped in, locked the doors, started the engine, and looked in all directions. No sign of him. Just a lone crow, hopping about on the sidewalk close to where he'd been.

She bowed her head. "Dear Father, thank you for keeping me alert to whatever that was, if anything. I, um, hope this prayer is okay with you. I'm still pretty rusty. I've returned to a place that once felt so good, and I can feel your comfort and your love warming me again. Please help me through whatever it is I need to do to make things right—with you, work, and my family, especially Mom and Dad. I'm feeling your presence, Lord. Please be with me now. Keep me safe here, so close to home."

She drove the car onto East 59th Street, heading through a landscape that appeared in two dimensions: one from decades past, with houses and shops that no longer existed; the other with oncoming traffic, newly remodeled homes, and fat, mature trees topped with giant canopies. The interplay between the two dimensions was both inviting and cheerless. Her sepia-toned recollections brought clarity to an unhappy present.

Kristin was so interested in seeing familiar streets in the old neighborhood that she paid no attention to the dark sedan two cars behind her.

She got out at the house she knew so well and knocked on the door. An older couple answered, greeting her warmly. Kristin explained that, many years earlier, she grew up in the home. "Oh dear, you must be one of Jack and Miriam's daughters," said the woman.

"Yes, I'm Kristin."

"My oh my. You're so beautiful," added Mrs. Terroni, hands clasped to her mouth. "We're so glad they sold us the home. Won't you come in?"

A few minutes later, Kristin called her father, but the call went to voicemail. She left a message. "Dad, guess where I am? I'm standing with Mr. and Mrs. Terroni, here in our old home. It brings back some great memories. Love you. Give my love to Mom." She ended the call.

The Terronis let Kristin roam freely throughout the house while she took photos with her phone. She went outside through the kitchen door, strolling through the backyard. More photos. Though Jack and Miriam moved from there just the year before, Kristin hadn't set foot on the property for many years. Her last visit had been brief, unhappy.

Her phone rang, but she ignored it when she saw it wasn't family. While she was walking around the house, there were the sounds of more calls and texts. Without examining the phone, she silenced it, refusing the intrusion.

The back yard transported her to a quiet, late night escape with Whitney, bottle in hand. The years had done little to change the setting, yet somehow, in just the past few days, she'd gained a very different perspective of what home is. In part, it was here all along, merely awaiting her return. She was then hit with the realization of how unhappy she was that her parents had moved away. A profound sorrow and deep love for her parents overwhelmed her. Recalling the anger and disappointment of her last departure and her refusal to return their love gripped her heart.

She stopped, on the verge of tears, wishing that she could dash inside to embrace her parents. The move had taken them away, surely toward a source of goodness for them—and further from her. Of course, they'd moved to Ohio. What could she possibly have offered them? All they knew was her unhappiness with them, her murderous career, no husband, no kids. Yet her sister's love for them was continuous. She and Chet had given them grandchildren. Wave after wave of regret buffeted her there in the back yard.

"Oh Mom, Dad. I'm sorry. I miss you," she mumbled quietly to herself, eyes closed.

The Terronis glanced out the window to see her, motionless, head held low. "She's so pretty, isn't she?" asked Mrs. Terroni of her husband. "She is," he replied. "But she sure looks sad."

Kristin attempted to walk off the emotions. Going back in the kitchen door, she thanked the Terronis. As she gripped the steering wheel, she realized that she meant to ask them for a drink. Well, she'd certainly make it her priority at the clinic. The dark sedan, parked just a few doors away, followed her car.

It wasn't long before Kristin could see the clinic in the distance. Just one more stop sign, and she'd be there. She'd googled it days earlier, enough to be sure what the place looked like (hadn't changed), its setting, and its approach from the street. She fought off recollections of the neighborhood and her trip to and from the clinic as a teenager.

What she didn't see immediately was the clamor that awaited her. She pulled over before going the final distance to the clinic's entrance. A large group of protesters had formed. In their midst, four microwave trucks had already raised their big, periscopic antennas. It appeared that all had reporters doing interviews with the demonstrators.

That's when it hit her: the phone! She snatched it from her purse and scrolled through the dozen or more notifications. She tapped a message from Moloch first: "Kristin: where are you? The clinic in Indy's calling. They made the mistake of saying to the media that you're in town for a meeting with them. The videotape of my interview was released this morning, creating a Fox news firestorm, but others have picked it up too. Reporters have been calling here nonstop. You'll have to handle it as best you can."

The PR agency had called and texted. Another call from Cyn, and several more texts, including a dozen calls from numbers with a 463 area code. Must be the clinic, local media, or both. She steeled herself and drove on, aiming for a parking space within the fence not far from the clinic's main entrance. Seconds later, the car following her slipped into the smaller staff parking lot around the corner.

Kristin stepped out, opening a back door to grab her purse and a portfolio. When she turned to close the door, thinking only of her need for water, she looked up to see a wave of reporters with microphones thrust forward, cameras in tow. They surrounded her.

No doubt the video gear was on as she attempted to maintain composure amidst the tight quarters and barrage of questions. "Dr. Soelberg. Dr. Soelberg!" they yelled. "Are you here today to harvest baby parts?" "Do you sell them profitably?" "Is this clinic meeting their quota for late term abortions and fetal tissue sales?" "Are you the top abortionist?"

She saw immediately that it was impossible to answer questions or provide a sensible response in the midst of such chaos. The only way out was to plow through them to get into the clinic. She forced her way to the door, and yanking it open, she was hit by a memory she'd suppressed for many years. This is where she'd left her child. The visage of a screaming, horrified baby with a tiny outstretched hand flashed before her.

Through that horrific vision came another extended hand. She looked up, about to grasp it, but followed the arm to a face she recalled from the park. Malbas had removed his shades to reveal ghastly, goat-like irises probing deeply into hers.

In a split second, her neglect to hydrate mixed with the combined shock of unexpected turmoil and horror closed in. Kristin collapsed as the clinic's staff—forcing their way to her through the stranger who appeared ready to perform CPR (or exactly what they didn't know)—rushed to her aid. The commotion developed into an immediate frenzy among the camera crews and reporters.

More cameras and onlookers appeared as EMS personnel rolled her into a stretcher. Images of her fall, the momentary glimpse of a man in dark clothes who quickly bent toward her and who was then hastily pushed to the side, the efforts of confused staff, then EMS care and ambulance transport—all ran in network news. The drama of her collapse appeared with scenes from Dr. Cynthia Moloch's restaurant interview. The late night news, repeating it all, also included an update of Dr. Moloch's resignation and temporary closing of their headquarters.

The crew of NBC's Channel 13 had been the first to rush behind Kristin to the clinic's door. Jan, the reporter (in heels and with an uncooperative notepad), arrived three seconds too late to see for herself what Glen, the cameraman, had captured. Later, reviewing the footage, she saw Kristin's last, fast-paced steps to reach the door, the alarm she showed at being pursued by so many, then the opening of the door and her wobbly collapse.

Jan did, however, arrive in time to see the strange man who reached for her and, for just a split second, the expression on his face. Had she just imagined it? The man appeared to snarl at Kristin. Recalling the event, Jan realized that she was probably mistaken. Yet, there was something else quite strange about him. It was the split-second glimpse she had of his eyes. Or had she imagined that too?

Things happened at the abortion clinic so quickly that Jan forgot to mention it to Glen while sitting in the van outside the facility. Always in a rush to package each report, they worked quickly to transmit the edited story to the station. In every instance, there was room to edit further if need be. Then, for Glen and Jan, it was time to move on to the next assignment. A few hours later, as they traveled back from the grand opening of a hog farm in New Palestine, Jan contemplated what she'd seen at the clinic door. She asked Glen if he'd seen anything unusual.

"What I can't see now is the freakin' road. May I please

have your sunglasses again?" he asked teasingly. "The sun's about ready to burn two holes in my head!"

She knew it was futile to argue with Glen. The big, playful guy with long, golden locks and ready smile always had a quick-witted response to anything—whether serious or funny, day or night. She removed the large, stylish sunglasses from her face and gave them to him. Even from behind the rims of her bejeweled sunglasses, he somehow appeared normal. "You look like Elton John—with hair. I hope your wife enjoys your humor, and I also hope that channel six passes us to see you at the wheel," said Jan as she adjusted the visor to reduce the sun's angular beam.

"My wife's become a stone wall to my humor," he assured her. "As for channel six, bring 'em on!" Just then, Jan received a text from the station's news director. "Hmm. Apparently, the doctor back at the clinic, the one who collapsed at the door earlier today, is now the organization's top dog," explained Jan as she turned to Glen, now enjoying the drive thanks to her sunglasses.

"The woman who just resigned—remember her from the network news? Her name was Cynthia something; she's the one that was videotaped during the sting operation at the restaurant in California," added Jan. "So, with her resignation, Dr. Soelberg's in the top spot, making her the nation's most prominent abortionist—the one who's now at the hospital. So, thinking more about her, what do you say Glen?" she prodded. "You were first to the door back there at the clinic. Did you see anything different or unusual?"

"You mean, more unusual than the nation's top abortionist collapsing at the door of their clinic here in Indy?" he replied.

"Well, part of that," Jan clarified. "The look on the guy's face who was there, first to reach for her…or his eyes, in particular."

"It happened too fast for me to focus on anything but her rush to the door, then steadying myself for good video as the door opened," replied Glen, finally offering a serious reply. "I mean, sure, I saw all of it happening before my eyes, but it was through the lens. That was my priority. Well, thinking about it, yeah. Maybe. There was something odd about him, but I was just too busy framing the shot, making sure I captured everything as it happened."

As the clinic's staff converged on them, Malbas was pushed to the rear. Seconds later, he merely walked away. He retraced his steps to the back door and then disappeared.

Reporters did stand-ups all night long at clinics around the country to localize the network news. No one knew where Dr. Moloch had disappeared to, but that topic lost most of its allure as the media shifted their attention to Dr. Kristin Soelberg's collapse and concerns about her ability to manage the company. News media were camped out at the hospital where Kristin was recovering, but they weren't allowed in.

Jack and Miriam monitored the news all night long; the last report they saw carried news of Dr. Moloch's disappearance and resignation. After calls to the hospital earlier in the evening, they made plans to fly into Indianapolis in the morning. Calls came in from family and friends through the evening. Hannah, Chet, Matt, and Sarah came over, offering comfort. It wasn't until Hannah saw a lengthier report during the 10 o'clock news that something caught her eye. Was it the guy in dark clothes? He was visible only momentarily. It appeared as though he was reaching for Kristin from inside the clinic the moment the door opened. Why did he look familiar?

Hannah was exhausted, wanting sleep, but the image of the man in the doorway, bending down to her collapsed sister, haunted her. She convinced Chet to stay awake with her until the news refreshed the story at 11 pm. Meanwhile, she pored over the news online, hoping to find better pictures of him. She found some still photos, apparently video-pulls, but their resolution wasn't sufficient to provide detail.

During the 11 o'clock news, Hannah was immediately struck with the realization that the man inside the clinic door, visible for just a second, appeared to be the very same one she'd seen on two occasions—the guy in the dark car. Chet watched in dismay as she froze the TV, then released it for the report to continue. Reversing, she did this several more times while recalling the instances when she saw him. "If it's not him, it's his double," she assured her husband.

ANGERED THAT HE COULDN'T GET to sleep, Jack's evening gradually came apart. Irritably, he got up to prowl online news. He watched several portions of the Cynthia Moloch interview, shaking his head in dismay. One of the stations offered the interview in its entirety. He grew more uncomfortable as it unfolded, dismayed that his daughter had worked directly for this disgraceful, appalling woman.

A few of the media commentaries flayed the organization. However, many of the old pro-choice stalwarts referred to the beleaguered cause and the value of fetal tissue for researchers, saying essentially that the end justifies the means. The organization's lawyers went on the offense, stating they'd file a lawsuit for libel, defamation, eavesdropping, and invasion of privacy. They claimed, "Dr. Moloch's career is destroyed. We'll defend the integrity of our client, the goodness of her professional character, and the many qualities of the new director, Dr. Kristin Soelberg, now recovering in a hospital from this horrible assault to decency."

When Jack trudged upstairs for a shave and shower, Miriam was already awake. After a quick breakfast, they drove to the airport for the flight to Indianapolis. At the hospital, Kristin's physician spoke at length with them, saying he was confident she'd soon regain consciousness. "Her vitals are good. Her blood tests reveal nothing alarming, but her blood pressure was high. It appears her condition is a result of exhaustion, trauma, and severe dehydration. It happens. Oh, and her babies—now at twelve or thirteen weeks—appear to be fine too."

WHEN KRISTIN AWOKE late that afternoon, she looked into her mother's eyes. Her father was asleep in a chair nearby. Miriam had one of Kristin's hands in hers. "Mmmom," she mumbled. "I love you."

Tears welled in Miriam's eyes. "I love you too," she replied quietly. "So much, sweety. Everything's fine. We're here for you." Miriam tapped Jack on the leg with her foot, stirring him. He looked over to see Kristin looking at him. He smiled, immediately coming to her other side, kneeling to get his face closer to hers. His eyes were as red as she'd ever seen them. He looked so sad and exhausted, but his eyes poured love into hers. "We got your message, honey, from when you were at the house with the Terronis. We came as quickly as we could."

"Oh, Dad, I love you. I'm so sorry. I'm…thirsty." The attending physician had warned them about giving her water but had asked a nurse to fill a Styrofoam cup with ice. The intravenous drip assured proper hydration; a mild sedative encouraged rest.

As Jack began spooning ice into Kristin's mouth, she was aware only of his tears and the gentle repetition of the plastic spoon's movement. Gradually, her thirst subsided. She slipped in and out of sleep, feeling a sense of rest she hadn't experienced for months. Jack and Miriam took turns sitting with her. Each sent text messages back to family: "All's well. She's been awake but is sleeping now."

EARLY ON HER SECOND DAY at the hospital, Kristin was moved to a regular patient room. Jack and Miriam had avoided conversations with her about work or the babies; an ultrasound had confirmed twins. Jack pressured Miriam to wait a short while to keep that latest news from Kristin until her condition was more stable. Reluctantly, Miriam agreed.

As Kristin recovered, she grew restless. She asked her father to track down her rental car, belongings, laptop, and phone. Jack needed a mission and was glad to jump in. He went to a sitting area near the nurse's station to make calls. He quickly learned that the clinic staff had secured her belongings and car. There was some confusion, he learned, about which car was hers. Apparently, there were two cars, both locked, in different lots on the clinic property. Jack didn't want to discuss it at the time, sensing that he had no need to debate the ambiguity of another car in their lot. *That's their problem,* he told himself.

The clinic's manager called him to say they'd deliver all of

Kristin's belongings. An hour later, they met in the hospital's front lobby.

Jack was aloof, judging that he had little to say to a woman who supervised a staff whose goal in life was to murder babies. When he arrived in the lobby, she rose from a chair to meet him.

"We're so sorry, Mr. Soelberg," she said. His stern expression suggested that he merely wanted his daughter's belongings. "We found everything and returned the car to the rental agency," she explained. It appeared that the woman had come with all of Kristin's stuff: a classy suitcase, light jacket, phone, laptop, purse, and portfolio. "I placed my card in the laptop should Doctor Soelberg have any questions," she added solicitously.

Jack looked at her, softened by her desire to help. "Thanks for your help with that, and for all of these," he said, looking at his daughter's belongings. He managed a thin smile.

"My name is Cécile," she said, extending her hand. He took it. "Mr. Soelberg, you'll recall I mentioned the other car."

Jack struggled to pull some recollection of it. "I vaguely recall you saying something about that."

"We guessed right as to which car was the one Kristin drove," she explained. "It was closest to the patient door. There was another, a charcoal-colored sedan, parked in a staff lot, not far from the staff's entry. When we knew we had Kristin's car properly identified, we knew we had another mystery to solve. The other car was taken to a county impound."

"Why does this concern me, Cécile?" interrupted Jack.

"Maybe it doesn't, sir," she replied. "But if you saw the videos and photos from the incident at the clinic doorway, there was a man who was there inside, the first one to reach her. We, uh—have no idea who it was. Perhaps he'd driven the other car and abandoned it."

Jack's stared at Cécile. "You mean to tell me that a strange man may have something to do with all...of this...and you have no idea what he was doing there, or who he was?"

"Well, no. We don't. He may have been one of the girls'—well, women's—father or boyfriend, or a driver. Things went so quickly into emergency mode after Kristin collapsed that we lost track of a few things. Kristin was our sole concern. We don't yet know who or where he is, but I'm confident we'll find him."

"I'll explain that to Doctor Soelberg," said Jack. "Please let her know if you come up with answers. I assume you know how to reach her." With that, he gathered Kristin's belongings and spun in the direction of the elevators.

LATER THAT EVENING, alone with her laptop and phone, Kristin quickly found the full video of Cynthia Moloch's restaurant debacle. The "procurement pros" had set their trap well. The video and audio quality were superb. Every embarrassing nuance and detail were there, including the spoonful of dripping Crème Brûlée as she delightedly offered details about dismemberment abortions. The YouTube video already had more than 18 million views!

Alone at the time, Kristin set her laptop aside and closed her eyes. A strange sense of apprehension swept over her. She was troubled but wanted to close it all out, wanting only sleep. Gradually, she dozed.

A few hours later, her parents entered quietly with Hannah. Seeing that Kristin was asleep, the three of them spoke softly and began to arrange some of her belongings. They'd learned at the nurse's station that Kristin would likely be released that day.

KRISTIN'S DREAM BEGAN with a peaceful walk through a field of flowers, maybe poppies. The nearby hills were dry. It was an arid place with snowcapped mountains in the distance. There was another sensation she became aware of two of…something, both in peril. As the dream clarified, two girls were revealed, yelling for…their mother? She realized that, side-by-side, they were both mostly covered, maybe in sand, their expressions contorted in fear. Tears and helplessness.

A crowd assembled around the girls. All were dressed strangely in long, flowing clothes. Faces in the crowd were stern, determined. Then one picked up something with weight, heft—and threw it at the girls. Others joined in as the objects, which Kristin quickly knew to be stones, began to pummel the helpless girls who bled profusely. A third girl— no, a young woman in a beautiful, spotless dress—ran to their aid. Quietly she danced around the girls, shielding the stones that seemed to have no effect on her. Yet, the more she tried to protect them, the more rocks were thrown by the crowd.

The girls' screams awoke Kristin. She too began to scream. Her mother, father, and Hannah rushed to her bed. Fully awake and now aware that Hannah was there, she couldn't make sense of the horror that woke her just seconds earlier and brought a nurse and physician quickly to her bedroom door. Her father turned to them and said, "She's fine. Just a bad dream."

Hannah moved closer to her sister's face, covered with fine, downy beads of sweat. Kristin's eyes closed momentarily, then opened to look deeply into her sister's eyes, quickly softening as she released the dream.

"Another bad dream?" asked Hannah, holding her sister's hands. "We've had our share of those lately, haven't we?"

Jack and Miriam hovered close behind Hannah, smiling into Kristin's eyes, now tearing freely. "I'm so glad you're here—all of you," uttered Kristin, barely a whisper. "Hannah, you came."

"Of course I did, sis. I'm so glad to be here. You sure gave me a scare. Hey, Sarah made you something." Turning toward her mother, Hannah said, "Mom, would you please grab that envelope inside my purse?"

Miriam quickly produced the long envelope. Kristin reached for it, smiling. She thumbed open the back panel and pulled out a drawing with Kristin's name at the top and signed by Sarah below. The crayon drawing depicted a woman flanked by two girls, arms mingled joyously. The girls smiled broadly and had enormous, banana-shaped eyelashes and red and yellow bows tying blonde pigtails. They wore dresses, appearing to be their Sunday best. It seemed that the three of them were moving toward a door with a cross above it. Smaller stick people were waving at them in the distance. Another girl with a broad smile appeared to be running toward them with arms open wide, hair streaming behind her.

"I think it's something of an invitation for you, sis," explained Hannah.

"It sure is nice. I love it. Please tell Sarah for me." She glanced at it again, mystified. But just as quickly, her thought was interrupted.

"You can tell Sarah yourself," said Hannah. "They're downstairs with Chet. We turned this into something of a family getaway, school or no school. You're much more important."

Kristin's eyes began to tear. A hand extended in between the two sister's faces. In it, a Kleenex, and—on one of the fingers—the wedding ring their mother hadn't removed for decades. Kristin's eyes followed the arm to her mother's face, beaming radiantly. "Mom, thank you."

Just then, Kristin's awareness of the dream and the drawing sharpened. "But…the girls? Wait—I just dreamed of two girls; it was awful. A third one was there with them."

"Sis—you can tell us about that later. I can assure you there's nothing at all awful about those two girls," said Hannah, moving her hand to her sister's belly. "They're healthy and well."

Kristin's eyebrows bunched as she formed an unspoken question. The expression of confusion was one Hannah and Miriam enjoyed, allowing it to linger just a moment longer. She turned toward her mother and father just as Chet, Matthew, and Sarah entered. Seeing her drawing in Kristin's hands, Sarah wedged herself closer to Kristin's bedside, jumping up and down while saying, "Did you tell her?"

Kristin smiled broadly. "My you've grown, little one! Last time I saw you—"

Sarah wouldn't let her finish. "That's you, Aunt Kristin. In the drawing!"

Kristin's eyes danced between the faces, stopping briefly at Chet and Matt, acknowledging each of them with a new smile. "I'm so glad you're all here. I'm so lucky to have you."

"And we're blessed by you, sweety, and your girls," said Jack.

"My girls?" was all Kristin could say through fresh tears of joy. Her eyes moved slowly from face to face, stopping at Sarah. "Tell me, honey. Who are they?"

"They're your girls. You're a mommy now! Twins!" said Sarah pointing to the drawing.

"That's right, sis," added Hannah. "Your baby is more—there are two of them. Two girls, confirmed by a sonogram. You slept through the entire procedure. There's no doubt, and each of them are fit as a fiddle. In fact, when the pictures were taken yesterday, their little arms were wrapped around each other."

Tears now poured from Kristin's face. Those gathered around her assumed, initially, that they were tears of joy. But Kristin's expression contorted into a cloudy mix of doubt and fear. Her mind raced through innumerable scenarios with a life—no, lives—flashing before her eyes as she tried to piece together the outcome of decisions she'd soon have to make. Dominoes were falling, yet unlike an intersection of carefully arranged tiles, only one of the paths would activate, tipping forward. She could choose just one path. It occurred to her that she was rapidly approaching that intersection.

Kristin, lying in bed with her chest and head elevated, reached for Sarah. Sarah understood the gesture and moved closer. Sarah hadn't expected her artwork to lead to a moment like this. Kristin hugged her, pulling her niece into the steel bedframe and mattress. Sarah awkwardly reached out, connecting with her aunt's arm and shoulder. Sarah's lips trembled when she saw that Kristin was crying.

Hannah and Miriam saw the inevitability of this moment developing now before their eyes. "Hey, guys," said Miriam, looking at both Jack and Chet, then Matthew and Sarah.

Could you please let us have a few moments?" The men immediately understood. Chet took Matt's hand while Jack reached for Sarah, reluctant to leave. They moved toward the door. Sarah glanced back as they stepped into the hallway, catching a glimpse of her mother and grandmother, with heads bowed down, close to Kristin's.

"Let's take a walk outside, huh?" said Jack.

16

GABRIEL REAPPEARS

THE THREE WOMEN WERE ENTWINED in a warm embrace for many minutes. A physician saw them and stopped at the open door. "Everything okay in here?" he asked. Miriam's head lifted. She smiled and thanked him, assuring him that everything was fine.

Then, Miriam realized she knew his face but couldn't place it. Even his voice was warmly familiar. "Doctor…" she began to say.

But he'd already moved from the doorway. Miriam quickly slipped around the bed, leaving her two girls. In the hallway, Miriam called out. "Doctor?" she asked. The man had made it only to the next doorway. He spun, turning toward her, and smiled. His light blue eyes pierced hers.

"Yes…Miriam?"

Immediately, she felt a weakness in her knees. The physician recognized the signs of vertigo, knowing that the woman who stood only 20 feet from him could soon lose consciousness and collapse. He rushed to her, supporting her easily. He helped her into a chair just inside Kristin's room. She struggled for clarity and whispered, "Gabriel. How…why, you haven't aged a day."

He smiled again and quietly replied, "No. I don't. It's

great to see you again. You look wonderful, Miriam. You may recall, long ago, I mentioned the twins. Not these lovely girls," he added, lifting his eyes to Kristin and Hannah, both of whom stared with wide eyes, "but the ones to come."

"Mom, are you okay?" asked Kristin.

"I'm fine honey. I just felt a bit unsteady for a moment. The doctor—well, Gabriel—knew just what to do."

"You know each other?" asked Hannah.

But before Miriam could reply, he answered. "We do. We're old friends, and I see you've grown to be a fine young woman, Hannah. You, as well, Kristin; I see you've recovered well."

Kristin and Hannah were confused. Gabriel appeared to be no older than Hannah, and though it didn't seem unusual for a hospital physician to know a patient's condition, he knew both of their names without hesitation. Another facet to the mystery for Hannah was that she quickly observed the lack of embroidered hospital insignia on Gabriel's long white clinical overcoat. All other personnel had a blue caduceus with winged staff on their hospital uniform.

Gabriel turned his attention back to Miriam, who smiled at him. He took both of her hands in his, grinning at her reassuringly. "You'll be fine, Miriam. The girls, too. And your family…the twins included. Remember now? I told you so."

She closed her eyes, recalling his words from decades earlier. She felt his hands leave hers, and she opened her eyes. He'd now returned to the doorway.

"I must excuse myself," he said first to Miriam, then looking at both Kristin and Hannah. Addressing them all, he added, "Nova only means well; take her words to heart. As for the guy with dark glasses, I'll see to it that he doesn't bother any of you again." With that, Gabriel smiled and walked away.

Miriam began to rise from the chair, but this time it was Hannah who bolted from the side of Kristin's bed. Halfway to the door, she said, "Mom, stay where you are." Kristin had a look of disbelief on her face as her sister dashed to the doorway to catch the doctor.

Hannah was out the door in an instant. She looked down the hallway in the direction he'd gone, then spun to look in the opposite direction. Gabriel was gone. She walked quickly down the hall, looking into all open doors. She made her way to the nurses' station and asked about him.

"Dr. Gabriel," said Hannah to the head nurse seated at the curved, central desk. "May I speak with him?"

"Is that his first or last name?" the woman questioned. Hannah raised her hands.

The nurse seated before Hannah turned to ask another nurse, standing nearby, "Who's on duty tonight? Anyone named Gabriel?" The nurse replied, "Not that I know of."

The head nurse asked Hannah, "Where'd you see him last?"

"He stepped into my sister Kristin's room, just a minute ago. Tall, muscular, blue eyes. Thirty-four, maybe. Doctor with a long white coat, but no insignia."

"Insignia?" asked the nurse.

"Hospital insignia. Like yours," said Hannah, pointing to the crest on her chest. "His jacket didn't have it."

"You're sure of this?" asked the nurse, now assessing Hannah carefully.

"That's right. The two of us and our mother were just speaking with him."

The head nurse turned back toward the other nurse saying, "Please take the desk. Get a few other nurses up here to check rooms for an unfamiliar…physician."

She walked out of the central station, locked eyes with Hannah, and said, "Let's go to your sister's room. It's Kristin, right?"

"That's right," responded Hannah. When they entered Kristin's room, Miriam was still sitting; she and Kristin were talking. Miriam was saying something about "before Hannah's birth."

That's the instant when Hannah recalled her mother's explanation of a man, a physician named Gabriel, the one who provided a second opinion that prevented the termination of Miriam's pregnancy a few months before she was born.

The head nurse spoke with the three of them, taking notes. Miriam made no reference to her first encounter with Gabriel, so Hannah decided against it as well. Each confirmed speaking with Gabriel.

Moments later, hospital security quietly locked the hospital down. No one was allowed in or out—except at the emergency room where the sliding glass doors were guarded. The director of security met with his staff at the main entrance. He explained the need for understanding as concerned relatives were either detained inside or asked for patience outside. Others pored over video monitors looking for evidence of the mysterious doctor who called himself Gabriel. Two video cameras—the one closest to Kristin's room and another near the nurse's station provided the only glimpse of him.

Staring intently into several monitors on a wall, one technician cursed the administration's unwillingness last year to upgrade many of the interior surveillance cameras to ultraHD cams. Unable to achieve the level of detail they wanted from cameras that were 30 and 50 feet from Kristin's hospital room, he and his supervisor commiserated over their misfortune.

"They threw all the money at the exterior vids, thinking that a threat—or any need for hi-def security pictures—was sure to come from outside," said the tech who tapped keys and moved the cursor across the only images they had. "Well, we can at least hope to capture better shots of him coming or going outside," said the supervisor who stood behind him.

The hospital's best screen captures from interior cams, magnified, were so grainy as to be essentially useless. They showed only a Caucasian man of undetermined age, with a full head of hair, who smiled almost continuously. To their disbelief and consternation, their search of images from the higher-def exterior cams offered nothing. It was as though Dr. Gabriel had somehow materialized from within, had not left the hospital, but yet was nowhere to be found.

Chet, Jack, and the kids, who'd taken a walk around the campus, soon found themselves stuck at the main entrance. Fortunately, the weather was ideal. Chet tried to call Hannah first, then Miriam, unsuccessfully. But he found that he could text them. After learning some of the details ("What? Gabriel—from before Hannah was born? The same age?"), Jack attempted to get inside by explaining to security that his daughter is a patient there.

The security officer explained that he couldn't let them in, though he'd pass along news of their plight to Kristin, Hannah, and Miriam. "They already know we're out here. Thanks. We'll wait." Jack shuffled back to rejoin Chet, Matt, and Sarah along with a growing crowd of people outside the main entrance. They noticed that a large group had assembled inside the doors as well.

MALBAS' OFFER OF $500, slipped discreetly to a gate attendant, was sufficient to gain release of his car from the county's impound.

A short time later, there was a disruption at the Highway 70 intersection along Harding Street, westbound. Four witnesses claimed to police, all consistently, that a dark sedan stopped at the light with a turn signal showing intent to enter the highway. As if from nowhere, a tall man—brilliantly white—approached the driver's door and effortlessly yanked the door from its hinges. As he reached toward the driver, there was a commotion as the driver tried to fight back.

"Malbas, at last!" said Gabriel.

There were flashes of light, like those made by a welder. The man standing outside the car pulled the struggling man from the driver's seat. He reached in with no expression of concern or alarm, with strength that immediately overwhelmed the other. There was a brief struggle as the flashes of light gradually dissolved. The skirmish ended quickly, and when it was complete, the driver of the car was nowhere to be seen. Then, the other man reached inside as though to look for any belongings, and then he too disappeared.

Officer James Dunn, first to arrive at the scene, was mystified. There was no sign of either of the men. No sign of a struggle, no blood, nothing. Two other police cruisers, each with two officers, arrived at the scene to help with the investigation and traffic control.

There were four witnesses—a banker driving to an appointment whose car was directly behind the dark sedan; a lone man in a battle fatigue jacket, on foot; and a mother and daughter walking in the opposite direction in the green space between Harding and the railroad tracks.

"The standing guy squashed the man in dark clothes, the one he pulled from the car, and there were several flashes of light during the scuffle that lasted no more than three or four seconds," said the banker who had a box office seat for the event.

The man in the Army jacket heard part of the banker's testimony. "I agree with that guy," he said. "Best description of it I could offer. Man, I fought in Desert Storm, Army, 4/66th Armor. I've never seen such a one-sided fight between two people. That dude in white overpowered the other one and just freakin' squashed him. I saw the flashes he referred to; then I blinked, and they were gone. Oh yeah, I do recall that the car's driver was wearing a dark derby hat."

Officer Dunn then approached the last witnesses. When the woman saw him coming, she straightened her spine, thrust her chin up, and without looking at her daughter, said, "I'll handle this."

"So, ma'am, may I ask what you saw?" asked the patrolman.

"It's doctor," said the woman.

"Huh? I'm sorry," he replied. "What's that?"

"My title. I'm a doctor. Dr. Lindsay Rothchild."

He noticed that she rolled the "R," sounding like Rrrroths-chiiild. He snuck a quick glance at the child who had her head down, swinging slowly side to side.

"Okay. So, um, doctor. What did you see?"

"The driver of the car was quickly subdued, rendered,

then reduced to nothing. There were several quick light pulsations. Then, he simply dissolved," said the mother, an assistant professor of postcolonial literature at Northwestern University. "We're on vacation; just the two of us," she added, as though to explain their presence at a crime scene.

Wondering if he should attempt to get her full title or to transcribe her exact words, Officer Dunn mumbled, "So the, uh, man from the car, was…."

"He was squashed," said the professor's 12-year-old daughter. She too had heard parts of the banker's explanation.

Officer Dunn then looked at the professor. She glanced at her daughter appreciatively and muttered, "I concur."

One patrolman had a prints kit; he attempted to lift prints from the detached door and the car. He was 20 minutes into the frustrating work when another officer said, "Hey, no sense getting any deeper into that. There's no crime, no body. Just a car left here in the intersection."

He made sense. It was as though the scene had been thoroughly cleansed—or that nothing had happened at all. Just a mess of old prints and smears.

They called Pop's Towing to impound the car. After a quick study below the car, Pop said to Officer Dunn as he pulled it onto his Jerr-Dan, "I don't get it. That car's tranny was trashed. Locked up solid too. No one coulda driven that thing."

"Yeah, that's right, chief," said Officer Dunn when he called in a summary report. "The banker's legit, and so are the others. They saw the car being driven into the intersection. Heck, the banker said he'd been behind the car for at least half a mile. But the tow truck driver said that's impossible. He said the car couldn't be driven. He said the tranny was shot, locked up tight. Well, it's on its way to impound now. As for the two guys involved—nothing. They're gone without a trace."

Officer Dunn shook his head in dismay, wondering how he'd verify what happened there at the intersection. Before his shift was over, he'd have to complete the report. They had the car and the car door, with hinges bent like taffy, but nothing else. Stolen plates on the car from somewhere in Ohio. No prints. No papers or wallet. Nothing. Well, he did have the witness statements. They'd have to do.

A BOY ON HIS BICYCLE, riding along the White River near the Indianapolis Zoo, heard faint police car sirens somewhere off near Highway 70. Maybe an accident. Spotting something unusual, he stopped at a trash can. Curious, he studied a neatly folded pile of clothing next to it. There were black boots, pants, a shirt, and sunglasses. Also, a funny black hat and a white doctor's coat.

He looked in both directions. Seeing no one nearby, he reached for the stylish Oakleys and put them on. From the trash can, an empty plastic shopping sack wagged in the breeze. He snapped it open, dropping the boots in, followed by the clothes and hat, then pedaled off toward home on Elder Avenue.

EVENTUALLY, JACK, CHET, MATTHEW, AND SARAH were allowed back inside the hospital. When the main doors opened, large crowds from inside and out converged. Security quickly established an orderly flow. "In on the right; out on the left—just like traffic."

When they arrived at Kristin's room, she was sitting up in

bed, fully clothed and freshly showered. Miriam and Hannah saw to it that all the loose ends were attended to. Kristin's bags were packed, and the hospital's exit paperwork completed. "We're ready to leave, Dad," said Hannah. Kristin just smiled.

Miriam looked at them and said, "Well, look at the stragglers. Menfolk—always a few steps behind."

Sarah looked at her grandmother. "Grams, what's 'menfolk?'" Everyone shared a good laugh.

Jack shook his head and said, "Well, let's get outta here before they lock the place up again."

They took the elevator to the first floor. Jack quietly pulled Miriam to the back of the procession. He whispered, "Gabriel?"

"The very same. Just exactly as I remembered him," she replied. "And he mentioned Nova." Miriam went on to tell him about their encounter with the enigmatic doctor, trying to recall everything he said. "And the twins. Remember his bringing that up decades ago, and how we were confused by it? He seemed to indicate that the twins he spoke of back then are the very same twins we now have pictures of, from Kristin's sonogram."

Jack shook his head in amazement, thinking it's just too strange to be true.

As they made their way to the rental vehicle, Chet pulled Jack aside. "Hey—the whole clan's all here, in your ol' hood. And we've gotta make sure Kristin feeds those babies, after all. Should we do an early dinner? I just googled nearby restaurants. There's a Chick-fil-A nearby. Want me to drive?" Jack's smile gave him the answer he'd hoped for. "You read my mind."

At dinner, Sarah and Matthew kept staring at Kristin. She enjoyed their attention. "You guys aren't used to seeing me, are ya?" she teased. "Well, your aunt in California isn't just a photo on the wall anymore; she's a real live person who can challenge anyone to a chicken nugget eatin' contest." Her eyes met Matt's. "You look like a pretty tough kid. Wanna challenge me?"

Matthew smiled, a bit embarrassed at the sudden attention from his mother's sister but gave her a confident thumb's up. Jack and Chet piped in, looking at Kristin, saying, "You'll regret that bet." Miriam had hoped Kristin would say something about "having to feed three of us," but it didn't happen.

While eating, Kristin asked about her parent's new home. Miriam talked about having more space than they could possibly need and the gardening. Jack winked, saying he liked the neighbors—especially the ones two doors down. Sarah explained that they found a hideaway named "heaven" and how she and Matt launched a surprise attack with nerf balls when her grandparents returned from the grocery store one day. Hannah spoke about work and her recent promotion. The lively conversation included antiquing, books they've read, even artwork—a topic Kristin knew more about than they'd thought possible.

Kristin also spoke about her new friend Mary, "a beautiful, brilliant sculptor," adding that Mary had given her a gorgeous leather Bible, a comment that drew looks of surprise and admiration. She shared some of the funny moments of Mary's visit and the exchange with Festus O. Yossarian, a topic the kids especially enjoyed. Hannah and Miriam appreciated the reference to Eleanor Roosevelt and the engagement ring left behind in a pot of water. Kristin also spoke about her visit to the old home and that the Terronis were so welcoming and sweet.

"Let's go," said Jack. "Let's drop in on them. We've still got an hour of daylight." Miriam counseled against it, at least in favor of calling first. "Jack immediately dialed them; a few moments later, he turned to the family and said, "It's arranged. Nineteen-hundred hours."

"Um, Grampa, that's seven o' clock, right?" asked Matt.

"That's right, sport," Jack replied, with a wink.

After leaving the restaurant, they drove to the ol' homestead. They also made plans to visit Fort Harrison State Park and to do some hiking around Geist Reservoir the next day.

Kristin nodded, saying that, as far as anyone at work's concerned, she's still recovering. "Which, I can assure you, is accurate," she added. "I can't think of a better, healthier recovery than the one I'm in the midst of right now."

Miriam reached over discreetly to pull Jack's hand into hers.

TWO DAYS LATER, Jack, Miriam, Hannah, Chet, Matt, and Sarah drove to the airport for an early afternoon flight home. Kristin asked to be dropped off at a Marriott, explaining that she had a full day of work to do and loads of email and voicemail to attend to. Her parting from them, there under the hotel's main entrance portico, was tearful.

Kristin enjoyed a restful first night. In addition to the work and feeling a rush of excitement to assume her new role, there was so much to contemplate.

She'd been driven by advancements in her career for so long, and now there were substantial threats to it—obstacles at the very least. And all the strange occurrences. Yet Kristin believed her career was tailored to her precisely. It had felt so right for so long. She excelled at it, sprinting between positions. And now, she was respected and admired as a woman, physician, and leader—a symbol of strength and accomplishment for women and their cause. This was her opportunity to excel.

Kristin was, however, aware of a deep current, a strange and powerful undertow that was pulling her in another direction. It forced her to pause and contemplate its meaning. There was no question it stemmed from recent events, but she forced herself to trust that her doubts and concerns would self-resolve.

The next day, she plowed through work continuously, ordering room service for breakfast, lunch, and dinner. Halfway through the day, she went to the gym for two hours. After her shower, she made a call to Shelby, the director at the clinic closest to HQ.

"Hi, Shelb. Thanks, I'm fine. All's well, and I'm pretty much recovered. Hey, um, switching tracks, I'd like your help with something. A procedure. Yeah. Actually, mine. Please see if you can secure a physician for it. I'll email you all of the pertinent info shortly. I'll come in fifteen or twenty minutes after normal closing on Wednesday. Could you and a few others stay a bit late for me? Low profile for everything, okay, especially in light of recent events. Thanks, Shelb. See you then."

After an early dinner, as she prepared to call their travel agency to ask about morning flights back to San Francisco, Kristin noticed a piece of paper protruding from the side pocket of her purse. Pulling it out, then unfolding it, she saw that it was Sarah's drawing—the mommy and her girls. Next to it was the sonogram image of her own two girls, embracing. It happened fast; Kristin's tears poured from a source she thought was high and dry. No doubt, Hannah or her mother had placed them there secretly.

Kristin fell back into the bed, pulling the sheets and cover up high. "Oh, Lord, please help me. What am I to do?"

When she recovered sufficiently to make a call, Kristin forced herself to the desk where her phone was charging. She dialed the travel agency to make arrangements for her flight. "Please check me in for the flight and have them text me the boarding passes." Kristin managed to complete her packing, seeing to it that she'd have everything ready to go for her ride to the airport early the next morning.

She thought she'd take a quick walk to the front desk for a newspaper. As she grabbed the card key she noticed a piece of paper partially visible below the door. Before pulling it in, she peered through the door's wide-angle spyglass; no one in the hallway. Too early for a checkout folio.

The moment she saw the handwriting, she felt weak. Picking it up, she retreated quickly to the bed, collapsing back into the pillows. Still holding the note, she slowly raised it to her face.

Dear Kristin—

I'm delighted that you've again reached for the Bible. Treasure Mary's gift. It's your lifeline. Remember how good it made you feel and how warm were those early years with your family at church? The warmth and goodness await you still.

Find Ephesians 2:10, Jeremiah 29:11, and Matthew 7:7. You are equipped to alter your path with Christ as your guide. I'll be with you as well.

You must know these truths, Kristin:

Because man is made in God's own image (Genesis 1:27), each life is of great value to God; Children are a gift from God (Psalm 127:3). He even calls our children his own, saying ". . . you took your sons and daughters whom you bore to me and sacrificed them…you slaughtered my children…" (Ezekiel 16:20-21).

The Bible says of our Creator, "In His hand is the life of every living thing and the breath of every human being" (Job 12:10 NLT). God, the giver of life, commands us not to take the life of an innocent person: "Do not shed innocent blood" (Jeremiah 7:6). The Sixth Commandment, written in stone by the finger of God, commands, "You shall not murder" (Exodus 20:13).

Infanticide is nothing less, Kristin, and punishment for it—unatoned—is a punishment long and desolate.

Make the blood good, Kristin. So much of it has been shed. You now have the opportunity to reverse its impact, to change it from senseless loss to prayerful atonement. Rise to your sacred, consecrated role. Forgiveness is there, especially for you (even for Cynthia). But you must reach for it.

In Hebrews 13: 20-21 it says: Now may the God of peace, who through the blood of the eternal covenant brought back from the dead our Lord Jesus, that great Shepherd of the sheep, equip you with everything good for doing his will, and may he work in us what is pleasing to him, through Jesus Christ, to whom be the glory forever and ever. Amen.

Blessings to you, Kristin, as you move forward, righteously.

—Nova

PS—The baby you've seen at night, Eve, is your aborted child. She's very much alive and well in heaven. She's now a fine young woman in spirit form. Eve looks so much like you, and she looks forward to telling you all about her life with Christ. Most importantly, Kristin, she loves and forgives you.

As for the other two girls in your dream, those in your womb and in Sarah's art—they are yours to hold and cherish, a gift from God. They will return your love bountifully. As will your Lord and Savior who now has a special place in his heart for you.

Kristin dropped to the floor beside her bed. Awash with tears, she joined her hands on the mattress, knees together on the carpet. "Oh, please, Father. Help me to understand this and to do what's right."

She remained there well past midnight. She prayed like she'd never prayed before, asking God for forgiveness and discernment. She forced herself into a desperate nothingness, an empty receptacle for God's direction.

With no concept of time, only that there wasn't enough of it that evening, Kristin gradually opened her eyes, spotting the David Jeremiah Bible that Mary had given to her. Pulling Nova's letter close, she first found Ephesians 2:10. There, she read, "For we are God's handiwork, created in Christ Jesus to do good works which God prepared in advance for us to do."

Then, Jeremiah 29:11 (ESV)—"For I know the plans I have for you declares the Lord, plans for welfare and not for evil, to give you future and a hope." Finally, she read in Matthew 7:7, "Ask, and it will be given to you; seek, and you will find; knock, and it will be opened to you."

An explanation offered this: God is more than willing to show us his will and plan for our lives, but he also wants us to show that we want to know it and follow it. He wants us to make an effort to seek his will. With that, he has promised that we will find it. So if you are asking and seeking and knocking and doing everything as to the Lord, then you can rest assured that he will show you his will for your life. His will may not always be what we expect, and it can be revealed to us in unexpected ways, but if we are truly interested, we will find it.

"In unexpected ways," mumbled Kristin as she slowly rose to lie on the bed. She immediately fell into a deep sleep. A dream returned but altered its path. In it, as Kristin's vision clarified, she saw the two girls who she knew to be her twins. They were no longer infants. Kristin was then aware of another presence, a beautiful young woman—appearing as much like an angel as she was human, who ran toward her girls. And yet, unaccountably, the angelic young woman somehow seemed familiar. Kristin then was aware of the strange, unfamiliar terrain. Like a moonscape, it was a dry, barren mountain desert region. She then realized her girls were in peril.

The twins appeared to be buried to their waists in sand. A rock-wielding mob, yelling in a language she couldn't understand, directed their wrath at her girls. Kristin's horror lifted when she saw that the angelic young woman had reached them, standing in their defense.

Wielding a strange power, the woman's stare was enough

to push the attackers back. They dropped their rocks while retreating. Then they stood motionless to watch as the young woman effortlessly pulled the girls up from the ground, embracing them.

Kristin was transported into the scene; she knelt beside the girls to console and protect them. They were still within sight of the unmoving mob.

Her girls then spoke to her in the same, strange language, yet she understood them. They explained that their father, angered by Kristin's embracing of the Christian faith, had abducted them. Traveling to Iran on a vacation, he and the girls traveled to his homeland and family. Their father had no intention of returning.

Several years later, the girls, at 12 years of age, were promised as sharia brides to a cruel uncle and his friend. The wedding was held, yet they refused the men and ran. The girls were found in the home of friends from school, a boy and his sister, both of whom were whipped mercilessly for harboring the twins. The uncle and his friend claimed the boy had sex with them; thus the brides were deemed guilty of adultery.

Only a lethal stoning, fully supported by sharia law, would properly settle the crime. Leading the brutal sentence for atonement was the presiding mullah, there at the head of the pack and wearing the brightest tunic. Their own father, Dr. Gilgamesh Arzhang, stood despondently in the back of the crowd with a stone in each hand.

The girls said they knew that Kristin, the mother they loved, now had a choice. They explained that they'd come to her in a vision, granted by a spirit named Nova, to show her how their lives would end. Kristin's decision would lead to one of three results: to abort them, to stay with Gil and give birth to them (a path that would lead to their half-buried corpses surrounded by bloodied stones), or to do as God has asked, leading to happiness and fulfillment for her and for them.

"We've met Jesus. And Nova," they explained to her. "Jesus is watching you now, Mommy, with such love in his heart. Nova is our guardian."

As Kristin turned her attention fully to the girls and away from the crowd, the people advanced toward them. Just as a large rock struck Kristin, she was jolted awake forcefully.

Still lying in bed but with eyes wide open now, Kristin tried to reassemble the dream but knew implicitly the meaning it held, foretelling three very different futures. Unsteadily, she rose to take a shower. Looking at the clock, she saw that it was 5:15 am. She made two cups of coffee. Still sluggish, she turned her attention to the last of her packing. At last, she reached for her Bible, turning to Genesis 1: "In the beginning, God created the heavens and the earth," she said softly.

OBSERVING THIS, BUT UNSEEN, Nova wiped a tear, surprised by its sudden escape; the stirring of her heart was an immense and welcomed relief.

Nova considered her good fortune. Her foray into the lives of humans, stemming from Eve's plaintive cry, had been so rewarding yet still incomplete. There were times that her special project redirected her activity away from earth's endless spillage, a river of souls on the move. She reflected on the significance of the tiny drama—in both the physical and spiritual worlds—that held her fascination.

Though many of the players were still in motion and fulfilling their divine purpose, Nova had been less attentive to it lately. Their prayers, tears, or the reading of Scripture always warranted a glance. She was satisfied to know that many of the humans who'd come together in this drama had, at last, turned toward the divine light.

Kristin's longing for the Word pushed her deeper into Genesis, where eventually she arrived at Genesis 41, the pharaoh's dreams. A jolt of wisdom and clarity led her to comparisons between her own role, professionally, and that of the feared leader of Egypt. After all, she was no longer Cyn's understudy. She'd achieved the leadership role, having accomplished so much professionally and at such a young age but by whose measure, and at what cost?

Kristin immediately knew she'd arrived at an important place in her reading. It fit her predicament well: it was the gift of Joseph's interpretation that brought relief to the pharaoh's tortured dreams. It was the interpretation of dreams that she most needed now. Yet, in a surreal but perfectly acceptable way, Nova (whoever she was) and her own girls had done just that. With this reading, clarity emerged.

Her babies were fighting for their lives, for their cause. And there were other, substantial considerations, including the plight of so many other unborn children. And God's very own direction, conveyed during her prayers, confirmed by the mysterious guardian. Nova.

A moment later, the front desk called: "Doctor Soelberg, your cab's here." Kristin closed the Bible, grabbed her bags, and left the room.

17

NOVA STEPS IN

Hannah knew that her return to work would have its challenges. It was always that way, with the abundance of mail, email, and voicemail to attend to. She drove to work early that morning.

As she opened her office, the phone on her desk began to ring. She dropped her bags and picked up the phone.

"Hannah—it's Dad. Sorry to call so early. I just got an email from Kay Zavala, the Army intel officer. Got a minute?"

"Sure, Pa. What's up?"

"Well, it appears that General Zavala has friends in the international intel community. A friend of hers in the federal police force in Austria knows something about the surgical tool. They confirm what Dr. Harley suspected—the tool you have is the Luer Cranial Perforator that was taken from the Museum of Conception and Abortion in Vienna."

Hannah listened as Jack found the place on his monitor he was searching for. "The surgical instrument was developed by a physician-engineer, Hans Luer, in 1858," he resumed. "Looks like there were only three in existence, and the only one with the striation in the ivory handle is the one that was sent to you.

"The tool led to the development of far more sophisticated and efficient ones," he added. "Apparently, new cranial perforators are electric, with outer and inner drills spinning at hundreds of RPM while vacuuming out all of the debris. To the senses of an unborn child, there's nothing more menacing than the sound and vibration of that machine."

Hannah told her father where to find the tool in their garage so he could box it up to send to Kay. She would forward it on to her contact in Austria, who would return it to the museum.

BACK IN HER NEW APARTMENT, Kristin made a quick check for email. Her voicemail had 18 new messages, most from the media wanting an interview. The PR agency had placed three of the calls, desperately wanting to schedule interviews for her with the *Today* show, Graham Norton, and Doctors Oz and Phil—all of whom requested time with her. Of course, there was every expectation that she would be portrayed as a victim of harsh intolerance, that she'd champion the cause of women and their right to choose.

Kristin figured that calls to the PR firm tomorrow would be soon enough—though no doubt they'd be angry at her.

She needed some quiet time. Her early arrival back to the apartment suited that nicely. She made a salad and a fruit smoothie, then settled into a comfortable chair in the living room, her phone and iPad balanced above the Jeremiah Bible. She felt the comfortable weight of the book and the electronic devices on her lap; for a moment, she thought about the conflict between them.

Opening her iPad, she scanned her calendar for the following day. She planned to get an early start at the office, with loads of calls to make and email to attend to. Then the procedure, her own, at 5:20.

Kristin knew that she'd now, at last, arrived at the intersection that offered one of three directions to take. Her work and the next day's schedule, topped off with a quick, outpatient multifetal abortion offered the continuation of one path—the one she'd worked tirelessly toward for years. The next option led to a commitment to Gili; she'd already dismissed that one. The remaining track was far less comfortable in many ways yet strangely inviting. There were so many uncertainties, among them a revised career path. There was simply no acceptable explanation for Nova, the mysterious notes, or the unsettling dreams; a thread of doubt stitched those pieces together.

There were nagging memories; what was it Mary had said? "Rest on God. Let him provide." Worst of all, the dreams. So haunting and yet purely imagined. Or, were they? As a physician and scientist, Kristin fought with what was already beginning to feel like her old self. Such a strange and uncomfortable feeling! She'd never really, truly known doubt or uncertainty since she'd left home. She wondered if, while striving to achieve her degrees and then professional status, she'd mentally barricaded, chained, and padlocked the door to home.

Had she worked so hard to reject everything home represented, and especially to snub the outstretched arms of her mother and father and their Christian faith?

She remembered a professor's favorite motto, "Science trumps fiction."

Kristin recalled that, not long ago, there was nothing more frustrating than soft, vague religious explanations. She'd bristle at references to an imperfect spiritual realm with its supernatural manifestations, none of it grounded in her safe, familiar world. She placed her trust in the foundation of cold, hard science. There were certainties tied to the laws of nature, or at least repeatable, proven probabilities. The closer she leaned into physical science, with its hypotheses and experiments, the more secure she felt.

Still, there were substantial concerns as she began to doubt some of the familiar dogma. Had many facets of her education entailed blind acceptance of deeply biased doctrine? There was subtle nagging as though from an inner voice. Kristin could feel now that parts of her well-entrenched, immovable self-image were eroding, giving way to bewildering uncertainty and vulnerability. And, wonderment.

She sat back, closing her eyes. What was she missing? Her brow was pinched in concentration. She wanted clarity, answers. Kristin excavated the far reaches of her mind, tearing further into neatly settled layers, her foundation. The further she dove, the more she became aware of the need to surface. She surrendered, allowing a sense of being lifted into a new and different place. Oddly, it felt good, warm, and restful. She was immediately aware of muscles and nerves, relaxing. There was a release of tension as her heart and mind were coupled.

"Lord God, please help me. I want to make the right decision," she whispered.

Her words, barely audible, shot aloft as though from a cannon. Nova winced at the explosion, forcing her to flee from a heavenly perch and into a space where she could enter the earthly dimension. She practically fell into Kristin's apartment. Though invisible to the human eye, she could walk among the living without being seen or heard. Mumbling to herself, she looked about the apartment, spotting the Bible on Kristin's lap, unopened. Portable electronics were cradled above it.

For Nova, influencing human thought was one approach, but the door had to be open, requiring either one's dream state or prayer. Either would do. Nova shook her head, anticipating a padlock, but instead found the door ajar. She mumbled, "Thank you for prayers, at last, Kristin," as she entered and quickly leafed through files. Memory banks for the human species were sometimes very complicated because the human mind interconnected so many thoughts and experiences. She navigated through years of Kristin's recordings, like a spaghetti tangle of magnetic tape.

"Thank you, Lord, for color-coding," she said as she deftly separated a tousled, interwoven mass of dark records and knotted strips of memory while probing deeper into Kristin's mind. Nova reached further through a deeply shaded nest of gloom, gently disjoining a profusion of dark strands, clammy with guilt, shame, and insecurity. Aha! There: ensnarled beneath them, she pulled light-emitting tendrils forward, those with goodness and love sewn in, scanning for just the right…"There you are."

Nova winced at the complex task of threading memories back into the human mind, bringing them into the foreground. It reminded her of winding film into a crabby old movie projector.

Seconds later, Kristin bent forward and clamped her eyes shut, focusing intently on a memory that began to percolate—slow to refine, pushing forward. Its clarity was remarkable; she was transported back to their old home. She saw herself, sitting up in bed. It was late at night; tears were streaming down her face. She was 17 or 18, her last year at home. She saw the bedroom window nearby that she had used so many times to launch late night outings with Whitney.

Kristin watched as her father tapped lightly and entered. She was immediately aware that, as he moved toward her, he was in prayer. His expressions of love and concern arose toward God like a sweet, fragrant aroma. She could hear his unspoken prayer and sensed the hurt she'd caused, knowing also that it was a wound shared by her mother. Her father moved with care, tired and worn through the experience of parenting. He was asking for God's forgiveness, at failing in his responsibility as her steward and guardian. He came to her side, sending more prayers aloft.

"Let me ask just one thing, honey," he said, placing a hand on her shoulder. "That, someday, in a situation when you feel even worse than this...remember this moment, then raise your eyes and your heart to God and simply say, 'Please be with me Lord. Show me what to do.'"

He waited a moment as new tears pushed outward and fell from her eyes. She looked deeply into his, holding his gaze.

"Promise me, honey," he asked her. "Promise me that you will."

"I promise, Dad."

The memory left her now with a sense of peace she'd not experienced before. Her lips parted, and she prayed, "Please be with me, Lord. Show me what to do. Give me a sign."

Nova saw the value of giving Kristin an anointed glimpse into her past. Sadly, she contemplated, it's a rarity for humans to have such a transcendent experience. Yet, Kristin's prayer was confirmation.

Gradually, Kristin opened her eyes. It was twilight. The large picture window near her chair provided a view of tree-tops, silhouetted against a shimmering sapphire blue sky, moments before sunset. It was the joining of two high jet trails, prominent in the window's frame, that took her breath away. They intersected perfectly, forming a flawless cross, luminous in the last trace of sunlight. She watched it, transfixed, as the sun's disappearing light brightened it momentarily, then faded.

"Lord, it *is* you," she whispered.

Kristin was then aware of the light fixture above the kitchen table, now glowing softly. She was certain she hadn't turned it on. She noticed the Jeremiah Bible, illuminated just below it on the table. It was open. Abruptly, she looked down at her lap to see the iPad, with her phone on top of it. The same Bible, now missing; she'd held it just moments ago.

"How could this be?" she moaned. Kristin rose unsteadily, sending the tablet and phone to the floor. She attempted to step around them, but one foot sent her weight directly onto the iPad, which emitted a quiet crunch. Ignoring it, she walked trance-like to the table and dropped into the chair closest to her Bible. Nova had been thorough; she'd opened the book to Mark 10: 14-15, circling it.

Kristin stared at the Bible initially, unable to focus. Standing beside her, Nova sensed that—at last—she'd reached Kristin.

Kristin read:

Then they brought little children to Him, that He might touch them, but the disciples rebuked those who brought

*them. But when Jesus saw it, He was greatly displeased
and said to them, "Let the little children come to me, and
do not forbid them; for of such is the kingdom of God.
Assuredly, I say to you, whoever does not receive the
kingdom of God as a little child will by no means enter it."*

Nova had harvested a few strips of palm leaves, plentiful
nearby, placing them in later pages of the Bible. Kristin
worked her shaking fingers as well as she could. She pulled
pages until she reached the first palm leaf. Opening the book
to reveal the full pages, her eyes were drawn to Nova's mark
at Deuteronomy 30:19. It read,

> *This day I call the heavens and the earth as witnesses
> against you that I have set before you life and death, bless-
> ings and curses. Now choose life, so that you and your chil-
> dren may live.*

Kristin's hands shook. With greater difficulty, she went to
the next bookmark, opening the pages to Psalms. Psalm 127:
3 was marked,

> *Behold, children are a heritage [gift] from the Lord, the
> fruit of the womb is a reward.*

There was one more green marker, but she was now con-
vulsing. Her entire body shook as though naked in the cold.
She was fearful, sensing the presence of a spirit, or something
with no explanation, very nearby. The Bible almost jerked
from the table as she opened it to Jeremiah 1:5, also marked:
"Before I formed you in the womb I knew you; before you
were born I sanctified you...."

Just as Nova was sure she'd delivered the coup de grâce,
Kristin's phone rang. The telltale signature for Cynthia Moloch
was a bluesy brass band jingle. Kristin stumbled across the

floor, reaching down to answer the call reflexively. Cyn was speaking before Kristin's mind could even make the connection.

"…been slammed by all the calls; they told me you haven't answered any of them! I'm done, and they don't seem to get it. I'm ruined. Now the board's telling me they may garner my 401K funds and my savings. It's insane! I never asked for—

"Cyn, Cyn—hold up," Kristin blurted out. "I'm just catching up with you."

"What? Where have you been for so long?" stammered the familiar voice. Cyn droned on for ten minutes. Kristin mumbled monosyllabic replies as the woman related her tale of woe. Still sitting in the kitchen, Kristin eyed the open pages and Jeremiah 1:5.

Cyn's sky was falling. She wanted sympathy and someone to commiserate with her. Just as she was inviting Kristin over for drinks, Nova reached her tipping point. Shaking her head, Nova said to herself, "You sure are stubborn, aren't ya?"

Then, audibly, she spoke directly to Kristin. "That's enough." Nova then reached through the last barrier again to intervene directly, visibly, into human affairs, something she rarely did. God's expectations of her were clear; this must end. Now.

Kristin, shocked by the voice out of nowhere, felt the phone leave her hands, wrenched cleanly from her grasp. It dropped to the floor. She rose and stepped backward, eyes wide, slipping silently into a living room chair. Stunned by what she'd just seen and heard, she attempted to comprehend it.

Her first reaction was to cry, but tears wouldn't come. Her tremors returned. Kristin closed her eyes tightly, expecting something horrifying. Her only recourse was prayer. She clenched her fingers into the chair; her legs trembled. She pleaded with God to be released from this threat. Over and over, she prayed. Her desperate petitions mixed, bumped, and collided.

All right, thought Nova. *Now we've got you where we need you. Rock bottom. Funny how a wee dose of fear will do that so easily, with just a sprinkling of shock 'n' awe.*

Deciding against another verbal approach, Nova spoke into Kristin's prayers: "You know me. I'm your daughters' guardian. I want no harm to them or to you. But you need to know this, dear Kristin—their lives are important; they're depending on you. That goes for the lives of countless others who'll bear your mark should this wretched, senseless killing continue.

"The sanctity of human life is not open for debate. It's a certainty; the gift of God's own hand," continued Nova. "As for the role you sought to achieve—you'll have a thousand good opportunities to replace it. And the best of them awaits you—motherhood. Sure, others will pick up where you and Doctor Moloch left off. But I'll deal with that later. Right now, my charge is to—"

"Change my heart," uttered Kristin.

"Yes."

"Is this . . ."

"Yeah, I suppose so," replied Nova. "It's an intervention of sorts."

"But I'm afraid," whispered Kristin.

"That's ridiculous," replied Nova, again in prayer form. "I'm not here to harm you. Just the opposite. In fact, I'll share this with you, Kristin. In your state of agitation, and doctor

Lei Jiāng's inability to perform your procedure properly, three of you were to die on that OR table tomorrow, not just two. Of course, I'm doing my best to be sure it won't happen."

"What?" mumbled Kristin, pitifully. "How?"

Nova replied. "The new abortionist, Dr. Jiāng, just off the boat from East Asia, is a career monster. He was the only one available on such short order. Let's just say his track record isn't so good. And his credentials are a bit, well, misty. Oh, I can assure you his mortality rate is 100 percent for the babies, but plenty of his grown patients leave clinics in ambulances with severe complications. Or, in a body bag. Sadly, as you know, doc, it happens."

"Shelby . . ." was all that Kristin could say, thinking of her friend at the clinic.

"Oh, your friend at the clinic doesn't know," replied Nova. "Not yet, anyway. No doubt Shelby and others would check the doctor's stats, but only after things go wrong for you. But like I said, I can't let that happen."

"The others...." Kristin cried. Nova immediately knew Kristin's concern was for innocent mothers.

"Look, Kristin," communed Nova. "They're all innocent, the babies especially, certainly more than the mothers are but—yes—they should all be protected. They're all God's children. Babies are the gift of life, offered only as God can. And soon you'll know for yourself. As for Shelby, I'll be sure to enlighten her.

"That other worry you just expressed, Kristin? Yeah, uh-huh; I can read your thoughts, too—not just the prayers. You were thinking you're not Mommy material, right?"

With her eyes still shut tight, Kristin's head bobbed up and down in agreement.

"I can assure you that you'll be a lot better at it than many," answered Nova. "And, you'll have a lot of help from those who love you and your children. God will be with you each step of the way. And then, of course, there's Miriam and Hannah, and your babies' cousins, Matthew and Sarah. Why, you've got an entire family waiting for you back home. You and those beautiful girls, that is.

"By the way, Kristin. The young woman in your recent dream, the angel who protected your twins in Iran…that was Eve, your very first baby. Though she was mentioned in my last note to you, you've now had a chance to see her in action. Oh, she's got class, that one."

Kristin's chin slowly dropped toward her chest. Miraculously, the jitters subsided. Her prayers began to weave a colorful, light-filled tapestry of hope and desire for Christ's love in her life and for her babies. She was aware that her prayers were now moving in unison toward an honest, heart-felt plea for God's mercy, love, and direction.

"That's my girl," answered Nova, into her prayers. "Be sure to ask Hannah about a cross that she has; it's for you, but must be returned to its rightful owner when the time's right. I'll leave you now, dear. Go, be the Gospel."

18

KRISTIN'S FREEDOM

LATE THAT EVENING, the phone rang just inches from Miriam's head. Woken and disoriented by the strange sound, Miriam was jolted into an immediate fear: is it an emergency call?

Jack was leaning up, staring at Miriam as she reached for the phone. Glancing at the clock nearby, he saw that it was 2:20 am. He turned on his bedside lamp.

Miriam picked up the phone. "Yes."

"Mom. Mom, it's me. I'm sorry to call so late."

"Kristin, honey. Are you okay?"

"Yeah, Mom. I am. I want you to know, I'm coming home."

"You're…what?"

"Mom—I need you and Dad to know this. I couldn't wait. God wants me to have those baby girls; I know that now. And the kids want their grandparents. I know that now too."

Miriam's eyes swelled with tears. She strained to see, finally thumbing the speaker button. "Honey, you're on speaker now," she explained. "Your Dad's listening, too."

"Dad. I love you both so much. I'm coming home." They spoke for a while about Kristin's immediate plans. Jack carried the conversation; Miriam wept, smiled, and prayed. She occasionally nodded to questions or blubbered responses as best she could.

Kristin explained what her attorney had told her: with all the upheaval leading to and stemming from Cynthia Moloch's resignation, she needn't be concerned about resigning with no advance notice. He wanted her to resign immediately, so that's what she did. Kristin added that she was ready to reassess all of it, and that her profession was the least of her concerns. "My babies are most important now."

Kristin paused. Jack was quiet. She heard Miriam's muffled crying, tears of joy. "I want you both to know that so much has happened recently—all of it an answer to prayers," continued Kristin. Miriam looked at Jack, who had tears of his own.

"Dad, there's something I need to thank you for, and hope you'll remember," she added. "I clearly recalled a night, at home in Indy, when you…."

"Said that someday you'd feel a deeper need to be with God," said Jack.

"Yes! Dad, it happened," blurted Kristin. More tears at both ends of the line. "I recalled that promise. My prayers have been so strangely answered. I have so much to tell you both, and Hannah."

Miriam and Jack were wide awake now, slathered in tears and praying as they spoke with Kristin. Their conversation was rich with love and shared prayers. Nearing the end of the call, Miriam asked Kristin if she could wait 'til early evening the next day to tell Hannah; they could surprise her together. Kristin readily agreed.

It was close to 3:30 when the call ended. After spending

some time discussing their conversation with Kristin, it took a while before Jack and Miriam finally drifted off to sleep. Well after sunup, Jack and Miriam invited Hannah, Chet, and the kids to dinner.

Before lunch, Jack returned from Target with a 10-inch "smart display." He spent much of the day playing with his new toy. The portable device he'd chosen for the connection with Kristin would allow everyone to enjoy the call.

Excitedly, he tore himself from the device to work with Miriam in the kitchen. By the time Hannah and her family came crashing through the front door, kids in the lead and smiling from ear to ear, the house smelled like shrimp and peppers, sesame oil, and a tantalizing mix of Asian spices. Jack was stir-frying the appetizer, tempura calamari, when Sarah and Matthew ran in to see what he was doing.

"Whoa, kidzos—careful. Not too fast; the oil's hot!" They watched, all smiles, as Jack lifted out the last of the squid. Miriam had already set the table with lit candles. At each place—silverware with optional chopsticks, salads, and large glasses of water with lemon wedges.

"Mom, Dad—this is amazing!" said Hannah as they gathered at the table. "Smells crazy!" added Chet. "What's the occasion?"

"Oh, nothing special," said Jack, shooting a quick wink at Sarah.

"I saw that!" exclaimed Matthew. "There's something they're not telling us!"

"Hey, everyone," said Jack. "Mom's ready to start the meal right away, so let's say grace and dive right in. How's that?"

Everyone quickly agreed, and glancing around, they all joined hands. Jack lifted his prayer, thanking God for the meal and so much goodness within the family through answered prayers, "especially for Kristin who can't be with us now."

Moments after their prayer, Jack and Miriam were sending dishes around for everyone. Jack offered warnings on two of them. "The Szechuan shrimp and vegetables has a bit of a kick to it, and the ginger chicken packs a punch too. If you need to, just push the peppers aside."

"There's also fried basmati rice—that's where you smell the sesame oil—with sugar peas," said Miriam. "The dish with scallops is the big bowl in the center." It wasn't long before dishes were moving in all directions.

"Well, Jack, what's the secret?" asked Chet. "Matthew seems pretty sure you're hiding something. He's usually pretty quick to pick up on those things, especially with you. Both kids're convinced your wink gave it away." All heads turned in Jack's direction.

"I thought I could keep the secret longer," said Jack. "Hmm. Gosh, I'm having a hard time recalling what it was. Well, uh…."

Miriam clasped her hands below her mouth, supporting her chin with two thumbs, enjoying the reactions and wondering how long Jack could extend the charade. Matthew and Sarah were the most vocal, attempting to tease it out of him.

"Gramps," said Matthew. "We all know it's a trick. If you don't tell us, I'll have to throw some calamari in the fish tank."

"We don't have a fish tank, mister know-it-all," replied Jack with a smile.

Sarah took a swing at it. "Grampa, you know I've always liked your stories at bedtime. But, not any more. No more bedtime stories unless you tell us."

"That's not fair!" exclaimed Jack. "Why, that's just gang warfare, you two. I know when to surrender." He looked at Miriam, who was still smiling quietly. "Miriam, rescue me, will ya? Tell 'em it's all a hoax and nothing's up."

Miriam dropped her hands to the table and surveyed the faces. "Well…," she started, making sure she had their attention. "We got some news late last night. Some really good news."

"Mom…what is it? Does it have to do with Kristin? My food's getting cold," said Hannah.

"Well, dear. Yes, it does. Kristin called to say something, and Grampa will tell you all about it!"

Whew. Jack was sure she'd give it away, but they'd rehearsed the deception while cooking together. He smiled at her resolve.

"Aw, c'mon, Mom!" said Hannah, still enjoying the moment. Chet lowered his chin, trying to contain his amusement but yielded to chest-heaving hilarity.

"Mom, 'fess up," said Hannah, again turning her attention back to Miriam.

Miriam glanced at Jack, then at her watch. Smiling, she said, "It's almost six, Jack. Go get your new toy."

As Jack left the dining area, the family enjoyed a new round of laughter at his expense. When he returned, Jack was carrying a sizeable electronic gadget.

"He's a pretty smart guy, that Jack Soelberg," said Chet.

"You bet I am," agreed Jack, returning the smile. "I've joined the digital age and am now master of this new device, almost as good as a Star Trek transporter beam." Sarah sat, still smiling and wiping "happy tears" from her cheeks, appraising her grandfather.

"Dad—you're kidding me," said Hannah. "You bought the latest, greatest electronic toy before we even had a chance to beat you to it?"

"Yup, that's me. Always known for my talents at staying ahead of the curve," replied Jack while setting the device down on the table next to Miriam. He activated it, then dialed Kristin's number. Within seconds, Kristin's face appeared. "Hi, all!" she said as Jack swung the large screen in a slow arc so that she could see everyone. There were abundant, joyous greetings.

"So, hey, sis—Dad's got this new toy, but we're also sure he's hiding some sort of secret. We don't know yet, but we're certain there's more to it," said Hannah. "Most of all, we're glad you could join us for dinner!"

"It's great to see all of you! Matthew and Sarah—have you guys grown since we were in Indy? My gosh, you look so grown up." Kristin had just finished a stir fry she'd made for herself, by design. She pulled her plate closer to a tall glass of water and repositioned her cell phone for a better FaceTime picture. "It's a bit early for my dinner. I made a small lunch today so I could eat with you."

Kristin thrust her nose into the camera and made wafting motions with her hands. "Smells great over there! I'm jealous!"

"Well, you see, Mom and Dad and I did in fact hatch a plan," continued Kristin as she pulled back to a full-frame view of herself. "That is, for me to join you for the meal. How'd we do? Are you surprised?"

"Aw, c'mon, y'all—I can't eat my meal like this!" complained Hannah, laughing. "I know for a fact there's more to it. 'Fess up!" Chet scooted his chair closer to Hannah, then put an arm around her and smiled, enjoying the exchange between sisters.

Jack looked at Miriam and nodded. Miriam moved close to the big screen and whispered to Kristin, knowing that all would hear. "They're ready, dear. Give it to 'em."

Kristin looked at the small image of her family. It was time to share the good news. "So, um, Hannah," she began. "Mom tells me you have a friend in the real estate business, and that you probably know a good OBGYN."

"Yeah. Well, I do . . ." replied Hannah with glances around the table, lingering longer as she probed the eyes of her mother and father. She then stared at the screen and smiled, enlarging her eyes for effect. "So...."

"Well, I'll be looking for a home nearby and a good doc for my baby girls. My plane arrives next Wednesday. I'm bailing out," said Kristin with the broadest smile her family had seen in more than a decade.

For a split second, there was total silence, then a deafening cheer. Everyone began to talk at once. It was an hour before the call ended, with shared excitement and stir fry at both ends of the call. Jack and Miriam got to bed early that night, enjoying the best night's sleep they'd had in months.

19

HELEN'S RELEASE

SEVERAL DAYS AFTER HER VISIT with Kristin in Gil's home, Mary went to a café for lunch just around the corner from her gallery. With her order in hand, she noticed there were plenty of empty tables. But Mary felt an urge, almost like she was being guided to explore the back section toward the café's rear door.

Mary looked once and then again to verify it; there sat Hell (Mary much preferred her full name, Helen) in one of the booths. Mary barely recognized her. She'd never before seen her natural auburn hair. And, she wore a beautiful multi-colored dress with a splash of jewelry.

"Is this seat taken?" Mary asked. Halfway through a large salad, Hell quickly closed a book. As she slipped it onto her lap, Mary caught the familiar title (*My Utmost for His Highest*). When she looked up, Mary was surprised to see her natural hazel eyes.

"Please do," she said, smiling as she pulled her plate a bit closer to avail table space for Mary.

Mary began to say, "I'm glad to see you…."

"It's Helen now. I ditched the old name. Time for change and a new direction," Helen said, smiling again. Mary returned the smile and put her sandwich and drink on the table.

"I must say I like your full name a lot more," replied Mary. She then added, "Excuse me for just a moment." Mary's head dropped, and she closed her eyes. Helen watched as her hands came together, and then her lips moved almost imperceptibly. Moments later, Mary lifted her head and looked directly into Helen's eyes.

"What did you pray about?"

Helen's question was certainly direct, so Mary figured that a candid reply was warranted.

"Well, Helen, I thanked God for the goodness I see in you. You've changed, and it's noticeable. In fact, I'm rather startled by it, so much so that I needed to lift you in prayer and thanksgiving. I hope that's okay with you."

They smiled at each other momentarily. Helen broke the silence with a friendly warning that, if Mary waited any longer to eat, her sandwich would grow cold. "Tell you what," added Helen, "you eat and I'll talk. Okay with you?"

Mary nodded as she took her first nip of an everything bagel with roast beef and smoked swiss cheese, grilled to perfection. Noticing Helen's eyes on the big sandwich, studded with garlic and onion bits, Mary laughed and said, "Missed breakfast this morning, and no clients that I know of this afternoon! They call it their 'Trail Boss,' but hey, if you don't mind me chomping through this like a cavewoman, I'm all ears. Want a piece?"

Helen laughed with her. "No thanks, but it sure looks good!" Helen's story began shortly after the LA arts event. Her boyfriend of more than nine months (Mary recalled seeing him a few times and remembered his eyes) was a salesman of medical devices; he'd grown impatient, preoccupied. Helen added that, shortly after they met, he moved in with her and paid her rent with cash. "He was nice enough, a great looking guy—but then I was more attracted to the dark, sinister types too. He loved to eat out at all the nice restaurants, always paying with cash. But, he only used his last name…or his first. I may never know."

Mary's face, too involved in a big bite of the Trail Boss, communicated bewilderment.

"Oh, his name is Malbas," added Helen. "First name or last, I have no idea. He told me it was a European custom to use just a single name. It sounded odd to me, but I took him at his word."

Helen went on to explain that Malbas had taken several back-to-back trips and was growing more frustrated after each return. When he returned from Ohio, he was restless and unhappy. She grew suspicious when he refused to talk with her about the source of his irritation. Had a big sale gone sour? Was he being demoted? He wouldn't say.

It wasn't long before Malbas flew off to Indianapolis. That is, if he'd been truthful about the destination. The more she thought about it, the more suspicious she became. He'd disappear without taking a change of clothes, and once, when she asked him what airline he flew on, he tried to slam the conversation shut, replying that he flew on whatever airline Western Travel arranged for him. The travel agency was just a few streets away; a good friend of hers worked there. Her friend at Western Travel assured her that they knew of no such guy.

Malbas had been vague about everything. About his Russian/Eastern European accent, he dismissed her interest in his heritage. He'd said that his parents were simply dead. He referred to a couple of brothers and sisters but offered no further detail.

She once asked about a previous love. "His face contorted into an awful snarl," continued Helen. "The only thing he was willing to talk about were his travels."

Apparently, Malbas had been all over the world and recalled astounding details about every country she could ask about. For hours, he spoke about Latvia, Cuba, Australia, Mongolia, China, Burma, and the Mariana Islands. He told her he'd found the perfect pizza in a small town in Ohio, smothered in anchovies and cayenne pepper. "Where haven't you been?" she stammered. Without missing a beat, he replied: "Alaska, Transylvania, the Shetland Islands, and Bozeman, Montana."

"Where's your mail?" she asked several weeks after he moved in.

"Mail?"

"Yeah, I thought you'd change your address and that phone bills or insurance papers might arrive here," she added. In reply, Malbas stammered something about having a safety deposit box at the post office.

"Now that I recall that conversation, I think he meant to say that he had a post office box. I checked at nearby post offices. Nothing. Of course, I had only 'Malbas' to go on. He had no paper trail. No bills, no bank accounts. Nothing.

"A few weeks ago, he just disappeared," added Helen. "He left behind a few pieces of clothing but nothing else. He had a cell phone that I've called every day. No replies to calls or texts."

"No family nearby? No friends or colleagues? No inquiries from customers or work?" asked Mary.

"Nope. Not a one," replied Helen. "So, I've begun to pay my rent again, and it seems I've closed one door to open another. I've since met a really nice guy who's given me a whole new outlook. Turns out his mother's a fabulous musician and his father's an artist. I didn't wear my 'goat' contacts the night I met him and decided that I didn't like them after all. As for clothes, when I returned home a week ago to get some of my old stuff, my Mom decided that since I'd chosen to ditch the all-black clothing, she liked shopping with me. Dad was glad to see me, too. Tomorrow, I plan to introduce them to Aaron, my new friend. He seems pretty serious about our relationship, so all of a sudden a bunch of good things have happened. Aaron says it's not just by chance; he says it's God's doing."

Mary's sandwich was gone, and her smile was studded with small flecks of garlic and onion. Helen laughed. She reached to the side of the booth to extract a wrapped toothpick from the table dispenser and gave it to Mary. They laughed again as Mary pushed the toothpick through its wrapper.

"As for Malbas: poof. He just disappeared," continued Helen. "I'm almost afraid he'll come around the bend any minute with plans to pick up where he left off. A week into our relationship, I told Aaron about him. The next day he told me that he prayed about it. In the morning he called me to say something sorta peculiar. He said that, in prayer, God told him that Malbas was gone for good."

Mary smiled, showing no flecks of garlic or onions this time, while enjoying the company of a completely changed, rejuvenated young woman.

"I'm so glad for you, Helen. Have you and Aaron spoken about his faith?" asked Mary.

"We have. He's taught me so much in such a short time.

You know, Mary—Christ is alive. He loves me and he wants me to be with him desperately," said Helen.

"'Faith never knows where it's being led, but it loves and knows the One who is leading'," replied Mary, smiling. "Here's another: 'We tend to use prayer as a last resort, but God wants it to be our first line of defense.'"

Helen's face conveyed confusion.

"They're not a perfect fit, but I remember both quotes from Oswald Chambers," added Mary.

"Oh, yes! You must've seen the book," countered Helen, pulling it from her lap; she'd forgotten it was there. It was an old version of Chambers' daily devotional. "I've never read anything like it. Aaron tells me there are a lot of great devotionals these days. His father said that he grew up with this one and insisted that I have it for a year. There's a page for each day. It's a bit deep, but I've found it to be an amazing source of confidence and insight. And, more importantly, a lovely way to know more about God's love for all of us. Even for me."

"And, even for me," smiled Mary. "Tell me, Helen—what are you doing now? How's your art coming along?"

"Funny you'd ask. There's been a nice change in that direction too," replied Helen. "Aaron's father referred me to a fantastic teacher. I've always enjoyed oils, but now I'm getting to new levels. And it feels like my fixation with death and suffering are behind me. No more Hieronymus Bosch."

As the conversation came to an easy conclusion, Mary asked Helen to stop in at the gallery with her new work. "We'll work out the details of a consignment sale if you like. And, hey—maybe even a part-time position if you're interested."

20

THE CRUCIFIX + THE TOOL

Kristin had already booked her one-way flight to Cleveland for the following Wednesday, so there were just a few remaining needs before leaving California. She spent most of the next day packing and making calls to her bank and creditors.

That evening in prayer, Kristin thought of Mary—the new friend who'd quickly become a source of warmth and godly counsel. As she read the David Jeremiah Bible that Mary had given her, now personalized with margin notes and highlights, Kristin decided to send her a quick text:

Hi, Mary. I'm studying the New Testament and thought I'd reach out. I've got important news to share. Is the gallery open tomorrow? You in? I'll stop by.

Her phone chirped seconds later.

You bet! Driving south?

Yes! I'd like to see you. I'll leave in time to do lunch if that works. The drive offers some thinking time and prayer time too. (The eyes-open sorta prayer!)

LOL. Perfect. See you soon!

Kristin's big change could've been unsettling, but there

seemed to be loving confirmation in all facets of her life lately—such as her ability to sleep for eight hours that night and the buoyant mood she felt as she scooped out a cup of homemade granola at sunrise. She'd kept Miriam's cereal recipe for a decade but had only just recently made a batch of it. If she was going to pivot and spin toward a better quality of life, this was the time to do things she'd ignored or avoided. Besides, a healthy diet now served three.

A quick glance in the mirror before leaving was early confirmation of her improved lifestyle. Gone were the signs of "terminal aging" she'd assumed were irreversible: bags under her eyes and deep furrows in her brow. *I must've been a real sight during that last trip to LA with Gil,* she thought, recalling the bitterness and discomfort that prompted restless sleep, twitching nerves, and chest pains. She didn't miss the hangovers, either. This trip to LA would be different. By a long shot.

Kristin listened to sermons by Dr. David Jeremiah and R. C. Sproul as she drove south. The messages were inspiring and intellectually and spiritually challenging. So incredibly wise. The voice in the back of her mind kept coming back to the same question: *How could I have been so self-absorbed and stupid to ignore God's simple directive: trust, obedience, and prayer?*

A burst of motorcycle taillights brought her attention back to Highway One. Eight bikes, traveling together, eased around a bend in the highway. She slowed, keeping her distance. The road was essentially scratched out of the mountainside—a sheer wall to the left and a precipitous drop into the Pacific on her right.

Her mind wandered again. Kristin considered the irony of

contemplating God's truths in Psalm 46 while driving parallel to (and on the wrong side of) the San Andreas fault. "God is our refuge and strength…Therefore we will not fear, though the earth give way and the mountains fall into the heart of the sea, though its waters roar and foam and the mountains quake with their surging…."

Prophetic of some giant, geologic slide—right here? I suspect it's just a matter of time, she mused. A year, a decade, a century? She imagined the mountainside and all that stone coming undone, sliding into the sea. The more convinced she became of the goodness of her decision to leave California, the concept of her own seismic fissure—now repairing and cementing itself closed—was apparent. She was sure that her new life's directive would bring wholeness to the gaping rift she'd created between herself and the God she loved.

With the windows of her car open, the sweet smell of wild chamomile flew at her in heady sea-breeze torrents. She ventured an occasional gaze out to the Pacific Ocean before Highway One turned briefly inland behind Malibu.

Kristin looked up suddenly to see that the bikers were all slowing to observe two workers on a platform, pasting the last panel of a large billboard into position. Three women, back seat riders, raised their hands while pointing skyward in affirmation. The bold message was for all: Every sinner has a past. Every child of God has a future.

"Thank you, Lord," she whispered.

As she entered the heat and congestion of LA, Kristin reluctantly turned off the spiritual guidance, swapping it for GPS as she followed directions to Mary's LifeLine Gallery. She was delighted to find a parking space nearby. Kristin was struck by the incongruity of her last walk here with Gil—recalling his forceful insistence that she leave Mary's gallery—and the serenity and confidence she now felt as she approached LifeLine. A small bell attached to the door jingled as Kristin entered and walked to the desk where a receptionist concluded a phone call, then looked into Kristin's eyes.

In an instant, Kristin was transported back to her visit to the nearby LSD gallery months earlier. She found herself looking into a strangely familiar face, a young woman with a pleasant smile and clear eyes. Yet as Kristin's memory gradually reassembled the pieces of a haunted visage with goat eyes, Helen spoke.

"Hi. You must be Kristin. Mary said to expect you. We've met before, but things have changed. I, um…."

"I recall," said Kristin. "Gosh, how things have changed. I'm so glad to meet you again," Kristin extended her hand.

"I had an unfortunate relationship, one that was taking me off course," explained Helen, standing, warmly grasping Kristin's hand.

"Isn't that funny? Me too!" replied Kristin, offering a hug. They embraced as Mary entered from a door behind the desk. Helen released Kristin just in time for the two of them to wrap their arms around each other. "Mary!" exclaimed Kristin. "I'm so glad to see you!"

"And to have you here again!" said Mary. She slowly released Kristin, turning to Helen. "Helen, you and Kristin have become reacquainted, right?" They both nodded, smiling. "What you may not know yet is we are all, now, sisters in Christ."

"What a gift," said Helen and again stepped toward Kristin. The three of them embraced with shared laughter.

"My oh my how God works wonders," added Mary.

"Each of us has come to Christ through very different circumstances, but the important thing is that we're here, and our commitment is real."

Mary asked Helen to show Kristin her new work. Mary had given Helen the gallery's most prominent display area. It was apparent to Kristin that Helen was immensely talented. Two of her five oil paintings were marked Sold. One of the pieces was different: it was a small pastel painting of two crimson, bean-shaped pods floating in a pool of deep blue. Kristin stepped closer to admire the skillful brushwork and textures. A simple maple frame completed it.

"That's for you," said Helen.

Kristin turned toward her with a look of confusion. "For me?"

"Yup. Mary and I spoke after you texted her last night; she said you'd visit and—well, I remembered scaring the wits out of you with my Bosch art! She also told me about your two girls. Well, there they are," explained Helen. "They may be further along by now, but this is what came to me this morning when I painted it. I just finished framing it 20 minutes ago. My way of saying I'm sorry for upsetting you that day."

"Helen, that's crazy, and amazing! I love it," beamed Kristin. A tear forced itself out as she reached again for Helen. "You shouldn't have done that. How can I thank you? This means so much to me. Especially now that…I'm leaving."

Both Helen and Mary locked eyes with Kristin. They stood for a moment, wordlessly, until Mary broke the spell.

"When you texted that you had news to share," interjected Mary, smiling brightly, "it was almost as though the

Holy Spirit tapped me on the shoulder and said, 'I'll let you in on her secret.'" Helen and Mary laughed; Kristin was stunned. "So I told Helen this morning my money's on your return home to be with family," added Mary. "Which also means you've likely made a career choice too."

"Ohio, right?" asked Helen.

"That's right," replied Kristin, wiping an eye. "And yes," looking at Mary, "a career choice. Talk about a nudge from the Holy Spirit!"

Mary and Kristin enjoyed a long lunch, sitting at the same table where she and Helen dined recently. Mary told Kristin of that meeting, and her surprise at Helen's revelation of her new faith in Christ. "You both became committed Christians at about the same time," said Mary. "I'm always in awe of God's mysterious ways!"

"Well, they're still new to me, but no less startling," said Kristin. They spent most of the time talking about Kristin's encounter with Nova. At last, they agreed that, once Kristin had settled in, Mary would visit. Mary explained that she took trips to New York at least once or twice a year.

Back at the gallery, Helen had wrapped Kristin's new artwork. Helen wouldn't accept anything for it. Though, with some prodding, Mary agreed to give Helen the cash that Kristin sealed into an envelope for her. Their parting was bittersweet, tempered by plans for a joyous reunion.

"My entire family looks forward to meeting you, Mary. You led me to Christ. My parents already refer to you as 'Saint Mary.'" They laughed and embraced.

FOUR DAYS LATER, Kristin boarded her flight for Cleveland. Her handbag's only oddity, the cause of momentary interest to the TSA agent staring at an X-ray image of the bag, was a small, well-padded painting. The TSA agent considered cutting it open, but took one look at Kristin—joyously radiant and unconcerned—and let it go. Two Bibles and a few other personal items caused no curiosity.

Kristin's flight was flawless and peaceful. Toward the back of the cabin, a physician named I. M. Gabriel, kept a watchful eye on her. At mid-flight, when she got up to use the restroom, he lifted his magazine.

At baggage claim, Jack and Miriam greeted her with many hugs. The doctor, observing from a distant spot, smiled when he saw their reunion. "Praise God," he said quietly, then disappeared.

Shortly after Jack turned off the highway, Kristin emitted a snort. "Whoa! What's that awful smell?" she cried. Though the windows were up, Jack smiled when he saw a farmer dressing soil in a nearby field.

"That my dear is the sweet smell of back country goodness—only the best of rural Ohio! Take a look over there," he said, pointing to a slowly moving tractor connected to a large wagon. From the rear of the wagon, a paddle-like contraption launched huge gobs of wet cow manure in a wide spiral. "We're surrounded on all sides by farmers, and this is what they do every couple of weeks, all year long. Ain't it great?"

Miriam turned to smile at Kristin. "Please excuse your father. He's trying to make the best of it. You'll get used to it. I have. Well, sort of."

While pulling into the garage, Kristin smiled at a banner stretched across the front entrance of her parents' new home—Welcome HOME, Kristin! As soon as they entered the house, joyous noise began.

Weeks earlier, Kristin learned from her parents that they had a spacious guest room for her—hers as long as she wanted it. But she hadn't expected one with its own bathroom and large windows that looked out on Miriam's garden, now in full bloom. As Matthew and Sarah tugged her baggage into the room, Kristin saw that her mother had gathered flowers, making gorgeous arrangements for each nightstand, the dresser, and both windowsills. When Kristin turned to say how happy she was, tears of joy got in the way but were soon replaced with laughter at the kids' antics; Matthew almost spilled one of the arrangements, and Sarah was jumping on the bed.

FIVE MONTHS LATER, Kristin, now rounding out nicely, continued to review local real estate postings. She'd made quick friends with Janet, a diligent realtor who'd found a few three-bedroom homes within her means. "If I'd had any reservations about leaving California, buying a home certainly isn't one of them, Mom," she said while the two of them ate salad in the kitchen. "My dollar has three or four times the buying power here."

Miriam nodded contemplatively. "That is good news, but there's a much bigger goodness in it for us," she said, looking closely at her daughter. "Jack and I have talked about this so many times during the past several weeks. You and your babies have blessed our lives beyond the best of what we could've imagined. It was wonderful for us to move here to be near to Hannah's family. But now this—you, here, and with your girls growing each day—it's wonderful beyond words, an answer to prayers."

"Oh, Mom, I'm so glad to hear you say that. My prayers

are being answered too." Kristin reached over to rest a hand on her mother's.

"Come to think of it, part of the blessing is in what you just said," added Miriam.

"Hm?" questioned Kristin.

"Well, your prayers and your commitment to Christ. How could I be happier? I'll tell you how: you've called me Mom. For months now. I didn't mention it because I didn't want to break the spell," continued Miriam. "It's just so rewarding, sweetheart."

Kristin slowly rose, then half-knelt at her mother's chair to give her a lingering hug. When there was a knock at the door, Kristin gave her mother's shoulders a squeeze before walking into the hallway.

Miriam heard a jovial welcome and a voice that was familiar, but one she couldn't immediately place. She turned the corner to see Kristin beaming. Janet, her realtor friend, had come to deliver some news. Miriam beckoned them toward the den.

"I have a very interesting story for you, and it leads to great news," said Janet. "Last week, Kristin, we explored the possibility of three homes. All suitable, all nice, and all passing inspection with flying colors. But the Asher's home, right here in the same development as yours, is just a block away," she added, casting a cheerful glance at Miriam. "It was least likely; we knew that. It's immaculate and has no issues. The professional couple was selling the home themselves, for sale by owner.

"They listed the home earlier this year, then took it off the market a few months later," continued Janet. "For whatever reason, they reconsidered. So, just 10 days ago, they re-listed it themselves, again as a 'fizbo,' though inviting agents with an incentive. But, one of the agent comments I found online—sorta strange—stated that the couple was reluctant to sell. Go figure. They've had more visitors through the home recently, and some very good offers, but they accepted none of them.

"Then you and I visited, Kristin, just as they were leaving the house to go somewhere. As you'll recall, they decided to stay. It seemed to both of us that, when they noted your pregnancy, they wanted to know more about you, becoming quite welcoming and chatty," added Janet.

Then, turning to Miriam, she said, "If Kristin didn't mention it, the couple asked about her pregnancy, learning about the twins; we could tell there were some emotions. Gradually, they revealed that they can't have children. A little while later, they asked about the position Kristin left in California. There was great surprise and then astonishment to learn that it was a decision based on Kristin's faith. There was a spark of excitement when both recalled the network TV news of Kristin's collapse, and presto—they had a real live hero in their midst.

"Here's the kicker," added Janet. "They called me an hour ago. Apparently, yesterday was a very big day. A lot of prayers were answered. I learned that the Ashers have been on a waiting list for a sibling adoption for more than four years. Yesterday morning, they heard from the adoption agency: their made-to-order family of three young children, siblings, was approved. They learned an hour later that their offer on a farm house was accepted. That's when they decided to sell the house to you, Kristin. It's almost like there was some heavenly orchestrating going on with pieces falling into place one after the other."

"You mean it? Just like that?" exclaimed Kristin, looking at her mother, then at Janet. "The home is mine?"

"Just like that," answered Janet. "Even though your offer was substantially less than some of the others they received, they'd like you to have the home because of your decision to leave the organization. They want to enable you and your girls to be right here, within walking distance of your family."

Miriam stood and held her arms out to Kristin, smiling. Kristin stood to hug her mother. "In all my years of real estate work, I think this is about the sweetest outcome I've been a part of," Janet said. "The Ashers hope to move next weekend, so you won't have long to wait."

"Oh, Mom—this is so amazing. It really is an answer to prayers, isn't it?" asked Kristin.

"Yes it is," said Miriam.

Later, Hannah congratulated her sister. "My oh my, sis," she said to Kristin. "Never in my wildest dreams would I have anticipated this. What an incredible joy to have you here, and soon as a mommy and a neighbor. God has blessed us mighty hard."

Before turning in for the evening, Jack phoned Kay Zavala, expecting to leave a voicemail message. She picked up on the second ring. Soon, Jack was giving the latest family news to Kay. She shared their success at getting the old surgical tool back to the museum. It wasn't long before they turned their attention to the enigma of Nova's letters.

"Jack, I've passed the notes around among several of the world's best graphologists—handwriting experts," she explained. "These are the folks who for decades have taught handwriting analysis at the highest levels and serve as forensic experts to the world's top courts. They're my mentors, the pros I turn to when I'm stumped.

"We're all mystified," she added. "Nova's notes, beginning with your first letter decades ago, and now most recently Kristin's letter, and all the others in between, are perplexing. Nova's intellect, theology, and perspective, and the nature of the handwriting itself, were beyond my reach, Jack. Now all of my mentors are baffled. We all agree that it's the toughest assignment we've seen. You may or may not want to hear the analysis, Jack."

"I do. That is, if you're willing to share it," he replied.

"Of course. After all, you shared the letters with us. No matter how we diagnose the letters' content or style—then add the profound mystery of the many decades involved, and Nova's intimate knowledge of your lives—she's outside our ability to define. She's an extraterrestrial, Jack. The mystery leaves us with the impression that she may not be of this world."

"That's amazing, Kay. That you and the other experts to come to the same conclusion," said Jack. "Incredible. As Christians, Miriam and I believe in miracles. It seems to me that we've come face-to-face with one."

THE NEXT EVENING, the family adults gathered after dinner to discuss Jack's most recent call with Kay. All of Nova's letters were placed on the table, arranged chronologically, beginning with Jack's first note, delivered the day after Hannah's was born, referencing his experience in 'Nam and calling attention to the attack that took the lives of his best friends. The documents, spread neatly across the dining room table, including a copy of the letter sent to Dr. Harley, ended with Nova's most recent dispatch to Kristin. The letters represented a spread of 35 years.

Hannah's photo of the surgical tool and the small crucifix necklace were placed below the note from Nova addressed to her.

The group's discussion was mostly glum; it seemed as though they themselves were surprised at its tone. Kristin had opened the discussion, a bit unsure of where to begin. But her comments at least got things off to a start. The antique surgical tool was discussed in detail, though Kristin hadn't seen it. Hannah and Chet described its working mechanisms. Kristin told them about the latest cranial perforators: "Fully-automated, high-speed excavating devices with a 100-percent mortality rate."

Kristin touched the necklace. "Oh, sis, that's for you," said Hannah. "Nova was clear about that. She said that you'd need to return it to its owner, when the time's right."

Kristin pulled it toward her, examining it with curiosity. "That's it? No more to go on than that?" she asked.

"Nope. Not yet," replied Hannah.

Jack told them about the tool's return to the museum and mentioned Kay's most recent revelations. Then they turned their attention to Nova's letters, the first and last of which drew the greatest interest. Initially, Jack found it very difficult to speak with his daughters about Vietnam, especially anything that led to "the wall."

Miriam helped move him through his retelling of the attack that would have surely sent him home in a body bag had it not been for the miracle of Nova's interference.

Jack referred to Nova as "his shield." Previously, he'd

spoken rarely of the war with Hannah but never before with Kristin. On this evening, she was next to him with one hand on her belly and the other draped around his shoulder as he spoke about how the lives of his good friends were lost. Miriam was so thankful that Jack could, at last, convey the weight of it. Miriam's prayers swirled aloft.

They talked about the other letters: their spot-on accuracy and timing, their poignance, direction, and love; even the references to Kristin's now-abandoned career. They also spoke about the mysterious doctor, Gabriel. Miriam and Jack retold the story of their initial meeting with him—and Miriam expressed how, when she saw him again in Indianapolis, he looked exactly as she remembered him.

Gabriel was a source of fascination, as was Malbas. After all, each of the sisters (and Samantha, Hannah reminded them) had encounters with the sinister character. The conversation moved as details were sewn in through recollection or through Nova's letters. Hannah became the default secretary, writing copious notes.

Eventually, Hannah and Miriam settled on the obscurity of the surgical tool.

Jack pondered his earlier conversation with Kay Zavala about the mystery of the cross and the tool. Thinking to himself, he remembered saying that they were symbolic of the cosmic battle between good and evil.

Hannah broke his thoughts, stammering, "How's that awful surgical tool fit into this? Decades ago, Dr. Harley had seen it at a museum in Austria, and then it came into my possession. Why?"

After a lengthy period of silence, with no attempts to unraveled the mystery, Miriam spoke. "Hannah, don't fixate over that despicable tool," she warned. "Let's all admit there are spiritual facets to this. Consider the strange, awful, and amazing occurrences that have happened in just the past several months. Also, the impact in our lives and this crazy mystery that we find ourselves immersed in. There's Jack's first letter from Nova directly tied to his survival of the attack in Vietnam. And, every aspect of Kristin's return to us, and the amazing blessings she's experienced—rather convincingly tied to her being here. So many parts of this defy explanation.

"Consider the timeless blessing of the cross," she continued. "The cross can be everywhere, at all times and in every dimension because Christ avails himself to every person on earth. He sacrificed himself for all of us. Christ knows and desperately loves all of us—each of us—completely, intimately. God knew us long before we were born, and the Holy Spirit comes to live within us should we choose. So, if enormous mysteries like these form an important part of our faith, right here and intertwined with our physical world, why should we obsess over a simple mechanical device that rose from its horrible past to play a role in God's plan?"

Hannah quietly nodded, yielding to her mother's insights.

"Mom's right," agreed Kristin. "She's helped me see it as a final connection. The cross and the tool. It seems that the mystery we've all been immersed in comes down to the tool, representing evil, hatred, and my involvement in the abortion industry; and the cross representing God's love and Christ's sacrifice for all humanity."

Jack looked in dismay at his eldest daughter. "Kristin, you just spoke words from my own heart," he said to her as he moved in for a long hug. She lovingly returned his embrace.

21

JACK FINDS A MIRACLE

SHORTLY AFTER KRISTIN SETTLED on the house that would become her new home, she, Hannah, and Miriam walked through it, visualizing changes. The sisters were quick to see easy, personalized alterations—new plumbing fixtures in the master bath, a wainscot treatment in the dining area, and draperies for the living room. Outside, Hannah was quick to spot ideal locations for a sandbox and swing set.

Kristin's next couple of weeks were an energized blur. She was buying furniture with special attention to the nursery. One day she scheduled the arrival of several trade pros. A painter arrived first. Then, furniture was delivered, and some window treatments came.

A plumber was an hour late, apologizing for the need to take a shower after his last call. He explained to her that a "tree root skewered a sewer main, and you don't want to know anything more about it, believe me."

Kristin quickly noted that not only was Joel the plumber naturally, effortlessly funny, he was about her age and, well, wasn't wearing a wedding band. He made her laugh throughout the day.

Outside, Kristin noticed that Joel's truck—Patriot Plumbing—was artfully wrapped with patriotic signage. She liked that. She also noticed the prominent rear panel cross, about two feet high with the words, "In God We Trust," draped around the cross. On the back bumper was a sticker: "Try Jesus. If you don't like Him, Satan will take you back."

Joel worked efficiently, replacing bathroom fixtures and the master bath toilet. Leaning against the vanity, she asked, "Why 'Patriot Plumbing?'" At the moment, he was assembling the flushing mechanism for her new toilet.

"Well, I served in Iraq, first, and then Afghanistan," he replied. "I owe it to my buddies—those I served with, some of whom never made it home." Instantly, she was transported back to a recent evening at her parent's home when her father explained his tears to her with, essentially, the same words.

That day, Kristin also received delivery of four skids of limestone that she looked forward to stacking neatly around perennial garden beds. The plumber was packing up his truck as the limestone skids were set in place in the side yard with a skid-loader.

"You're ambitious!" he exclaimed, as though noting her expanded size for the first time. "Oh, it'll give me something to do while my girls sleep 12 hours a day," she replied, smiling.

"Twins? Congratulations. And, I hear they always do that," replied Joel. "Twins, that is. Memo to Mom first thing in the morning: We the undersigned, after 12 hours of uninterrupted sleep, hope to schedule our daytime naps to best meet your needs. Wanna stack rocks in the garden? Just tell us when. We won't make a peep!"

"Ha! So, do you have kids of your own?" she ventured.

"Nah. Not yet anyway. First comes marriage, then the baby carriage," he countered.

"So, no Mrs. Patriot Plumbing?"

"Haven't found her yet. Maybe it's my aversion to beer and smoking. Or that I love puppies, apple pie, and the American flag too much. How about you? Is your husband away on a sales trip? Convention?"

"Well, thankfully no knot was tied. I left him behind in California. I found that Cali wasn't right for me in a lot of ways. Grew up in Indianapolis but came to Ohio because of my parents and my sister's family. They live right here in the neighborhood."

She watched him closely, noting a faint smile.

Deftly switching tracks, he turned toward her house. "You've got good ground in this neighborhood. You'll like gardening here; the soil is deep, rich loam. I noticed that side bed you've got over there. It's got real potential. With ample shade, it's a perfect spot for a variety of hostas and liriope. Plant a dogwood or American redbud in the corner. Perfect."

"How's a plumber know so much about soil, trees, and gardening?" she asked.

"Grew up on a farm just a few miles from here with parents who love to garden," he said. "I guess some of it rubbed off. Dad's a Vietnam vet who took over his parent's farm after the war and never looked back. He lost a leg but that didn't slow him down. I have eight siblings and a bunch of nieces and nephews. Somehow, I'm the uncle they most want to play with."

"Amazing. I couldn't help but notice some of your signage, Joel. Do you attend a church around here?"

"Occasionally, my family's church. Too often, I collapse on Sundays. Mostly, I read. History, science, my Bible. I'd like to find a church that's growing and really engaging. It's on my to-do list. Let's just say I'm awaiting miraculous inspiration." He'd buried a double-entendre in there, but she didn't catch it yet.

As Joel finished packing up his truck, Miriam and Jack walked up, holding hands. "All done for the day, honey?" asked Miriam. "Almost, Mom. Hey, let me introduce you to Joel…."

"Miracle," said Joel, smiling. He extended a hand first to Jack, then Miriam. Jack, Miriam, and Kristin all looked at him.

"Oh, I get that look all the time," he said. "Miracle's the last name, plain 'n' simple."

"Hmm. I knew a captain in 'Nam named Miracle," said Jack. "That is an unusual, memorable name."

"Maximus," replied Joel.

Jack stared at Joel, then the truck, trying to put pieces together. Then he studied Joel's face. "Well, I'll be. So you're related to Captain Miracle! AKA, Maximus Miracle or Captain Max. We always thought it was funny—sort of like Captain America. He was a great officer—my first company commander over there. Now if I recall correctly, he lost his legs, right? I was there when the artillery round came in, but your father was a lot closer to the explosion."

"Yes sir. They were able to save one leg. Dad lost the other, but it didn't slow him down a bit. He's still farming. A few of my brothers, sisters, and I help out whenever he and Mom need us, but it's a blessing that he's still doing so well. You served with him, sir?"

"I did. And please call me Jack," replied Kristin's father, now fully engaged. "So your dad is Maximus Miracle. Incredible. You look a lot like him, son. How far is he from here?"

"Oh, just six or seven miles. But, at the moment," he said, glancing at his watch, "maybe twice that. He and Mom are probably at Beiler's Diner by now. Wednesday nights're usually their 'Beiler's outing' for an early dinner."

The men chatted for several more minutes, ending with soldierly backslaps. Kristin and Miriam had given them some space, drifting back several feet. "He was a soldier in Iraq, then Afghanistan, Mom," whispered Kristin. "And, single. Did you see his truck signage? Says he's looking for a good church and the right 'miraculous' woman."

"I sorta wondered if there might be some chemistry when we walked in on your conversation," said Miriam. "I was really taken by his last name. It certainly fits into recent events around here, doesn't it?"

Before leaving, Joel leaned out of the window of his truck. "Kristin," he called out. She turned to him. "Remember the hostas, liriope, and redbud. No charge for your gardening plan. Great choice with the limestone. It'll look great."

She smiled at Joel and waved.

LATER THAT EVENING, assumed to be her last night at Jack and Miriam's house, Kristin was one click of the cursor away from buying an entire playroom full of rock maple building blocks and a fully equipped dollhouse. Looking over her shoulder, Miriam smiled. "Aren't you rushing it just a bit, sweety? You know, Hannah and Chet have a trove of toys to give to you, and there's always Craigslist. And, come to think of it, with all those brothers and sisters, Joel's probably got loads of toys at his disposal too."

"Mom! That's crazy. You know that. We just met," Kristin replied. But she was smiling. In fact, she couldn't get him off of her mind. The online distraction to search for educational toys helped momentarily, but her mother's intuition brought her right back to Joel.

"Have you told Hannah about him?" asked Miriam.

"Yeah. I mentioned him. We just got off the phone."

"Uh-huh. I thought maybe you had. Handy guy who can fix anything. Local roots. Good looking. Unattached. And, he's a Christian soldier, well, Marine," said Miriam. "I'm pretty sure your father's favorably predisposed."

Kristin's phone chirped. She looked at it to find photos of hostas, liriope, a dogwood, and a redbud with a text message from Joel. "Now on sale at Stambaugh Nursery."

Miriam noted Kristin's amusement, smiling. Just then, another image came through from Joel. He'd skillfully drawn the corner of her home, indicating ideal placement of the plants. The text message said, "Couldn't help myself; just throwin' it out there."

"It's a great plan, Joel. Thanks!" she replied.

The next day, while still at the nursery, she decided to tease him with an offer. "Got the plants and then some," she texted. "The redbud looks a bit twiggy, but they assured me that it'll bloom beautifully in April. If you want to demonstrate your farming skills, I'll be planting on Saturday."

That afternoon, he texted in reply. "How's 9 am Sat? I'll bring a shovel."

"Sounds Gr8."

Saturday morning at nine, a freshly washed, deep green Ford F250 pulled up at Kristin's curb. The door opened and out swung a pair of weathered boots. Joel's long jeans were clean, even creased. She watched from the front window as he reached into the bed for a shovel and then opened the back door for a large cluster of cut flowers. She had the door open, greeting him with a smile before he could touch the doorbell.

"Howdy," she said.

"Howdy, ma'am," he replied with a plausible John Wayne drawl. "I hear you've got some gardening to do. We won't, um, plant these though," he added, extending the flowers. "But if you've got a vase, I'm sure they'd like to pretty-up your kitchen."

Kristin welcomed him inside and found an old, blue glass Mason jar left in the pantry by the Ashers. The flowers were a perfect fit. She filled the jar with water and placed it on the kitchen counter.

Outside, Joel was pleasantly surprised to see that she'd purchased a bale of peat moss and several bags of gardening soil and fertilizer. They spent most of the morning planting perennials and the six-foot redbud; Kristin wanting to put more physical labor into the task than Joel allowed, given her near-burst condition.

An hour into Joel's visit, Jack and Miriam walked by un-noticed, both smiling as though they'd pulled off a successful reconnaissance mission. They got a glimpse of the gardening work in progress. "Prayers aloft," whispered Miriam as they turned the corner.

Kristin and Joel ate lunch together on the back porch. She'd flawlessly replicated her mother's fresh lemonade recipe. She served BLTs with a garden salad. "You don't eat like a plumber," she said, chuckling.

"Oh, Mom made sure we kids had some etiquette. In my trade, though, it's all about clean hands," he replied.

"Oh, yeah, I guess that'd be important," she said, smiling.

Throughout the day, their conversation ranged from growing up to school experiences, his military service, and her work in California.

"I'm so glad that you left that work," he told her as the sun angled westward. He was tossing his shovel into the bed of the truck, dusting off his pants. She'd walked him to the truck's door. He turned to her and, for just a moment, was tongue-tied.

"Kristin—I, uh, have a confession to make."

"Uh-oh. Here it comes." When he didn't laugh, she regretted it. There was an extended pause.

"Joel, I'm beginning to wish I wouldn't've said that."

"It's okay," he replied. Then, with an awkward start, he revealed that there was once an intended Mrs. Joel Miracle. While he was in college, close to completing a degree in engineering, his girlfriend Julia became pregnant. Unknown to him at the time, Julia aborted the baby. The experience pulled her into three torturous months of self-recrimination, concluding with her suicide. Both lives were lost. The day after her funeral, he went into the recruiting station to become a Marine.

"I'm so sorry," Kristin said.

"It's okay. The Marines knocked it right outta me. It was a package deal: six years of recovery, active-duty patriotism, and boy-becomes-man all in one. Gave me the money to complete my degree, but then I realized I didn't want a desk job after all. So, this. I also realized never, ever again to be cavalier with a relationship, saving babies for the sanctity of marriage."

She immediately looked at her toes. The force of his own words struck him. "Hey, Kristin—I'm sorry. I didn't mean it that way...."

"No, it's okay. I deserve a reminder now 'n' then about the life I left behind. Looks like we've both discovered a few of each other's secrets and sensitivities, huh? Yet, God's given me concrete reasons to know that I'm not only forgiven, but that the best lies ahead—including the lives of these two," she said as both of her hands moved to her tummy.

He smiled, then reached for the door's handle, seconds before lifting himself into the truck. At that moment, it seemed as though he was attentive to her every nuance. She leaned forward slightly. So he risked the reach and a hug. She turned to the side just enough not to put the babies between them. She held on a moment longer than he'd expected, enjoying each extra second of her embrace.

THE FOLLOWING WEDNESDAY, Kristin set up her Mac in a space she'd arranged as an office. The first email to find her was from Mary. "Hey, Kristin—looks like I'll be in New York City within the next month or so. Would there be a good time to visit? Can't wait to see you."

Kristin's eyes fell immediately on a calendar. She'd highlighted Thanksgiving Day: her OBGYN told her eight weeks earlier to expect delivery around the end of November. "Wednesday, Thursday, or Friday," ventured her doc. "But I'd place my bet on Thanksgiving." Kristin replied to Mary, suggesting a mid-December visit.

Late in the afternoon, recalling what Joel had said a week earlier about his father's regular mid-week trips to Beiler's Diner, Jack and Miriam decided to eat dinner there. Jack hoped that he might bump into his CO from decades ago, Captain Miracle. As they walked into the diner, Jack quickly surveyed the interior, noticing a "Stammtisch" sign hanging over a well-used corner table and, below it, a man and woman sharing a meal.

The place was packed and, though the Stammtisch table sat six, Jack and Miriam knew the German sign meant "reserved for regulars." They began to move back toward the entry to wait for a seat, and Jack looked closely at the man; he was just three or five years older, and there were facial characteristics that reminded him of his old CO. Jack risked a quick glance under the table. A glint of metal, going into the left shoe, confirmed it. Jack turned to Miriam. "Honey, it's him. That man was my company CO in 'Nam—Maximus Miracle."

"Go ahead, Jack," she encouraged, "Introduce yourself." But of course she knew he would. Jack moved toward the table. As soon as the man noticed Jack's lingering glance, he stood up. Without asking for an introduction, he simply said, "Won't you join us? Don't let the sign scare you. This table's wide open to friends."

Jack turned to Miriam, smiling, and waved her forward. Jack then turned toward the table, stood erect, and snapped a salute. "Captain Miracle, it's an honor to see you again, sir."

Maximus saluted in return, then moved toward Jack. "So we know each other, soldier?" he asked Jack.

"Yes, we do," replied Jack as the men first shook hands, followed by warm hugs and back-slaps. Jack recounted the explosion that took Captain Miracle's leg and recalled how the helicopter, brought in for him, was almost knocked out of the sky by antiaircraft fire. Before long, the soldiers were comparing notes while the women became acquainted.

It wasn't long before Miriam learned from Barbara that she met Max while serving as a Navy nurse on the USS

Repose hospital ship, filled to the gunnels with wounded soldiers. Though Max had lost his leg, his charisma and heart won the interest of his caregiver. Barbara's tour of duty ended three months after Max returned to the family farm. He was soon to learn that work on the rural homestead, and then the love of the nurse who came for a visit and stayed, were the best rehabilitation a man could hope for.

THE NEXT DAY, Jack knocked on Kristin's door. He wanted to tell her how impressed he was with Maximus and Barbara Miracle. He recounted a few moments from their visit with them at the diner.

"And...Joel?" she asked.

"Huh?"

"You say you're impressed with mom 'n' pop Miracle. But, what about Joel?"

"Oh! Yeah, of course. Hey, what a fine young man. I guess I should've said something to you about him too. Just smack me when I forget how to be a dad, huh? Well, here's why I came over—Max and Barbara invited us out to visit their farm this weekend. Wanna join us? They tell me Joel will be there, something to do with harvesting corn. "Hey, but wait," he added. "Is that a weekend we should be putting on alert for the twins?"

"Not yet, Pa," she replied sweetly. "That'd be two weeks too soon. Getting close, though. My doc says we can expect 'them on Thanksgiving Day."

ON SATURDAY MORNING, Jack, Miriam, and Kristin arrived at Miracle Ranch, a 280-acre farm just ten minutes from their own neighborhood. The property included a large,

1860s limestone farmhouse and bank barn, three Harvestore silos, a field decorated with round haybales looking like giant shredded wheat, tobacco hanging in a drying barn, and big machinery hard at work in a tall carpet of field corn. Maximus, Barbara, and a gaggle of black labs, a mother and eight pups, came out to greet them.

After introductions, Kristin quietly made her way to a bench below a giant oak tree near the home's front door. Maximus and Barbara had already heard from Joel about Kristin, but they refrained from telling her that she'd quickly become an all-consuming topic with him.

Maximus and Barbara broke away from Kristin's parents momentarily to join her. "Joel's in the harvester," Barbara told her, pointing to a gargantuan machine with what appeared to be a huge, spinning paddlewheel in front. At the rear of the machine, a large truck followed, taking a steady stream of corn seed. Gradually, the equipment eliminated the standing corn. "That's a big lawn mower," said Kristin. Max and Barbara laughed. She added, "The truck behind Joel's harvester will soon be full, so he'll join us shortly. I'm sure he knows you're here by now." Maximus made a point to say how glad he was that they could visit.

As Joel's parents moved away, the black labs moved in. The mother, Ella, collapsed her weight against Kristin's thigh, then placed her head in Kristin's lap as though to say, "I understand! Only two of them in there? It'll be a piece of cake."

The pups climbed all about her legs, weaving about her as a mass of yipping fur, paws, and tails. One of the puppies reached for her continuously. Laughing, she picked up the little guy, placing him on her lap. The pup was surprisingly mellow, satisfied merely to be with her, licking her hands. She pulled him up to her face, his little tongue darting out continuously.

At that moment, Joel sat beside her, having jogged the distance from his now idle machine. "I think I'll name him Gunner," he said. Kristin turned her head to him and smiled.

"He's special," she replied. "I can't believe how he chose me. I was just sitting here, enjoying the view. It's like he claimed me as his."

"He's got a real personality," said Joel. "Gunner will be a great bird dog."

"Bird dog?" she asked.

"Yup. The best kind: waterfowl." Joel explained how purposeful dog breeding led to champion waterfowl dogs great for duck and goose hunting. "Ella fetched the birds. But they're also exceptionally good family pets. This breed's got it all the black lab is. In my opinion, they're the finest of dogs." They sat close together, enjoying Gunner and the other pups.

"Grill's hot!" Maximus yelled to Joel.

"That's my cue. Dad was in charge of getting the grill ready," explained Joel. "My job—the appetizers. When we eat, you'll see why having a good waterdog's so important."

Joel walked toward the garage and from there into the kitchen, returning quickly with a tray piled high with morsels he placed on the grill. He turned the heat down and returned to the bench; lingering tendrils of sweet smoke stuck to him.

Ella reclaimed her pups, then curled up on the cool garage floor to feed them. Joel pointed out to Kristin that the big truck was about ready to join him for the final corn haul. "I'll make one more round with the harvester then join you for lunch. There's only another 10 or 15 minutes of field work left to do. Okay with you?"

"Sure," she replied. "Need me to turn whatever it is you've got on the grill?"

"Mom said she'd do it, but if you don't mind, great." He looked closely into her eyes, taking her hands into his. She was a bit surprised by the intimacy of it but happily allowed the moment. "Thanks," he said, smiling. "Did I tell you I'm so glad you're here? See you soon for lunch."

Kristin watched him jog back to the harvester. The truck was slowly lumbering toward him. Soon, they were working together as the last of the corn yielded to their efforts. She slowly raised herself, going to the grill. Lifting the lid, she was assailed by a smell so delightful it made her stomach growl. She admired dozens of bacon-wrapped and toothpick-pinned morsels bubbling in the heat. She could see green pepper poking out from inside, with onion and oozing cheese. There was also some sort of cubed meat or a cut she didn't recognize. She carefully turned each one, then closed the lid.

Kristin joined the others just as they made their way from the barn. Maximus was explaining the business of farming and how their property was insufficient to provide enough income for everyone in the family. He was pointing to distant fields. "We now do contract farming throughout the area. Two of Joel's brothers and one of his sisters pretty much run the place now. They burn the long hours. Joel chose well to start his plumbing firm. He helps out occasionally, mostly in the spring and fall."

Joel returned to Kristin's side as the group was making their way back to the house. "I just turned off the grill, Pa," he said, glancing at his dad.

They gathered in the kitchen. Maximus led them in a

joyful prayer. He thanked God for a "soldier's reunion," new friendships, a bounteous fall harvest, and for the blessing of Kristin's twins.

They took seats around the large dining room table. First out was a steaming platter heaped with the freshly grilled appetizers. Maximus looked at his son. "Joel, would you like to tell our guests what we've served?"

Smiling, Joel quickly surveyed the faces. "Ladies and gentlemen, today's menu begins with Canada goose and mallard duck breasts, some of which are stuffed with jalapeno pepper and onion, some just with onion and cream cheese. I call 'em bird poppers. These are fresh, taken at various locations nearby, yesterday. Each is wrapped with our own smoked bacon, drizzled with Ma's finest glaze. We can thank Kristin for helping with the grillin'. Enjoy!"

Kristin was reluctant to try the jalapeno poppers, but the first one was a hit. They disappeared quickly and were followed by a huge garden salad, then Barbara's turkey-and-rice-stuffed peppers.

After the meal, they took a walk down a farm lane passing through the just harvested cornfields strewn with discarded husks, stalks, and silk. Ella followed them with a noisy party of pups. The lane dropped down toward a small creek and a pond where the puppies entertained them. Ella went in for a swim so, of course, the pups followed in her wake like furry amphibians, ears floating wing-like beside whiskered faces, puffing eagerly behind their mother. Everyone laughed heartily when Ella emerged and shook off, jettisoning water in bursts; the puppies eyed her and, in seconds, mimicked her technique.

Gunner shook so vigorously that he toppled over, then

trotted proudly over to Kristin for warmth. She sat below a magnificent sunset maple, dressed in full, fall regalia. As she played with the puppy, Joel knelt beside her. He offered Gunner a cornhusk teething toy.

Suddenly, Maximus blurted out, "Now I remember you, Jack! I've been trying all day to recall you in 'Nam. You were the guy who always had his nose in a history book. Never swore. Didn't smoke cigs or dope. And, if I'm right—the one time the guys got you to drink beer, you were sick for two days!"

"Oh, it's so nice to be remembered," laughed Jack. "Yup, that was me. You filled my canteen with water all day long. What a hangover. Sure taught me a lesson!" Jack stood, put an arm around him, and said, "Captain Max, it's great to know you again!"

22

TRANSCENDENT EXPERIENCE

ON WEDNESDAY AFTERNOON, the day before Thanksgiving, Kristin had just ended a phone call with her mother ("Still no cramps or other signs, Ma. Looks like I'll make it to another day. Maybe my doc was right about Thanksgiving.") when a call came through on her cell phone. She'd already assigned a ring tone to Joel. She greeted him warmly.

"Hi, Joel!"

"How's it goin' Kristin?" he asked. "Gosh, it's already five or six hours since I last spoke to you."

"Oh I can tell the kids are getting ready to make their exit, but…Joel, wait…something's happening. Oh, my—my water's breaking right now. I'll have to give Mom 'n' Dad a call."

"Hey, no. Let me take you. Please." She could hear Joel breathing hard into the phone. Then the sound of the truck's ignition. He'd activated the speaker on his cellphone. Over the ruckus of tires spinning and stones flying, Joel was yelling.

"…so just give me three more minutes, hon. I'm on my way! Two-and-a-half minutes now!" She could tell from the sounds of the truck that he'd reached the hard top and was quickly barreling in her direction. Momentarily, Kristin was torn. She'd imagined her parents taking her to the hospital, but this—Joel's rush to her aid—was fully unexpected. And entirely delightful.

She fully knew every facet of the coming adventure. Sure, there'd be some pain, even excruciating pain, but she was healthy and knew every detail about her own condition and the health of her two girls, now ready to greet the world. Knowing that Joel would be there within a minute's time, she texted both of her parents: "FYI + no worries. Babies R on the way. Joel's taking me to the hospital. See U there!"

Kristin grabbed the small travel bag she and Miriam packed a day earlier, turned off the TV, then the lights. She was locking the door just as Joel's truck came screeching around the bend. The driver's door flew open before the wheels came to a stop. "Kristin! Thank God!" Within a flash, Joel was beside her, helping her toward the truck. As they trotted the last few yards, he breathlessly spewed a chain of questions: "This is really it, huh? Are you and the girls okay? Did you call your parents? Am I okay to go the hospital dressed in jeans, boots, and a flannel shirt?"

"Slow down there, buster," she scolded him, smiling. In addition to the bag she carried, Kristin had grabbed a towel on her way out of the house. Before getting into the truck, she folded it onto the seat. "We're all good, and when I'm seated—please wait 'till I'm strapped in—I want you to ease this beast down the road, okay? No heroics. Everything's fine. I texted Mom and Dad. And you look like the most handsome dude ever to take a woman to the hospital."

With eyes riveted on the road and guiding the big truck toward town at just five or ten miles over the speed limit, Joel stole a long look at Kristin. His heart was melting: she was a heavenly visage, serene and indescribably beautiful, now flush in maternal splendor. Within those few suspended seconds, his gaze of absolute adoration fixed on her. At that very moment, Kristin was the Sistine Madonna, backlit by a billion celestial diamonds, exuding beauty from within. She was Mona Lisa and a full harvest moon, gloriously exquisite.

Their eyes met.

A moment later, Joel was stammering. Kristin looked at him, hoping to help him verbalize whatever it was he was attempting to say. "It's okay," she told him. "Everything's fine, Joel. Remember—I know a thing or two about pregnancies. This is textbook stuff."

"S-so we have a few minutes?"

"Yes. Of course. Everything's fine. Contractions have only begun. We have plenty of time."

Suddenly, Joel pulled the truck off the road into a gravel lot a mile from the hospital. He turned toward her, unstrapping his seat belt. Kristin watched, mouth and eyes wide open, as Joel pushed himself closer to her.

"Joel…what are you doing? You know I'm going to give birth to these two girls, right? My parents are likely to pass us if we don't get back on the road." She laughed, looking at how out-of-sorts he appeared to be. Joel's breathing was irregular, constricted. Shaking, he reached across her knees to the glove compartment, then grabbed something within it. Whatever it was, he clasped it tightly in his hand. Kristin looked into his eyes, puzzled and amused.

That's when he opened both hands, forming them into a cup. Within the fingered basin was a small, elegant box. He looked into the depth of her eyes, his gaze clear and beseeching.

Kristin's hands formed over her mouth and nose as though in prayer, tears coursing in streams to each side. She squinted, trying to stem the flow.

He slowly opened the box to reveal a magnificent gold ring with a cluster of diamonds. "Kristin, I know this is the worst imaginable time to ask, but…I want you to be my wife, forever. And for your girls to be our girls from the moment we enter that hospital. Will you…marry me?"

Immediately, Kristin's head bobbed up and down, her hands still in position across her nose. When she moved them from her cheeks to Joel's face, she was smiling. "Yes, my good man. My sweet Joel. I will marry you, and these girls will love you as their only earthly father." They embraced. Gradually, the sound of Joel's hazard lights stirred recollection of where they were.

Two minutes later, when they arrived at the women and babies center, nurses quickly moved Kristin and Joel toward the maternity ward. When they gathered again at the entrance, the gaggle of nurses spoke quietly among themselves. "Wasn't that amazing? Did you see the love in that couple's eyes?" "Not a shred of fear or stress. That's happiness." "Women are supposed to come in here screaming and hysterical. Men, stressed and bloodshot. You'd think those two were on Cloud Nine."

Just minutes behind them, Jack and Miriam arrived at their birthing suite. The attending physician was explaining to Kristin that her obstetrician was on the way. Kristin nodded, then looked at her parents. She beckoned Joel closer, holding his face close to hers with one hand. "Mom, Dad. Joel and I have something to tell you." That's when she moved her other hand to her swollen belly, now draped with hospital linen.

Though Jack was fully swept into the excitement, he was oblivious to the sparkling cue on Kristin's finger. Miriam saw it immediately. She smiled broadly and turned to Jack. His moment of confusion lasted just another second. When he stole another glance at his daughter, a glimmer of refracted light caught his attention.

"Well, I'll be darned. Congratulations!"

Jack and Miriam closed the distance to Kristin and Joel, embracing them. "Sweety, we're so glad for you," added Miriam. "This, all of it, is an incredible, miraculous answer to prayers."

Kristin smiled. "A new and better adventure begins. Joel and I are so happy. During the past several weeks, we've talked lots about our lives, each other, and our futures. "This cowboy proposed to me on the way here! Now, he'll be with me when the girls arrive," said Kristin while casting a smirk at Joel.

"Oh, and they told me that I'd have to surrender the ring—risk of swelling and that sort of thing." Kristin's obstetrician, now gowned and washing at the sink, confirmed that with a nod. A short while later, the physician coached Joel about how best to help and encourage Kristin.

Joel took a few minutes to call his parents. He began the call with, "Mom, she said yes!" His parents wanted to visit, but he asked them to wait 'til morning. His mother soon busied herself with calls to others in the Miracle family.

By nine-thirty, Jack and Miriam bowed out. To take her mind off of the painful contractions, now coming more rapidly, Joel looked into Kristin's eyes. "You remember how

Gunner chose you that day under the tree at our farm? Well, I think that's when I chose you too. If you'll have me. I mean us," he said.

"You mean you adopted Gunner from the litter? He's ours now?" she asked. He nodded, smiling in return. More contractions, coming in faster succession.

Joel and Kristin turned their attention to final ponderings—the girls' names. They'd shortened the list though now, as a family-to-be, Joel softened to Kristin's plea for his help in naming the twins.

At 2:10 am on Thanksgiving Day, they welcomed the girls, Nova first, then Mira—a name derived by combining both grandmothers' names, Miriam and Barbara. Following brief periods of absence for gentle washing, weighing, and tests, the girls were returned to Kristin to suckle, their blue eyes wandering about in soft, watery movements.

"Miracle babies, that's what they are," Kristin said to Joel. Joel smiled in return and bowed his head in prayer.

Later that evening, a nurse gave Joel her approval to move the heavy recliner closer to Kristin's bed. Both of them dozed briefly when the babies slept. "I guess they didn't read the memo about 12-hour naps," said Joel.

Morning came quickly. Kristin's obstetrician reappeared, explaining that she had another patient two rooms down. "All systems go. You'll be able to take your girls home by midafternoon." They thanked her profusely.

When visiting hours began, the Soelbergs, Miracles, and Methaneys all took turns in small groups. Jack and Miriam insisted because they visited the night before, that Max and Barbara go first. Matthew and Sarah ran back and forth excitedly between the waiting room and birthing suite. Joel's siblings came and went separately, all thrilled at the opportunity to mingle with their new relatives and to see the twins. By mid-day Joel and Kristin were exhausted.

Most of their guests left the hospital, knowing the "new Miracles" would soon be on their way. Jack, Miriam, and Hannah lingered. And, for the rest of their lives, they wondered if their reluctance to leave was accidental or preordained.

Kristin's physician made one last visit with the new mother and her girls, and the nursing staff rotated out. Ten minutes later, Miriam, Jack, and Hannah talked about who would stay to help Kristin, Joel, and the girls with their departure from the hospital.

There was a knock at the door. Miriam looked up and gasped. Jack immediately followed her gaze to a face that floated out from his memory, buried for decades. Gabriel stood smiling; beside him was a beautiful woman with long dark hair and olive complexion. They entered, gently closing the door behind them.

"Gabriel," whispered Jack with an expression that conveyed his astonishment. Miriam, sitting, brought her hands to her mouth. "You came back," she muttered. Hannah, beside her, wrapped an arm around her mother. Recalling Hannah's observation of his white cloak in Indianapolis, Kristin assessed his attire to find the appropriate insignia, also worn by the woman.

"We couldn't fool Hannah last time," said Gabriel, addressing Kristin. "That is, with the lack of a jacket insignia. I was in a hurry at the time and overlooked it. We sure put that hospital into a tailspin, didn't we?" His smile turned into a chuckle.

Joel focused his attention on the tall physician while pulling from recollection parts of a story told by Kristin during one of their long talks. "Gabriel," he said, turning to Kristin. "You mean—."

"That's right, Joel," affirmed Gabriel. "It's good, at last, for us to meet." His eyes wandered among them as he smiled warmly. "But if I may, I'd like to introduce to you one of my close associates, a woman dear to my life and work. By now her name is familiar to you. Nova is an envoy who's had a very special assignment among you that began decades ago in Vietnam."

Miriam's head spun to look at Jack. Her eyes were flooded with tears. She wiped at them to clear her vision. Jack's head moved slowly from side to side. "Incredible," he whispered.

"Yes, Jack—I was your shield." Turning to Joel, Nova added, "I also served alongside your father, Joel. One of these days, ask him to unearth the letter I wrote to him while he was recovering. I believe there's a folder in the attic. Like Jack, Max was very fortunate, though I'm sorry I couldn't protect him fully. He lost a leg but gained a life rich with blessing—including Barbara. And now, with your coming marriage, and with these two lovely, blessed girls, we complete the circle.

"Congratulations to you both," she continued with a broad grin, turning her full attention to the new family. "Speaking of circles, I understand that there's now a ring involved. Soon, two, I'm sure." Her eyes came to rest on Kristin and Joel.

"The ring is a symbol of God's love for you, for all of you," she said as her eyes settled on the tightly bundled baby girls. "The ring signifies God's immeasurable, eternal love and faithfulness, with no beginning and no end. Also for your fidelity and devotion to each other and God.

"Now you're a family, blessed through all these years, and for many to come," she added. "I must say, I'm honored at baby Nova's name. I've come to admire sweet Mira, as well."

Astounded, Joel and Kristin merely nodded in reply. The room was quiet for several seconds. Gabriel and Nova took measure of Joel, Kristin, and the girls, then Jack, Miriam, and Hannah.

Gabriel smiled, then looked at Miriam. "Maybe you'd like a few explanations," he said. "First, I must say that this is exceptionally rare, not only this level of involvement among people, but especially facing you here, today, for closure. Last time Nova and I worked this closely was a century ago. So it's a real pleasure that we could share in this mission among all of you. This is the culmination of many years' work. Jack, I want you to know that your Amigos are all well, gladly serving as warriors for Christ. Someday, you'll meet them again."

Jack's reaction was immediate. He fell against the back of the couch, huddled and whimpering. Miriam put an arm around him.

Turning to Joel, Gabriel said, "And while I'm on the topic, Joel, your military buddies—those who didn't return home alive—want you to know they appreciate your prayers, and the loving attention you gave to their families when you returned. I also explained to your girlfriend, Julia, from long ago, that I would speak with you. She sends her heavenly love—to both you and Kristin. She's with her son now, your son—and they're both filled with joy to know of these two beautiful girls," he added, adoring them with soft eyes.

Joel's eyes filled with tears. He tried to smile, looking at Kristin in a weakness she'd not seen before.

"At its root, all of this ties to prayers and surrender," continued Gabriel. "Jack, you may recall your mother telling you before leaving for 'Nam—and repeatedly after that—that she would always be praying for you. Her exact words were, 'Remember: 9, 12, 6 and 9. I'll be at my bedside, head down, there for you.'"

"I do remember that," sputtered Jack. "I haven't thought of Mom saying that for decades."

"You were a fine soldier, Jack. One of the best," said Nova. "I'm not referring to skills or—how do they say it in the military?—'dedication to the mission.' Initially, it was your character, godliness, and empathy for others that brought you to our attention. That's when we saw a prayerful swirl—the perfectly timed co-joining of your prayers and your mother's prayers, lifting as one, sometimes four times a day, from different parts of the world. So, we looked more closely.

"With that sort of scrutiny, we tend to scroll your life forward and backward for a better understanding of God's plan," added Nova. "We quickly found Kristin and Hannah, the tool, and the cross; even Helen and Malbas—all entwined and with ties to things of immense importance to the Trinity. I knew at that moment we'd 'opened a geode'—a term that Gabriel and I use to describe hidden treasures. When we looked inside, there were magnificent surprises with clearly marked places for our involvement. With you, Jack, we found geodes in every direction."

"That's when we knew it was time to step in," asserted Gabriel. "As you know, Nova was there to protect you at the wall. That was no small accomplishment for her, I can assure you. Especially since she, like you, deeply loved your good friends Roscoe, Ringo, Speedy, and Billy Yank."

Jack emitted a desolate cry. Miriam embraced him as his entire body rocked in grief, new tears spilling onto his khaki pants.

Nova and Gabriel looked on with loving eyes, watching Jack and the others in response to his grief. Slowly, Jack lifted his head.

"Several days after the attack that took their lives, Jack, do you remember your prayers, lifted to God in deep sorrow? It was the night before your freebird flight home," asked Nova.

"No. Well, maybe parts of it," replied Jack, barely able to form the words.

"You called your parents earlier that day from a phone at division headquarters. They knew you were homebound," she continued. "But you had a deep sorrow to work through, stemming from your war experiences. After the call, you went to your barracks room. You looked at your watch, and as you'd done so many times during the past year, you'd calculated the time of your prayer to precisely match the prayers of your mother—12 hours behind. At 2100 hours, you knew your prayers would be in perfect synchrony with hers. That's when you made a commitment unlike any other before it.

"Jack, your mournful prayer was this, exactly: 'Lord God, I loved my soldier friends, my brothers here in 'Nam. Many of them will not join me to return home alive. You spared me, and I feel so unworthy. I surrender my life to you now, Lord, if I've never made it clear before. Please, take me, Lord. Do with me what you will. I never want to get in your way again. I commit my life to you, to your purpose. Lead me and I will follow. As your Son Christ suffered and died on the cross for me, I will myself now to die on that cross with Him. Please, Lord, take what remains of me and give me a new life with Christ, your loving, holy Son.'"

Nova looked at Jack, shoulders heaving, awash in tears. "Yes, yes," he said, looking up at Nova, then to Gabriel.

"Your prayer was answered, Jack. And you kept your end of it. You really did," said Gabriel. "You've lived a good and godly life. Just look at the many blessings. The good news is, you're not done yet. You and Miriam are rewarded with plenty of time to enjoy the fruits of your faith and love, including these two new girls."

Turning his attention to Joel, Gabriel added, "Well, son, I suppose by now you know you've gotten yourself involved in something rather unusual."

Joel's expression was one of shock and bewilderment. Yet, he bore the revelations with poise. Gradually, he looked at Jack (whose bloodshot eyes locked on his), Miriam, then to Kristin—smiling apologetically—and then to Gabriel. "I've fallen in love, and I know it's where I belong," he replied.

"You're right, Joel," acknowledged Gabriel. "A finer family you won't find, and yet the gift to them is that you're of the same stock. We've heard your prayers as well.

"Oh, and the two of you may want to make plans for an extra bedroom or two in a few years," he added. "I have it on pretty good authority that you'll have two boys. Um, that's one at a time, Kristin." Kristin looked up at Gabriel and smiled, then turned to Joel, who reached for her hands.

"What about the dreams and the letters? The cross, the surgical tool, and the awful problem of abortion?" sputtered Hannah.

"Mostly resolved, my dear," replied Gabriel. "Importantly, we've taken some big leaps forward in the fight against the scourge of that horrible depravity. The battle will go on. We can thank God—and Nova's astounding efforts—that Kristin's no longer involved. In fact, she helped to turn the tide. Who knows, maybe these two young girls will someday have a role in defeating abortion once and for all. Bear in mind that God's will...*will*...be done. When the time comes, and we'll never know when that is, abortion will cease to exist entirely. God's timing and the depth of his love is a mystery, even to us. Have faith."

"The beautifully crafted tool with the hideous purpose was Malbas' prize possession," said Nova. "Fortunately, the tool's back where it belongs. Malbas, too. As for the cross, Kristin, please keep and protect it. Someday you'll know exactly what to do with it. More importantly, allow the life of Christ to grow in your lives. That is its gift to you now."

"Humankind is amazingly resilient but only when God is in the equation," added Gabriel. "Each of you has learned this. So don't ever forfeit the love of Christ. Rest in his love but be vigilant for him. In his letter to the Philippians, Paul wrote, 'I can do all things through Christ who strengthens me.' Those are words to live by.

"Our purpose here is served," said Gabriel. "Just know that your lives will be lovingly observed and appreciated."

To Kristin, Gabriel added, "Your friend Mary has shown her devotion to Christ in many ways. Please convey our deep love and appreciation for her.

"Hannah," he added, turning his smile to her, "please convey our love to Samantha, whose love of Christ is growing beautifully. And to Chet—his steady love for you, and Christ, is wonderful. We are so blessed to have been a part of this journey with you all. What we most desire would be the strength and nourishment of your prayers. Please keep us in your devotions; they support us in ways we're unable to describe.

"Wait, please," Hannah blurted out. "Can you tell us more about yourselves, or what heaven's like? To…see God? Are you angels?"

Miriam's head swung to her daughter with an expression of dismay.

"Oh, Hannah," Nova replied. "We'd love to share more with you about ourselves, the world we live in, or the nature of our work, but we simply can't do that. Some day you will know. I can tell you only this…that when a faithful Christian's life on earth comes to an end, a new beginning unfolds with indescribable warmth and love, glorious and full of splendor. In the presence of God, followers will experience a fullness of joy that I can't even begin to explain."

Gabriel turned once more to look at Miriam. He gave her a warm smile. Then Gabriel and Nova left the room swiftly, closing the door behind them.

That evening, Hannah called Samantha, giving her an abridged explanation of what happened. "That's so amazing, Hannah," replied Sam. "I wonder if they've had anything to do with my easy, restful sleeps lately. No bad dreams."

"Well, come to think of it, Sam—neither have I. It's been weeks."

23

A Mother's Sustenance

Mary Bruneau's flight from LA to Cleveland arrived at four pm, five days before Christmas. Kristin and Hannah met her at baggage claim while Joel remained at home with Nova and Mira.

As they waited for her bags, Mary explained that, in a week, she would continue on by train to spend three days in New York City. She'd then fly to Paris for a reunion with her husband and his family.

For Hannah, it was quickly apparent why her sister had formed such a warm relationship with Mary. Mary was inviting, genuine, and filled with joy. *How odd*, she thought, *that these two women—opposites in many ways and each one, once in love with the same man—had found each other amidst Kristin's crisis only months earlier.*

On the ride home, Hannah was entertained to learn more about Gil, the man's art collection, and his wild, eccentric forays into the cultural abyss of high-society LA. They all laughed riotously with recollections of the bird, Festus O. Yossarian.

"Some people never change," said Mary, adding that Gil now had a new live-in. "His place is still party central from what I've heard." Mary revealed that Gil's new flame was the woman from LA with an elaborate snake tattoo on her shoulder.

"Yes," replied Kristin. "She was sending smoke signals to Gil throughout the entire arts fair weekend there in LA. I can only be thankful now that they both got what they wanted."

The conversation turned to Kristin's blooming relationship with Christ. Mary was delighted to learn about Kristin and Joel's new church family, and a Bible study group they'd recently joined.

Hannah and Kristin also shared new insights into the many letters from Nova, at least one of which dated back to the Vietnam war (the letter to Joel's father Max was yet to be found). They spoke about the maternity suite visit by Gabriel and Nova just weeks earlier. Mary was astonished and delighted to learn that her love of Christ had come to the attention of both Gabriel and Nova. First, there was Nova's reference to Mary in the letter, and now this!

"Oh Kristin, Hannah—what a strange and wonderful mystery this has been," said Mary while turning to look at each of the sisters. "Maybe someday we'll understand what the entire picture looks like. It must be very important."

As they exited the highway, the conversation seemed to gain momentum and clarity. They spoke about the many pieces in play and others involved: the surgical tool, the cross, Dr. Harley, Cynthia Moloch and the awful business of abortion, and Kay Zavala's handwriting research.

Shortly after Hannah pulled the car into Kristin's garage, Mary was introduced to Joel and the girls, then Hannah's family, and finally to Jack and Miriam, who served a late meal for the travelers.

Joel offered to spend the night at Kristin's so that Mary, Hannah, and Kristin could spend the evening together with no concern about the girls. He took residence in the den (he and Kristin made a vow against premarital sex).

The ladies began with a long walk around the neighborhood for exercise and to enjoy the Christmas lights. Gunner stopped occasionally to pee, drawing sweet, falsetto praise from Kristin.

One startling discovery emerged. While talking about the gallery, Mary spoke about Helen's amazing transformation. That led to a conversation about her relationship with the brooding, ominous man in dark with goat eyes. Kristin and Hannah wanted to know more; they prompted Mary to call Helen, who soon texted two photos of Malbas. So that was their dark stalker! It was an astounding revelation, especially considering what Gabriel said about having dealt with him conclusively.

Back at the house while Joel, Mira and Nova slept peacefully, the women's conversation bore into the early morning hours. Eventually, Kristin settled into pillows with both girls—Mira snuggled in at one breast, Nova at the other. Their mother's sustenance, and her embrace, provided everything they needed. Kristin wrapped them with a cover, as much for humility as to keep the girls warm.

Mary and Hannah looked on, smiling. They contemplated the wonderful oddity of this moment. After all, it wasn't long ago that Mary learned of Kristin's initial plan to end the pregnancy. And from Hannah's perspective, her sister had spent a career helping women avoid this very experience—one she now knew her sister cherished more than her own life.

As Hannah prepared to leave, pulling on boots for the quick hike to her home, she asked her sister, "Now that you know motherhood, could you imagine it any other way?" Both she and Mary waited a moment for Kristin's reply. It didn't come verbally. Kristin's lower lip trembled. She reached around the sleeping twins to wipe tears, then smiled.

Kristin immediately found herself in prayer; it was a sacred moment of thanksgiving that concluded with an intense plea for God to strengthen and support Nova and Gabriel, wherever they were. When she opened her eyes again, Hannah was gone—walking home while raising her hands in prayer.

Mary was placing pillows back on the couch. "Good night, Kristin," she said. "See you in the morning." Kristin heard the guest room door open, then close. She sat, curled comfortably in the big overstuffed chair, cradling the twins. Hours later, she woke when the girls stirred. She fed them again, then went to take a peek at Joel, asleep on a couch in the den.

Moments later, she tucked the girls into their cribs. As she pulled up her own covers, Kristin rested a hand on the pillow beside her while pondering the night she'd be able to share her bed with the man she loved.

THE METHANEYS, MIRACLES, SOELBERGS, AND MARY gathered the next afternoon at "Miracle Ranch." All of Joel's siblings and their families—whose progeny, the dozen-plus kids now making up "Max 'n' Barbara's many minions"—were there to meet the woman known as "Saint Mary." Some of the young cousins merely stood and stared, spellbound as they took in the visage of the beautiful brunette. They'd heard that she was from California, meaning that she'd beamed in from a distant world.

"She certainly has a zeal for life," whispered Miriam to Jack as they watched her gather the children for a spontaneous sculpture lesson. She used a freestanding coat rack to suspend a small collection of paper plates and cups—with colorful ribbons that connected to each child. She then tied the art lesson to "God's ability to perform Many Marvelous Miracles—just like all of you!" The adults smiled in wonder, marveling at her extraordinary talent.

ON SUNDAY, Mary, Joel, Kristin, and the girls met with the Methaneys and Soelbergs in the church lobby. The joyous crowd was pressing in on all sides. Shortly before the service began, Samantha and Rob arrived. Hannah quickly ushered them into their family circle, making sure that Kristin and Mary understood the significance of their presence.

The church service included many of the best traditional Christmas hymns. As the pastor closed the service, he said, "I have a very special announcement. Joel and Kristin, would you please stand?" As Joel, then Kristin stood, each holding one of the girls, they turned to face the congregation.

"Right here, in the sanctuary tomorrow, I will join in marriage Joel Miracle and Kristin Soelberg," continued their pastor. "This is a most impromptu event; Joel, Kristin, and I made the arrangements yesterday—only Jack and Miriam and Joel's parents were informed. Plans for the service were sprung suddenly, not unlike Joel's proposal to Kristin a month ago, shortly before Kristin gave birth to Mira and Nova.

"You're all invited," he added. "The service will begin at 10 am. No gifts. No food. Come as you are. I'm told that

Joel's best man will be his father, Max. And Kristin has two Maids of Honor, her sister Hannah, and Mary Bruneau—will you both please stand?" Startled, both Hannah and Mary stood, then turned to face the congregation beside Kristin. "We all know and love Hannah. But Mary, I'm told, is single-handedly responsible for bringing Kristin back home and to our church family!" Joyous applause erupted.

An exuberant fest of back-slapping, hugs, and conversation followed the service. Samantha and Rob were radiant.

Sam pulled Hannah aside in the parking lot. "I didn't want to upset the flow of things to say that Rob and I would like to join you here each Sunday. We really enjoyed the service and the people—everything about it."

"That's great, Sam!" said Hannah. "Can you join us for a meal at Mom 'n' Dad's?"

"We'd love to," replied Samantha. "But from here, we're due at Rob's parent's place. We have some news to share with them."

"Oh? Good news I hope."

"Oh, Hannah—the best. We're so happy. I'm now seven weeks pregnant!"

Hannah's joyous reaction—something of an explosion—immediately drew stares and surprise. Matthew and Sarah ran to her side. Kristin and Mary joined them and, learning of the news, were quick to share hugs and congratulations.

"We were just getting used to the notion that we'd be a family without children of our own," said Sam.

"Well, it looks like God had a different plan for you," said Hannah. "Consider this too. Your new church family awaits you.

MARY, KRISTIN, JOEL, THE BABIES, AND HANNAH'S FAMILY gathered at Jack and Miriam's house shortly after the service. "You two certainly know how to throw curve balls," said Hannah to Joel and Kristin as everyone gathered for lunch. "Is this how you'll keep us on our toes from now on?"

"A secret you didn't even share with Mary!" exclaimed Jack. Mary smiled at Kristin, confirming it.

"Well, it's just so much fun to do some things on the fly. And just think of all the money we saved on a little ol' event that needn't be expensive, Dad," replied Kristin. "All that maddening, cuh-razy preparation, avoided entirely. Tomorrow's ceremony, after all, will be a holy matrimony. The idea really came together when I learned that I fit so well into Mom's dress. And, Mary gets to join us!"

"You what?" Miriam blurted out.

"Mom—while I stayed here at the house with you and Dad, I found your old wedding gown in a closet one day. "It fit perfectly, so I took it to the cleaners with a rush order."

"Oh, honey, that's amazing. I'm so glad," replied Miriam. "I mean—some of those preparations would've been enjoyable, but I'll get over it."

"Thanks, Mom. It was just a matter of when, and we knew the sooner, the better."

By meal's end, the conversation had covered all facets of the service, from the availability of the pastor, an organist, and the church sanctuary, to the ordering of flowers—all tended to covertly by Joel and Kristin. Joel's brother Stan agreed to do the photos.

That evening, after Kristin had nursed both girls, Joel remained at her house to be with them. Kristin, Mary, and Hannah took a quick walk back to the Soelberg home. The ladies enjoyed fluffing up the gown and veil as Miriam perfected the fit. They chose just the right footwear for Kristin and a pearl necklace—the perfect accompaniment to the small crucifix on loan from Nova. A few hours later, they acknowledged that the wedding preparations were as well set as they could be, given a 24-hour notice.

THE NEXT DAY, Joel, Kristin, Mary, and the girls arrived at the church an hour before the service. Kristin and Mary made their way to a conference room where Miriam and Hannah waited with the gown and other accouterments.

Joel went in another direction, directed by Jack, Chet, and Matthew into an office where he was soon joined by his brothers and Max. It was a raucous occasion. Jack and Max watched as Joel donned a dark blue suit adorned with a cheerful tie and floral boutonnière. Joel completed the arrangement with a new pair of blue suede shoes and argyle socks.

"Stunning," said Jack. Max smiled, put an arm around Jack, and said, "This is gonna be a great adventure. Happy to have you by my side again, soldier."

Joel soon found himself at the front of the church where he stood facing the minister. The music swelled to a crescendo as Jack led Kristin down the aisle, then placed her hand in Joel's. He spun to take a seat beside Miriam.

The service unfolded beautifully. Joel and Kristin, radiant in their love for each other, made one special request of the guests before exchanging their vows. The pastor gave the microphone to Kristin.

Kristin turned to address the church body. "Family, friends, and guests. Before we make our commitment to each other here before you and our Savior Jesus Christ, Joel and I have a special request. Our mentors, Nova and Gabriel, cannot be here with us today. I'll lead us in prayer, and then ask that—whenever you can—lift *them* in prayer."

Kristin's prayer was moving. She spoke of the depth of her love for Nova and Gabriel and their love of Christ. "If not for Nova and Gabriel, my life, my soul, and the lives of my beautiful girls would be lost. And I'd have never found Joel. Nor would I be here among you today. Someday you may know more about Nova and Gabriel, but Joel and I ask that you now join us in silent prayer for our most special shepherds."

The only sound in the church was the murmur of prayer.

"Thank you," said Joel, "for all of your prayers. And now, without further delay, let's do this!"

Joel and Kristin turned toward the pastor. As the ceremony continued, Joel's brother Stan was seen occasionally at one side of the church, then another as he took photos.

One image the newlywed couple wouldn't see, as their vows were exchanged, was the one framed by the hands of Nova, standing beside Gabriel, as she whispered, "click, click." Gabriel smiled, amused by her antics as they watched from above. The two of them stood effortlessly on a beam—one among many, twenty feet above the floor—spanning the width of the sanctuary.

"That was quite a tribute and heartfelt prayer led by Kristin, wasn't it?" said Gabriel. "We asked for their prayers, and we got a giant reply. The strengthening is remarkable, isn't it?"

"It is. It's amazing to feel so boosted and uplifted," she replied. "They really came through for us, didn't they?

"By the way, the view's great from here," Nova added. "I

know we've got work to do, but this is a moment I just couldn't miss. You understand, don't you?"

Gabriel turned to her and smiled. "I wouldn't've missed it for the world."

SHORTLY AFTER MIDNIGHT on Christmas morning, a gentle snow fell, leaving behind a four-inch blanket. Families descended upon Jack and Miriam's house, the first stop in the day's visitations. Their collection of Christmas music became the backdrop for the joyous occasion. The only disappointment for Joel and Kristin was the knowledge that the next day, they'd take Mary to Lakefront Station to catch a train to New York.

On the way there, Mary couldn't help staring at the magnificently carpeted hills. "It's so cleansing and peaceful," said Mary, staring in wonder at the gleaming landscape.

Joel and Kristin made plans with Mary for a week in Maine to be timed with Mary's next trip to New York City. "It'll be our honeymoon," said Joel cheerily. "Hey, with the girls, it'll be perfect."

It was a tearful parting. Joel hugged Mary warmly, saying, "Thank you...for all that you've done."

ON NEW YEAR'S DAY, Kristin, Joel, the girls, and Gunner popped in unannounced for a brief visit with Jack and Miriam.

A fresh pot of Jack's favorite rum-flavored coffee drew them to the kitchen. Thinking aloud, Kristin said, "Y'know, I can recall pouring real rum into my coffee before lunch not so long ago. Come to think of it I haven't had a clear head on New Year's day for ages."

"I'm glad those days are behind you, hon," said Joel as he poured a coffee.

"I guess I wasn't aware of how much the drinking had become a part of your life," said Miriam. "But there were a few times that Hannah shared her concerns."

"I'm sure. And I don't blame her," replied Kristin. "I learned the hard way that the Cali lifestyle wasn't so healthy after all."

After leaving the Soelberg's home, Joel and Kristin drove to Miracle Ranch. There, they left Mira, Nova, and Gunner with Barbara and Max, relaxing by a fire in the living room so that they could tend to a mission they'd looked forward to for weeks.

"What's up, bud?" Max asked Joel. "Oh, nothin', Pop. Kristin and I just want to find my old yearbook and other stuff in the attic." Well, it was at least partially true.

"Oh, Joel—it's an awful mess up there," protested Barbara. "I sidestepped the spider webs and dirt to get Christmas decorations weeks ago. Don't take Kristin up there."

"Mom, I've got this," assured Joel. "I'll plow through the dirt first."

The old, six-bedroom farmhouse had two floors, topped by a spacious attic. Kristin and Joel climbed the home's main stairway, then turned right into a room that was once Joel's bedroom. Kristin watched as he thumbed a metal latch that held the attic door shut, swinging it wide. Cold, stale air rushed out from the opening.

The base of a narrow stairway was littered with dirt, dead flies, and moths. That, and the smell of old wood and bat guano. Joel grabbed a whisk broom off the bottom step. He swung at a tangle of interwoven spider webs, climbing as he went.

Moments later, as Kristin watched from the relative safety of the bedroom, the broom flew back onto the lowest step. She looked up to see only Joel's arm and hand, open in a gesture to join him. Reluctantly, she peered around the corner to find her husband smiling, halfway into the attic. She took his hand. They climbed into the loft that was lit by two loosely hanging bulbs and muted window light.

A track of footsteps led through dust across the attic's wide-plank floor to a stack of empty boxes, all marked "Christmas décor."

"Yup, those are Mom's tracks, just like she said," mused Joel as he diverted his attention from the empty boxes to aim for the larger pile in the middle of the attic. Under the roof's main, central beam were books, chests, a few dressers, and a collection of boxes, all covered with dust and bat droppings.

"Thanks to Mom's insistence to organize everything, it looks like these boxes are all labeled." In short order, Joel found his high school yearbook and two boxes labeled, "Max, 'Nam."

"I think we found them," he commented. Joel quickly surveyed the other boxes, moving some aside and restacking a few others. The flurry of movement created a small dust storm. Kristin stepped back as Joel opened and searched the first box. Health records, assignment orders, and citations.

Halfway into the next box, Joel found a folder with health reports, a description of Max's injury, Purple Heart citation, and his DD-214 (honorable discharge). Joel was fanning the contents when a long manila envelope fell out. In large handwritten letters, along the envelope's length, it read, "Maximus

Miracle, Patient # O-4236Y aboard the USS Repose Hospital Ship, South China Sea."

He turned to show it to Kristin. "Oh, my gosh, Joel," she whispered. "That's Nova's writing."

Joel carefully pulled a single, heavy paper page from the envelope. Folded twice, it enlarged substantially as Joel carefully expanded the page. Mesmerized, they examined the page held directly under one of the hanging, 60-watt light bulbs. The note was short, but the artwork, entirely unexpected, occupied most of the large page.

Dear Maximus—

What a life you'll have! So sorry about the chaos of your injury. Time heals, and there's so much before you. Have peace through life's coming struggles because much goodness awaits you. The Lord God and his gracious Holy Spirit will guide you through the darkest valleys. Fear no evil, for you are with God, and I will be with you. You will dwell in the house of the Lord forever. An important mission for the Unborn awaits your and Barbara's son. —*Nova*

PS—here's some scripture for you, Max:

Consider it pure joy, my brothers and sisters, whenever you face trials of many kinds, because you know that the testing of your faith produces perseverance (James 1:2-3).

Suffering produces perseverance; perseverance, character; and character, hope (Romans 5:3-4).

The pen and ink drawing that occupied most of the page was a superbly rendered aerial view of a church sanctuary with two people—a man and a woman with long dark hair—

standing side-by-side on an exposed collar beam high above a congregation. The woman standing on the beam formed a rectangular frame with both of her hands around a man and woman, below, apparently a bride and groom, standing with a pastor at the front of the sanctuary. Christmas decorations included a crèche. Then there was the bride's flowing white gown. The groom, wearing a dark suit, wore bright blue shoes and colorful socks. In the periphery, a man aimed his camera at the bride and groom.

"The note certainly connects to others with her reference to 'Unborn,'" said Kristin. "This note may be dated from the same period as my father's first letter."

"And she's quite the artist," said Joel.

"Yes, she is," replied Kristin, unable to take her eyes off the page.

"But something's really unusual here," added Joel. "Look at the detail. Kristin, wait…that's your church. Our church. Look at the beams, and the Christmas decorations including the Nativity scene, with all of the figures moved back to make room for our wedding. That's you in your mother's dress! Just look at the details; they match perfectly. And that's me, there in blue suede shoes and argyle socks. And…Stan with the camera!"

"Oh my gosh, you're right, Joel. This is amazing," she replied. "That means, the man and woman above, there in the rafters—and they match so well—are Gabriel and Nova. Maybe it means that this is where they were and what they were doing when we exchanged our vows.

"So, she drew herself as she was framing a 'picture' of us from above," continued Kristin. "And look, there are your parents standing next to mine at the head of the crowd. She obscured some of the details purposefully but made sure that you and I could see ourselves…and that's Max and Barbara. My mom and dad are identifiable too. It's really incredible."

Joel slowly swung his head from side to side. "So this means, with Dad's letter buried here in his belongings from the war, that he came to Nova's attention before she shielded your father at that wall—and that she envisioned our own wedding and gave Dad a glimpse of it decades ago."

"Amazing," said Kristin, still staring at the drawing.

"So, Dad lost his leg, and it was the care he received at the hospital ship that saved him. That's where his primary nurse, my mom, entered his life," muttered Joel. "It all connects Dad with your father and you and me…long before anyone else could've known. She envisioned the wedding, down to the last detail, decades ago!"

MAX AND BARBARA WERE HOLDING the girls when Kristin and Joel returned to the living room. When Joel showed Max the old manilla envelope, he registered both acknowledgment and surprise. "I wondered where in the world that had gotten to," said Max.

"What is it, hon?" Barbara asked, swiveling with a bundled Mira to face him.

"Well, it's been a long, long time since I've seen it," replied Max. "What I recall of it was confusion, thinking that someone on the ship was just playing a prank. At the time, I was sure that someone on the medical staff, or maybe a friend of yours, made it for me. There's a drawing I didn't understand, and a reference to you, I think."

Joel withdrew the paper, taking it to them. Barbara and Max stared at it in rapt attention. Their concentration held as they viewed the illustrated note. Barbara, seeing it for the first time, paused at seeing her name—saying, "Max, what is this?"—and then she recognized the church sanctuary. Gradually, she recognized the depiction of herself, Max, and their son Stan. Then the bride and groom.

"I had no idea what it was, but it was interesting enough that I must've kept it," said Max.

"Dad—do you recognize the setting shown in the drawing?" asked Joel. They watched as he tried to make sense of it.

Barbara looked at Joel and Kristin and said, "Let me get this straight. You found this in one of Max's military boxes, up there in the attic, untouched for decades? And you," she added, turning to her husband, "never told me about it?"

"What should I have said so long ago?" said Max defensively. "It was so odd, and half the troops and as many medical staff were smoking weed. I just thought someone was high as a kite, and they aimed their fun at me. But, clearly, an inner voice told me to keep it, so I did."

"Mom, Dad—this has been in the envelope for what, 50 years? And Nova knew exactly where it was," said Joel. "We didn't mention it to you immediately because we didn't want you to tear up the attic looking for it. That's the real reason we went up there today. So, here it is, and we can see now that she'd given you an accurate look into your future, so long ago."

"My gosh," said Max. "After the war, and dealing with all the rehab required before they'd fit me with a prosthetic leg, I was so stressed out. I forgot about this. But one thig I do recall: I easily memorized and leaned on Romans 5:3-4 and James 1:2-3—which I still repeat as part my daily devotions. So that's where the seed was planted."

"Kristin says she can tell without a doubt it's Nova's handwriting, and it appears she also played a role in connecting you and Mom, Dad—not unlike our own providential meeting," said Joel, looking at Kristin.

"Incredible. As for the drawing—at least the scene that's depicted below the roof beams—it's true in every detail," said Barbara. "I love her detail in the dress, Kristin. And your socks 'n' shoes, Joel. But what's also amazing is what's happening above. How do you explain that?"

"Nova drew herself and Gabriel, standing there on the exposed trusses, high above the congregation. It's the two of them, for sure," replied Joel.

"There's even some whimsy or humor in it if you look at how she's acting out the framing of a picture," added Kristin.

"Well, I'll be," whispered Max, unable to take his eyes off the drawing. "She knew it all along. My struggle, our relationship, Barb...and Joel...and our faith. And if Joel's right, she hitched the two of us!"

"So, that's Nova," said Barbara reverently. "Just as amazing, she was helping to assemble the pieces of our lives—your lives—way back then. It seems she knew every detail about the wedding; that's clear in the drawing. For all we know, she and Gabriel even placed us into Hannah and Kristin's battle against abortion. After all, the magnetism between you and Kristin, Joel, can't be denied from the moment you first met.

"And from that, Max, you were reconnected with Jack. With Miriam, he uprooted their lives rather miraculously to be brought here to be with family. Just look at how the pieces have fallen into place. So, there she is, frolicking on the beam, making it clear to us that there's joy in everything."

"Mom and Dad are going to love this," commented Kristin. "And so will Kay, the handwriting expert who took such an interest in Nova. I recall Gabriel's words when we met with him the day the girls were born. He said they wanted to give us 'closure' to everything that had happened. It wasn't long after that when Nova mentioned the letter to Max, even telling us where to find it."

24

CLOSURE

SLEEP DEPRIVED, KRISTEN WALKED over to Jack and Miriam's house mid-morning. She'd wrapped the girls in soft blankets to shield them from the last remnants of cool, late-March weather. Small patches of snow gave the neighborhood a ragged, contrarian appearance. Quietly, she nursed the twins from a chair in the guest bedroom, watching through the big window as squirrels jumped between backyard oak trees. When Nova and Mira were asleep, side-by-side in the crib, she slipped silently into the den. There, she curled into a soft, roomy chair.

Miriam had placed coffees on a tray. Smiling to herself, Miriam knew she'd eventually have a conversation with Kristin about the rigors of growing into family responsibilities. Still in the kitchen, she whispered to Jack that this was the likely occasion for their daughter's visit.

"How do you know that's what she wants to discuss?" asked Jack, leaning close to Miriam.

"Call it woman's intuition," she whispered. "I've learned to interpret every movement a mother makes. And, well . . . she sorta said as much shortly after she arrived with the girls."

Jack smiled, always amused by this warm, witty woman

325

he'd come to love so deeply. "You're still the same, you know."

"Hmm?"

"That humor of yours. Just as natural and easy as hot dogs 'n' apple pie."

"Oh, Jack. You can do better than that."

"Not today I can't. I'm tongue-tied just thinking of the pending 'you're a big girl now' conversation."

Miriam laughed as she entered the den, trailed by Jack.

Kristin looked up with tired eyes. "What's so funny, Mom?"

"Oh, your father. He's an entertainer, but you know that."

"The big soldier's afraid of a faceoff with his daughter, right?" interpreted Kristin.

"Now who's got a sharp intuition?" replied Miriam, aiming her comment at Jack as they settled into a couch opposite Kristin.

After a brief exchange about the girls and news from Miracle Ranch, Kristin's expression became pensive. Jack and Miriam knew to wait it out.

"Mom, Dad—what a whirlwind couple of months we've had, and I know that a lot of the turmoil stems from my life," she began. "You did your best many years ago to prepare me for true happiness, goodness, spiritual growth, and motherhood. For a whole bunch of reasons, all of them wrong, I rejected every part of it. I'm so sorry."

Jack was quiet. This wasn't what he'd anticipated. Miriam quietly accepted her daughter with loving eyes.

"The best part is that you steadily, consistently gave me your love," she continued. "Unconditional love. There were times when I really tested and challenged that love, but it was always there. So now I'm a mom with two of the most beautiful girls a mother could ask for, a fine husband whose love for me takes a back seat only to his love of Christ. I couldn't ask for more. Your love and prayers for me made it all possible.

"I realize now that I've almost entirely rejected the lifestyle I was so blindly passionate about only a year ago," she added. "Come to think of it, it feels like my new values blow me right off my old set of tracks. So what am I now—a conservative? I now see that our traditional values run deep, and are mostly grounded in integrity and decency, empathy, respect for moral authority, the ethical treatment of others, and a deep hatred of evil. But, I had to see it for what it is. It's hard to believe how blindly I was involved in the awful business of abortion, in lock-step with feminists who worship autonomy. Just makes me shudder. And to know now how clear God is on that one. Life is precious and sacred.

"I guess, if anything, I'm admitting that in all my years away from home I was so wrong and self-absorbed that I couldn't truly learn, grow, and mature," Kristin said. "It's so sad to think how our culture has embraced so much evil— disguised by cries for 'tolerance' and 'empathy.'"

Jack and Miriam watched as their daughter fought back tears. Unsteadily, she took several sips of coffee. It appeared that a sudden thought nudged her sadness aside. She smiled introspectively.

"I love that quote by Mark Twain, Dad. Something like, 'When I was a boy, my father was so ignorant I could hardly stand to have him around. But when I turned 21, I was astonished at how much he'd learned.'"

Jack and Miriam chuckled, nodding.

"So here I am, now a new mother of babies just coming

to see the world as a maturing woman," continued Kristin. "It just amazes me and keeps me up at night to think of God's grace and how he's so blessed all of us through the nightmare of where my life was headed. Nova and Mira are a big part of it, a potent persuasion. Children really get you to reassess life, don't they?"

Miriam smiled, agreeing. "Yes, honey, they sure do. As our first, you created changes in our lives not unlike those you're going through and contemplating now."

"I'm so blessed to have had the foundation of faith that you provided for me throughout my early years," added Kristin. "And one thing I know with certainty—that your prayers were always with me, even though there were times that I didn't deserve or acknowledge them."

"Well, you said it yourself, sweety," answered Jack. "It's unconditional love—at least to the best of our ability, imperfect as we are. And someday soon you'll have plenty of opportunity to give back what we gave to you—just as Christ taught us. Come to think of it, I don't ever know if I've told you about your own name."

"What do you mean, Pop?" Kristin replied.

"Have we ever mentioned, or have you ever considered the origin of your name? As a Soelberg, your first name is also of Scandinavian origin. Kristin. It means 'follower of Christ.'"

Kristin stood up, placing her empty cup on the small end table, and moved to where her parents sat on the couch and wedged herself between them. She said, while placing her arms around her father, "No, Dad, I never knew that. But I'm so glad to know it now. I'll want the name to fit for the rest of my life."

For a moment, Kristin's head rested on his chest. His hands moved to embrace her. As Jack held her, longer than he could recall since she was just a small girl, she leaned warmly into him. Kristin then rolled into her mother, placing Miriam's face in her hands, eyes only inches apart. From both sets of eyes, joyous tears first simmered, then flowed. As they hugged warmly, all sharing tears, Jack contemplated the astonishing goodness of this moment.

Later that evening as they got ready for bed, Jack said to Miriam that Kristin's visit, and their shared time on the couch with her, was one of the best moments of his life.

A FEW WEEKS LATER, while serving breakfast to Jack and Miriam at their small, eat-in kitchen table, Kristin and Joel shared their plans for a late May drive to meet Mary at the airport in Portsmouth, Maine—with plans for a week in Lubec. While talking about the small coastal town and the latest news from Mary, the three of them took turns feeding the girls, who'd just begun to sample baby food.

"Joel and I have had long discussions about work, for me, that is," said Kristin, switching tracks. "His business is doing well, especially now since he found the new guy to manage the team, so I think for the foreseeable future I'll just be a mom."

"That's amazing, Kristin. I know it comes with some sacrifice," said Miriam.

"It does. But I'm okay with it. In fact, I know it's right. There's also some other news."

"Oh? What's up, kiddo?" asked Jack.

At that moment, Joel sprung up from the table to fill a cup of coffee. By now, Kristin was well aware of Joel's weaknesses, including an inability to disguise certain emotions. Happiness sat at the top of that list. Miriam was perhaps the world's finest interpreter of body language, and Joel knew it. Half a second longer under her gaze and his expression would undoubtedly have betrayed his delight.

Jack and Miriam looked at each other, eyebrows raised expectantly as Joel made noise at the coffee pot, assuring them that his quick departure was legitimate. They turned their attention back to Kristin, and she held the moment quietly just a bit longer, watching her parents.

"Um, I think this is what they call a pregnant pause," said Jack, smiling.

"Precisely," replied Kristin. She gave it just another second or two, enjoying her parents' expressions as they evolved from bewilderment to gathering excitement—Miriam well in the lead. "You, um, baited that one, Dad. That is, to confirm it. I'm pregnant again, now eight weeks!"

"Hallelujah!" sputtered Jack. Miriam, who'd already made an accurate assessment, moved in to hug Kristin.

"Thank God that didn't last a second longer," stammered Joel. "That was a painful pause, and I didn't have anything to do with it!"

"Um, Joel, I hate to break the news to you, but yes you did!" was Jack's quick reply. The eruption of laughter lengthened as Kristin and Miriam also turned their attention to Joel whose discomfort was immediately visible. A bright red flashed from his cheeks and melted into his forehead and neck. He slapped his forehead with both hands, enjoying their humor at his expense, an endearing self-deprecation.

Miriam, still at Kristin's side, hugged her daughter again. Jack got up to join them. The twins' little voices added gently to the joyous occasion. *Oh, what the heck,* thought Joel as he moved in for the group hug.

H<small>ANNAH LEFT FOR WORK EARLY</small> on a Friday morning. She'd anticipated this day for weeks. It was her last day to complete the boxing up of her belongings to move out of the lab/office space she'd come to know as her home-away-from-home.

She cleared her shelves and packed the coffee maker. She removed three large, framed posters. She pulled the plug on her desk lamp, one of the last items to go.

Standing in the doorway, Hannah looked back at the now-altered space. The office was no longer hers. Finally, her eyes were drawn to the desk that would remain. She was reminded of the Fed Ex box that arrived there a year earlier with the surgical tool and note that ignited the chaotic, even miraculous series of events with ties to her family, professional, and church life. And there were the mysterious connections to the abortion industry.

Hannah was interrupted by the arrival of a few other early-starters, lab techs and bioscience researchers who also preferred some quiet time to begin the day. She stepped back into the now vacant office to sit in a chair along the wall. There she dropped her face and closed her eyes, hands resting in her lap.

Father God, I thank you for the way that you've rescued me and Kristin from this awful experience. I thank you for the past year and how you've brought so much goodness into it.

Lord, we were so blessed through Gabriel's and Nova's involvement, so I must ask for you to strengthen and encourage them in whatever challenge they may now be dealing with. Please give them endurance. Whatever pressures they may now have, please help them soar with the power of your supernatural love. Lord, please bless this new office for Samantha. Let it be as good for her as it was for me, especially now as a woman who's new to Christ and your amazing grace. Amen.

Just as Hannah began to rise from the chair, she heard a light tap on the doorframe. Dr. Harley and Samantha greeted her warmly.

"Hey, you—it's day number one, and I'm so proud of you!" exclaimed Hannah, rushing to give Samantha a hug. Sam's bulge was now seven months along, and she carried the baby admirably. Hannah then gave a hug to Dr. Harley, who was smiling broadly.

"Her first day, thanks to your recommendation that we bring her in as a candidate, Kristin," said Harley. "She'll be here for a few weeks, and then out for 12 weeks to start her family. But that's a small sacrifice to make, given Samantha's many qualities!"

Hannah's new office, just two doors down from her old space, would be the office previously occupied by Dr. Harley. Harley's latest round of NIH grant approvals nudged him into a windowed third-floor office in the center's new research wing.

JOEL AND KRISTIN COMPLETED their finishing touches to the remodeled spare bedroom that Mary had slept in, now repurposed as another nursery. They favored shades of blue as they chose compatible colors for the walls and curtains.

"You think he'll like it, hon?" Kristin asked Joel as they

moved the last piece of furniture into place, a combination changing table and shelf unit.

"What's not to like?" asked Joel. "After all, lil' Gabriel will have the best mommy ever." He smiled at Kristin, then took a second glance. "You know...it just struck me how incredibly beautiful you are. There's some sort of radiance to a woman with child. In fact, you now remind me of the day I first met you a year ago."

Kristin took two steps closer to her good man and kissed him. "Hmm. That's right. It'll be a year in three weeks, three days and...seventeen hours."

"Gulp. Guess I'd better call the florist."

"Very funny, Joel Miracle. I'm amused by you, but sometimes more than at other times."

DAVID AND JONATHAN ENDURED a long, torturous legal battle. The abortion organization was so rattled by the departure of their top two execs that they choose to fire the old legal team, replacing it with a much more aggressive firm. The new group tossed all available resources into the fray, seeking vindication.

With one-third of its clinics closed, the organization's attorneys went all out against David and Jonathan. Jonathan served six months of a five-year sentence. David was sentenced to 10 years in prison, deemed guilty of tampering with confidential governmental records, invasion of privacy, libel, and other charges. His legal team, working pro-bono to defend the pro-life cause, chose to appeal the decision.

David was using the time to write a book about the experience. He and Jonathan became two of the most sought-after personalities for conservative talk shows, conferences, and symposia. Several media representatives chose to visit David while he was serving in Pelican Bay State Prison, recording their interviews there.

David had another visitor one evening, several months after entering Pelican Bay, 20 minutes before lights out. While working on his manuscript, David was suddenly aware of a presence along with a serene, calming sensation that he instinctively knew was from the Holy Spirit. Nova gradually materialized before him while looking sweetly into his eyes. She held an index finger to her lips.

"He can't hear me, David," said Nova. His cellmate, just 10 feet away, was reading in bed. "Please don't acknowledge me. I am Nova, an agent of our Lord. I've served for years in the battle against abortion and want you to know that our Father, our God, recognizes the goodness of what you and Jonathan and others have done in the fight against it. My next visit will be to Cynthia Moloch who I know you've been faithfully praying for. You prayers will be answered. I'll visit her next."

David's expression gradually transformed from astonishment to acceptance. Without taking his eyes off of hers, he nodded to affirm her words.

"David, I'm amazed at your strength and devotion to God. You are a good and faithful man. As I now look to complete my duties in this mission, I promise to look after your family," she added. At this, David broke emotionally.

"Please don't worry. You will be released much sooner than the duration of your sentence," she said. "We've already seen to that. Please continue to use the time to work on your draft. It will serve you and the Kingdom well. You've found your calling, David.

"I now leave you in the name of God. You are loved and dearly appreciated." With that, the apparition of Nova—who David knew unquestionably to be real—began to dissolve. He whimpered, "No, no—please don't leave."

His cellmate turned to look at him. "Hey. You okay?"

DR. CYNTHIA MOLOCH HAD LOST her home, her savings, and her artwork collection, and she'd saved little for retirement.

Cyn's attempts to find employment were unsuccessful. She gradually learned that most of the prospective employers merely wanted to meet the international pariah in person. One hospital director mockingly offered her a cosmo and Crème Brûlée during their brief interview. He laughed raucously as she ran from the boardroom in tears.

Throughout her adult life, Cynthia's library of sensations rarely included happiness or pleasure apart from those that stimulated her artificially. Laughter with family and friends or colleagues, prayer or meditation, brisk walks in the countryside, or (especially) the delight of play with children—all of these were foreign to her. Cynthia's drug of choice, alcohol in its many forms, was wretched compensation for the lack of these virtuous rewards.

It was evening, and just as she'd told David, Nova began to take shape next to Cynthia. Nova found her in a ramshackle efficiency apartment. Next to her on a small table was an open bottle of Absolut vodka.

Using both hands, she began to raise a .45-caliber revolver, one round in its chamber. Mascara ran down her face in salty rivulets as she moaned miserably.

Before appearing to Cynthia, Nova had interpreted her piteous mutterings.

Abruptly, Cynthia was aware of a strange and unfamiliar presence. At the same time, she was unable to raise the pistol further. A warmth enveloped her as a cascade of endorphins was released, coupled with a baffling sensation of delight. Momentarily, she looked up, wondering if she'd somehow been transported from one world to the other. There were spiders along the ceiling and wall paint carelessly smeared on a window frame. She glanced at the unfired pistol. As Nova's face appeared before her, the gun fell to the floor. Cynthia was unable to speak, yet she was vibrantly alert, charged with a strange energy.

Nova reached out to stroke Cynthia's hair and smiled warmly into her eyes. "My dear, I'm here to rescue you…from you," Nova began. "You've made many mistakes, but God's heart is softened for you because your life collided with Kristin's. The carnage must end, Cynthia. Satan has held you too close for too long. It's time for you now to move toward the light. In God's own words [Deuteronomy 30:19 NET], 'I have set life and death, blessing and curse, before you. Therefore choose life so that you and your descendants may live!'

"The womb must never be violated, Cynthia. Yet the evil of abortion continues. In man's existence, life here on earth is heaven's womb. It's only a place to begin, yet there is no beginning if it's cut short. Life in the womb is sacred, cherished by God.

"I'm here to offer you the goodness of hope, and God's love for you," added Nova. "You now have a role in giving others hope while offering an option to abortion. You'll meet an elderly couple who've looked for years to make a lasting gift to humanity. They will find and recognize you. God's plan is already in play. Please use the next few days to begin plans for a national consortium of shelters for homeless mothers. Only you, Cynthia, are uniquely prepared for this mission. You've been chosen. Yet, ultimately, the choice is yours. God's grace is upon you."

Nova pulled her into an embrace. Cynthia melted into her arms. When Nova released her, Cynthia stared at her in wonderment.

"Please tell me who you are," uttered Cynthia, regaining her voice.

"I am Nova. Soon enough, Kristin will call you. Not only will she tell you more about me, but she will again be your successor." With that, the visage of Nova gradually dematerialized.

AFTERWORD

Unborn began on Sunday morning in January 2019. Church that day included Bible study; we spoke about how legislation in several states had legalized late-term abortions, even as a baby exits the birth canal.

Class attendees stammered, "Who'll tell their story?" and "Who'll stand up for them?" "Christians aren't doing enough!" Our pastor's message that morning contributed, asking, "How will you find and fulfill your calling?"

After returning home, I took a brief nap—just long enough to know the mind indeed works while sleeping. I woke abruptly with the word, "Unborn" on my lips. I wrote it down, knowing there was an undercurrent. I had the distinct feeling that God coupled that gifted word with an admonishment, something like: "I've rather had it with your distractions; if when you sleep is the only time I've got you to myself, that's how we'll go at it." *Unborn* was underway. It's my first attempt at a long-term (shall I say, full-term) writing project, borne in just the right way—inspired by God.

Research begun, I was soon deeply saddened to learn that early terminations, even infanticide, were horrors brought on by early man, though not with the frequency we now see. Today, among the world's many nations, with America now in second place behind China, unborn souls have created the weightiest burden for heaven: babies are aborted much faster than humans leave earth by any and all other means!

FROM MY HEART

Unborn was not written to shame, judge, or malign women. Far from it! The purpose of this book is not even to

338

disagree with women's rights and freedom of choice. To have a child or to end its life—those are personal choices. Yet, there are eternal consequences. God will ultimately judge us for our every thought, action, and deed.

I'll admit to a seething hatred of organizations that have mobilized against helpless babies into which God has breathed life. They do this under the guise of offering "family planning" and health-sustaining services to women who are mostly naïve to deliberately schemed institutional manipulations and deceit.

I believe it's my God-given commission to stand against the giant, grinding bloody machine—so shrewdly positioned as a source of help and empathy while offering fast, easy solutions to the inconvenience of living children. I hope that *Unborn* helps to uncover and illuminate their hell-bent deception.

Finally, I pray that adoption becomes the choice to outshine abortion. It offers the fulfillment of dreams for millions of couples while giving the blessing of life, joy, and promise to every unwanted child.

Endnotes

1 A viable fetus or baby can be born and have a reasonable chance of survival at just 21 or 22 weeks of age. By contrast, a nonviable fetus (typically prior to third trimester, or with a disorder or abnormality) has no chance of survival outside the womb.

2 The World Health Organization (WHO) list heart disease, stroke and pulmonary disease, among many others, as chiefly responsible for removal of human beings from this planet. They also show that reported abortions are responsible for 57% of all deaths worldwide: https://righttolife.org.uk/news/abortion-was-the-leading-cause-of-death-worldwide-in-2019

3 According to *OurWorldData.org*, about 140 million people are born into the human race annually. Mortality rate to the human species, globally, averages about 55 million/year.

4 Guttmacher.org—The key source of information about unintended births and abortion rates states that the average number of abortions, globally, stands at 73 million/year—far higher than deaths by any/all other means of death combined (and of these, only about 50% of abortions are considered to be from "safe" sources).

5 Abortions are significantly underreported globally, perhaps setting global abortion rates more accurately as high as 100,000,000 to 150,000,000 per year. Of course, abortion-biased organizations, which far outnumber those dedicated to the truth about this method of birth control, do not offer more accurate data.

About the Author

Lona Schäfer has been married for decades and has lived in Europe as well as in numerous cities across the USA. Lona has written for many years (mostly magazine articles), though *Unborn* is Schäfer's first book, and its sequel is moving toward completion. Raised in a Christian home, Lona was not born again until recently—attributing that glorious moment to "revisions" stemming from a real immersion into John Bevere's book, *Driven by Eternity*. It's Lona's hope that *Unborn* will impact the lives of young people who face life and death decisions because, after all, God's Word makes clear the value of life. For security reasons, Schäfer's true identity and location are being withheld.